# THE
# HOLLOW
# EARTH

*Books by Rudy Rucker:*

Geometry, Relativity and the Fourth Dimension
Spacetime Donuts
White Light, or, What Is Cantor's Continuum Problem?
Software
Infinity and the Mind: The Science and Philosophy of the Infinite
The Fifty-seventh Franz Kafka
The Sex Sphere
Light Fuse and Get Away
The Fourth Dimension: Toward a Geometry of Higher Reality
Master of Space and Time
The Secret of Life
Mind Tools: The Five Levels of Mathematical Reality
Wetware
Mathenauts: Tales of Mathematical Wonder

# THE HOLLOW EARTH

The Narrative of Mason Algiers Reynolds
of Virginia

EDITED AND WITH A NOTE

BY RUDY RUCKER

**WILLIAM MORROW AND COMPANY, INC.**
**NEW YORK**

Recognizing the importance of preserving what has been written, it is the policy of William Morrow and Company, Inc., and its imprints and affiliates to have the books it publishes printed on acid-free paper, and we exert our best efforts to that end.

Library of Congress Cataloging-in-Publication Data

Rucker, Rudy v. B. (Rudy von Bitter), 1946–
    The hollow earth: the narrative of Mason Algiers Reynolds of
Virginia / edited and with a note by Rudy Rucker.
      p.    cm.
    ISBN 0-688-09413-9
    1. Poe, Edgar Allan, 1809–1849, in fiction, drama, poetry, etc.
I. Title.
PS3568.U298H6  1990
813'.54—dc20                      90-31029
                                    CIP

Printed in the United States of America

First Edition

1  2  3  4  5  6  7  8  9  10

BOOK DESIGN BY A. DEMATO

*For*
*Martin, Greg,*
*Sylvia,*
*Georgia, Rudy, and Isabel*

# CONTENTS

# THE
# HOLLOW
# EARTH

# 1

## Leaving the Farm

I WENT TO Poe's funeral yesterday. There was a minister, four mourners, and a grave digger. The grave digger called me a damned nigger and chased me off. Otha should have been there to see.

Eddie wanted to write the account of our "unparalleled journey," but he's dead any way you look at it and Otha's in the Umpteen Seas. That leaves me and Seela living as penniless, free Baltimore Negroes, with the winter of 1849 coming soon. I'm writing as fast as I can.

My name is Mason Algiers Reynolds. I am a white man; I am a Virginia gentleman. My unparalleled journey started thirteen years ago, when I left my father's farm in Hardware, Virginia. There were five of us on the farm: Pa, me, Otha, Luke, and Turl.

I woke in the dark that last day at home. I'd been dreaming about being buried alive. The dream was tedious more than it was scary. In the dream I couldn't see anything; I could just hear and feel. First there was the noise of the folks praying over me, and then came the bumping of the coffin being carried out and lowered into the ground. There were some hymns, and then they shoveled the dirt in on me and it was nothing but black.

Right after I woke up, everything felt like a coffin—my bed, my room, Pa's farm. But then I got happy, remembering that I was fifteen and that tomorrow I would drive the wagon to town.

I got up to pee out the window. The moon was low, and the predawn breeze brought the smell of rainsoft fields. We'd made it through another winter, we Reynoldses, and tomorrow was today. Pa was sending me and Otha to Lynchburg to sell three barrels of whiskey. We needed seeds, a new plow, some books for me, and a wife for Otha if we could find one. All winter I'd had nothing but our accumulated subscription copies of *The Southern Literary Messenger* to read, which is where, come to think of it, I'd gotten the idea of being buried alive: from Edgar Poe's tale "Loss of Breath."

Beneath the surface, my thoughts were still running down the tracks of that bad dream, wondering about the worms that eat corpses. Were corpse worms the same as the purple crawlers that Otha and I used for fishing? Or were corpse worms the fat white grubs with hard heads that bite? I'd once read in the *Messenger* that if an angel from another star were to come and do a census of Earth, she'd think this was a planet of worms, since there's more of them than of any other living creature. Beetles would come in second, as I recall.

In the barn, our new-farrowed sow was grunting, warm and slow. I said a prayer and went back to sleep.

Turl woke me up for real, yelling up the stairs that it was time for breakfast. She was a handsome yellow woman who never tired of telling all of us that she was too good to be a slave. According to Turl, her grandmother had been a Hottentot princess and her grandfather a Spanish buccaneer. It was no secret what she thought of the rest of us: Pa was a drunkard, I was a dreamer, Otha a baby, and Luke a mule. The only one of her relatives she ever said anything nice about was her sister's little son, Purly, at the Perrows' in Lynchburg. We all put up with her because with Ma dead, Turl was the only woman to care for us men. When she was feeling sweet, she could cook and sew and clean to a fare-thee-well.

But today wasn't one of Turl's sweet days. Breakfast was a sloppy cold porridge of watery grits and rank fatback. Turl slapped some of it in bowls for me and Pa, and took the rest of it out to the slave cabin, holding her mouth stiff and stuck out. I was glad to be leaving today.

"How's the boy, Mason?" said Pa, coming in from the barn. He'd already been out to feed the stock. He was big and strong and he had a black beard. Sometimes I wondered how Ma could have stood to kiss him—in the picture we had of her, she looked so delicate that it seemed like a rough beard would have torn her face. I took after Ma; I was blond and short, with pale brown eyes. Ma'd died aborning me. Occasionally I worried that Pa hated me for it; not that he was ever harsh with me—far from it. Pa could be rough on other men, but he still had his gentleness to let out, and mostly it came to me.

He walked over and rested his callused hand on my neck. "Are you ready for the trip, son?"

"Lord yes, Pa! I've been packed for two days! Soon as we eat our breakfast, I'll help load the barrels into the wagon."

"Luke and Otha and I can do that, Mason. My boy's too fine to coarsen up his hands. He's going to be a university man!"

"Aw, Pa. You sit down and eat, too."

We sat and ate for a bit, and pretty soon Pa commenced to chuckle. "Tastes like Turl's upset."

I stuck my lips out to imitate Turl's mad face, and Pa laughed harder, making a deep rumbling sound like a bear. I set my dish down on the floor and let Arf finish it. He'd been lying under the table waiting, the way he always did.

"Looks like Turl'd want her son to have a wife," Pa said. "With her womb all dried up, that's the only way we're going to raise any more head of pickaninnies."

"Otha's scared," I told Pa.

"He won't stay scared long, young buck like him." Pa wiped his mouth off and stared at me. "Would you be scared of a wife, Mason?"

"No sir. Leastways I don't think so. Not if she was as kind and beautiful as Ma."

"Be careful of the women in the Liberty Hotel, Mason. They beautiful, but they not kind. After you sell the whiskey to Mr. Sloat, go straight to Judge Perrow's and stay on there with his family. I'm putting a demijohn of my best mash on the wagon for him."

"Yessir. I'll give it to him." The good thing about Judge Perrow was his daughter, Lucy, a reckless blond girl several years my senior. Last year Pa'd brought me into town for Christmas, and Lucy had played a kissing game with me.

"Good. And, Mason, it might not be a bad idea to just buy Otha a gal from the judge's household, or from one of his friends. Those poor niggers at the slave auction, there's no telling what they've been through. I recall the judge had a nice pickaninny gal called Wawona. Look at the Perrows' Wawona before going off half-cocked." I winced at the thought of doing business with sour old Judge Perrow. It was no secret that he thought of me as an unmanly bookworm. Last Christmas dinner when I'd tried to talk about one of Edgar Poe's stories in the *Messenger*, the judge had launched into a long tirade against Poe's character and against literary thinking in general. I was already known to all our family and friends as a good reader and writer; indeed, whenever Pa or my uncle Tuck needed a letter written, they came to me. When I'd taken exception to the judge's remarks about literature, he compared me to a chicken-killing dog and asked if I'd eaten a dictionary. It was hard to see how he and a girl as nice as Lucy could even be in the same family. Pa saw my expression and sighed. "Just make sure the new girl is broad-hipped and healthy, Mason, and try not to pay more than sixty dollars. Don't give Otha too much say-so; he changes his mind every ten minutes anyhow."

There was a whoop out in the barnyard, and then Otha was at the door. "Lez go, Mist Mason! Lez go to town!" He was dressed in his Sunday clothes, Pa's castoffs carefully patched by Turl. Otha was three years older than me and a foot taller. He was lanky like Turl and coal-black like Luke. His head was small and round, and his big mouth went a third of the way around. Yesterday he'd been scared, but today he was raring to go.

Luke was out in the barnyard waiting with the wagon and the three barrels of whiskey that Pa'd distilled this winter. In the summers we grew corn, and in the winters Pa turned the corn into whiskey. It wasn't just that Pa liked whiskey; this was the handiest way of getting our crop in to market. One barrel of whiskey was worth the same as five hundredweight of corn.

Otha helped Pa and Luke roll the barrels up some boards and onto the wagon. Arf got excited and started barking. He had the noble profile and the feathery legs of a retriever. His legs and ruff were white, but his head and body had the tawny coloring of a collie. I'd grown up talking to him like a person. He had a way of moving his eyebrows and his feathery tail so expressively that I often felt he understood me. Now in the farmyard, his tail and eyes were merry as he pumped his barks skyward. There was no sign of Turl. Pa went back in the house to get Judge Perrow's demijohn.

"Goam git us a sweet gal, Mist Mase?" said Luke. He was a strong man with a dazed air about him. It was as if he'd given up thinking years ago.

"Ain' no us, Daddy," cried Otha. "Goam git me! Ah'se de one fixin' to jump obber de broom wid de new gal." In our part of Virginia, a master married slaves to each other by having them jump over a broom handle that was held a few feet off the ground.

"Sho you is!" said Luke. "Jes like me an' yo mam." He glanced back at the slave cabin and lowered his voice. "Doan bring back no thin mean yaller bitch, Marse Mase, I swear to God. Bring me a black gal wid a big butt."

"Ain' goam be yo gal, Daddy," said Otha one more time. He tried to laugh, but the sound came out all cracked. I knew he wanted to leave as bad as I did. Things were too tight on our little farm.

I went in the barn and got our mule. His name was Dammit. Pa'd given him a big breakfast of corn, and he was in a mood to ramble. Otha and I hitched Dammit to the wagon tongue and drove him forward a little, checking how the barrels rode. They were heavy enough so that Otha and I'd have to walk, but that was no matter. It was turning into a sunny April day and the mud had stiffened up pretty good.

Finally, Pa came out with the judge's demijohn. I could smell from Pa's breath that he'd sampled it. Without me there to watch over him, he'd probably stay drunk for a week. Poor Pa. I hugged him goodbye, and Otha started Dammit toward the gate. We all knew Turl still had her licks to get in, and now there she was in her cabin door with her face all wet.

"Otha!"

"Mam?"

"Otha, ain't you goam say goodbye?"

"Goodbye, Mam." Otha looked desperately unhappy.

"Otha, why you wanna leave yo mam?" She started across the barnyard toward Otha. If I was man enough to take the wagon to town, I was man enough to stand up to Turl. I stepped in between her and Otha, blocking her way.

"We'll be back in a few days, Turl. Goodbye."

"Git outten my way, you whelp."

She raised her hand as if to slap me, and I wondered what I could do about it. Pa spoke up before it went that far. "Turl!"

She stood there a moment, a proud thin woman afraid of losing her son. Otha urged Dammit on through the gate, and then I was out of the barnyard, too. Arf slipped out the gate after us, his tail held demurely down. I scolded him, and he cringed, but he kept right on coming. Luke and Pa and Turl stood there watching us, Turl with her hand still up in the air. Finally, she started to wave. I prayed we wouldn't bog down in the muddy farm track that led over the hill to the highway—not that the highway was anything more than a dirt road three ruts wide. If we could only get out of the grown-ups' sight!

Otha was thinking just like me, and if Dammit had balked then, I think we would have stove in his ribs. But Dammit pulled and the wagon rolled and in just a few minutes we creaked up over the crest of the rise that separated our farm from the highway. We looked back and gave the parents a last wave, little realizing we'd never see them again, not that we would have stopped even if we'd known. We were right sick of life on that farm.

It was a fine day, the last day in April. There was enough wet in the ground so the sun had a weak, watery feel to it. The highway was muddier than I'd expected, and every so often Otha had to get behind the wagon and push while I urged Dammit from the front. Arf liked it best when Dammit would balk and I'd have to pull at the mule's bridle. Arf would help out then, barking and snapping and coming as close as possible to getting kicked, all the while glancing up at me for approval. Going down hills, Otha and I would hop on the wagon and drag the brake levers against the wheels. It was hard, muddy work, especially for Otha, but our spirits rose higher and higher the closer we got to Lynchburg. Otha began chaffing me about Lucy Perrow—I'd had no one else but Otha to confide in that time she'd kissed me—and I let him in on Pa's plans about Wawona.

"Whut she look like?" Otha wanted to know.

I only remembered pigtails and a wide smile, but I talked her up to Otha, secretly hoping we wouldn't have to go to the auction. There'd be ugly rednecks there, and I'd be cheated sure as night.

The green-hazed woods were full of blooming white dogwoods, peeping out at us like shy girls. There were bright redbuds, too, and best of all, the big purple bell-blossoms of the paulownia trees that only bloomed every few years.

I knew the way to Lynchburg from having made the trip with Pa before. The highway meanders along next to Rucker Run

Creek for some eight miles, at which point you find yourself on a high bluff looking down at the James River and at the town of Lynchburg on the river's other side. The creek cascades right down the cliff, but a body has to drive left and loop all around to get past the bluffs to the James.

Before hopping on the wagon to ride the brakes down the loop, Otha and I paused a moment to rest. I unharnessed Dammit, and we led him over to the last pool of Rucker Run for a drink. He slurped for a bit and then began cropping at some of the early plants that stuck up green through the mud. Arf splashed across the creek and into the underbrush, in search of small critters. When Arf hunted, he flexed his ear muscles so that his flap ears would hang an extra half-inch farther out from his head. It gave him a harried, overalert look.

Otha and I washed some of the mud from the road off ourselves, and then we skirted around the edge of the pool, right out to the edge of the cliff where the creek went waterfalling down. It was a lovely view of Lynchburg from up there, all framed by the water and the flowering trees. The little town was on a hill that sloped down to the river.

"I'm a bird," sang Otha. "Ah sees evverthang, and when ah poops, look out!" He pointed out across the river toward the top of the hill. "Looky dar, Mase, see de carriage ridin' obber de hilltop wid de two dogs runnin' after? Ah bet dass yo Judge Perrow. Wawona, here ah comes! And, Lord Lord, see all de folks down to de market, Mase. You reckon it's Saturday? Whoooee! See dar down in de ribber, dey loadin' up a boat! How 'bout you send me and my new gal to Richmond fo' a honeymoon?"

The boat Otha was pointing to was the sort known as a bateau. The bateaus weren't cruise boats, they were flat-bottomed barges designed to carry tobacco down the shallow, rocky James to Richmond. They were rough and uncomfortable; crews of slaves poled them downstream and up.

The tobacco warehouses were on the first street up from the river, as were the cigar factories and the flour mill. The next street held the wholesale merchants: the feed stores, the slave traders, and the like. Another block up was Main Street, with its market square, its fancy stores, and the Liberty Hotel. Higher yet was the crest of the slope on which Lynchburg flourished, and on this crest was the great domed structure of the county courthouse, flanked by the offices of the bankers and lawyers who fattened on the city's trade.

We were brought back to the present by the howls of Arf. With great floundering and yelping, he came crashing toward us through the underbrush. His ears were flat to his head. Close behind him was a filthy half-naked boy of ten.

"An Injun!" exclaimed Otha.

Arf splashed across the pool and threw himself down at my side, panting with his mouth wide open. Now that he'd stopped running, he looked totally relaxed. Had the Indian boy threatened him? Or had it been the other way around?

"Hey," I called to the dirty red boy in the breechcloth. He wasn't so much *dirty* as he was marked. That is to say, the black marks on his chest and face were regular stripes rather than random splotches. "Why you chasin my dog?"

The boy made a gesture and melted back into the woods. "Injuns'll eat dogs," said Otha. "Especially in the spring."

"What was that he did with his hand?" I asked. "Was he waving goodbye?"

"He moughta been puttin' a hex on us. Lez move on, Mason." Otha didn't call me Mist or Marse when it was the two of us alone.

By the time Otha and I got down past the cliffs to the ferry, it was late afternoon. The ferry house was a wretched shack near the edge of the river. As the James flooded every few years, all the structures at its edge were temporary. I was glad to see that today the river was running clear and slow. I led Dammit and the wagon down onto the cobblestone apron that was the dock. The ferryman and his wife lived in the ramshackle ferry house; the wife sold biscuits and slices of ham.

"Buy us some food," urged Otha.

"Can't," I told him truly enough. "We don't have any money till we sell this whiskey to Mr. Sloat."

A hawser led across the river from a ring set into the cliff side. Its other end was similarly fastened: It served as a guide for the ferry. Right now the ferry was on the river's other side, just upstream from the bateau wharves. I waved to the ferryman and finally, slowly, he set his craft in motion. The ferryboat had hoops that hooked over the hawser, keeping it from drifting downstream. The ferryman had two slaves, each with long poling sticks.

As the ferryman drew near, his wife stumped out to the porch of the ferry house and began quizzing me. "Who you? Ah know ah seen you befo', but you done growed!" She bent her mouth in a smile.

"I'm Mason Reynolds, from Hardware."

"Ah knowed it!" she shrilled. "Don't you and yo boy want some food, Mist Reynolds? Ah can give you a steam catfish on a naahce little loaf o' bread."

"I don't have any money yet," I explained. "Until we sell these three barrels of whiskey."

"Lord! And how was you plannin' to pay my husband?" There was nothing kind or gentle about this old woman. She reminded me of a splintered tree branch slimed over with river scum. She looked smooth, but she'd cut you fast. She was so excited about the fee, she took a step toward us, which set Arf to barking. He had a special deep-chested bark he used on strangers, a bark quite different from the tip-of-the-nose bark he did when he was simply excited.

"I'll pay him on our way back," I said. "Surely you trust a gentleman." Pa was fond of saying how he and I were gentlemen, but this old woman wasn't having any of it.

"Dirt-farmer whiskey-seller kind o' gentleman! How 'bout if you leave that demijohn with me for safekeepin'?" The old bitch had spied out the extra wicker-covered whiskey bottle I had for Judge Perrow.

"You'd drink it dry," I exclaimed.

"Two dollars," said the ferryman, who'd just stepped ashore. "Twenny-five cent each for the mule and the Negro, fifty cent for the young *gentleman*, and a dollar for the loaded wagon. Right this way, and set the brakes good for the ride."

"He says he don't have any money," cried the ferryman's wife. "His wagon's full of whiskey!"

The ferryman smiled broadly. "Fetch a jug, Helen, and the gentleman'll tap us off a gallon."

"We get three dollars a gallon for our whiskey," I protested.

"An' I get three dollars for ferryin' it," said the man calmly.

"I'm mighty hungry," Otha reminded me.

"Get us two fish breads," I called after the old woman, who was in her house looking, no doubt, for the world's largest jug. She reappeared presently with the food in one hand and the jug in the other. She'd brought us each a small loaf of bread split in two and with a whole catfish on it, still warm from the steamer, its eyes all white. I set mine down on the wagon, but Otha boned and ate his right away. I got the demijohn out of the wagon and trickled the ferryman's jug full. He watched with a pleased smile as his jug swallowed up about half of what the judge had coming. When I went to put the demijohn back in the wagon, my loaf and fish fell on the muddy ground. Arf bolted the slippery gray catfish with a nasty gasping sound. Nobody noticed, and I was too disgusted to say anything about it. I led Dammit onto the ferry, urging him to pull our wagon up the sloping planks that led aboard. Dammit couldn't quite make it, and when I asked Otha to push the wagon from behind, he was slow about it. Losing all patience, I cursed Otha for a lazy black fool. In truth, I suppose I was abusing my companion to look big to the ferryman and his wife. Slave master Mason Reynolds! Otha gave me a puzzled look and leaned his strength against the stalled wagon.

Finally we were all afloat, gliding across the green James River for Lynchburg. There were huge rapids upstream from us, and cooling bits of mist came drifting down on the early evening breeze. The ferryman pulled at his new-filled jug, sighing with pleasure and gazing up into the darkening sky.

"Do you like it out here on the river?" I asked Otha.

He eyed me suspiciously, still smarting from my harsh words of a minute ago. "We out here, Mase, and ain't neidder one o' us can swim." There were lights on in Lynchburg. The closer we got to the town, the bigger it looked.

"I'll act right by you, Otha, you can count on me. I was only yelling at you because Arf ate my fish."

"Arf ain' de fool," muttered Otha. "An' neidder is I. *You* de buttho'." He swallowed the last word, but the ferryman's two slaves caught the tenor of his remark and grinned at me with expressions that dared me to object. I was just a fifteen-year-old country boy, and they were full-grown men of the city. I kept silent, stroking Arf and biting my lips. This was an example of what slave owners always said: Give the crow a kernel, and his flock will eat your field.

The ferry grounded up onto the Lynchburg landing ramp. I coaxed Dammit forward, Arf and Otha followed, and there we were, big as life, on the Lynchburg waterfront, six o'clock of a Saturday evening, April 30, 1836.

Otha came up next to me, and we stood there, the two of us, staring at all the people. There were heaps of darkies, whole gangs of them, with their own black bosses. One gang was swarming over a bateau, loading it up with hogsheads of tobacco. Others of the gangs were hauling things or being idle. There were fussy little white bankers and merchants dithering around here and there, and knots of rednecks, too. It was more different people at once than I'd seen total all winter in Hardware. I stood goggling; breathing in the smells, mostly bad, and listening to the hubbub of the wharf, with its waves lapping, timbers creaking, and barrels rolling on beneath the noise of the wharfmen's hollers and goodbyes. Behind those noises I could hear the great hum of Lynchburg's thousand voices and the ceaseless grinding of her thousand wheels.

Someone tapped my hand. I glanced down to see a four-foot white man with a heavy pistol strapped around his waist.

"Hidee," said he. He had an upturned nose that showed the insides of his nostrils.

"How you," said I.

"What's your load?" asked the dwarf, as if he couldn't smell the sheen of good corn whiskey that had sprung through our barrels' dray-battered staves. I figured him for a damn thief. His gun meant that he worked for some one of the gangs of thieves that called themselves government. United States, Virginia Commonwealth, or Town of Lynchburg, they were all the same according to Pa—they all just wanted to drive the honest man down. Pa'd warned me not to answer any questions on the wharf or we'd end up giving out money to every thief who thought he had the right to ask for it.

"A gentleman's business is none of your affair," I said, calm-like. "My boy and I are heading into town. A good evening to you. Otha, get in back and mind the cargo." I hopped up on the wagon seat and smacked Dammit with the bridle. We clattered up the sloping cobblestone street. The dwarf yelled after us, but Arf barked and snarled so hard the little thief was scared to follow. Every now and then Arf did himself proud.

After the long day's haul, Dammit was inclined to slow down on the slope up to Main Street. I kept after him, now smacking him, now talking about oats. Fortunately enough, the Liberty Hotel was right at the corner where we crossed Main. We pulled around into the courtyard in back. A hostler came out of the stables, a sharp-faced blond boy not much taller than me. He seemed right watchful of things and even had a pistol to hand in a holster hanging on the wall. I asked him to give Dammit some water and a half pail of cracked corn. Brushing down the mule could wait till we got to the Perrows'.

Otha went over to the kitchen shed and started chaffing with the cooks. To see him there so free and easy, you'd think he'd been hanging around Lynchburg all his life. For my part, I felt small and no-count. Standing in the courtyard, I could see through a small open window into the hotel saloon. There was a lively crowd in there, no doubt about it. Men were singing and cursing, and there was pretty women laughing loose and bold. The sight of them cheered me right up. They were the women Pa had warned me about! As soon as I could finish up my deal with Mr. Sloat, I hoped to get a closer look at some of those famous women. I lifted Arf up into the wagon bed to guard the whiskey, and went in the hotel back door.

The back door led into a dark wood-plank hall. There was a staircase on my left and some smoke-blackened frame paintings on the wall on my right. About ten paces in, the hall opened up into a lobby with stuffed chairs and a small Oriental rug on the floor. Pa'd never taken me here before, but he'd told me about that rug. It was marvelous, all red-and-blue-bordered, and with twelve squares marked off, each square with a different kind of zigzag explosion in it. I bent over to get a closer look at how it was made.

"Don't bed down just yet, country cousin," said a voice. "The rooms are upstairs. Would you care to register?"

I turned around, blushing, and saw there was a fat man at a desk in the rear corner of the lobby. He wore gray trousers and a shiny black tailcoat. I blushed harder, realizing that with my rough shoes, simple blue breeches, and loose white blouse I looked no better than the stableboy outside.

"Are . . . are you Mr. Sloat?"

"You have the advantage of me, sir." Sloat cocked his head questioningly. His eyes were dark and bright in the white dough of his face.

"I am Mason Algiers Reynolds of Hardware, Virginia."

Sloat picked up a pencil and chewed the tip. "The whiskey Reynoldses?" I'd expected him to be pleased, but he merely looked distracted.

"I have three twenty-gallon barrels on my wagon in the courtyard outside. Pa said you could pay four dollars a gallon, which would make two hundred forty dollars, would it not?"

"Would it not." Sloat shook his head and gave a short, mirthless laugh. "God save me from petty Virginia gentlemen with manure on their shoes. Come closer, son, and don't step on the rug." Pa'd warned me that Sloat was a sharp one. The rock bottom I could take for the whiskey was two dollars a gallon, though last year Sloat had paid two fifty and this year we were hoping for three.

"It's unusually good mash this year," I said. "Last summer's corn came in extra sweet." I thought of Judge Perrow's already opened demijohn. "Would you care for a taste, Mr. Sloat?"

"Your mash may be better than last year . . . Mason, is it?" I nodded, though I wished he'd call me Mr. Reynolds. "Your mash may be better, but my custom is worse. Prices are down. The very most I can pay per gallon is . . ." He stared at my eyes, and I could have sworn that he was reading my mind. "Two dollars a gallon." He knew he had me, and he pressed right on. "Let my men unload your wagon, and you can settle in here as my personal guest . . . Mr. Reynolds." Another sharp glance at my eyes. "For a valuable supplier like you, everything my hotel offers is free: room, board, and . . ."—he rolled his bright little eyes toward the saloon door on the other side of the lobby— ". . . and one night's companionship."

One of the women laughed again, long and wild, like there was no tomorrow. Nobody would have to know. I could go to the Perrows' tomorrow and say I'd just come into town. Otha would back me up if I . . . But where would Otha sleep? Not in my room, not with a woman there. "What about my manservant?" I asked Mr. Sloat.

He shrugged. "Have the hostler put fresh straw in your mule's stall. There'll be room enough for both of them."

I knew I couldn't do that to Otha. He was here to find a wife, and I was going to put him with a mule so I could bed a whore? He'd tell Pa for sure. I followed Mr. Sloat down the hall to the courtyard, still thinking.

Some of Mr. Sloat's men rolled our barrels down into the hotel cellar, and then Mr. Sloat took me back into his private office, a dark little room right behind his desk in the hotel lobby. It had a peephole in the door so Mr. Sloat could keep an eye on everything. There was another peephole set into the left-hand wall.

Mr. Sloat had a big rolltop desk and a metal safe with a lock on it. The safe door was ajar. He gave me a sharp look and then hunched over the safe till he'd found the $120 he owed me: six gold double-eagle coins. They were so heavy I worried they'd drop through my pocket.

"So," he said, pushing the safe door almost closed. "That's our business, and I thank you, Mr. Reynolds. Did you want to have supper in your room or at the bar?"

"I . . ." I'd been thinking about what to say, but it was hard getting it out. "I have to go on to Judge Perrow's tonight, Mr. Sloat. But if . . . if you really mean that about . . . companion-ship . . ." The women through the wall were laughing hard and high. "Just for an hour," I said finally. "Just to see what a woman is like."

Mr. Sloat smiled like I'd made him very happy. Perhaps it was his pleasure to mislead the young. "Go on into the bar and pick one," he said, leaning back and waving his fat hand at the door. "There's four of 'em there, fat and fresh and ready to go."

I scuffed my feet and shook my head. The women wouldn't believe I had Mr. Sloat's go-ahead, and the drunk men would laugh at me. They'd tell all their coarse friends. Pa and Judge Perrow would find out. *Lucy* would find out. I couldn't go in the bar and ask a woman to come upstairs.

"Look through the peephole if you're ascared," said Mr. Sloat coaxingly. He gestured at the little glass bull's-eye set into his office wall. "Look in there and make your pick and I'll send her upstairs to you." He was uncommon keen on this. I was such a hayseed, I couldn't see why.

I stared through the peephole for a long time. At first it was hard to see, but then I got my vision and began picking them out. It was two older women and two younger, two of them blond and two of them dark-haired. I didn't want to choose the young blond one, on account of Lucy, so I told Mr. Sloat the young dark-haired girl would do. He sent me on up to room number three.

It was a plain enough room, with a shuttered window that opened onto the courtyard. I sat on the bed for a while, and nothing happened. Finally, I cracked the shutters and peeked down in the courtyard. It was the last breath of twilight. Our wagon was right down there, with Arf lying on it licking his balls and Dammit standing next to one of the wheels, sleeping. I wondered where Otha had gotten to.

"Welcome to Lynchburg, Mason," said a sweet voice behind me.

I jerked back and the shutter slapped shut. It was the young dark-haired woman, sure enough, smiling at me and holding a candle. Seen up this close, her hair had some kink to it. A quadroon, I expect, but Lord knows she looked clean and she smelled sweet. She set the candle down and came right to me before I could start worrying about what to do. Her name was Sukie.

Pa'd never quite explained the details of sex to me, but at the end of an hour I knew all about making babies and I'd seen exactly where they come from—though it meant getting some candle wax on the sheet. I bounced with Sukie three times, just to make sure I understood. It tired me out so much I dropped right off to sleep. It was Otha yelling down in the courtyard that woke me up.

"Mist Maaaaason?"

The room was pitch-dark and the woman was gone. I got up and banged into things till I could get the shutter open.

"Mistuh Maaaaason?" I could see him as a dark patch against the courtyard's pale cobblestones. Off to the right, the kitchen fires were burning.

"Hsst, Otha, I'm coming."

"Whut you doin' up dere?" he said, all mock innocence until he burst out laughing. Darkies always knew everything that white folks did. I left the shutter open and dressed by the faint light of the town outside. I realized I should have hidden my gold, but—thank God—my pocket was still heavy with it. Next I started worrying that the Perrows would be able to smell the sticky perfume of Sukie's body on my loins, so I dropped my pants to splash myself off with the water in the basin. How late was it?

I hurried downstairs and found Otha lounging against the wagon. He looked more loose-limbed than usual and more content.

"What time is it, Otha?"

"I ain't got no clock, Mase. All I know is it be dinnertime come an' gone. I traded a few pannikins of our whiskey to de cook for supper. Whoooee, it were good. Beefsteak from a cow, Mase, all fried up wid taters an' onions an' washed down wid city-made beer. I don' nebber wanna go back to no farm."

There was lots of noise from the hotel bar—I thought I could hear Sukie singing. Warm lights filled the windows in every direction. It couldn't be later than eight or nine. "We better head on to the Perrows', Otha. I'm all done here."

"Ah see you is." He grinned broadly. "Were she sweet?"

# 2

# Murder

IT WASN'T till the next morning that I learned Sukie had replaced all my gold pieces with lead slugs.

I woke up to the sound of church bells and rain. Lucy had said we'd be going to St. Paul's Episcopal Church downtown today. I knew the Perrows had a closed coach, so the rain didn't matter. The idea of taking Lucy to church touched something deep in me. I was a man now, no doubt about it, and before too many years I'd be getting married. First I'd go to the university, of course, but after that . . .

I lay in bed for half an hour, listening to the rain and running over the happy memories of my wonderful interlude with Sukie. I wondered if there was any chance of seeing her again. Already the exact sensations of the act were a bit a hard to recall. It had been smooth in her, smooth and warm.

The drive to the Perrows' had been easy—with his belly full and the wagon empty, Dammit hadn't minded a bit. Otha had thought to pour the judge's remaining whiskey into a tight small jug from the hotel kitchen. The judge had graciously accepted it, never knowing that twice as much had gotten away. Mrs. Perrow was fluttery and hostesslike as ever, happy for some distraction from the judge's endless talk of politics. The slave girl Wawona had been brought in for my inspection: She was firm and sassy and interested in Otha, who was bunking down with the rest of the Perrow slaves. The judge said we could have her for sixty dollars. Lucy above all had been thrilled to see me. She'd pressed more than one kiss on me out on the stairs before bed. I'd gone to bed happy and woken up the same. Everyone loved everyone.

"Oh, Maaason!" Lucy's voice came drifting up the kitchen stairs. "Get up, sleepyhead! It's May Day! You said you'd take Ma and me to church!" Judge Perrow was a freethinker, and the Perrow women were happy to have a man accompany them to church this once.

"I'll be right down, sweet thing!" The gallant words sprang easily from my lips. What a change Sukie had wrought, quiet radiant Sukie, goddess of the night!

What a change indeed. After I'd washed up, I reached into the pocket of yesterday's breeches and pulled out . . . six gray lead slugs.

The rain kept right on like nothing had happened, and Lucy called me again just the same as before. But I stood there thunderstruck, staring down at the gray metal in the window's gray Sunday light. Of course Sloat had wanted Sukie to come up to me. Sukie had robbed me, and she hadn't even done it for herself.

"Mason! Am I going to have to come up there and fetch you?"

Slowly, I took Pa's good clothes out of the portmanteau. It was a white linen shirt along with black trousers and a tailcoat. I'd looked forward to wearing these fancy clothes when Turl had hemmed up the sleeves and pant legs for me, but now it was all ashes. Even the bright red cravat Pa'd given me failed to lift my spirits. I shoved the lead coins in the side pocket of my tailcoat and walked numbly down to the kitchen. Lucy was at the table, and Wawona's mother, Baistey, was at the stove.

"Some ham and eggs, Mason?" said Lucy. "You'd better eat fast, there's not much time. Walloon has blacked your shoes." She had a bossy edginess that I'd never seen before.

"Ham and grits," said I, still fingering the lead coins in my pocket. "When is the church service over?" I was going to have to go see Sloat.

"It starts at ten," said Lucy, "and it's nine o'clock now. See my watch, Mason? Lieutenant Bustler gave it to me for Christmas." She stretched out her arm to show me the little gold brooch watch she held clutched in her hand. It was the smallest watch I'd ever seen—no bigger than an inch across—and it even had a fast-moving thin hand that counted seconds. "Wasn't that dear of him?" went on Lucy, turning the watch over and opening its back. "See here? Lieutenant Bustler's picture." The cameo showed a pie-faced man with muttonchops and a high collar.

Baistey set my ham and grits down in front of me and filled me up a big glass of milk. There were butter and blackberry jam to put on the grits. For a few minutes I ate without thinking. When I noticed Lucy again, she was looking at Lieutenant Bustler's picture and now and then glancing over at me. I had the feeling I was supposed to ask her something, but I didn't know what.

"Will Bustler be at church?" I said finally.

"No," Lucy quavered. "Lieutenant Bustler is serving the naval department in Norfolk, Virginia. I'd thought, Mason, that he would take me with him, but the fates would have it not." She gave me a look that said she had much more to tell.

"I wouldn't trust him," I blurted out. The upset of losing all Pa's money had me on edge. "Your Lieutenant Bustler looks too flat-headed for anything *but* soldiering. What kind of a fool is a military man anyway, Lucy? A fool to fight other fools at the head fools' say-so." I'd heard Pa say this many times.

All of a sudden Lucy was in tears. "You're so right, dear Mason. I trusted him too much. He . . . he caused me to fall and, oh, Mason, *everyone knows*!" With her face red and twisted in the morning light, she looked less lovely than I can say. My heart went out to her.

"Hush that talk, Lucy. You'll find a husband soon enough. You just wait and see. Pshaw, if you last till I'm out of the university, I may come acourting you myself." The implicit admission that I was not courting Lucy *right now* made things worse. She cried harder, and Baistey left the room, no doubt heading for the African Baptist Church with the rest of the slaves.

I walked over to the kitchen door and stared out at the rain. There went Turl's sister, Calla, carrying Turl's two-year-old nephew, Purly, a cute little pickaninny with features as fine as a new-minted coin. The lead was heavy in my pocket. Someone was scratching at the door. I opened it a crack and Arf surged in, soaking wet. I caught him, but not before he'd executed a big shake, which showered Lucy's pale blue dress with muddy spots.

"Goddamn you," she screamed in sudden anger. "Stupid bookworm with a stupid dog. I don't need your pity, Mason Reynolds!" Before I could react, Lucy had stormed upstairs. I fed Arf a big slice of ham, dried him with a kitchen towel, and snuck him up the back stairs to my bedroom.

"Good dog," I told him. "You stay here." He stared up at me and blinked his eyes twice, the way he always did when he pretended he understood. I shoved him down on his side and hoped he'd go to sleep.

Was the trip to church still on? And what was I going to say to Sloat? Too bad I didn't have a gun. I thought of Judge Perrow's gun collection. I hurried back downstairs and through the kitchen to the gun cases in the den off the hall. They were locked, but as luck would have it, the key was right in the first desk drawer I tried. Wonderful. I got the case with pistols open and took myself a four-shot pepperbox pistol, small enough to fit in my tailcoat's inside pocket. There were rapid footsteps all through the house now; the women were almost ready to go. Working quickly on the floor, I got my pistol charged and loaded. I swept the spilled powder under a rug, locked the case, and dropped the key back in the desk.

"There you are, Mason!" sang Mrs. Perrow, popping into the den. "Lucy's changed her dress and we're all ready to go! Get your shoes!"

The weight of the judge's pistol balanced out the weight of Sloat's lead. I sat through the church service with equanimity, enjoying the rare sensation of being part of a crowd.

St. Paul's Episcopal Church, Lynchburg, Virginia, had a minister called Spickett. He was an older man with thinning hair and a smarmy accent. His sermon was about our stewardship of the Negro race. It hadn't been so long since the black preacher Nat Turner and his followers had killed off some fifty white people, and folks were still buzzing about it. We all knew that if the slaves ever *really* revolted, there'd be hell to pay. Maybe we should free them first. But what would the blacks do then, and what would happen to the South? We looked up at Reverend Spickett, waiting for his answers.

Reverend Spickett's text was Jesus' "Suffer the little children to come unto me." The darkies, according to him, were our children, given by God unto the white race's care. We were to be firm yet gentle, ever mindful of the fact that the Negro was our ward, a subordinate human species whose ongoing growth must eternally trail the wake of the ever-wiser white race. Here the reverend got to his point: Although *someday* the time might come when it would be proper to teach certain Negroes to read, that time was not now. *No Negro should read, whether or not he knew how.* Nonetheless, it was fitting that all God's children should find Jesus Christ through the divinely inspired words of the Bible. Therefore, St. Paul's was adopting the African Baptist Church as a mission and had begun sending a deacon over to their Sunday services to act as a reader. Congregation members were urged to increase their offerings today to help with this holy work of stewardship.

There were a number of rich planters' families in the church, and they filled the plates right up. The unspoken point was that Nat Turner had been a Negro preacher who read books. My mind wandered, and I started thinking what it would be like to own

Sukic. She was just about black anyway, wasn't she? But if I was so much wiser than her, how had she turned my gold into lead? And why could Otha beat me at checkers whenever he really wanted to? These vague thoughts damped down into a trance as I sat there staring at the pretty colors of the stained glass over the altar. It was a picture of Jesus standing on an orb, with clouds all around and a bright light overhead.

We took communion, and we sang some hymns. I had fun picking the different voices out of the singing and then looking around to see whose they were. I felt like I knew lots of the people by the service's end, not that anyone rushed up to say how-do. There seemed to be some truth to Lucy's belief that her affair with Lieutenant Bustler had made her a social outcast. But Mrs. Perrow was good friends with Reverend Spickett, and she dragged me over to meet him.

"This is Mason Reynolds from Hardware."

"Ah, yes. I know your father. A real man." Spickett peered at me like I wasn't much compared to Pa. I hadn't gotten my growth yet. "Is he well?"

"I left him well. He had me bring our whiskey to town."

"I'm sure Lynchburg needs more whiskey!" said Spickett cheerfully, and turned to shake the next person's hand.

"That reminds me," I told Lucy and Mrs. Perrow on our way out of church. "I have to stop by the Liberty Hotel and speak to Mr. Sloat."

"You can't expect us to go in there!" exclaimed Lucy. She was all set to plunge into another of her snits. "Really, Mother, can you *believe* Mason's manners?"

"Can your business wait till tomorrow, Mason?" said Mrs. Perrow.

"No ma'am, it honestly can't." I could see the hotel from the church steps. "Suppose I go over there alone and meet you all back at the house."

"And leave us unescorted?" wailed Lucy. I was liking her less all the time.

"If you'll be quick, Mason," suggested Mrs. Perrow, "we can take the carriage down to the market square and meet you there."

"Wonderful." I helped them into their carriage, which was driven by their black boy, Walloon. I rode up on the front bench as far as the hotel and jumped off there to see about my gold. The lobby was empty. I went behind Mr. Sloat's desk and pushed his office door open. He was in there right enough. His face was mean and startled, but he was quick to set it in a lecherous smile.

"What kind of squozin' did you give my Sukie, Mason? She's flown the coop! Did she say anything to you about leaving?"

"You're a damned liar, Sloat!" I pulled the lead coins out of my pocket and threw them on his desk. "Give me back my gold!"

His eyebrows went up and down a few times, and then he forced out a laugh. "She robbed you too, did she? She took a suitcase of my silverware! But we'll catch her, boy, don't you fret."

Sloat was a slippery one all right. He'd told Sukie to rob me and now she was lying low, I was willing to bet. But who would help me prove it? "Have you called in the law?" I said finally.

"Just on an informal basis. Sheriff Garmee's a friend of mine. I believe you know him too, Mason. Little fellow, wears a gun?" Sloat squinted his eyes at me and chuckled nastily. "Sheriff said you was right short with him down by the wharf yestidday."

I sighed so heavily it sounded like a groan. These city slickers had me coming and going. If I pulled my gun on Sloat, I'd land in jail. It was no use standing there with him smirking at me, so I left his office.

Just on a hunch, I went out the hotel's back way quiet-like and stood in the courtyard staring up at the windows. Most of them were shuttered, but—by God, yes—two of the windows up on the top floor were open, and there sitting by one of them was Sukie, looking in a hand mirror and combing out her curly black hair. I hurried out to Main Street before she could catch sight of me.

There were upward of a dozen carriages driving slowly around the perimeter of the cobblestoned market square. The clouds had broken up, and the sun was gleaming on the puddles. All those fine horses and coaches made a brave sight. It looked like May Day after all. Lucy spotted me and waved laughingly from her carriage window. I sprinted over and sprang nimbly onto the little step by her door.

"Good afternoon, lady fair!" I was trying to make up for this morning. Soon I'd talk things over with Otha, and we'd do what we had to do. I already had the makings of a plan. Wasn't no way Sloat was getting away with the Reynoldses' whiskey money. Sloat didn't realize what he'd gotten himself into. No indeed.

"Are you talking to yourself, Mason?" said Lucy. "What's the matter?"

"Nothing a-tall." I plastered on a smile.

Otha, as it turned out, had taken quite a shine to Wawona. After Sunday dinner, I went back to the kitchen and asked him to come outside with me. The Perrow house was up at the top of a long sloping field leading down to the river. There were vegetable plots in the field and a few acres of tobacco. With the torn bits of gray clouds drifting across the pale blue sky, it made for a lovely view. Otha couldn't stop talking about "that little girl."

"I'll buy her for you," said I. "But you have to help me get the money."

"Whuffo' git what you done got, Mason? Wawona cost sixty dollar an' Mist Sloat done give you one hunnert an' twenty."

"I'm telling you. That girl last night, that Sukie, she took the gold out of my pocket and gave it to Mr. Sloat. I went and asked him about it today, and he pretended she'd run away. But she's still right there in the Liberty Hotel. I saw her through a window. More than likely our money's right back in Sloat's safe where he got it in the first place."

"Damn and *hell*." Otha's lanky frame twitched in horror. "You teasin' me, Mason! 'Cause what was dat you was jinglin' in yo pocket last night?"

"Lead."

"Damn and *hell*. I want Wawona, Mason, you white folks owes me dat. Ain' my fault you done lost de money to a fancy ho'. Tell de judge you gwine pay him on account. Dat little girl comin' home wid us tomorrow." His voice softened. "She sweet as can be. I held her han' in church."

"Was there a white man reading the Bible?"

"Ah ain' pay him no mind. Bible pages be white, but de ink be black. Nat Turner say God be black, what dey say."

I glanced around uneasily. "That's no way to talk, Otha. We're not out on the farm here. We're in Lynchburg, and if you think Judge Perrow got rich by selling slaves on credit, you're dreaming. You got to help me steal that money back."

"An' git caught and whupped an' git sold to auction fo' to pay yo fine? You gwine be de one to tell Turl, li'l messymess?" This was a childhood nickname that Otha still mocked me with from time to time. I hated it, as well he knew.

So that I wouldn't be in the demeaning posture of looking up at Otha, I glared into the distance. "If you gonna mouth at me like that, *nigger*, we might as well take our losses and go on home. You and me and Dammit and Arf. I expect there's plowing to do."

Otha made a high keening noise in the back of his throat and peered down at me with his big yellow eyes. "Tell me yo plan, damn fool."

The two of us walked downtown right around dusk. I still had Pa's trousers and tailcoat on. This was the longest I'd ever worn them. They were loose on me, but after yesterday I knew better than to play the rube in breeches. Otha followed me by the accepted three steps, and Arf hung close to Otha.

We loafed past the Liberty Hotel entrance, checking that

Mr. Sloat was on duty at the desk in the lobby. And then Otha took Arf and rolled him around in a big mud puddle, making sure to get his own feet good and caked. I hurried around to the hotel's back courtyard entrance and slipped on in. By the time I got as far as the lobby, the excitement had already started.

"No suh," Otha was saying. "Ah ain' goam leave till I sees Mistuh Bustler." He and Arf were standing in the middle of the Oriental rug, Arf shaking and Otha scuffing his shoes. There was no Bustler here, of course, but it amused me to have Otha use Lucy's pie-faced seducer's name. "Miz Bustler's powerful upset. Ah's real sorry to 'sturb you folks, but . . ."

*"Don't stand on the rug!"* Sloat screamed. *"Are you deaf!"*

"Ah's might' sorry, suh, but Miz Bustler done tole me as how she ain' goam . . ."

Sloat's chair smacked against the wall and he went puffing across the lobby. In his passion, he didn't see me waiting there at the head of the back hall. I darted around the corner and into his private office with my coattails flying. Out in the lobby, Sloat was screaming, Arf was barking, and Otha was still maundering on in stubborn slave talk.

I went right to the safe and yanked on the door—it was open. I tried drawer after drawer until I found the right one. A small metal drawer at the bottom held several handfuls of gold twenty-dollar pieces. Should I take them all? Frightful thought! Was I not a gentleman? I took the six coins due me and whipped back into the lobby, aiming for the safety of the dark back hall . . .

It would have gone off smooth as snot on a doorknob if Arf hadn't run over to dog my steps. Sloat was still busy trying to shove Otha off his precious rug, but Arf's excited rush for me made him look around. He turned just as I stepped out from behind his desk—me with the gold coins glinting in my hand.

"Mr. Mason Reynolds," said Sloat, his voice calm even though his face was still red. "This is *your* boy here, I do believe." He raised his voice back to a scream. "Sheriff Garmee! Arrest these two!"

As soon as Sloat called him, the damn midget from yesterday was there in the saloon door, his upturned nostrils making black holes in his humorless little face. I took off down the hotel's back hall as fast as I could run. Arf and Otha followed close behind.

The blond stableboy out in the courtyard got a hand on me, but Otha shoved him off. Glancing back, I saw the stableboy pull the gun out of the holster hung by the stalls. The gun in my inside pocket was slamming against my chest. I yanked it out and fired a shot back toward the hotel, and at the same exact time the stableboy fired off a shot after me. I knew for sure he'd fired because the bullet whizzed right past me, making a tearing sound in the air. There was a scream. We ran around the corner to Main Street and took the first alley down toward the river. Folks turned to watch us clatter by. We took a right on the next street down and slowed to a walk so as to not attract any more notice. Another alley popped up, and we took that the rest of the way down to the river.

It was dark and quiet down there. Back up in the town, people were yelling . . . yelling more than seemed fitting for a simple settling of scores.

"You done messed up for true, Mason."

"We better cross the river and walk home. Do you think we should try to swim? Hell, dogs can swim, Otha. I bet we can too."

"What about de wagon an' de mule?" said Otha, shaking his head. "What about dat little girl?"

"We can't go back to the Perrows', Otha. Yesterday I told Sloat I was staying there. That's the first place they'll look for us."

"Your pa goam be bleak obber dis."

I knew just what Otha meant. When things went wrong, Pa'd get quiet for days on end, and usually drunk as well. But things could still work out!

"Listen, Otha, unless Sloat gets a paper to seize the wagon, Walloon can drive it out to us. And, Otha, Walloon can bring

Wawona. There's none of this city law out on the farm. All we got to do is cross the river and walk home. I got the money back, didn't I?"

"I don't know, Mason. Did you?"

There was a sudden hubbub of voices nearby. Sheriff Garmee!

"This way, men," he called in his nasty tenor. "We're lookin' for a blond little fellow, a long nigger, and a dog." They had torches, but they were still a few hundred feet away.

"Hsst!" said Otha. "Git in de bateau!"

The bateau that the slaves had been loading with tobacco was tied up right nearby. We slipped down into it, fast and bumpy.

Arf stood up on the wharf staring down at us. "Come on," I hissed. "Come on down here, Arf." He snuffled and backed off. I lunged and got hold of the loose skin of his neck. Man's best friend had to let out a yelp, of course, which set off hallos from the sheriff's torch gang. I yanked Arf down into the bateau, and a few seconds later the three of us were stuffed under a tarpaulin with some barrels of tobacco and bags of provisions. It was lumpy and close, but we didn't dare move. Two of the searchers came within an ace of lifting up our tarp, but then a noise up in Water Street led them back uphill.

The tarpaulin smelled of pitch and the river, and the bateau rocked slowly in the current. Before too long, the three of us were asleep.

# 3

## On the River

FEET Someone stepped on my back, and I woke. The first thing I saw was Otha's muddy toes, right in my face. There were voices and footsteps all around: black voices and bare feet. Pinpoints of light showed through the tarp. It was dawn, and the bateau crew was setting out for Richmond.

I held myself still, bracing steady against the foot on my back. "C'mon now, Custa!" yelled someone. "Pick up yo pole and lean into it, son. Dis ain' no steamboat and we ain' 'bout to set no sail!" Grudgingly, the foot moved away. Arf pushed his snout forward and gave my mouth a lick. I shoved his head down against the bateau's wet planks. Otha and I had wedged ourselves in head to tail, with Arf in between us. It was hard to tell in the faint dotty light, and with just his foot to judge from, but Otha looked as if he were still asleep. He liked to sleep.

"Look out, Richmond, here come de Garlands again!" whooped the same voice as before. With great wallowing and splashing and banging of poles, our boat seemed to be making its way out into the James River's stream.

41

"'Turn it, boys, and head it on down!'' Feet ran up and down the two long walkways built up onto the bateau's gunnels. The hull groaned, turned, and picked up speed.

"Go left, go left, go leee—Custa, hang on!'' We struck something with a heavy jarring crash. Another crash and another, and then shouts and laughter. Otha's foot twitched: I pinched it hard. He thought for a while, and then his invisible hand gave my ankle a twist and a pat.

The hammering of the rocks lasted another few minutes, and then we were in a smooth stretch. The polers moved up and down the bateau with steady strides. When it seemed sure we must be out of sight of Lynchburg, I began struggling to sit up. It took a minute, what with Arf and my tailcoat and Otha's legs tangling me. I was a little dizzy from the strong smell of tobacco. By the time I finally wormed my head and shoulders out from under the heavy tarp, the whole bateau crew was pointing and jabbering. My collar was awry and my red cravat had come partly unwound.

"Lord help us,'' cried one of the crew, a chunky boy my age. "It's de bloody ghost ob de stableboy!'' Arf pushed his head out next to mine then, and the chunky boy gave a falsetto scream. "It's de ghost an' de devil!'' With that, he fell overboard.

"Git holda Custa, Marcus!'' cried a wiry little man standing by the steering sweep. His was the voice I'd heard before. He had high cheekbones and bright darting eyes. "He cain't swim! Fetch de ax, Luther! Dis ain't no ghost, it's de murderer!''

A bullet-headed, barrel-chested blue-black man surged back from the bow, snatching up an ax from a toolbox. He yanked the tarp off me and crouched over me, weapon at the ready. Arf growled furiously.

"Dere's anudder one under dere too,'' called the steersman. "Ah sees his feet! Come on out, long legs!''

While two of the crew members hauled plump Custa in over the gunnel, Otha extricated himself from the tarpaulin to sit at my side. I was glad to see his face. He'd be able to soothe these savages.

"Hush de dog, Mason," he said to me quietly. "I knows dis man."

I threw an arm around Arf and squeezed him reassuringly. Arf yipped at my first touch, but then he settled down.

"Wo ain' no murder, Unc Tyree," said Otha, looking up at the steersman. Otha had that special honest look he always put on for talking to grown-ups. "You mought not 'member me, but you be cousin to my ma, Turl, who work out at de Reynoldses in Hardware? Dis here Mist Mason Reynolds. We . . ."

"I knows you, Otha," said Tyree. "Whole town knows 'bout you and yo young marse robbin' Mist Sloat and shootin' his hostler dead. Sheriff Garmee, he got a hundred-dollar price on Mason Reynolds' head, dead or alive."

"What about me?" asked Otha.

"You ain' worth nothin' dead, long legs. Wif yo master a fugitive, you's a runaway up fo' auction, ah 'speck. Less'n you goes back to yo farm."

"We both want to go back to the farm." I put in. "I didn't murder the stableboy. It was an accident. And that was *my* money I was taking from Mr. Sloat. Just put us off here, Tyree, and we'll make our way back to Hardware." I sat up straighter. "And tell your boy to put down the ax."

"Who you callin' *boy*, boy?" said the blue-black man, named Luther. "Sheriff'll pay me hundred dollar to chop yo haid off. Nuff to buy me free, and mah missus too."

"Ah seen him first," shouted Custa, soaking wet and back on board. "*Ah* gits de reward."

"Share and share alike," sang a deep-voiced man with a perfect physique. "Right, Moline?"

"Ah'll be de one to chop his head off," said the last of the five bateau-men. "Killin' a white boy wouldn't bother me none at all." He looked like he meant it. He was as strong and well-formed as Marcus, but some mishap had removed his front teeth and left his nose smashed flat against his face. His eyes were small and angry. "Feed his body to de catfish and we'll have less weight to pole!"

Otha formed his face into an expression of exquisite contempt. "Ah may be country, but you boys is fools. You really 'speck some white sheriff to hand each ob you a gold double-eagle? Widdout yore marse Garland say nothin'? You really 'speck to walk into Lynchburg carryin' a white boy's head? Dey'd make de rest ob you match yo ugly face, Moline."

Everyone ruminated on that for a minute. The bateau continued drifting down the James. It was a bright day, with a few puffy clouds. The river's smooth green-brown water mirrored the clouds perfectly. The stream wasn't but twenty yards wide here, and it would have been easy to swim to shore had I known how to swim. But even if I got to shore, these Negroes would chase me down. And, I now realized, even if I could get away, even if I could get back to Pa's farm, there'd be bounty hunters coming after my head. My only hope was to enlist this crew's support.

I rose to my feet. Sensing that my sprung collar and wadded cravat detracted from my appearance, I tugged them off and shoved them in my soiled tailcoat's side pocket. I could feel my pistol through the fabric of the coat. Bullethead Luther made a menacing gesture with his ax, but I fixed him with a stare that rocked him back. "I'll make you men an offer," I said, looking up and down the length of the bateau. Wiry Tyree, big Luther, puppyish Custa, handsome Marcus, and angry smash-faced Moline. "*I'll* pay you the hundred-dollar reward. Deliver me and my man Otha to Richmond, and the money shall be yours. I give you my word as a gentleman."

"Lissen at him," said Tyree. He pursed up his thin-cheeked face and spat into the river.

"You all ain't gettin' nothin' if you pole back to Lynchburg, Unc Tyree," said Otha. "Nothin' but sore backs an' trouble. Sheriff likely to think you took us on purpose and changed yo mind. Specially if dass whut ah tell him. But effen you takes us to Richmond, you gits a gold double-eagle each. Mist Mason ain' no lie."

"Lez see de gold!" shouted Marcus.

I shoved my hand in my trouser pocket and fingered the six coins. I glanced questioningly at Otha. He nodded. Holding myself extra steady, I drew the coins out and displayed them in my cupped hands. They glinted wonderfully in the bright river sun. I turned this way and that so everyone could see them.

"Six coins," I said. "It's all I took. If I give one to each of you men, that'll leave just one for Otha and me to share."

Luther set down his ax and reached up as if to take one of the gold pieces. He looked like a boy reaching for a beautiful butterfly.

"Not yet!" said Otha, slapping Luther's hand away. "Y'all gits de coins when we's in sight o' Richmond!"

"Sloat and de sheriff sayin' yo marse stole a thousand dollar, Otha," complained Tyree. "Whar de rest ob it?"

"Oh, it were *tin* thousand dollar," said Otha. "And we spent it all to buy this here yaller dog. He be so smart he kin say his own name." Arf stretched, bowed, and shook himself three times.

"His name is Arf," I said, putting the six coins back in my pocket. "Let's head for Richmond!"

"*Lean into it, boys,*" sang Tyree. "*Lez* git dere early and claim our gold!"

The trip took five days, where usually it would have taken seven. Otha helped a bit with the poling, but that certainly wasn't my place. I spent the days sitting on a barrel in the middle of the boat, staring out at the gentle scenery of Virginia. The river was lined with big ashes and elms, thick-trunked giants that reached far out over the stream. There was tangled scrub behind the elms and on the river's many rocky little sandbars. The thickets were just starting to green up, and it was still easy to see the roll of the hilly land. Now and then we'd pass a plantation of great cleared fields surrounding a mansion. There were poorer farms, too; the white farm kids would hear us coming and come down to the river to wave. When that happened, I'd lie down flat in the bateau bottom with Arf.

Nights, we'd camp out at the river's edge in a clearing beneath the elm trees. There'd be a fire, and Moline would boil up a mess of pork and dried corn. The crew'd all fill up to busting, and then they'd sit around the fire talking and chewing tobacco for an hour before they dropped off to sleep. Arf and I ate the same food as them, though Moline always acted like he didn't want to give me any.

It was interesting for me to hear their songs and stories. I'd never been this close to a gang of slaves. One of the reasons Tyree was boss was that he knew a lot of chants and legends that went right back to Africa. According to Tyree, his father's father had been an African medicine man, and the power and the knowledge had been passed right on down to him. Every night, the first thing after eating, anyone who'd gotten a cut or a bruise or a sprain during the day would show it to Tyree, and he'd rub on some herbs and chant in African. After watching him a few times, I let him work his magic on an elbow that I'd smashed against the hull. His spooking really did make the throbbing some better.

After Tyree's healing they'd sing a couple of spirituals—but with the words changed around so that the songs were about running off to the North instead of dying and going to heaven. And then they'd start in on the ghost stories. Custa knew dozens of tales about killings and ghosts. After listening to a few of his chillers, I'd spend the whole night with that poor dead stableboy's sharp little face hanging over me. In my dreams, the stableboy looked more and more like me. We could have been friends, or even brothers, and I'd shot him without even needing to. I considered throwing my damn pistol away, but I couldn't quite turn loose of it. There was always the possibility one of the men might decide to take my money in the night.

The money was another big topic of conversation. Twenty dollars wasn't enough for any of the men to legally buy his freedom, which was something they all seemed to want, Luther most of all. By law, slaves weren't allowed to have money—any more than they were allowed to read—so by law, any sum short of the sixty to a hundred dollars' slave price was only good for hoarding. But—though they avoided clearly saying so in my presence—if a slave were to run away and head North, twenty dollars could make a big difference in escaping the paddy rollers—the patrollers who hunted runaways. And there were certainly pawnbrokers in Richmond willing to do trade with slaves. A house servant might bring a filched silver spoon to the back door of such a pawnshop and leave with a jackknife or a bolt of cloth or a box of peppermint candy. The crewmen spent a lot of time debating the merits of this and that shop, with the house of Abner Levy being mentioned most frequently.

Their chatter ran in various levels of comprehensibility. If they really didn't want me to understand, they could layer on so thick an accent that I might as well have been listening to the cawing of crows. I watched the scenery pass, now looking at the land, now at the river's sinuous flow. I couldn't bring myself to think about what lay ahead. The whole afternoon of the fifth day, the men's talk was incomprehensible jabber. Something was up. That evening, we grounded the bateau on a sandbank just above the shallows and rapids of Goochland. Two other bateaus were already here.

"Tormorrow mornin' we goes into de canal 'bout quarter mile up dere, Mist Mason," Tyree told me. "And den it's twenty-some mile to Richmond." The James's flow was accelerating and there was a graveyard's worth of white-foamed rocks ahead, bright in the gathering dusk. Up to the left where Tyree pointed was the granite bulwark where the James River and Kanawha Canal branched off from the river. There'd be toll takers up there, men likely to remember my passage if the sheriff eventually searched this far. "It be best fo' us if you an' Arf stay under cover all day tomorrow."

"All right," said I. The thought of our trip ending made my stomach tighten in fear. I'd never been to Richmond.

"You mought's well pay us now, Mist Mason," put in

Luther. "Lessen dere some confusion later on." He was smiling and happy about getting his money.

"Come on," put in Moline, pushing his ugly face toward mine. "Lez have dat damn gold, white boy." No amount of money was going to make *him* happy.

"I said I'd pay you in Richmond," I said uncertainly. Were they planning to turn me in after all?

"You goam pay us now," said Tyree. "Stead o' slippin' off in Richmond, like you mought be fixin' to do."

Didn't they trust me? They were all squeezed around me in the middle of the boat. I glanced at Otha, who gave me a shrug and a nod. I took the bitterly won gold coins out of my pocket and handed one each to Tyree, Luther, Custa, Marcus, and Moline. Five gone, and one coin left for me and Otha. He looked like he thought I ought to hand it over to him, but I shoved it back down in my pocket.

There was a regular beaten-down campground here; the two other bateau crews already had their fires going. There was a certain amount of visiting back and forth and plenty of that incomprehensible crow-cawing. I was the only white man in the campsite. After our fire was going, Moline put on the fatback and cracked corn. As usual, he served all the others first, only tonight there was no food left by the time he got to me.

"Too bad, Mason," he said jeeringly, and took his own big plateful of food off to eat. Although I was very hungry, I was damned if I was going to beg these niggers for food. Tomorrow I'd be shut of them. A few of them—Custa and Moline and Marcus—were grinning up at me, but I didn't give them the satisfaction of saying anything. Instead, I found a soft spot and lay down to sleep. Someone must have fed Arf, because after a while he came over and lay down with me. I half expected Otha to bring me some food, but he never did.

I woke up suddenly in the middle of the night. Arf was gone. The fires were burnt down to red glows, and the moon was high. My stomach was so empty I couldn't think about anything

but filling it. I decided to get myself some corn from the supply
sack and boil it up. I found the sack all right, over by the fire
where Moline had left it. I carried the kettle down to the river and
waded out to get a scoop of clear water. I stood out in the river
for a minute, watching the moonlight quivering off the ripples
and listening to the steady roar of the rapids coming from downstream. Standing there, I woke all the way up and realized there
was something wrong.

What was wrong was that I was all alone. There were still
some rags and wads of clothing lying around, but none of the
crew was there by our fire. Peering over to where the other two
crews had been, I could see that their campsites were deserted
too. Yet all three bateaus were still down on the sandbank—I'd
just seen them.

I boiled a little corn mash, keeping my ears pricked all the
while. Sure enough, I could hear something back in the woods,
a steady humming that blended in with the river noise. Now and
then the humming rose up into a yell. I bolted down my half-
cooked cracked corn and headed through the trees, turning my
head this way and that to catch the noise. The ground turned
swampy and the humming noise grew. There was an orange glow
up ahead. I pushed twenty yards further, trying not to crackle the
underbrush, and then, peering through the branches of a sassafras
sapling, I could see.

There was a clearing of raised ground with a bonfire in the
middle. All around the clearing, the wet ground sent back streaks
and patches of the firelight. On the far side of the bonfire were a
tent and a huge old oak tree, lightning blasted and half rotted out.
Perched inside the tree's hollow was a huge man with skin as
white as paper. He had curly white hair and thick lips and could
have been an albino Negro. Yet his whiteness was so total and so
extraordinary that he seemed rather a member of some different
race.

Standing in a knot on the near side of the fire were fifteen or
twenty slaves; among them were all of the six I'd been traveling

with. They were chanting some repetitive phrase that I couldn't make out. Now and then the huge man in the tree would beckon, and one of the slaves would go up to him.

A man from one of the other bateaus took a bag of corn up; when he set down the bag, a big snow-white arm extended out of the tree and handed him a leather pouch on a thong. The man tied the thong around his waist and skipped back to the others with a smile on his face. He kept pressing the leather pouch down against his privates; I expect it was a spell for having children. Diverse exchanges occurred, turn by turn, and then came Tyree. He had a little bundle of tobacco that he must have filched out of one of the hogsheads on our bateau. The paper-white man's mouth made a big welcoming hole in his face when he saw Tyree; it seemed like they were old friends. In the firelight it looked as if the weird man had bright red teeth. He dug around in his tree for a bit and then gave Tyree three little sacks in trade for the tobacco.

I was just wondering if any of the boys would be bone-headed enough to give their medicine man one of my gold coins when Moline did it. He pulled out his coin, held it high in the firelight, and marched right up to the tree with that big white man lurking in it like a termite. Next thing I knew, Moline and the magic man were dancing around the fire together. They made a frightening sight: Moline with his dark, hating, smashed face, and the big treeman white as the inside of a toadstool. In the firelight I could see his face more clearly than before. Though he had a Negro's big lips and kinky hair, his nose was thin and pointed and his forehead was flat and high. At first I'd thought he was fat, but now as he moved around I could see all those bulges were muscle. He wore nothing but an oddly patterned loincloth. I wondered if he might be from the Feejee islands, perhaps come to America on a whaling ship. It was a strange thing seeing him.

He was working himself up into a frenzy, yelling something over and over—it sounded like *"Lamalama tekelili."* His teeth really were red. The bateau-men were dancing and yelling *"La-*

*malama,"* too, and goddamn Arf was in there as well, I now noticed, frisking right along with the war dance, so excited that he was practically walking on his hind legs. After a little more dancing and yelling, Marcus got worked up enough to give his gold to the big albino too, and then the fellow ran into his tent and got out a sword. They all cheered him and called him Elijah, and he cried out back something that, just this once, I could understand only too well: "Kill the masters!"

As he cried out, Arf sped away from the circle of men like a clot of mud thrown off a spinning wagon wheel. He bounded through the underbrush and ran right into me. I was glad he didn't bite me.

I decided to get back to the campsite. Arf showed no inclination to lead, but by using the moon and the sound of the river to guide me, I found my way back to where I'd been sleeping. After Arf and I'd been lying there a half hour, the men came traipsing back. I had my gun clenched in my hand, just in case Marcus decided to stick that big sword in me. But they dropped off to sleep without bothering me. I lay awake till dawn, wondering about what I'd seen.

The next morning Moline was missing and Marcus had the sword, but nobody offered to explain why. I didn't press them; I was ready for the trip to end. Arf and I got under the tarpaulin, and the men maneuvered the bateau into the canal. My mind had been blank during this whole river trip, but now it was teeming. Elijah, Pa, Sukie, Lucy, Sloat, and the dead hostler's faces all swam before me. Should I warn people about Elijah? How soon could I return to safe Hardware and Pa's proud plans for my future? What would become of me in the big city? How could I live? I was only fifteen years old!

I dozed through most of that long last day. Over and over the stableboy showed me the hole in his forehead, over and over I used a candle to see between Sukie's legs, over and over Elijah screamed, *"Kill."* The canal was busy, and each time I heard a strange voice I jerked awake, thinking it was the evil midget

Sheriff Garmee. In my dreams he became small enough to crawl through a bunghole, and each of the roaches that crossed my face felt like him.

Finally, it was dusk and we were bumping into the canal basin. Once again Custa stepped on me, and once again Arf licked my face. "Right here's fine, Unc Tyree," I heard Otha say. And then, "Come on out, Mason."

I sprang out from under the tarp. We were in the canal basin, a landlocked lagoon in the midst of Richmond. Up ahead of us was a wharf with some dozen bateaus in various stages of un- lading. But right here on our left was a low stone embankment edging a nearly deserted square. Without a pause, I grabbed hold of the wall and swung myself up onto land. Otha passed Arf up and then joined me on the canal side. The crew was eager to be off lest they be seen with a fugitive. We bid them a hasty fare- well, and they went poling off toward the bateau wharves.

"How 'bout mine, Mason?" Otha held out his pale-palmed hand for the last double-eagle. Seeing all the other blacks get coins yesterday had been too much for him.

"*Mister* Mason, please, Otha. People might hear. Don't forget you're my slave. I'll keep the coin. You know that what's mine is yours."

"Sho'. Do dat make *me* mine? Ah b'lieve ah's ready fo' dat."

"Are you asking me to free you, Otha? Why in hell should I? Can't you see we'd do better to stick together?" This was no time to say so, but I had a half-formed plan of renting Otha out as a factory worker if need be.

"You de one messed up, Mase. You de one lost mah bride money and kilt dat boy. Ah could still turn you in, you know."

"Sure you could. Turn me in and get sold down the river by Sloat. Get sold down to 'Bama, where the masters whip instead of jawin'!" I was getting really angry. I'd seen enough black faces in the last five days to last me a lifetime. Otha's expression was hard and dark. He stuck his hand out again.

"Gimme de money, Mason. We's splittin' up."

Behind Otha I could see a street leading uphill several blocks to some kind of green field. The lower part of the street held offices, but higher up were beautiful homes with shiny brass doorplates and lace curtains in the windows. The whole big world was waiting for me. Would I never be free? In sudden revulsion, I drew the coin out of my pocket and slapped it into Otha's hand. "Go on then, stupid nigger. I'm dead sick of trying to boss you. Go on and get. Sign up with crazy Elijah for all I care."

Otha pocketed the coin without a smile. "Don' call me nigger, you white mess." He turned on his heel and marched across the square, heading toward the wharf where the bateaus were unloading. Arf trotted after him.

"Come here, Arfie," I called. "Come on, boy, you stay with me." Arf stopped and looked back at me, cocking an eyebrow. Otha kept walking. "Come on, Arfie!" Arf flapped his tongue at me and scampered after Otha. I'd raised Arf white and now he'd turned into a damn nigger dog. They could both go straight to hell.

I stalked up that pretty street I'd had my eye on before. My heart was pounding so hard I could barely see. I hadn't gone but two blocks before I banged into somebody, a well-dressed man in one of the new-fashion frockcoats.

"Pardon *me*," he said sharply, raking me with a look that made me realize how really poor I must look. After he marched off, I crouched in front of one of the elegant houses' brass doorplates, using it for a mirror.

I still had Pa's tailcoat and trousers on, but after five days of riding the bateau, they were right motley. I was stained all over with mud and water. Dog hair, dead insects, and bits of vegetation were pasted to me. My shirt, socks, and underwear stank so that even I could smell them. My shoes were invisible beneath a layer of dried river slime; more of the slime matted my hair. The only possession I had in my pockets besides my collar and cravat was that cursed pepperbox pistol, still loaded with three shots—

though after the days on the river, the powder was surely too sodden to catch.

I needed to find lodging in an inn, where I could bathe and have my clothes laundered. Yet with my appearance like this, who would extend me credit? I wandered further uphill until my street butted into the field I'd noticed before. The field covered the whole hilltop, and there was a low black iron fence all around it to keep livestock out. In the middle of the field, at the top of the hill, was an enormous white building with columns. I realized it had to be the state capitol, which Mr. Jefferson had modeled after a Roman temple he'd seen off in France. I swung over the fence and sloped across the field to get a good look at the building. It was a simple design: a long rectangular box with a triangle roof on top and the big columns at either end. The columns were so tall that looking up at them made me catch my breath. Even if politics was all thievery and lies, those boys certainly had a grand stage to play it on. I went on across the rest of the field that was Capitol Square and went another block till I got to a street called Broad Street. There were all kinds of shops there, with lots of people and carriages moving around. It was close on to dusk on a Friday night. I needed to find lodging before the streets got dark.

Off to the right there was a church called Monumental Episcopal. Maybe the preacher there could help me. I started up the church steps, but before I could even get to the door, a fine-dressed woman frowned out at me and asked me what I wanted. She had some cloths in her hands like she was there to fix the altar. I didn't feel I could introduce myself, so I simply said I was looking for a place to stay.

"Do you know horses?" she asked, looking me up and down. She had a hard little nose and a lot of rouge. "I believe my brother is looking for a stableboy."

*Stableboy.* The word made me run chills all over. "I'm sorry, ma'am," I informed her. "I'm a gentleman."

She let out a laugh and closed the door.

I walked another block down Broad Street. The boys on the bateau had said something about this street, and when I got to the next corner I remembered what. The pawnshops were supposed to be off this street somewhere, near the capitol. I could pawn my pistol and get cleaned up enough to find a position befitting my station.

I took an empty alley that went to the left behind the church, and then I took another alley off that to the right. Another left, and sure enough, there was a building with three gold balls hanging over the door. ABNER LEVY, read a small sign under the balls. I felt myself smiling for the first time in days.

There was a gaslight on in the shop and a man in there, a stocky fellow with dark hair and thick lips. He flashed me a ready smile.

"Good evening," said I. "Would you pawn a pistol?"

We were alone in the shop and the pistol part put him off a bit. But once I'd handed it to him butt first, he brightened up.

"Shouldn't leave these loads in here," he said, tapping the powder out on the counter. "Wet powder can go off unexpectedly when it dries. I didn't catch your name."

"Lieutenant Bustler," I said easy-like. "Of Norfolk, Virginia."

The dark-haired fellow raised his eyebrows at that, me being fifteen, fair, and five foot two. But there wasn't anyone else there to hear my lie, so he let it pass.

"I can let you have a month's loan of three dollars on it," he said presently. "If you come back before June sixth, you can redeem your pistol for four dollars."

"That's fine," I said, not wanting to fuss.

He wrote out a pawn ticket and counted the three dollars into my hand. When he leaned over to write the ticket, I noticed that he had a little round cap on the back of his head.

I went back to Broad Street and headed the way I'd come from. There was bound to be an inn somewhere near the capitol. There were all kinds of people on the sidewalk: gentlemen, ladies, farmers, slaves, and free blacks. In my tatty condition, I was ashamed to look any of them in the face lest they take me for a beggar or a drunk. A few more blocks and I saw the gold sign of the Swan Inn. I headed right in.

Fortunately it was murky in there, so the woman behind the counter couldn't make out just how shabby I was. With a minimum of conversation, I engaged her to give me a room, to send up supper and a bath, and to take my garments down for a wash. All this would cost me two and a half dollars, payable in advance. I paid her, and a serving girl escorted me upstairs. An hour later I was asleep in my bed, clean and well fed.

# 4

## Eddie Poe

I WOKE UP earlier than I wanted to. I tried to go back to sleep, but it was no use. Today was the start of my new life in Richmond; there was no shirking it. My clothes were in the hall outside my door: cleaned, pressed, and folded. My shoes sat next to them, freshly blacked. If I could find a position at all, I had better find it today.

I dressed with care, enjoying the touch of the clean cloth on my clean skin. My room had a fine looking-glass; I adjusted my cravat to cover the creases in my collar and then spent a few minutes regarding myself. My blond hair was clean and straight, my pale face had a bit of color from the days on the bateau, and my hazel-brown eyes were clear and rested. If only I were a bit taller and had hair on my face! I formed a smile—no, that looked too scampish. I tightened my thin lips in resolve—that was better. A competent, well-born young man, ready to succeed.

But at what? I walked downstairs and passed through the tavern, assuring the innkeeper that I would return. If I did the thing right, I might hope to spend another few days there on credit. My feet led me toward Capitol Square. Today I noticed that the templelike capitol was not the only building in the grassy field. There was a smaller domed building in the field as well. A passerby told me that the smaller building was the Richmond city hall. It occurred to me that I might find employment there. After all, I could read and write excellently, which was a skill our pastoral commonwealth could ill despise. If I were indeed a thief and a murderer, then might not the political arena be the place for me?

Only a few offices were open in the city hall, it being nine o'clock of a Saturday morning. In one office a red-faced man dozed, with his feet on his desk. Another room held a thin man scribbling furiously with a quill pen. In still another office a strapping young man in shirtsleeves tried to explain something about a certain street repair to an underling. The largest office held three men behind desks and five more men sitting on a bench, everyone in trousers and tailcoat. I slipped onto the left end of the bench, where there was space. The room had a pleasant smell of cigar smoke. I noticed that there was a fourth desk with no one at it. Maybe that was the spot for me!

Now and then, one of the men at the desks would look up and call, "Next." The rightmost man on the bench would get up and go sit in a chair by one of the desks, and then he and the deskman would shuffle through papers together. As time wore on, I scooted down closer to the business end of the bench, and a few new arrivals came and sat down to the left of me. Finally, it was my turn.

"Next!"

I tightened my lips and marched over to the desk by the window, where the man was waiting. He was a baldpate, with a greasy fringe of gray over his ears. He wore spectacles that flashed in the sunlight. His mouth was much thinner and tighter than I could ever make mine.

"Is this a debenture or a deed in trust?" he asked me.

"I'm Mason, ah, Mason Bustler," I told him. "A gentleman."

"To be sure." He held out his hand. "To cede the notarized instrument of the parties in bailiwick?"

I made as if to feel in my pockets. "Suppose we use one of your papers. I can read and write. Better than that, I've got *literary style.*" That's what my uncle Tuck had said about a ten-page letter I'd written for him, and it was true. With all the close reading I'd done, I could write as flowery as in a magazine.

The baldpate sat back like he didn't know what I was talking about. "You waive conveyance of the warranty?"

"I'm looking for a job." I hooked my thumb over at the empty desk. "Looks like you fellers could use an extra hand."

The baldpate took off his glasses to see me better. It didn't seem to help. "Affidavit of all property representation must be filed within ninety days," he told me. "In lieu of putative tenure."

"Can I start today?"

"Nincompoop." He put his glasses back on and made a shooing gesture with his hand. "Next!"

I knew what *nincompoop* meant all right. On my way out, I noticed what looked like a thick discarded newspaper on the floor; I scooped it up and took it with me.

It was a fine sunny May day, with weeds and clumps of grass pushing up shoots in every spare corner of Richmond's muddy lots and streets. I wondered if I might have better luck in the capitol. Not likely. I set myself down on a clean patch of grass to read my paper.

I was pleased to see it was a copy of the April issue of *The Southern Literary Messenger.* That issue hadn't made it out to our farm yet. Scanning down the contents list, I saw an article called "Maelzel's Chess Player" by Edgar Poe. He was my favorite new writer; he had a horrifying or humorous tale in the *Messenger* almost every month. I read "Maelzel's Chess Player" straight through right then and there.

It was an essay rather than a chiller like I'd been expecting, an essay about a chess-playing machine that a Mr. Maelzel had been showing around the country. Edgar Poe argued that it couldn't really be a machine or *it would always win*. Instead, wrote he, there had to be a midget hidden inside the machine, and he had a diagram worked out to show how. I finished the article with a sense of satisfaction and sat there for a while thinking about how it would be to have a job hiding inside a chess machine. I didn't know how to play chess, but I did play a good game of checkers, if not quite so good as Otha's.

Flipping back to the front of *The Southern Literary Messenger*, I noticed that their editorial offices were at 1501 Main Street, Richmond. Reading the editorial matter (which I normally skipped over), I learned something I hadn't realized before: Edgar Poe was now the *Messenger*'s editor! What luck! Edgar Poe would understand my predicament—he'd seen trouble himself. According to Judge Perrow, Poe had been kicked out of the university for gambling. I'd go and ask him for a job!

I made it to Fifteenth and Main without even having to get anyone's instructions. Like Edgar Poe says, man's highest ability is his power to ratiocinate.

When I came to the appointed street corner, it was a quiet dusty noon. A hog slept in a shallow wallow at one edge of the street. There were brick buildings all around; 1501's Main Street storefront held a shop selling jewelry and optical goods. A sign by the building's side entrance indicated that inside were the offices of *The Southern Literary Messenger*, T. W. White, Prop. Though no man was in sight, the door opened to my touch. I found myself in a large plank-floored room filled with ink-marked papers and printing equipment.

The printing press dominated the room; it was a ponderous black iron machine, wonderfully scrolled and ornamented, with powerful-looking screws and levers on every side. The far wall held a huge double door that I supposed gave onto a loading dock and an alley. Piled next to that door were stacks of newsprint and stacks of finished papers—issues of the May *Southern Literary Messenger*. The near wall, which ran along Fifteenth Street, was lined with tables lit by large windows to the street. Dust motes jigged in the steep-slanting light. It was so quiet that I could hear someone talking in the shop out front.

Some of the tables held ragged-edged printed sheets laid out for proofing, and some were strewn with bits of metal: letters and punctuation marks. There were sticks and trays with letters lined up into mirror sense, and pots of pitch for sticking the letters into place. A long, low case resting on the tables held scores of small drawers—one drawer for each version of each letter. As no one was about, I pocketed three handsome italic letters: *M*, *A*, and *R*.

To the left of the door I'd entered was a staircase with a pointing hand painted on the wall. I went up.

Upstairs I found a large, bright room with windows on two sides. There were masses of print stuffed into shelves and tottering in stacks: manuscripts, magazines, newspapers, and books. There was a single empty desk with a sign reading T. W. WHITE, PROPRIETOR. Well-used sheets of flypaper hung from the ceiling. The whole building smelled of ink.

"Hollo?" I called presently. "Is anyone here?"

I heard a dry, delicate cough.

There was a small square office jutting out into the room's space from the right rear corner. The office door was half open and on the door was written in gold leaf, EDGAR ALLAN POE, EDITOR ALLOPATHIST AND POET, ABANDON ALL HOPE YE SHAMS WHO RAM HERE. I peered in. A young man lay easily stretched out on a morocco divan. He looked up at me with no great interest.

"I assume you are Mr. Poe," said I. "I am Mason Algiers Reynolds of Hardware, Virginia." He nodded very slightly. As this was of all men the fantastic Edgar Poe, I felt I could speak honestly. "I have inadvertently killed my double. I am a fugitive, and I stand in need of employ."

He widened his eyes a bit, eyes that were deep pools of darkness set beneath a high and somewhat too prominent brow. Should I forget everything else about Edgar Poe, I will never lose the image of his eyes. Poe's eyes seemed to look in as well as out—at all times scrutinizing his mind's play of fantasies as keenly as the happenstances of the world without. His eyes were wondrous portals between two worlds. As for the rest of his face, he had a straight mouth, a pleasing aquiline nose, a small mustache, and wavy dark hair, already a bit thin at the temples. But his eyes were everything; they were lamps to my soul's fluttering moth.

"What is your age?" he said presently. His voice was low and clear, and as he spoke, the line of his mouth sketched a bewildering range of expressions: from contempt to boredom to amusement to interest to genuine concern. "And why do you speak of a double?"

"I am fifteen, Mr. Poe. I say double because the boy I shot—purely by accident, mind you—was blond like me and just my size. I feel terrible about it, and Sheriff Garmee wants me dead or alive. I was only getting Pa's whiskey money back from Mr. Sloat at the Liberty Hotel in Lynchburg. I was supposed to buy a wife for our slave Otha with the money, but one of Mr. Sloat's fancy women stole it from me."

"Whoring and killing at age fifteen," mused Poe. "A lively lad. A Virginian. You have not brought your African to my office, I trust?"

"No sir. Otha took off on his own when we got to Richmond yesterday. I've read your stories in the *Messenger*, Mr. Poe, and I like them enormously. I practically know 'Berenice' and 'A MS. Found in a Bottle' by heart. I read and write better than anyone in Hardware, or even Lynchburg. Do you think I could have a job? Only you mustn't tell anyone else my real name. Call me Mason Bustler."

"Come in then, little brother." He made a rapid gesture with his delicate white hand. "And close the door."

I stepped into his office and closed the door behind me. Besides the divan, the office held bookshelves, two straight wooden chairs, and a desk piled high with papers. More books were stacked here and there on the floor. There was a window in the wall behind Mr. Poe's desk. I took one of the wooden chairs and sat down. "I could help with the printing," I suggested.

"A very printer's devil," said Poe. "Your name is Mason? Does your father adhere to the Accepted Lodge?"

"The Freemasons? No sir. We are Episcopalians. Ma's dead and Pa drinks. All I own is fifty cents and a pawn ticket for my pistol."

"You forget your bucolic health," said Poe with a smile. "And the outsized raiment on your limbs. You've cast yourself adrift, Mason, and the tides of fate are sweeping you to sea. I know the feeling, I know it well." He paused and regarded me for a bit, his expression subtly changing with the rapid flow of his thought. "I will help you," he said presently. "Though first I must jot down my morning's musings. Today I've set aside my cursed book reviews to work on a new tale. Do you drink spirits?"

"No sir. I don't want to be like Pa."

"Nor do I wish to be a wild eyed slaving farmer, Mason, but today is the biblical Sabbath and Mr. White is in Petersburg. Allow me, as I say, to preserve the fruits of my interrupted labors and then you and I shall off to the pothouse, young killer, young devil, young Mason *né* Reynolds *appellé* Bustler. *Bustler*—the name has the sound of an odious, sanctimonious fool. You would do better to keep your own name. I am close friends with one Jeremiah Reynolds, a brilliant man with a global mind. He will come here next week, perhaps to make my fortune. I have a wonderful plan for a trip of exploration. But now, silence!"

He swung his legs to the floor and moved nimbly to his desk. Taking pen in hand, he wrote rapidly for the better part of an hour. At no time during his steady penning did he so much as glance at me. Not wanting to disturb his labor, I passed the time by looking through the books stacked on the floor by my chair. I noticed a book of letters and recollections of the poet Coleridge, a pamphlet called "South Sea Expedition" by the Jeremiah Reynolds whom Poe had just spoken of, also some travel books on

Switzerland, Spain, and Pennsylvania, and at the bottom of the stack a geographical treatise with the full title: *Symmes's Theory of Concentric Spheres; Demonstrating that the earth is hollow, habitable within, and widely open about the poles, By A Citizen of the United States.* This odd treatise caught my fancy, and I delved into it.

*Symmes's Theory* started out with a slew of prefaces, apologies, and advertisements to the effect that Captain John Cleves Symmes, "the Newton of the West," was a great genius whom the world did little appreciate. There was so much about Symmes that I soon reached the conclusion that he himself had written the book. Once all the strutting and throat clearing was over, it turned out that Symmes believed our planet is a huge hollow sphere with big open holes at the North and South poles. According to Symmes, each of these holes is some four thousand miles across. Symmes held that it should be possible for a ship to sail over the lip of one of these holes and onto the Hollow Earth's inner surface. The inner surface was supposed to be covered with continents and oceans just like the outside. Symmes had some further theories about other hollow spheres concentric to the main one, but these extra spheres struck me as unnecessary garnishment to the inspired flapdoodle of his initial premise: a Hollow Earth.

The idea tickled me so much that I eagerly read further, forgetting all about Edgar Poe busy at his desk. Symmes, or his mouthpiece the Citizen of the United States, had a list of reasons why our planet is in fact a hollow crust. Centrifugal force tends to squeeze all of a spinning planet's matter out into a spherical shell. If you put the end of a magnet up to a sheet of paper with iron filings, the filings will naturally arrange themselves into a hollow ring. Wheat stalks and birds' feathers are hollow. Heavy mountains sit on top of light soil. The material around Saturn arranges itself into rings. The poles of Mars look dark because the poles are actually great openings to the hollow inside. A correct interpretation of the Hebrew words *theoo* and *beoo* shows that instead of starting out, "The earth was without form and void," the Bible actually reads, "The earth was without form and HOLLOW!" And finally, as a clincher to it all, it makes sense for the planets to be hollow because "it displays *a great saving of stuff.*"

A great saving of stuff. I liked Symmes's thinking. I'd always had a yen to explore; what an adventure it would be to discover a whole new world, the world that lies inside! How would it feel to sail over that great thick lip to the interior? What would be the conditions inside the Hollow Earth? And why hadn't any travelers yet brought back reports of great continent-size holes in the arctic and antarctic seas? The Citizen of the United States had two answers. First of all, the earth's magnetic field reverses direction on the inside, which means that along the great round verges of the holes the field runs east/west, leading to a phenomenon that the Citizen termed "winding meridians." An explorer who tries to follow his compass toward the North or the South Pole will inevitably end up sailing east or west along the rim of one of the great verges. And even if the explorer eschews compass measurements for the more reliable method of celestial navigation, his attempt to enter the hole will be gravely hampered by the "great walls of ice" that ring the holes both north and south. The battlements of these icy hoops have occasionally been sighted by storm-driven whalers and sealers, yet none *that we knew of* has ever survived an attempt to venture beyond. Symmes felt that the best way to reach the Hollow Earth would be to head north over the ice fields from the northernmost shores of Siberia.

"It is well," said Poe, breaking into my dreams of exploration. "My hero is launched; I thirst and tremble. With bandy-legs White from the scene, I shall dare the forbidden precincts of Hogg's Tavern." Noticing the book I held, he smiled broadly. "How do you like Symmes's theory, Mason? He is a madder drunken farmer than your pa."

That was typical of Eddie Poe, I would learn; typical of him to fasten on some one little thing you told him and to come back to it over and over. I was in no position to stick up for Pa right then, so I ignored the slight and spoke to his question.

"I wonder what it would be like inside the Hollow Earth. Do you think there might be a sun on the inside?"

"A sun! Interesting notion." While he spoke, Poe busied himself rolling his fresh-written sheets up into a scroll that he bound with a ribbon. "I had Symmes's theory in mind when I wrote my 'MS. Found in a Bottle.' Of course there, to end the thing, I filled the hole with a great black maelstrom. Have you ever seen a maelstrom?" He stared at me with his dark eyes.

"A giant whirlpool? No. Though there were plenty of little eddies in the James coming down. I rode here on a bateau with a crew of slaves."

"Did you converse with them?"

"Of course. You should hear the stories they tell around the fire at night, Mr. Poe. Some of the tales go right back to Africa."

"*Absit omen,*" said Poe, making a two-fingered gesture at me. "Spare me the company of Pa and the slaves. And don't call me Mr. Poe, little brother, call me Eddie. I am no Mister Such-and-So, I am an international genius of twenty-five."

We headed out of the office, with Eddie going back twice to make sure he'd fastened the locks. Outside, we crossed Main Street catty-corner to Hogg's Tavern.

"I spent the night at the Swan," I told Eddie as we went in. "Maybe we should go there and if they see me with someone as important as you they'll give me credit."

Eddie was very cheerful now, and this supposition of mine made him shake with laughter. "Do you think writers are wealthy men, Mason? Pillars of society? I am penniless, though I despise to remain so." He said the last sentence in a whisper, as now we were in Hogg's Tavern. The place was nearly empty. Eddie made a commanding gesture and addressed the publican. "Ho, Hogg, two twists of tobacco, if you please."

Eddie examined his tobacco briefly and then placed it back on the counter. "I don't much like this tobacco, Hogg. Bring us rum and water in its stead." We found seats on a bench by the wall. The bench had horsehair cushions. It was nice being there. Hogg brought us a pitcher of water and a noggin of rum with two glasses. When Eddie lifted the noggin, I put my hand over my glass.

"Please," I told him. "No strong drink for me. I've tried my fill of Pa's whiskey a few times and I don't like it. It makes me dizzy and sick."

"Lucky lad," said Eddie. "Pedestrian carking farmer. You talk, then, while I imbibe. Tell me your misadventure in dramatic detail."

I told him the whole story of how I'd left the farm, made a mess in Lynchburg, and fled to Richmond. He was particularly taken by the fact that I still dreamed of the dead stableboy.

Eddie's behavior changed noticeably with each of the four toddies of rum that the noggin held. During the first drink he remained cheerful and cutting, with the second glass he became deep and thoughtful, with the third glass he grew fluttery and maudlin, and the fourth glass started him to speechifying on Symmes's Hollow Earth theory. With his tongue loosened by the rum, Eddie freely confessed that he believed Symmes's theory from the bottom of his heart.

Just last month Eddie's friend Jeremiah Reynolds had delivered a speech to Congress in favor of a United States exploring expedition to the south polar regions. Although Reynolds had once been a follower of Symmes, he dared not speak to Congress of the Hollow Earth. Instead, he had urged polar exploration for such petty put-up reasons as better trade and better maps.

Eddie was disappointed that Reynolds had missed his opportunity to lecture Congress about the Hollow Earth, and the farrago he now poured out to me was what *he*, Edgar Allan Poe, felt Jeremiah Reynolds should have said. Eddie's reasons for believing the theory were not scientific at all. His reasons for belief had to do with what he termed poetic necessity.

"The womb and the skull," he intoned, sitting up straight

and wagging his finger at me. "The womb, the skull, and the Hollow Earth. If a man's head be but a ball of empty bone, why not our world as well? And what is the womb but a cave of muscle and thew? Is it not fitting that farmer Symmes makes our verdant orb a grinning *memento mori?* But who or what has eaten the moist brain or fetus that nestled once within? Some hero must drive to the Pole and seek out the worm that slumbers not! It may be, young Mason, that you are the one to carry it through." His dark eyes were magnetically fixed on me; their depths spun like whirlpools.

A moment passed. Eddie blinked and poured out the rest of the noggin. Only a few drops were left.

"The great wall of ice is the final barrier between us and the southern pole. Like a virtuous woman, Earth hides her nether mystery behind a chaste and frozen corset. The frozen hoop lies between us and the hole, Mason, but is this not the age of aeronautics? Cannot a ballooning flight of fancy overspring the most beetling wall? I have written Reynolds all this, and next Saturday he comes to realize my plan. Some call me hoaxer, but I am in my way a man of science. Only science can save me from the melancholy similes which crowd my brain." He gazed gloomily at his last bit of rum.

"Foul," sighed Eddie then. "Birth and death are both foul beyond imagining—to be sealed up into the flesh of another, to be nailed into a box! I suffocate. I must have air!" Draining the last of the rum, he started to his feet and tottered toward the tavern door, with me dogging his steps.

"Sirs," called Hogg. "I believe you have forgotten to pay for your rum and water."

"Pay for my rum and water!" exclaimed Poe, his mouth set into a hard line of anger. All at once his footing was quite steady. "Didn't I give you the tobacco for the rum and water? What more do you require?"

"But, sir," said Hogg, looking a bit uncertain. "I don't remember that you paid for the tobacco."

"What do you mean by that, you scoundrel? Isn't *that* your tobacco lying *there?* Am I supposed to pay for what I did not take?"

"But, sir—"

"Savo your snares for the unwary!" snapped Eddie, and marched out into the street. He hurried off down the block so rapidly that I could barely keep up with him. His shoulders were shaking; when I finally fell into step with him, I saw that he was chuckling and talking to himself.

". . . a most excellent diddle," he muttered. "Most capital diddle indeed. It is well that watchful White postponed my first visit to the Hogg. Today I wear the diddler's grin!" He spread his lips wide in an unnatural leer and turned his head to stare at me.

I was confused. "I . . . you didn't . . . I mean, Hogg was right! You owe him for the rum. The tobacco doesn't have anything to do with it."

"The tobacco has everything to do with it, Mason, as surely as a magician's hat has everything to do with his hares. Am I not penniless? Yet do I not thirst? I work, I am penniless, I thirst, *ergo* it is my right to diddle Hogg. Fix your mind on the first two premises of the syllogism: *I work; I am penniless.* Mr. White's magazine, Mason, the magazine where you seek employ, this same *Southern Literary Messenger* began with a circulation of five hundred and under my editorial hand has risen to a circulation of two thousand. *Yet I am penniless.* My best energies are wasted in the service of an illiterate and vulgar man who has neither the capacity to appreciate my labors nor the will to reward them. I wander drunk in the streets of pawky Richmond with none but a fifteen-year-old farmboy to witness my degradation."

Poe groaned theatrically and turned a corner that led down toward the James River. There was a harbor down there, with a steam packet-boat and several large sailing ships at anchor. A cool fresh breeze wafted up from the harbor. The day was still fair, with a warm afternoon sun. I'd never seen ships before; the sight of their gently swaying masts thrilled me to the core.

"The tavern at Rockett's Landing is our next stop," said Poe. His gait was unsteady, but he was nowhere near so intoxicated as he'd seemed when we left Hogg's. "They know me well, so the diddle is out. I must implore you for the loan of the half-dollar you mentioned. In return I promise you reasonable lodging and a position as printer's devil. I have not tasted drink in a fortnight, and now I would sup the Bacchic madness to its lees. Allopathy, young Mason, is the scientific treatment of plague by a poison whose symptoms counter those of the disease. Drink is the allopathic remedy for the maelstrom of madness whose watery slopes I ride. The long sea tale I began today . . ." He waved his scroll of papers in my face. "This tale should make my fortune, Mason, and if the fool publishers will not help me, I must find some other way to become a wealthy man. A bank note is but ink and paper."

I handed Eddie my half-dollar coin. If he was really going to lodge me and get me employment, the price was well worth it. But, why, on such a lovely day and in such an exciting city, why did he have to get drunk?

"I'll wait outside the tavern," I suggested. "I want to look at the ships."

"Wise lad," said Eddie. "Do this for me—come in and seek me out before sunset. See that I get home to Mrs. Yarrington's boardinghouse on Bank Street at Capitol Square. I lodge there with my dear aunt and sweet Sis. Should I sleep and wake in this tavern, my suicide could result."

"Can I stay at the boardinghouse, too?"

"You'll sleep beneath my eaves, small petrel." He gave me a final salute with his scroll of papers and disappeared into the Rockett's Landing Tavern.

I spent a pleasant few hours poking around the harbor. After watching the side-wheeler packet boat steam off down the James for Norfolk and Baltimore, I found out more about the sailing ships. There was a small schooner, a two-masted brig, and a slightly larger three-masted bark called the *Grampus*. I managed to get aboard the *Grampus*. The sailors were friendly, but they kept a close eye on me. They'd found a stowaway slave on board that morning. I helped a bit with some loading, and one of the men gave me a chunk of bread and saltpork. It was my first food of the day, and it came very welcome. I hoped Mrs. Yarrington set a good table; even more, I hoped she would take me in.

As I worked with the sailors, I thought of how Eddie had diddled Hogg out of the rum. If that was the way of the world, I was a fool to have not taken a few more gold pieces from Sloat's safe. To hear Eddie tell it, T. W. White was a niggard. Nevertheless, the prospect of being a printer's devil pleased me. I could master the printer's trade in a few years. A printer could go anywhere and find employ. If today I found Richmond wonderful, with its riverfront and its capitol on the hill above, nevertheless I'd want someday to move on, perhaps to Baltimore and New York, perhaps to Europe, or perhaps to some wild new lands on a bark like the *Grampus*.

The sailor who'd fed me took me belowdecks to see their forecastle. Their bunks were cramped as coffins. It seemed odd that to go the furthest you had to be hemmed in the most. I wanted to see the world, but now that I'd escaped Pa's farm, I wasn't yet ready to squeeze into a sailor's bunk.

When dusk fell, I went into the Rockett's Landing Tavern. I found Eddie pale-faced and clutching a half-empty glass of dark rum. I sat down next to him, but the liquor had really taken hold of him and he barely knew me. He was at a table with two other men, one of them a deeply tanned Scotsman who was the first mate of the *Grampus*. He'd been buying drinks all day.

"I took a twenty-dollar gold piece off a slave I found stowed away this mornin'," the Scotsman told me. He had long hair and a ready smile. "The rascal wanted to pay his passage. Can you believe it? Would ye like a glass of rum then, young fellow?"

"No thank you," said I, feeling sick. "Which one was it? I mean, what was the slave's name?"

"He didn't want to tell us," laughed the mate. "Big black brute of a nigger he was. We whipped the answer out of him right enough. His name was Luther Garland."

It put a heavy stone on my heart to hear this. I remembered Luther reaching up for the gold that first day on the river, reaching up with a human spirit's innocent desire to be free. Now he was whipped and shackled and on his way back to Lynchburg.

"Did he say where he got the money?" I heard myself asking.

"Didn't say a thing but his name," said the mate. "He was bawling so hard even that was hard to understand. Drink up there, Eddie, and make us another speech!"

"Eddie has to go home," I told the mate. "I'm to take him."

"He promised me a poem," said the mate, reaching across the table to poke Eddie in the chest. "He said he'd pay for his drinks with a poem written out for my wife, Helen."

"To Helen," muttered Eddie. "Copy it down."

At the mate's cry, the innkeeper brought pen and paper. Eddie recited a poem and I wrote it down. It was a fine piece, though as I copied it out, I remembered having read it before in the *Messenger*. The mate liked it, once I told him what all the words meant.

TO HELEN

Helen, thy beauty is to me
   Like those Nicean barks of yore,
That gently, o'er a perfumed sea,
   The weary, wayworn wanderer bore
To his own native shore.

On desperate seas long wont to roam,
   Thy hyacinth hair, thy classic face,
Thy Naiad airs have brought me home
   To the glory that was Greece,
To the grandeur that was Rome.

Lo! in yon brilliant window niche,
How statue-like I see thee stand,
The agate lamp within thy hand!
Ah, Psyche, from the regions which
Are Holy Land!

Eddie gulped the rest of his glass and shuddered. I got to work getting him home. I had to put my arms around him and dance him out of the tavern. On the street, I draped his arm across my shoulder and started up the long slope to Capitol Square. Eddie kept letting his head fall back so he could stare up at the sky. I think he could have walked better than he did, but he was content to let me do the work. He knew what was up all right, the hoaxer. He knew I needed his patronage, and he remembered our morning's conversation well enough to stick in a remark or two about "being drunk like Pa," though he wasn't. No matter how much Pa drank, he could always walk straight.

Finally, I found Bank Street at the edge of the hilltop field that was Capitol Square. Eddie began picking up his feet a little better, and we arrived at a boardinghouse door. As soon as we stepped into the hall, a door upstairs flew open.

"Eddie?" called a woman. "Is that you?"

"It is I, Aunt Maria," said Poe, his voice low and contrite. "In the arms of a devil. I've slipped. A wretched prodigal, I eat husks with swine." He shrugged himself free of me and stood there unsteadily. "Thank you for your aid, young man. Farewell."

"You promised me lodging!" I protested. "And a job!"

Footsteps came stitching down the stairs. A strong-looking woman with a moon face confronted me. "Go on then, you young imp. Haven't you done harm enough, getting poor Eddie drunk?"

"I didn't get him drunk," I protested. "I've been taking care of him. Let me introduce myself." I bowed and cleared my throat. "I am Mason Algiers . . . Bustler. I met Eddie at the offices of the *Messenger* and he told me . . ."

"Go on, devil," said Eddie, gesturing at me with his scroll of papers. He'd hung on to the scroll; at least he'd stuck to that. "Come back Monday."

"He owes me fifty cents, Aunt Maria," I told the woman.

"My name is Mrs. Clemm," she said tartly. "You were wrong to lend Eddie money for drink."

"Please," I told her. "Have pity on me. I need a place to sleep. Once Eddie comes back to himself, he'll remember that he promised . . ."

"We certainly don't have space for you in our rooms," said Mrs. Clemm. She leaned forward and sniffed at my breath. "At least you are sober. You could speak to Mrs. Yarrington."

While we were busy arguing, Eddie had stepped around us and started up the stairs. He was gripping the bannister with both hands. Now the door upstairs opened again and a voice called out.

"Eddie! Mama sewed me a new dress! I'll sing for you in my new dress!" The voice was higher than high, and sickly sweet. I peered up past Poe's hunched form to get a look at the speaker. She had a round face like her mother, but where the mother was lankly muscled, the daughter was softly rounded. Now, taking in Eddie's condition, the girl cried out in a wordless torrent of liquid sound. I stared fascinated at her vibrating throat, wondering how she could produce such a noise. Eddie took his hands off the bannister to reach up toward her. Right away he lost his footing and fell backward.

I surged forward in time to catch him, and now that I had hold of him again, I led him the rest of the way to his door.

The plump girl's keening accompanied our progress. It sounded like I imagined an opera would sound. She cut off her noise sharply when Eddie reached the door. She curtsied and favored me with a smile that pocked her cheeks and chin with a dozen dimples. "You're too good," she said as Eddie fell into her round, outstretched arms.

I turned to find Mrs. Clemm behind me. "Lay him out on

the bed, Virginia," she told the girl. "Lay him out and put a basin handy for when he gets sick." Virginia bore Eddie away. "I'm glad he's safe," said I to Mrs. Clemm. "Will you help me lodge here? Please understand that I am of good family, temperate in my habits, and am a great admirer of your nephew's writing. Where is the Mrs. Yarrington of whom you spoke?"

"Mrs. Yarrington does not live here. I run this house for her." She looked me up and down once more and reached her decision. "Very well then, Mr. Bustler. You may engage the garret room. The lodging and board is three dollars a week. You are too late for supper, but breakfast is at eight."

"Thank you, Mrs. Clemm," said I. "I'll pay you every Saturday at noon."

# 5

## The Bank of Kentucky

MY GARRET ROOM was really just half of an attic. My part of the attic was separated from the storage part by a row of large up-ended trunks. The walls and ceilings were raw laths and rafters. My bed was a straw-stuffed tick on the dusty floor. Each morning I had to go down three flights of stairs to the courtyard to empty my slops and to fill my washbasin. But I was happy in that room.

Mrs. Clemm's food was nourishing, if plain, and the other boarders were decent folk. My room had a small gable window looking out over the Richmond roofs; at night it was a joy for me to gaze at the lit city. Best of all, instead of being knotted into Pa's farming and drinking and slaving, I was out in the world learning a modern skill.

Eddie stayed in bed all day that first Sunday. I had planned to accompany the Clemm ladies to church, but at breakfast Mrs. Clemm informed me that they were not religious. With no one to escort, I skipped church myself and spent the time till dinner wandering around Richmond. I went as far as Screamertown, the neighborhood where the free blacks lived. Many of them were craftsmen, working out of small shops in their tiny yards. I kept an eye out for Arf and Otha, but there was no such luck.

That afternoon, after we all shared a dinner of boiled ham and cabbage, Virginia played piano and sang in the boarding-house parlor. She had an exceptionally powerful voice for a girl of only fourteen. There was definitely something odd about the muscles of her throat. The noise made me think of hog slaughtering and of the big knife Luke used for cutting the throats of our hogs. Virginia had no inkling of my feeings; indeed she seemed to have taken a liking to me, and she favored me with many smiles during her pauses for breath. When she smiled, her full cheeks bulged up and squeezed her eyes into slits. The singing went on and on, but I felt it would be ungentlemanly to get up and leave. Finally, it was over. I went to bed with a headache.

Monday morning I was down to breakfast early lest Poe slip off to work without me. Breakfast was tea, warm milk, oatmeal, and molasses. I ate steadily till Eddie appeared. Though I was the only one left at the table, his glance slid past me as if I were just another boarder.

"Good morning, Eddie," said I. He twitched and spilled some tea on the table.

"You must call me Mr. Poe."

"You remember me, don't you, Mr. Poe? Mason Bustler?"

"I thought your name was Reynolds," he said, sullenly stirring a gout of molasses into his tea. "Jeremiah Reynolds is coming to visit next week. Are you related?"

I shook my head. Reynolds's South Seas pamphlet said he was from Pennsylvania, but my family had been in Hardware since 1710. "You mustn't call me Reynolds, Mr. Poe, because . . ." Not wanting to say it, I cocked my thumb and forefinger and pretended to shoot a gun. "My double?"

"Confused fancies," said he, drinking down his tea with a sick expression. "You are a nightmare come to roost."

"Please, Mr. Poe, you said you'd recommend me to Mr. White for a position as . . ."

"As a devil." He glared at me with his dark eyes snapping. "Have I not enough worries plaguing me?"

"I'm to pay your aunt three dollars a week," I offered. "And I'll do anything else I can to help you—errands, copying, anything."

He thought for a while and finally gave a curt, grim nod. "Very well then, Mason. You pester me till I am half-mad, and then offer to do anything? Indeed you shall do anything, and sooner than you think." He stared at me a bit longer and then rose to leave. "Run upstairs and tell my aunt to give you the scroll of papers I forgot."

At the *Messenger* offices, Eddie introduced me to Mr. White and to Glendon, their printer. White was red-faced and wobbly, while Glendon was a lean, long-haired man with a heavy mustache and a deep Southern drawl. As a test of my skills, White, Glendon, and Eddie watched me proofread a column and set a line of type. For some reason, getting the letters in the correct mirror order for typesetting came naturally to me. I was hired as Glendon's assistant at a salary of six dollars a week, with the understanding that I would also act as an office boy whenever Glendon didn't need me.

The first few days of work went by quickly. Glendon did most of the actual typesetting; I heated pitch and put used letters back into their little drawers. I also helped tend the big iron press, a beast of a machine balkier than Dammit had ever been.

It wasn't far to the boardinghouse, and I went back there for dinner at noon every day. Eddie tended to stay in the *Messenger* offices, busy with his new sea tale and with his editorial work of correspondence and reviews. Virginia always sat next to me during dinner; she'd gotten out of me that I'd grown up on a farm, and she loved to ask me questions about baby animals. I humored her, even though the squeaky voice that came out of her thick throat never failed to set my teeth on edge.

Saturday we got off for the day at noon. Glendon said I was working out fine, and Mr. White gave me six silver dollars. I felt wonderful. Just before I left, Eddie stuck his head out of his office and called me in. He held a handwritten letter in his hand. Something about it seemed to have upset him. Pacing back and forth, he demanded that I give him the three dollars' lodging I owed Mrs. Clemm.

"I'd rather not, Mr. Poe," I told him. "I'd feel better giving her the money myself."

"Aunt Maria trusts her affairs to me in every way," said Eddie, impatiently sticking out his hand. He'd been sober all week, but now I wondered if the fever for drink was on him again. Mr. White didn't pay him weekly like he did me. Eddie only got paid on the last Saturday of every month, which meant that right now he was as penniless as he'd been last week. If I gave him the three dollars, he would likely spend it in a tavern and blame me. I kept my money tight in my hand in my pocket.

"I'm going on back to the house right now," I said, backing out of the office. "It's dinnertime. Why don't you come on with me, Eddie. You don't want to end up like last Saturday."

With an ill will, he accompanied me back to the boarding-house. Mrs. Clemm had made a cabbage-and-cauliflower soup that you could smell from the sidewalk. I went into the dining room and sat down next to old Dr. Custer, a retired physician. Virginia scooted into the seat next to me and asked me how long it took tiny fuzzy baby chickies to peck their way out of the shell and if any of the sweet babies ever suffocated before breaking out. Eddie, seated at the end of the table, glared at the sight of us talking together. I wished he'd just trade places with me. Mrs. Clemm was at the other end of the table, and across from Virginia and me were the middle-aged widow Boggs and the two Reddle brothers. The Reddles were identical twins named Rice and Brownie. They both had jobs at the plug-tobacco factory. I'd known a few fellows like them back in Hardware.

As Mrs. Clemm was ladling out the soup, one of the Reddles rocked over to one side and let out a big fart. Quick as a whip, the other one said, " 'Tain't no need to apologize,

Brownie. Smells the same as our dinner anyhow.'' They laughed like hyenas and then Virginia started giggling, too. Nobody else thought it was funny, though, especially not Eddie. He jumped out of his chair so hard that it fell over backward. He took Virginia by the hand and led her out of the dining room and upstairs. I went ahead and ate my soup. It was a meal, and there was coarse bread for dipping in it.

After dinner, I gave Mrs. Clemm my three dollars' room and board and went out to sit on the porch. I had half a mind to go down to Screamertown and look for Otha or to go down to the canal basin and ask around about what had happened to the rest of the boys on the bateau. I couldn't stop thinking about them. Had they all cut and run like Luther? And was the word out about me fleeing to Richmond? How was Pa getting along without me? Maybe I should get some paper from Eddie and send Pa a letter.

Just as I was thinking of Eddie, he appeared. Before I could utter a word, he was standing over me, standing so close that I couldn't get out of my rocking chair. His face was twisted in spite and rage. "You are a sinuous, plausible weasel, are you not?" He gave me a poke that set my chair a-bucking. "You murderer. You drag me to taverns, you presume upon me in every way, you worm your viper self into my enchanted garden, and now you labor to turn my sweet Sissy against me." He raised his hand menacingly. "If you were not such a lowly stinking beast, I'd challenge you to the field of honor." He struck at my head, but I ducked the blow. This made him even angrier. He gave me another poke in the chest. "You need horsewhipping, foul country lout! Get to your feet if you dare!"

Eddie just wasn't the kind of person who could physically scare you, but even so there was no way I could get to my feet, what with the chair rocking back and forth so hard and with him standing so close that my knees bumped his. He took this for a victory and stalked off across the field of Capitol Square, casting a last gloating glance back at me. "Do your damnedest, fiend, yet *I* shall have her hand!"

I sat there wondering what was the matter. Something about Eddie's whole performance struck me as insincere. Mrs. Clemm appeared on the porch. "Is he gone?" she asked me.

"Yes, he headed off that way," I told her. "He's all het up."

Mrs. Clemm cocked her head and looked at me thoughtfully. "Are you sweet on my Virginia?" she asked me finally.

"No ma'am."

She sighed. "I didn't think so. Virginia likes talking to you, Mason, because you're a boy closer to her own age. But she's Eddie's. It was meant to be. I had my dreams of bringing Virginia out into society, but Eddie's a genius and he needs us so much. They're to be married right away. That's the only way he'll have it."

"They're getting married because of me? Believe me, Mrs. Clemm, I have no designs on Virginia."

"It's not just you, dear," said Mrs. Clemm. "I've always thought that Eddie and Virginia living in rooms together could cause talk. It's better all around to marry them, and with Eddie in such a passion, it might as well be today."

She went inside and Rice and Brownie Reddle came out, on their way to the taverns. They asked me if I wanted to come along, but I said no. Brownie gave me a plug of tobacco, and then they were on their way. Back in Hardware I'd gotten used to doing nothing, so I was comfortable just setting on the porch with my chaw, enjoying the feel of the three silver dollars in my pocket.

"Pardon me, young fella, is this the home of Edgar Poe?"

There was a solid man of medium stature looking at me. He had a short nose, a broad face, and skin that was deeply weathered and tanned. I knew Eddie still had some bad debts, so I didn't answer the man directly.

"What's your name, sir?" I asked him.

"Jeremiah Reynolds," said he. "Come to see Mr. Poe from Washington. I sent him a letter advising him of my arrival today."

I got to my feet and made him welcome. "Eddie's been talking about you. He went out, but I reckon he'll be back soon. My name's Mason Bustler. I . . . I know some Reynoldses in Hardware, Virginia."

"I'm from everywhere *but* Virginia," said Reynolds, setting down his travel case and taking a seat. When he smiled, which was often, his leathery skin creased in many wrinkles. "So, Mason, what is your trade? And what does Mr. Poe say about me? Good things, I trust?"

"Mr. Poe's taken me on as a printer's devil at the *Southern Literary Messenger*," I said. "And about you . . . he believes in the Symmes theory that there's big holes at the North and South poles leading to the inside of the earth. He was disappointed that you didn't tell Congress about the Hollow Earth in your speech last month."

"Ten years ago I was a firebrand like our Eddie," said Reynolds, chuckling a bit. "I traveled from city to city with Mr. Symmes giving speeches. He was an odd duck, our Symmes. He's dead now, you know; his grave in Ohio is marked with a great hollow sphere. Symmes and I made some converts, and Congress approved an expedition, but nothing came of it. In the end I had to lead my own expedition to the high southern latitudes. We made sixty-seven degrees; a thousand miles south of the Falklands. Surely you've heard of the South Sea Fur Company and Exploring Expedition?"

"Was that trip the subject of your pamphlet?" I said politely.

"Indeed." Reynolds beamed. "It is a pleasure to meet a young lad of such erudition! You have profited from your association with Mr. Poe! Yes, I led my own expedition for the southern Hole, but very soon the crew—ignorant money-hungry sealers—rebelled and forced us to turn back. Rather than return empty-handed, I had the crew put me off in Chile, where I spent some years tramping about. It took me nearly five years to get back to what we call civilization. Civilization indeed, that pack of purple-bottomed Jacksonians that is our poor young nation's Congress. The Symmes Hole is real, young Mason. I have specimens and tales to prove it. What think you of this?''

He drew a thumb-size white lump out of his pocket and passed it to me. It was an animal's tooth, marked all over with lines into which some native craftsman had rubbed ink. Along the length of the tooth was a thin map—the map of Chile, with all its intricacies of islands. Carved in less detail was the eastern, Patagonian, coast of South America, and even more sketchily presented were the jagged battlements of the southern wall of ice. The striking thing about this crude globe was that a hole had been drilled in the tooth tip, and the tooth's interior had been to some degree hollowed out. Etched on the inside was a mythical landscape of fruits and great beasts.

"The natives speak of a Hollow Earth?" I said, handing the tooth back to Reynolds.

"Indeed." He nodded, his genial face grown solemn. "They call it the land of Tekelili, and their gods are said to live there. When a volcano erupts, it is the gods reaching out from Tekelili. I have more than the natives' reports, Mason, much more. I hesitate to speak openly of these things—I do not seek the ridicule of poor Symmes—but as you are a friend of Eddie's, you will understand. Did you know that in the southernmost climes of Chile the seals and migratory birds head *out across the water towards the Pole* when the season grows colder? And that there is a great white whale named Mocha Dick who turns his flukes, and sounds, and never resurfaces till three days have passed? He swims through a deep ocean hole to surface on the seas of Tekelili, Mason. Would that I could ride there in his belly.''

"Isn't Congress going to vote for an exploring expedition?"

Reynolds laughed wearily. "I believe now that they will finally vote the money for a proper United States exploring expedition, but the expedition will be, as Mr. Poe fears, of little ultimate use. A scheming pock-faced poltroon named Captain Wilkes is even now machinating to take command of the expe-

dition; there is no hope of his pushing past seventy degrees southern latitude to the eighties and on towards the final polar ninety,
where the great mystery must be found. The high southern latitudes hold wonders beyond imagining. There is a whole new
world there for the men with the courage to vault the walls of
ice!'' He paused and shook his head, and then he fixed me with
his blue, twinkling eyes. "I'm past talking about it, Mason. The
time has come to act. You say you are a printer?''

"Yes sir. I'm learning to be one. I want to be able to travel
wherever I like. The *Messenger* has one of the new iron presses;
it's quite a machine.''

"Yes, yes, Mr. Poe wrote me of it.'' Reynolds's weathered
cheeks grew flushed with excitement. "And you are quite in Mr.
Poe's confidence? Do you know then why I have come?''

Before I could answer, Eddie reappeared, striding angrily
across the sloping field of Capitol Square. It developed that in
order to get a marriage license he had to post a temporary bond
of $150—a bond that would be nullified as soon as the marriage
was actually performed. But as there were a number of debtors'
claims outstanding against Mr. Edgar Allan Poe, his signature
was not sufficient for the posting of a bond. In order to get his
marriage license, he would have to physically place gold or bank
notes in the value of $150 in the court officer's hands, if only for
twenty-four hours.

"That's more than miser White pays me in two months!''
Eddie fumed. Now that his marriage plans were well under way,
he'd set aside his supposition that I was his mortal rival. The
court officer could serve as his new bugaboo. "The truly ludicrous aspect is that I am to receive the money back as soon as we
are wed. To the meager sapience of this petty harassing mole of
a bailiff, nothing but disks of rare ore or scraps of bank-printed
paper can serve as a proper signifier of gentility and worth! Would
it not be more fitting that I lend him the manuscript for my *Tales
of the Folio Club?* I have the manuscript back from Harper and
Brothers, Jeremiah. Every door is slammed in my face.'' Eddie

moaned and threw himself into a chair. "Jeremiah, I know you have come to discuss my balloon plan, but whatever shall we do for money?"

"We shall print it," said Reynolds in a quiet tone. "I have followed your earlier suggestion."

Eddie jerked galvanically and glanced around. No one but he and I and Jeremiah Reynolds were on the porch. Inside the boardinghouse, Virginia was playing the piano and softly singing. She sounded lonely and scared. In front of us was Bank Street, with its steady traffic on foot and horse. Market was over and people were going home. Eddie hurried into the house and spoke briefly with Virginia, and then he was back out, all energy, leading us to the empty offices of the *Messenger*.

Once we were safely inside, the chuckling, leather-faced Reynolds opened his case and drew out two engraved-steel printing blocks that showed the front and back sides of a fifty-dollar gold certificate on the State Bank of Kentucky.

"How did you get these?" I asked Reynolds. "Are these stolen, or are they copies?"

"They are neither," Eddie grinned, picking up one of the blocks and peering at the finely detailed engraving. "There is no State Bank of Kentucky. It was my thought that we might diddle the Virginians out of some considerable stocks of goods ere they notice the lack of any such institution. But I had little hope my plan would truly bear fruit. Jeremiah, these are capital specimens of the engraver's art!"

"Thank you, Edgar. James Eights has done them for me with the understanding that the money is to be used solely for the outfitting of the polar balloon expedition you have proposed."

"Stupendous," said Poe. "Can you mount them in the press, Mason?"

I took the blocks and examined them in the late afternoon light. They were quarter-inch-thick plates of fine hard steel, etched with a convincing amount of ornamentation and legalistic folderol. The main legends read STATE BANK KENTUCKY, FIFTY

DOLLARS, and GOLD COIN. One side of the bill bore a large picture of a frontiersman shooting a black bear with a long rifle; the other side showed a steamboat, a band of horses, and a field of hemp. The images were very plausible. They would print well.

"Have you any ink but black?" inquired Jeremiah Reynolds.

"Deuce!" exclaimed Poe. "We have not. Green or yellow would be the thing, eh? Mason! Run over to the Richmond *Whig* and see if John Pleasants can spare us some green ink. He inked his Christmas issue all in green this past year, I well recall."

"Stop right there," said I, handing the printing blocks back to Reynolds. "You want me to openly fetch the ink for printing these bills? If there is no State Bank of Kentucky, it will be less than a month before everyone knows the bills are fake. The people at the *Whig* will remember me. And then what, Eddie?"

"You are already wanted for murder, Mason *Reynolds,*" said Eddie coldly. "If you are to be a criminal, why not be a competent one? Give Pleasants another false name, dunderhead. Tell him you work for Thomas Ritchie at the *Enquirer.*"

"What?" said Jeremiah Reynolds, staring at me in wonder.

I had been a fool to tell Eddie my bloody secret; silently, I vowed never to pass such confidences again. The dead stableboy was my weight to bear alone.

"Mason killed a boy during a bungled robbery in Lynchburg," said Eddie coolly. "His true name is Reynolds, but he has changed it to Bustler. He lives in transit. He will print our bills for us, and then, to be perfectly safe, he will move on."

"Move on where?" I demanded. "I like my position here!"

"Mason," said Eddie quietly. "You are one of fate's chosen children. You are nimble. I think that you and Jeremiah shall ride our balloon over the walls of ice and into the Hollow Earth. I had planned to go, but"—his voice cracked momentarily—"I am soon to be married, and I have not the heart to leave a trembling new wife."

"No need to blush, Eddie," said Jeremiah. "It is enough to

be a genius—you need not be an explorer as well. The young man will serve well in your place. And how apt that his true name is Reynolds! Surely we are related! It is a wondrous thing!" He drew a ten-dollar gold piece out of his pocket and handed it to me. "Go, cousin Mason, and fetch the ink. Edgar and I must talk."

The *Whig* offices were ten blocks away. I walked with a troubled mind. With my own money, I had thirteen dollars in my pocket. Whether I fetched the ink or not, Edgar Poe would have me out of Richmond in a week. I wondered if I oughtn't best go down to Rockett's Landing and get the packet boat for Norfolk right away. The stableboy's death had been an accident, but to print false bills was cold-minded crime!

Still I pressed my steps onward to the *Whig*. I was dazzled by the sheer effrontery of Eddie's plan. Counterfeiting the money of a nonexistent bank! How fitting a scheme this was for Edgar Allan Poe: Poe, the poor, half-educated orphan posing as an American man of letters; Poe, the sham priest of our nonexistent culture. Watching him work in the office this week, I'd quickly learned to see through him. The manuscripts he sent to New York publishers kept coming back rejected. The reviews he wrote for the *Messenger* were simple tirades butted in with generously scissored out excerpts of the pages in question. The multilingual sayings he set into his essays were culled wholesale from foreign phrase books. There wasn't an honest bone in his body, and he still owed me fifty cents.

When I got to the *Whig* building, I paused and glanced down toward the riverport. Dusk was starting to fall, but I could see that there was a new bark in the *Grampus*'s place. The *Grampus* out to sea! I imagined the ship in New York, in the Marquesas, in the unknown cannibal islands of the far south. If I understood Eddie and Jeremiah aright, they planned to launch a balloon from near the great southern wall of ice. What an adventure *that* would be, especially if Symmes's theory was correct! First to sail and then to fly! The expedition would be dangerous, but it was in every way preferable to the stunted existence of Hardware and Lynchburg, preferable even to Richmond and my learning of the printer's trade. My heart leapt and I let out a shout as, once and for all, I resolved to go along.

At the sound of my voice, a dog came rushing out of the alley by the *Whig* building and jumped on me. He was white-legged with a tan head and body. He pushed his feet into my stomach and stretched his head up toward my face. His feathery tail was beating a mile a minute. It took me a minute to understand that it was my dear old Arf.

"Arfie! What are you doing here, Arfie boy?"

Arf licked and whined and rolled on his back. I knelt down and petted him for a long time. He lay there squirming, with his front paws folded over like a dead rabbit's. When I stopped petting him, he sprang up and shook his head vigorously. The way he shook his head was to stick it far forward and then to rotate it back and forth so fast that his ears slapped like the wings of a pigeon taking flight. The head shake was Arf's way of punctuating his changes in moods. Now that we were through greeting, it was time for something else. He stood there next to me with his tongue lolling out.

I walked down the dark alley Arf had come from. The *Whig* building's big side doors were open there; the men were just loading a wagon with bales of tomorrow's Sunday edition. "Where's the boss?" I asked one of the men on the loading dock.

The man hooked his thumb toward the doors. I lifted Arf up and went into the *Whig*'s print room. A meaty, long-haired man with a twisting lip asked me my business. He was dressed for the evening and on his way out.

"Two things. I need some green ink, and"—I kept petting Arf so the man wouldn't get a good look at me—"I'd like to know more about this dog."

"An ingratiating cur, is he not? He is a canine eponym, this dog Arf, an animal of such sagacity that all his race must speak his name." He talked in an amused, patrician drawl. "I don't believe you and I have had the pleasure of meeting, young man. I'm John Pleasants."

"I'm Jeremiah Allan. I'm working for Mr. Ritchie over at the *Enquirer*. Mr. Ritchie needs the ink for a special pamphlet of poetry."

"Old driveling Ritchie print green poetry?" exclaimed Pleasants. "I believe I've heard everything now. Are they to be pastoral poems, then, and printed on paper of grass? Bovine rhymes to feed a bawling cow? Green ink! I paid three dollars a can for ours, so let's set it that your old dotard pays me ten. Don't neglect to tell your Mr. Ritchie that I'm diddling him, young Allan."

"All right," said I, still fondling the dog. I didn't care about any feud Pleasants had with Ritchie, and if I was going to be printing money, I certainly didn't care about ten dollars. But what was Arf doing here? "So this is *Arf*, eh? How'd you hit on a name like that, Mr. Pleasants?"

"Alas, so great a stroke of genius is too African for my pale mind. The noble Arf, complete with fleas and mange, was a love offering to that ebony Venus who dusts our rooms when there is no silver to steal. She is Juicita, he is Otha, and Arf the symbol of their tender bond. I hope he follows you home."

Arf did follow me, of course. By the time I got to the *Messenger*, it was too dark to work, and Eddie thought it unwise to attract attention by lighting the lamps. Reynolds and Eddie went down to the Rockett's Landing Tavern, and I took Arf home to Mrs. Clemm's. I fed him some scraps and let him share my straw tick bed. I asked him where he'd been, but he just sniffed my fingers and flapped his ears.

I spent all day Sunday printing up fifty-dollar gold certificates of the State Bank of Kentucky—ten thousand dollars' worth. We'd found a stock of rag paper at the *Messenger*, and the bills looked fine. Still drunk from the night before, Eddie put a red-ink "bank president's signature" on each bill with his own hand, each signature a different anagram of his name: Peale O.

Garland; A. Prodegal Lane; Learn A. Godlcap; E. Apalled Groan; Loan A. A. Pledger; Gaol Pan Dealer; and so on, through two hundred variations. Jeremiah, a bit of a scribbler himself, was amazed at how rapidly Eddie produced the anagrams; Eddie said it was a simple application of cryptographic principles. I thought Eddie was being needlessly brazen.

The better the bills looked, the more I worried. People would accept them, and we would be counterfeiters. Would it really be so difficult to trace the bills back to the green ink I'd borrowed, to the Edgar Allan Poe whose anagram stood on every bill, and to the presses of *The Southern Literary Messenger?* We agreed that it would be unwise to pass any of the bills in Richmond, where Eddie and I were known. Deciding who should carry the money was more difficult. In the end, we settled it by making three stacks of it and each pocketing a stack. As soon as Eddie had pocketed his share, he announced his intention to turn three of the bills in to the Richmond City court officer tomorrow. Jeremiah and I protested strongly, but Eddie insisted that although the main purpose of these bills was to finance a polar balloon expedition, it was equally important that he and Virginia be wed. So you'll have an excuse for not going, I couldn't help thinking. Three of our fresh bank notes must serve as his marriage bond.

"That fool of an official won't study the bills," explained Eddie, sipping at a bottle he'd produced from somewhere. "He'll read the three number fifties, strain through a calculation, and be content. The clergyman Asa Converse will wed my Virginia to me Monday, and Tuesday morn the new husband and wife will set out on a honeymoon. Sweet words. I'll give out word that we are going by coach to Petersburg, but in fact we will take the packet boat to Norfolk. And of course I will redeem the bond before our departure."

"I'll leave for Norfolk today and rent our safehouse," said Jeremiah. "I'll use the last of my honest money for the rent. Mason, will you come with me?"

It was all happening so fast. Leave today?

"No, no," said Eddie rapidly. "Mason must stay close to the nuptial pair. He is our cocky bachelor; though small and young, our Mason is a man of the world. He starts the honeymoon with Virginia and me. Don't look distraught, young killer!" I was frowning and wondering what Eddie really had in mind. His true purposes were always hard to read. He jabbered on. "Jeremiah and I have the thing worked out in every detail. In Norfolk I will pose as . . . Colonel Embry, a Kentucky breeder of fine horses, and there I shall purchase all things necessary to our expedition—the silk, the caoutchouc gum, the wicker, the stove, the heavy garments, the instruments, et cetera. These things we shall privately convey to the safehouse which Jeremiah has honestly engaged, and before the false bank notes are found out, Colonel Embry will have melted into the pellucid sea air. *Il est disparu.*" Eddie paused and drank again from his bottle. "What's that beast doing in here?"

"That's my dog Arf. I found him yesterday."

Eddie stalked over to the corner where Arf lay. Arf flattened himself against the floor and rolled his eyes up, nervously watching Eddie's twitching face. Arf had been in the print shop with us all day, but Eddie had only now noticed him. It was the alcohol, I suppose, and the fact that he was so excited about his wedding and about all the money we'd printed. Several times today, Eddie had picked up big wads of our new bills and had rubbed them on his face, afterward insisting that he only did this so that the bills wouldn't look too new.

"Praise the gods it's not a cat," said Eddie, giving Arf's ribs a gingerly prod with his toe. "I can't stand a pussy—they scratch and they yowl. A cat attacked me once. I struck back, and the fiendish creature sank her teeth and claws so deeply into my hand that I could not get free." He lurched over to me, clenched his fist, and shoved his sleeve up to expose his forearm. "You see?" There were indeed some faint scars on the thin white tube of Eddie's arm. "I struck the monster against the pavement," continued Eddie, acting it out. "She screamed as her ribs cracked, and I laughed at the sound. I beat the ill-shapen bony mass till her blood ran and mingled with mine. Yet no release! Do what I would, the needle teeth and pinion talons stuck fast. Her body's knives were like stitches sutured into my flesh. Blessed cool rationality saved me, or I would bear the fiend on me to this day."

"What did you do?"

"I quenched my arm in a rain barrel. Ding dong dell, pussy's gone to hell."

Monday morning, Eddie was still in a state, though not quite so bad. I went to the *Messenger* office and told Mr. White that Eddie would be gone to Petersburg on honeymoon this week. White looked dubious and asked me if Eddie was drunk. I denied it, and mentioned that I too would need a few days' leave. I didn't like to quit the job outright, even though my return seemed unlikely. White granted my request offhandedly; he and everyone else at the *Messenger* was preoccupied by the day's news of a slave rebellion in Goochland County, west of Richmond.

While I was busy with Mr. White, Jeremiah Reynolds accompanied Eddie to city hall and forged a signature to a marriage bond certifying that fourteen-year-old Virginia was twenty-one. At noon, Jeremiah left for Norfolk on the steamer. In the afternoon, the Reverend Asa Converse came and married Eddie to Virginia. Eddie was obviously intoxicated, even though I'm sure he wished to be sober. He was in the midst of a bender like the ones that took Pa every so often, with no way out but a miracle or collapse. After the ceremony, we had a big dinner. At first I thought Virginia had no more idea of what a wedding really meant than would a child playing dolls. But there were looks she and Mrs. Clemm exchanged, and then, right after the cake, there was the kiss that she gave Eddie. She put the full strength of her oddly muscled neck into that kiss, pressing her face as tight against Eddie as a shoat against a sow. The kiss put cold sweat on Eddie's big brow.

I went to bed early, and then I woke up from Arf barking right in my ear. The window was pitch-dark, but there was light from the attic stairs. I cuffed Arf and listened. A tiny noise came from the stairs, a high sound that made my skin crawl. Eddie was there, still fully droood and taken very stiange. The pupils of his eyes were huge and black. Somehow he was able to hold a lit candle in front of him. Close behind Eddie was . . . Virginia. She wore a white gown, and her loosened dark hair hung down to her shoulders. Her mouth was set in a bold, frightened smile.

Eddie marched up the stairs like an automaton; he did a slow tour about my room and then took a place by my bed tick. He stood frozen there, a human candelabrum. Finally, he nodded his head. Virginia, still smiling rigidly, pulled off her gown and lay down on her back on my bed.

It was clear what was expected of me. I, being fifteen, was randy enough to comply.

Throughout our congress, Virginia all but ignored me, so engrossed was she in staring up at Eddie's face. Finally, as I expired, Virginia heaved and shook. The candlelight trembled terribly; the candle clattered to the floor and all was dark.

# 6

# Virginia Clemm

THE FACT that neither Eddie nor Virginia nor I spoke a word that night made a big difference. With no words to tether it, our strange, never-to-be-repeated orgy drifted to the border between reality and dream.

We greeted each other normally at breakfast, Eddie wobbly and Virginia gay. I had my tailcoat, collar, and cravat on for the trip. As no one else was present, Eddie instructed me to go down to Rockett's Landing and buy three five-dollar passages to Norfolk with a State Bank of Kentucky bill. It was safe enough, he insisted. I was, after all, a social nonentity. Meanwhile he would go to city hall and reclaim the three bills he'd left there yesterday. Virginia would pack. I was to hand them their two tickets as we boarded the boat, but we were not to converse. In Norfolk, Jeremiah would lead them to the safehouse, and I would follow.

"Why are there so many secrets, Eddie?" asked Virginia.

"Don't fret, Sissy. Wouldn't you like some new gowns? And a piano with candleholders? And a house and a garden all our own?"

"Oh yes!" She clapped her hands in delight.

94

"Well, then," said Eddie with a wan smile. "The secrets are because I made a lot of money, and the government men won't like me spending it. We're going to trick the old pinch-faces. Even though we're going to Norfolk with Mason, we'll tell everyone that you and I are going alone to Petersburg."

"I must never lie to Mama."

"Please lie just a little, Sissy."

She tossed her head and gave me a quick flash of that same fixed smile I'd seen last night. She was neither so dumb nor so innocent as she behaved. "All right then, Eddie, but I want Mason to bring his nice hairy dog."

"You like Arfie, Virginia?" My voice caught in my dry throat. I was sorry I'd gotten involved with her at all. The pliant succubus of last night was again swathed in Virginia's daytime persona of tight, greasy hair braids, spotted chalky skin, and strained high voice. Beneath the table Arfie started thumping his tail. He always noticed when someone said his name.

Virginia giggled shrilly. "Big noisy boy tail!"

It was raining outside, a steady spring drizzle. I took Dr. Custer's umbrella from its peg and left our house through the back door. Under Eddie's influence, all sense of ethics was leaving me. My thick wad of new bank notes rustled in the breast pocket against my heart. Arf trotted after me; he didn't mind the wet. The streets were full of men running this way and that. This seemed unusual for a Tuesday morning, and after a few blocks I noticed something else unusual: No blacks were to be seen. I stopped a hurrying ragged man and asked him the news.

"It's the niggers," he gasped, wiping the rain from his eyes. He was unshaven and had missing teeth. Ordinarily I wouldn't have spoken to him. "They've gone shit crazy! Butchered two families of whites in Goochland yesterday and kilt fifteen more in Richmond last night! Some of our boys strung up three of 'em at the edge of Screamertown this mornin' and would of done more, only the damn soldiers come to stop us! Who the hell's side are they on, hey?"

"I don't understand. What were the killings about?"

"Rebellion! Those murderin' savages want what *we* got! Want our houses and our clothes and our women and our smoked hams! It was a damn preachin' nigger set them off, a giant freak white nigger name of Elijah! Soldiers done caught him and his lieutenants; they bringin' 'em in to city hall! Come on, son, we gotta git 'em!" He finished catching his breath and hurried on up toward Capitol Square.

Elijah! Since coming to Richmond, I'd hardly thought about the strange firelit gathering I'd witnessed in Goochland. True enough, Elijah had yelled, "Kill the masters," but it had seemed like playacting more than a real plan, even if Moline had stayed with him. But now Elijah had gotten some of the slaves to rise up and kill, just like Nat Turner had done back in '31. The whole idea seemed as impossible as a dog attacking his master. Arfie poked my leg with his nose and I glanced down at him.

"You were dancing around Elijah's fire too, Arfie. You're a bad dog." He stared up at me with his dark eyes and nose like three black dots. We continued walking downhill.

There was a long line of people buying tickets for the noon packet steamer to Norfolk; they were worried the slave revolt would spread across all Richmond. With such excitement, the ticket agent didn't pay any mind to the unusual nature of my Kentucky bank note. He gave me thirty-five dollars' change in good solid-gold coin. No doubt about it, we'd done a profitable day's work on Sunday.

It was ten-thirty now, and I couldn't sit still. I kept thinking about weird white Elijah and about the feel of Virginia's pale, shuddering flesh. The memory of our congress was like a sore on my gum—unhealthy and painful, yet delicious to the touch.

I shoved my hand in my side pocket to see if the pawn ticket for my pistol was still there. It was. I resolved to run back into town to get my pistol from Abner Levy, and perhaps to catch a glimpse of Elijah on the city hall steps.

There was a good-size crowd in front of city hall, mostly riffraff like the fellow I'd spoken to. A double line of armed soldiers led from the city hall steps to Broad Street. I climbed into a tree so I could see. Before long, two wagons loaded with soldiers and black men came splashing up. Seemed like they'd arrested every loose Negro they'd set eyes on. The wet, ragged mob surged forward toward the wagons, but the soldiers held them back, and then here came two more wagons full of potential rebels. The mob stopped pushing entirely. Nobody wanted to tackle that many blacks at once. One last wagon arrived; this one held a bunch of soldiers and two men in chains. One was great big Elijah, standing straight up and yelling. The other was a dark man with a mashed face. It was Moline, wearing an army captain's coat. He yelled something that got both the slaves and the mob to hollering.

The soldiers started easing Elijah down off the wagon, and then all hell broke loose. I couldn't quite make it out, but it looked as if Elijah flat out busted the chains that manacled his feet and hands together. One minute he was being bundled up onto the city hall steps, and the next he was a pale angry pinwheel, kicking and hitting in every direction, his red teeth glittering like rubies. The mob went for him, some shots were fired, and then the wagons full of prisoners emptied. All at once, Capitol Square was like a dug-up anthill, with whites and blacks running every which way, slipping and sliding in the pouring rain. A black boy came scrambling up the same tree I was in. He saw me, bugged his eyes, and climbed right on past me toward the top.

I couldn't see Elijah anymore for the mound of people on him, but it was pretty clear things were going to get worse. Time was running short, and I'd seen enough. Arf was waiting at the base of the tree. He followed me across Broad Street and down the alleys to Abner Levy's pawnshop.

Levy had just finished drawing his blinds—I could tell because they were still swinging. I knocked hard until he opened the door a crack. He was out of breath. I told him I had the money to redeem a pawn, and he let me come in. Arf pushed in with me.

I put my pawn ticket and a five-dollar gold piece on Levy's

counter. "I left a four-shot pepperbox pistol with you," I reminded him. He picked up the money and the ticket and turned around to rummage in a cupboard.

Meanwhile, Arf gave himself a good shake and started sniffing around. The shop had a rack of fancy dress coats, cases with watches and jewelry, a variety of fine little tables, and several big trunks. One of the trunks caught Arf's interest in particular. He sniffed at it, gave it a good scratching, and then put his feet upon it and began to yelp.

"Get that dog out of here," yelled Levy angrily. "Why does everything have to happen at once? Shut him up, I tell you!"

I pulled Arf away from the trunk, but he leapt back at it, barking really hard. I noticed the lock was undone, so I decided to take a peek inside. Levy hollered at me to stop, but he was on the other side of the counter. I lifted up the top of the trunk, and there, curled up on his side, was Otha. He rolled his big eyes over my way and realized it was me.

"Marse Mase!" Otha sat up and threw out his long arms. "You looks mighty good indeed!" He jumped out of the trunk and did a little dance, unkinking his long limbs. His pockets rattled. Though he was soaking wet and a bit muddy, he was dressed to kill: yellow leather shoes, black velvet pants, an oddly cut purple jacket, and a watered silk shirt with a cravat of green brocade.

"Have you been in the trunk long, Otha?"

"No time a-tall. Ah only ran in here just befo' you, Marse Mase. Ah'd a been here earlier, only ah was delayed when some soldiers swept me up fo' bein' loose an' good-lookin' wifout no 'mancipation paper." He threw his arms around me and hugged me. "But ah don' need no paper effen ah got my little marse!" I couldn't help but hug him back. There were lots of hard things in his pockets. Arf capered around us barking.

"You ran in here?" I said finally.

"Soldiers had me on a wagon by city hall, and when 'Lijah

busted loose, I got away. Levy here done promise to send me to Baltimo' in exchange fo' some goods." Otha sprang over to the counter. "Ah don' require freightin' no more, Mist Levy, so ah'll jest have cash money fo' de silver teapot I done gib you." "I'm afraid that's impossible," said Levy, tightening his lips. "The risk on my part has already been undertaken. Your vacillation changes nothing."

"Is you gwine ship de empty trunk to Baltimo'?" yelled Otha. "No you ain't. You owes me fifty dollar!" He'd certainly acquired a lot of city manners in the last eleven days. And where had he gotten the expensive clothes and the teapot he'd just given Levy? "Ah wants mah money!" insisted Otha.

Levy addressed his attention to me. "Here is your pistol, Mr. Bustler. Thank you for your business. And . . . in the future, if you please, I prefer not to have slaves and animals in my shop." He handed me my pistol barrel first. It was unloaded. The clocks on Levy's wall said quarter to twelve.

Otha reached across the counter, grabbing for Levy's neck. I gave him a sharp poke in the side. "The money doesn't matter, Otha, believe me." I took Otha off to the side of the store and let him peek inside my breast pocket at the wad of bills.

"You stick with me," I told him with a certain amount of pride in my voice. "You've done well for yourself, but I've done better."

"Effen you done better, den do me some good. Tell Levy to gib me a big ole bowie knife."

"Anything, if we can just get going." I gave Levy another five-dollar gold piece—it all was beginning to seem like play money—and he got an excellent big knife out of his weapons cupboard. I gave Otha the knife as we left the shop.

We were down at Rockett's Landing a minute before noon. It was still drizzling. The wharf was crowded with people trying to get on the boat. All places were sold. I spotted Eddie and Virginia, him with his head up under an umbrella and her behind a thick pearly veil. I brushed up against them and passed Eddie his tickets. As we boarded, I tipped the purser five dollars to let me bring my slave and my dog.

Eddie and Virginia squeezed into the jam-packed passenger cabin, but Otha and I stayed out on the deck. We found a dry spot under an overhang and leaned against the bulkhead, with Arf huddled in against our feet. The whistle shrieked, the paddles beat, and our steamer moved out into the rain-pocked James.

"Well, Otha, how'd you get so rich? You weren't in with Elijah, were you?"

He didn't answer me directly. "Moline joined 'Lijah in Goochland, and Marcus took word to de rebels in Richmond. Luther ran North. Custa lost his ten dollars gamblin', an' Tyree drank his share up. Dey was de only two left to take Garland's bateau back to Lynchburg."

"Luther got caught," I told Otha. "Doesn't seem like those gold pieces did anyone much good."

"Did me plenty o' good," said Otha, adjusting his cravat. "Ah bought me some fine clothes and started sparkin' de help at rich folks' houses. Had me three gals on a string in no time, Mase. Dey'd sneak out for me to love 'em, and dey'd bring me silver fo' to save up to buy 'em free." He jingled his coat and then patted the rustling bulge over my heart. "Don' you call me crooked till you tell me how *yo* pocket got so full."

I glanced around. No one was near, but even so I stretched up on my toes to whisper in Otha's big ear. "I printed it, Otha. Thousands of dollars' worth. Two other men and I are going to spend it all in Norfolk."

"Whuffo'?" His eyes were wide.

A crewman rounded the corner and leaned against the bulkhead to smoke a pipe. I gave Otha a smile and a quiet nod. It was good to have him back, and to have him wondering what I was doing. With a big smart slave like Otha, I didn't have to feel so small.

It was raining in sheets when we got to Norfolk. Reynolds was there on the dock all right. He, Eddie, and Virginia piled into a carriage, and I got into the next one with Arf and Otha. Our route lay along the waterfront. There were dozens of ships at anchor in the harbor, and scores of lighters and dories at the docks. We rounded a point and then, for the first time in our lives, Otha and I glimpsed the open sea.

There was a sand beach with rain running down it and the surf running up. I hadn't known that seafoam would be so white. The shapes of the waves fascinated me; I didn't see how they could lean over so far before they came apart.

"Don't dey look like claws, Mase?" said Otha. "Draggin' everything out to sea?"

"They look like horses to me," I said. "Charging white horses that we can ride away."

"Whar we goin', Mase?"

"The ends of the Earth."

Jeremiah Reynolds had rented us a barnlike wooden building in a sandy lot just around the point. Curved timbers lay scattered in the yard like the ribs of dead cattle. The weathered gray building bore a faded sign saying BURRIS BOATS—it had once housed a builder of dories and skiffs. The main floor of the building was a great empty room with a stove at one end. Stairs led up to a loft, which was fitted out with two bedrooms. Burris the boatbuilder had lived here with his family until cholera had wiped them out two years ago. The superstitious locals had left the building to stand empty, and Reynolds had been able to rent it very cheaply.

Blessedly, the iron stove was well stoked. Otha and I took off our jackets and began to dry ourselves. Arf flopped down on his side right next to the stove. For a moment there, it felt like we were back in the kitchen on our farm.

"Here now," exclaimed Eddie, coming down from the loft with Virginia close behind him. "This won't do! Who let you in, nigger?"

"Don't talk to him that way," I cautioned Eddie. "His name is Otha. He's from Hardware; we came to Richmond together."

"He is your slave?" Eddie inquired.

"I expect so."

"Then tell him to remove himself to . . ." Eddie's voice trailed off as he glanced out through the back window. All but one of the sheds back there had collapsed; our little settlement's only standing outbuilding was a privy. "He can't stay in here with us," said Eddie. "There is a lady present."

That did it. Growing up on the farm with us, Otha'd never heard much abuse from whites. And now that he'd tasted freedom in Richmond and seen Elijah's uprising . . . he grabbed a fistful of Eddie's shirtfront and began to shake him.

"Ah's jest as much a man as you, little bulgehead." *Shake.* "And if you's shittin' yo pants so bad,"—*shake*—"ah'd say you de one belong in de privy!"

I pushed in between them, but not before Eddie had drawn a tiny pistol from his waistband. "Put the gun away, Eddie," I cried, fumbling my own pistol out of my coat pocket and pushing its muzzle into his ribs. "Calm down!"

Eddie's face was corpse-white. There were beads of sweat on his brow. "Are you prepared to give me a gentleman's satisfaction, young Reynolds? Are you prepared to answer for your servant's vile abuse?" Though my pistol was in his ribs, his gun was jammed up under my chin. The big difference was that his weapon was loaded. Virginia watched us in tense silence. Must I promise to duel Eddie for what Otha had said?

Jeremiah broke the impasse. "Otha will sleep down here by the stove, Eddie, while you and Virginia will stay on upstairs. Mason and I'll take the other upstairs bedroom. I've laid in enough bedding for us all. Let's not lose sight of what we're here for, men! Just another few weeks and we'll be launching our trip to the Hollow Earth! Come, come—if two races can't get along here in Norfolk, how shall we manage in Tierra del Fuego and beyond? Apologize to Mr. Poe, Mason, there's a good lad."

Though *I* hadn't said anything to apologize for, I went ahead and did it. After what had happened last night, I owed him something. "I'm sorry what Otha said, Eddie. And, Otha, I'd appreciate it if you'd let me do the talking here."

Eddie postured a bit more, but the crisis was over. Otha went off to the big room's other end and began violently to practice throwing his bowie knife to stick in the heavy wooden door. I helped Jeremiah cook some of the provisions he'd laid in. He'd used his Bank of Kentucky bills, so we had quite a spread. There were cucumbers, tender new potatoes, slices of ham, and a bushel of live lobsters. Although Eddie pretended to know all about lobsters, I think only Jeremiah had cooked lobsters before. At his direction, I threw the big green seabugs into boiling water. Arf pricked his ears up, and it seemed to me I could hear them scream.

While the lobsters boiled, Virginia used a piece of coal to draw a rectangular tabletop on the main room's big wooden floor. When she'd finished with the table, she drew round circles for plates, and a big fluffy blob in the middle for a flower arrangement. She washed her hands in the tub of rainwater we'd brought in and stood back, beaming at her housekeeping.

Jeremiah fried up the potatoes and ham while I peeled the cucumbers. Eddie opened up a bottle from the case of champagne Jeremiah had ready. When Otha asked Eddie for a drink from his bottle, Eddie told him to open his own bottle, which he did. When Otha drew masses of silver flatware out of his pockets to set our places, Eddie began to laugh. Before long, the two were toasting each other.

The flesh of the lobsters was succulent and piping hot. With two candles on our "table" and the rain beating outside, I felt like a romantic prince in a gypsy band. Something of the same mood imbued the others. Jeremiah got himself a bottle of champagne as well. He, Eddie, and Otha grew very merry. The strange setting was to Virginia's liking; she sang for us after dinner, her face blooming with youth and beauty. Here at land's end, in our dim storm-whipped banquet hall, Virginia's voice, which had been so shrill and pinched in Mrs. Clemm's boardinghouse, was filled with grace and wonder. When she'd finished singing, she skipped outside to bathe herself in the rain. I resolved to make love to her once again, and fetched Eddie another bottle of champagne.

Before we went up to bed, Jeremiah Reynolds spoke a bit about the voyage he and Eddie had planned. The idea was that we should assemble a huge balloon that would be filled with an extraordinarily buoyant coal gas produced by a brazier of charcoal sprinkled with certain salts. The balloon, brazier, and balloon cabin were to be assembled to make a huge crate, which we would engage to carry by ship as far south as the wall of ice would allow.

"Who all goin' in de balloon?" Otha asked. "Is you goin', Mason?"

"I think I am."

Virginia darted in from her rainshower, loose wet dress flowing, and went tripping upstairs. I'd never seen her look so clean and fresh. She paused on the stairs to stare back at Eddie. He smiled and blew her a kiss but made no effort to rise.

"Of course you'll go, young Reynolds," said Jeremiah, clapping me on the shoulder. "It's the opportunity of a lifetime. You and I and Otha shall go. Eddie would have come, but his duties lie here with his writing and with his young wife. As wanted men, you and Otha are natural sailors." He stretched and rose to his feet. "You'll like the rough and tumble of shipboard life, Otha. All men are equal before the sea. You can help Mr. Poe purchase our equipment, and Mason can help me assemble it. If you're truly a Reynolds, Mason, then once you see our cunning equipage, you'll jump at the chance to use it. Engineering has its own imperatives." He yawned again. "But now I'll off to bed."

Eddie gave me a sharp look just then. It struck me that he didn't want to go up to bed with Virginia. The tone of some remarks I'd heard him make—his fears of eyes, of mouths, of cats, of whirlpools—these remarks all suggested that he had a horror of a woman's most private part. It seemed unlikely that such a man would wish to crawl inside a great Symmes Hole in Mother Earth's nethermost clime. Perhaps Eddie's abrupt marriage to Virginia had been done not so much because he was jealous of me as because he needed an honorable excuse for backing out of the trip he'd promised Reynolds to undergo. First I was to explore Virginia, and then the Hollow Earth—all this in Eddie's stead.

Elaborately focusing his attention on me, Eddie drew out a metal pipe and a small glass vial. "Have you ever smoked opium, my young devil? It is most stimulating to the mind's eye."

"No thank you," said I. "I'm going to bed too." I wondered if Eddie could sense the pulse in my veins and the stiffening in my masculine member that came with night visions of Virginia. But no matter. If he was to spend the night down here drinking and smoking opium, Virginia and I would have free rein.

"Well then, black Otha," said Eddie, sending a thin blue coil of smoke up from his pipe. "How about you?"

Otha slowly nodded his head, a big loose smile on his lips. I knew from our experiments with Pa's whiskey that he had a stronger head for liquor than I. "Ah's had me a full week, Mist Poe," said he. "Done took three girls in Richmond to see 'Lijah do his juju, done drank champagne wid white folks tonight, so now ah guess ah's ready fo' yo' sweet dreams." He rolled his eyes over at me and winked. "Din' tell you bout 'Lijah, did I, Marse Mase? Warn't just my good looks and promises dat bound dem three gals to me, it were dat *ah knew de prophet.* Our whole bateau crew got in wid him, some fo' an arm and some fo' a toe."

"I saw you dance around the fire with him that night in Goochland," I said.

"Ah knows you did. Arf showed you to us. 'Lijah could juju de men an' de beasts. He come fum a long way away. Gimme dat O, Mist Poe."

I left the two of them smoking together and went upstairs. Jeremiah was snoring, but Virginia had locked her door. I called to her as loud as I dared, but there was no answer.

The next two weeks passed like an avalanche. Every day

Eddie and Otha went out to buy more goods with Bank of Kentucky bills. Every day I worked with Jeremiah at assembling the exploring apparatus. Every evening we feasted, and every night I dreamed of sweet Virginia.

Posing as Kentucky Colonel Embry and his manservant Oscar, Eddie and Otha made a convincing pair, even when, as sometimes happened, they were glazed and vacant from poppy smoke or draughts of the opium tincture known as laudanum. Their initial antipathy had established a tone of mutual frankness between them; with the frankness and the drugs, they got along very well. Eddie rented them a room at the Hotel Norfolk and took all deliveries of goods at that address. Otha lugged the boxes and crates over to our boatyard after dark. Despite his fear of the sea, Otha was enthusiastic about the notion of exploring the Hollow Earth. He was of the opinion that his pale prophet Elijah might have come from there.

The equipage for our trip was elaborate. First we had to sew together our great silk balloon. The silk came in rolls that we sewed into huge strips, half of them black and half of them white. The strips were trimmed into long, tapering gores, and then the gores were sewn together lengthwise to form a huge pear-shaped bag. Virginia was of much assistance in the sewing. Once the great striped bag was completed, we painted its surface with four coats of the liquid rubber known as caoutchouc. Following this, we rigged a huge network of silken ropes to contain the bag and to attach it to the cabin.

The cabin itself was of wickerwork. Of course no such thing as a ready-made wickerwork balloon cabin could be purchased; instead, we bought a number of large square wicker baskets (locally used for carrying catches of fish) and reassembled their sides into the big box that we required. Our cabin box had a swinging door, two shuttered windows, and a hole in its ceiling for our stove's flue. Fastened to the walls themselves were navigational instruments, most especially two highly sensitive chronometers: one with a pendulum, and one with a spring.

The stove was a lightweight affair fashioned from sheets of brass. A metalsmith constructed it for "Colonel Embry" to Jeremiah's specifications. The stove included a round chimney flue, which would lead up through our cabin roof to feed lighter-than-air gasses into our silk-and-rubber balloon. Packed in with the stove was a jar of the special salts that Eddie said would dramatically increase the lifting power of our stove's coal gas.

As this was to be an expedition that must initially pass across the Antarctic wastes, we obtained a number of quilts with which to line the cabin walls. Jeremiah showed us how to increase the quilts' insulating powers by opening their seams and padding them with goose down. As a precaution, we attached two steel runners on the base of the cabin so that should our balloon be downed, we could pull our cabin across the ice like a sled. Jeremiah went so far as to rig up silken traces with harnesses for the intended crew of him, me, Otha, and Arf.

Our dinners together were lavish affairs. Eddie was in a fever to spend or gamble away all of our remaining dollars before the counterfeit nature of the bills was found out. I tried to hold some of my bills back, but he took them all from me. Champagne we had always, and game, veal, seafood, and fruits of all sorts. I had the feeling of a noose closing in on us. Norfolk was not so large a town that no one would connect Eddie's spending to the activity in our backyard; nor was Kentucky so distant that its lack of a state bank would not soon be found out.

I often sought to get Virginia alone and talk to her during those two weeks, but she was as elusive as a cat, now skipping up to her room, now running out to wander on the beach. Even on the more and more frequent nights when Eddie did not come back to us at all, Virginia kept her door locked to me. As if to torment me further, she made much of Arf at all times, fondling him and feeding him bowls of delicacies. So lovesick did I become that I even hoped Eddie might use me as his member again . . . but Virginia's relations with Eddie were now minimal as well. Eddie was drinking much and gambling heavily.

Eddie's original justification for starting his now nightly gambling bouts had been to turn some of our Bank of Kentucky notes into gold coin. But here, as in everything else, Eddie knew no moderation. In his first two days of gambling, he won enough so that Jeremiah could indeed set aside enough gold for three shipboard passages south. But then Eddie's runs of losses began. He was out all night, every night. Otha stopped going about with Eddie, and lent his energies to running out for this or that last item for our trip: shot and powder for my pistol, extra clothes, bottled juices, dried meat, and the like. Eddie slept alone in the Hotel Norfolk—if he slept at all—and in the afternoons he would appear in our workroom, pale and shaking, though trying hard to front a demeanor of nonchalance.

It was clear that the sight of his neglected Sissy filled Eddie with agonies of shame and self-loathing. So strong were these emotions that he often spoke sharply to her, sometimes even screaming with what seemed like hatred. Though his tirades were not wholly comprehensible, it was evident that Eddie regretted his decision to marry instead of traveling with us beyond the pole. Under the stress of his neglect and his attacks, Virginia once again took on the greasy, unattractive appearance that she'd had back at the boardinghouse. Once again her voice grew tense and shrill, and our boatyard echoed to the mournful mewling of her songs.

Finally, our preparations were done. We stowed our hardtack and pemmican in the wicker cabin with its instruments, stuffing the folded balloon in there as well. With its doors and shutters sealed, the cabin made a massive crate six feet by six feet by ten. Working together, Otha, Eddie, Jeremiah, and I were able to inch it across the big room's floor to the great side door. With the help of two more men and a wagon, we would be able to get it to our ship.

For our trip, Jeremiah Reynolds had chosen a fast-sailing schooner called the *Wasp*. Veteran of several trips to the antarctic seas, the *Wasp* was laying in provisions for a sealing voyage and would be leaving Norfolk on June first. Invoking the captain's duty to American science—and additionally promising to tell him first of any fine sealing islands we flew over—Jeremiah convinced him to transport the three of us and our wicker balloon box to the very edge of the antarctic wall of ice.

On Tuesday the thirty-first of May 1836, the day before the *Wasp* was to sail, Jeremiah, Otha, Arf, and I walked down on the docks of Norfolk to examine our ship. I asked Virginia to come with us, but she tearfully insisted she must wait in her room for Eddie. She said that he must take her home to her mother today. When I tried to comfort her, she said that I was a silly yokel and that she was sorry she'd ever let me touch her. She blamed me for her troubles with Eddie and said that if only she could be alone with him and her mama, then everything would be *arcadian* again.

It was a lovely day outside, with a clear sky and a light breeze. Jeremiah pointed out that the horizon was hazy; this meant, he said, that tomorrow the weather would be fine as well. We found a man willing to row us out to the *Wasp*, which was anchored in Norfolk harbor a few hundred yards west of Town Point. Arf liked the boat ride, but Otha was in an agony of fear.

"We gots to learn how ter swim, Mase!"

"Praying's more help than swimming if the *Wasp* goes down at sea," laughed Jeremiah. "Hell, man, we're going in a balloon later on even though we don't know how to *fly!*"

The *Wasp*'s Captain, Guy, was too busy to see us, but one of the mates, a tall, well-formed Virginian named Bulkington, advised us that the *Wasp* would be sailing on tomorrow's ebb tide, half an hour before dawn. We and our cargo had best come on board today. Yes, the dog was welcome, especially if he could kill rats. Bulkington lent us three crew members and the ship's heavy sealing yawl, which rowed back to the dock behind us.

While Jeremiah, Otha, and the three crewmen rode a flat freight wagon, or dray, to our lodgings, I stopped by the Hotel Norfolk to rouse Eddie. In keeping with our plan of keeping

Eddie's Kentucky colonel persona distinct from our expedition's outfitting, I had not yet visited the hotel. It was a comely sandstone structure, several blocks from the wharf. When I told the man at the desk I had an account to settle with Colonel Embry, the clerk gave a little whoop.

"You a card player, too? You'd better throw in with Lieutenant Bustler; he's already gone upstairs. One flight and then to the right."

I went up the hotel's richly carpeted stairs and took the hall to the right. A hubbub of sound drifted from an open door. Inside, I found three men in naval dress. One of them had the muttonchops and pie face that I remembered from the locket portrait Lucy Perrow had shown me . . . how long ago? Only a month? I resisted a crazy impulse to introduce myself as Lieutenant Bustler.

"I'm Mason Bulkington," said I. "Where's Colonel Embry?"

"Are you a friend of his?" demanded Bustler, too pig-arrogant to introduce himself. I resolved to rag him.

"Everyone honors the colonel," said I, "though I don't have the breeding to call him a friend. I'm here from the confectioner's to present a bill. The colonel had me take a pound of chocolates to a lady this morning."

"What lady?" demanded one of the navy men. "Where?"

"A belle named Lucy Perrow," said I glibly. "She's here in this very hotel with her father. Touchy man, Judge Perrow. When I delivered the chocolates just now, he said he'd horsewhip the colonel as soon as he got through taking the starch out of some damn ponce called Lieutenant Bustler." I laughed easily, pretending not to notice the cloud on Bustler's face. "The judge meant business, too, I can tell you. He had a brace of pistols on, and a big black whip slung over his shoulder. Do you fellows know any Lieutenant Bustler?"

"Don't you be asking us questions, boy," blustered Bustler. "Your fine colonel cheats at cards!" The next minute, he and his friends had hurried off down the hall and out of the hotel.

I looked around Eddie's room. There were a few empty bottles, but the carpetbag he'd kept here was gone. I hoped with all my might that Eddie had taken Bustler for plenty of gold and that he and Virginia were safe on their way back to Richmond. Bustler wasn't in the lobby, but the sheriff was. He was deep in conversation with the clerk; they were leaning over a couple of Bank of Kentucky bills and jabbing at them.

"Counterfeit?" said the clerk unbelievingly. "Counterfeit?"

"No such bank!" said the sheriff. "We just found out!" Eddie'd cut his departure mighty fine.

I ran all the way to our boatyard. Otha, Jeremiah, and the three crewmen were struggling to get our wicker box up onto the wagon, while Arf barked furiously. I added my strength to the task, and the drayman got down off his wagon seat and joined us as well. The box was heavier than I'd expected, but finally we had it on the dray.

I whispered to Jeremiah that things were unraveling, and ran into our home of two weeks to see if Virginia or Eddie were there. The big room was empty, and the rooms upstairs were empty of life as well. Virginia's things were still lying about. I cast about for some message from her, but there was nothing. Perhaps she'd been too rushed to pack. I prayed she and Eddie were well on their way, and hurried after our slow-moving dray.

# 7

## Aboard the *Wasp*

WRITING THIS ACCOUNT of my adventures is slower work than I
expected. If it weren't for all the tekelili I shared with Eddie Poe
down in the Hollow Earth, I don't think I'd be able to do it at all.
I first set pen to paper on October 10, the day after Eddie's
funeral, and here it is Christmas Day, 1849. My skin remains
very dark; I've found work as a waiter in a Negro restaurant.
Seela and I have a Christmas bird and a hot stove to roast it in.
We have much to be grateful for.

When I began this narrative, I supposed it possible to produce a simple consecutive listing of one's memories, but I find,
in the writing, that memory is a feathery branching tree. The dray
that bore our box—should I mention that its wheels were hooped
in iron, that these wheels clattered terribly on the street's cobbles,
and that the sound reminded me of the first machine I ever saw:
a crank-operated corn shucker belonging to Cornelius Rucker,
owner of the farm next to ours in Hardware? Do I have time to
mention the walk Otha and I took on the beach one day earlier,
and to tell of the segmented leathery object we found, a mollusk's

egg case, with scores of perfect tiny shells in each of its membraneous disks? Can I mention that Virginia's last words to me were *I'm just a girl*?

I must prune and press forward.

On board the *Wasp*, our balloon box was stowed down in the hold, Jeremiah and I were shown to a cabin, Otha was lodged with the crew, and Arf was given the run of the ship. We set sail at dawn, June 1, 1836.

Given the prevailing trade winds, the natural course for a ship running for the South Seas is to sail southeast to cross the equator near Africa, and then to sail southwest to hit South America near Rio de Janeiro. This is what we did. The *Wasp* crossed the equator on the twelfth of July in longitude 26°W and we reached Rio on the fourth day of August. Rio was a revelation, a truly interracial city. I slept with another prostitute there, also wrote Pa a letter telling him I'd gone to sea. Though it was winter in Rio, flowers were blooming; more than anything, I was struck by the sight of the hummingbirds feeding on the blossoms. Otha and I took advantage of the good weather and calm waters by finally learning how to swim.

We replenished our stores and traveled down the coast past the Rio Negro, crossing 40° southern latitude. The wild South American coast of this region is known as Patagonia and is inhabited by a shy, gray-skinned race of men. Our sealing yawl landed in several of the bays, taking a few score of sealskins.

These takes were by no means satisfactory, as several thousand sealskins were needed for the *Wasp*'s voyage to be a success. Bulkington told me that Captain Guy had plans to eventually shape our course in search of untouched sealing islands presumed to exist beyond 65° S, the antarctic circle.

For those as ignorant of navigation as I was at the start of the *Wasp*'s journey, I should explain that every point on the equator has 0° latitude, and that the southern pole is the unique point with 90° southern latitude. The 90° symbolizes the fact that from the center of the Earth, there is a ninety-degree angle between a line to the equator and a line to the South Pole. A drive for the Pole is a drive for higher and higher latitudes.

Longitude, I may as well add, is a measure of one's angular deviation east or west from the prime 0° meridian, which runs north-south through Greenwich, England. South America lies in western longitude; most of Africa is in eastern longitude. Near the Pole, the longitude lines get so bunched together that one can effect large changes of longitude rather easily. But changing one's latitude stays just as hard.

On September 19 we reached the Falkland Islands, at lat. 52° S, long. 57° W, near the tip of South America. The Falklands are of good soil, with luxuriant meadows and many head of wild cattle. Though there are no trees, the lowlands supply an excellent peat or turf for burning. No humans live here, but the feathered tribes are very numerous, particularly the penguin and the albatross.

These two dissimilar birds form huge rookeries together— temporary camps for hatching their young. The chief rookery on the Falklands was nearly bigger than our farm back in Hardware. It was set on the rocky shore by the water. The birds had smoothed out their rookery by moving all the loose rocks out to form the walls of three sides of a square. The big square was divided up like a checkerboard, with alternating nests of penguins and albatrosses. The arrangement struck me as a symbol of how the two races, black and white, lived together in the south.

We stayed in the Falklands till September 26: overhauling our sails and rigging, obtaining a new supply of fresh water, and taking on board twenty-eight barrels of albatross eggs packed in salt. The plan was to run southeastward before the prevailing winds until crossing the latitude of 60°, and then to head back westward, beating our way as far south as the ice would allow. Captain Weddell of the English navy had achieved a latitude of 74° S in February 1822, and Captain Guy felt we might be able to do as well. If we could find a new, untouched seal rookery, we could well harvest as many as five thousand pelts.

Though Jeremiah was a pleasant, good-humored cabin mate, he had an annoying tendency to give me advice. I soon wearied of his homilies. I think he felt I was a bit of a criminal, not quite worthy of bearing the Reynolds name. He dined each day with Captain Guy, leaving me to share the mates' mess. Of all the mates, I got on with Stuart Bulkington the best.

Like me, Bulkington had grown up on a farm between Lynchburg and Charlottesville. He had a deeply tanned face and brilliant white teeth; it was a joy to see him laugh. For reasons he was unwilling to divulge, Bulkington had been steadily at sea for seven years now. He filled me with tales of the lands he'd seen, and though I had few adventures to reciprocate with, he seemed satisfied by my willingness to listen and to comment. We were kindred spirits, I felt: two men with troubled pasts.

Since Otha was not strictly bound to work, he stood somewhat apart from the crewmen. And in any case the handful of black crew members were near savages: Tasmanians and Feejee islanders with sharpened teeth and tattoos on their faces. Otha's best friend on the *Wasp* was a half-breed fellow called Dirk Peters, son of an Indian squaw and a fur trapper. When Otha was not with me, he was likely to be practicing knife throwing with Peters, who was a great one for whipping a bowie knife out of his boot top and flinging it at his target. He'd killed a penguin on the Falklands this way, sticking him right through the heart, which feat had impressed Otha mightily.

This Dirk Peters was short and ferocious-looking, with snaggleteeth that peeked out through thin, unbending lips. The straight mouth gave him an air of sadness, while the dancing teeth suggested he was merry. In truth he was, so far as I could tell, an empty-headed drifter who lived only for the moment. Not only Otha but Arf as well took a liking to Peters, who liked to pull the dog's ears and talk to him in a dialect he said came from the Missourian tribe of the Upsarokas. Over my great protests, Peters and Otha passed one idle afternoon by tattooing a spiral Upsaroka good-luck symbol around Arf's navel, on his belly just above the

tip of his penis sheath. Tranced by Peters's chants, or by some of
the opium that Otha still seemed to have about him, Arf endured
the ordeal with no complaint.

We spent a week sailing about southeast of the Falklands in
search of the missing Aurora islands. These small, round islands
had been sighted in 1774, 1779, and in 1794, but no one had been
able to find them since. We were unsuccessful, and on October
18 we made South Georgia island in lat. 53° S, long. 38° W. This
is a steeply mountainous island, with its peaks perpetually snow
covered and its valleys overgrown with strong-bladed grass. Captain Guy sent the yawl and two boats ashore in search of seal, but
after three days they returned empty-handed. We circumnavi-
gated the whole island without spotting a single seal.

We continued our course due east, driven by the powerful
prevailing westerlies, with strong wind and much heavy weather,
including snow and hail. We often spotted the free-floating islands of ice that are known as icebergs. On October 24 we reached
Bouvet's Island, in lat. 54° S, long. 3° E. A boat went ashore and
returned the next day with eighty fur-seal skins. The sailors had
clubbed twice as many to death but had not had the time to skin
them all. Arf and I rode to shore with Bulkington's boat the next
day to watch the men taking the skins off the remaining seals.
The procedure was to cut off the flippers and tail, make an inci-
sion around the neck and along the belly, and then to peel the skin
off like a jacket. Arf nosed the fresh carcasses with interest, but
he was not bold or hungry enough to tear a piece off.

It was a melancholy view on the beach there, two thousand
miles from Cape Horn and a thousand from the Cape of Good
Hope. I felt dizzy and unsteady on the unrocking land. The raw
red flesh of the flayed seal carcasses was the only vivid color in
sight. The sky and sea were gray, and the island was a mass of
glassy blue-gray lava. The beach was of pale, crumbling pumice
stone.

Out past our ship were scores of antarctic ice islands that had
come aground in the shallows around Bouvet Island. Some of

these huge icebergs were as much as a mile in circumference. In the slow spring warming (remember that seasons are reversed in the southern hemisphere, so that their October, November, December, January, and February are as our April, May, June, July, and August), pieces of the ice islands were occasionally dropping off and crashing into the sea with eerie roars that mixed with the cries of the seafowl feeding on the dead seals' flesh.

It seemed strange and cruel for men to come all this way and slaughter wantonly. Even if it were possible to reach the Hollow Earth, would it be right for us to pave the way for our civilization's further depredations? Or, more horribly, what if those inside the Hollow Earth were to come out and treat us the way we treated seals? I spoke with Jeremiah about these questions that evening, but he seemed not to take them seriously.

"This is a pretty fair sort of world, Mason, if you don't expect too much. There are a great many good fellows about. Captain Guy, for one, is a brick and a jolly toper. And your friend Bulkington seems right enough. Quit your vaporing! Don't you think those seals' jackets will look better on the pretty Knickerbocker ladies in the city of the Manhattoes? And as for Hollow Earthlings coming out after us—I wouldn't worry. It's likely as not to be dark in there, with nothing but mushrooms."

"I thought Symmes said there's a sun inside," I protested. "Right in the center."

"Yes, but our Newton of the West hadn't much of a head for mathematics." Reynolds grinned. "I have it on the authority of a professor from Johns Hopkins that there's no weight on the inside of a hollow sphere. If we could get past the ice and sail over the South Hole's lip into the Hollow Earth, we'd soon enough float off the ocean's surface in there. And if there was a sun in the middle, we'd fall into it and burn, and so would anyone on the inside who didn't cling fast."

There was a half-gale blowing outside and our porthole was battened shut. A flickering light of seal oil lit our little cabin with its table, chair, and two bunk beds. Arf lay sleeping on the floor.

Puzzled by what Jeremiah said, I drew a diagram on the flyleaf of the atlas he'd brought along. The picture I drew was what you'd see if you could take a thin vertical slice right through our Hollow Earth. You'd see a big ring of matter, broken by two holes at the bottom and top: the North and South holes that Symmes postulated. My picture showed two thick semicircles not quite meeting at the bottom and the top.

"Symmes said a ship could sail over the edge and then sail around on the inside," I said, drawing three ships, one on the outside, one on the lip, and one on the inside.

"Yes," said Jeremiah. "But the *real* Newton's integral calculus proves him wrong." He put his blunt finger on the ship inside the Hollow Earth. "Sure enough, the ocean and dirt right under that ship attract it." Now he swept his finger over the whole rest of the Hollow Earth-rind. "But all this matter is, so to speak, *overhead*. It pulls the ship up. It's far away, but there's a lot of it. My Professor Stokes tells me that Newton's integrals balance it all out." He sketched a fourth ship, floating free in the Hollow Earth's airy interior. "*This* is what happens. And if there were a heavy little sun in the center, it would pull all loose things down into it. Pfft! Too bad!"

"But if there *is* a sun and we go in, then . . ."

"*We'll be safe*. That's another reason why we're going there in a balloon instead of a ship. As long as the Hollow Earth's full of air, a lighter-than-air balloon will float up *away* from any central sun. We'll let out gas to go down in the Hole, and we'll toss ballast to get back out. If there is an Inner Sun, then as long as we're inside the Hole, we'll float around and the Hollow Earth'll just be like a kind of roof. There may be birds nesting on it, or apes in hanging-down trees—who knows?"

I tried to imagine it and gave up. "But you think there might not *be* an Inner Sun, Jeremiah?"

"The Hollow Earth could be black and empty, with rocks drifting around like the small planets called asteroids. Some little light would come in the Holes." Jeremiah shrugged and gave me his bluff, honest grin. "Thunderation, Mason, I don't know *what* to expect. That's why I want to go in there! Man gets to be my age, he'll go a long way for a surprise."

There was a great roar outside and then, a moment later, our ship pitched horribly. One of the giant ice islands nearby had shifted its center of balance and spun over. I slept uneasily that night, dreaming of a ship that fell up through a crowded sky toward the sun.

The next day we sailed around Bouvet Island looking for more seal rookeries, but so steep were the cliffs that not another spot could be found where a seal might land. We put out to sea and ran southeast before the squalling west wind.

On November 13 we crossed 60° S latitude. The wind moderated, the weather cleared, and we found ourselves in a vast field of drifting ice. Most of the pieces were rounded pancakelike floes, but many were heaped up like crystal fairy castles or like mountains of glass. The brilliant morning sun reflected off the myriad angles and sent out rays of every color. We were dazzled by the brilliant beauty, but our wonder soon changed to alarm. Huge chunks of ice and snow were irregularly falling from the floating ice mountains. If one of those chunks landed on or near us, we'd sink like a toy paper boat. Providentially, we were not very near any of the floating ice mountains.

The weather was very mild and pleasant, with not enough wind for us to make any rapid headway. Pieces of ice kept seizing up around our ship's hull, which made our progress that much slower. Yet if a strong wind had arisen, we would surely have been dashed to pieces.

Vast numbers of sea birds flew from one ice mountain to the other—albatrosses, petrels, ice birds, and many other strange species that no one had ever seen. I wondered if they roosted inside the Hollow Earth and migrated out here through the South Hole. Swimming about and clambering on and off the icebergs were also penguins in great numbers. To complete the lively scene, a great number of right whales and porpoises showed themselves in the clear water south of the crystal field we found ourselves in. The whales were leaping totally out of the water and shaking themselves for joy.

On the third day, we awoke to find that the sheets of ice had parted, and we found our way out into the clear water south of the icy drift. The water was teeming with shrimp and squid. The wind shifted around to the northeast now, so we resolved to sail back to the westward, holding a southern course so long as it would be practicable. We passed through several huge bands of ice, yet each time we were frozen in, the ice loosened back up. Captain Guy had a genius for finding more clear water. With the lengthening of the days it seemed, perhaps paradoxically, that the farther south we got, the more open space there was. Despite the warming temperature, the weather remained highly variable, with frequent hail squalls from the west. The greatest fear at all times was that our small wooden ship might fetch up against an iceberg hundreds of times our size.

On December 1 we crossed the antarctic circle at lat. 65° S, long. 15° E. In this latitude there was no field-ice, though there were many icebergs. Captain Guy was still enjoying the challenge of picking his way farther and farther south, but now the crew was beginning to grumble. We had taken no seals for over a month and were in daily risk of losing our lives. Fresh water we had plenty, but other provisions were running low. Taking all this into account, Jeremiah concluded that we had best bring our balloon box up on deck, so that we could leave whenever the captain judged it prudent to head back north. There seemed to be no sign of the new sealing islands that Captain Guy had hoped to find. He told us that if we found nothing soon, he would shape a northwest path toward the seal-rich archipelago of islands lying between us and Tierra del Fuego.

The balloon box was wedged into a wholly inaccessible recess of the hull. To make things worse, three boatloads of extra provisions had arrived on the evening of the last day, and these had all been packed in around the balloon box. It was the work of a full day for Otha, Jeremiah, Peters, Bulkington, and me to haul the boxes and barrels out of the way, and to wrestle our great wicker box up onto the deck. It was difficult work in the hold, suffused as it was with a vile smell of decay that I supposed came from the sealskins. Our box had an extremely foul stench of its own, and we wondered if our provisions had spoiled. Imagine my horror when, on grasping the stinking box, I heard a weak voice from its inside.

"Get me out," said the voice. "For the love of God."

In a minute we had torn the box's door open. I staggered back and vomited. Eddie and Virginia had been sealed in the box all these months, and one of them had long been dead.

With a superhuman effort, we lugged the box to a position near the hold and winched it up onto the deck. What a contrast between that box and the clean antarctic air! So smeared and tangled were the two lovers' bodies that it had been hard to tell who was who, but now I could see that it was Eddie who had survived and Virginia who had rotted into bones and black grease. Eddie's eyes were quite mad; Bulkington drew up bucket after bucket from the sea and dashed the cold water in Eddie's livid, twitching face.

Jeremiah drew the balloon bag out and let the breeze clean out the box's interior. All our bottled juices and spirits were gone; also the dried meats and the hardtack. Evidently, Eddie'd had room to squirm about in the cabin. Yet we'd found him in the arms of dead, rotting Virginia. It was a horrible thing to imagine a man seeking out so macabre an embrace.

The whole ship's crew was in a furor of excitement and disgust. I think they might well have thrown Eddie overboard with Virginia's remains had not Jeremiah intervened. He carried the weeping Eddie into our cabin and began nursing him. Otha and I set to work putting the balloon cabin to rights, and Bulkington helped us lash it to the deck. This last step was important as now a sudden gale was rising from the north.

For the next three weeks we were driven southward. Over

and over, Captain Guy tried to beat his way to the north, but a powerful current joined forces with the winds and the drifting fields of ice. We passed 70° S latitude, and then 72°, and finally, on Christmas Day of 1836, we reached a latitude of 75° S, closer to the Pole than any men had ever been before. Birds filled the southern sky, which was brilliant with the reflection of some vast unseen snowfield. There seemed little doubt that a landfall was imminent.

With the antarctic summer at its peak, we had sunlight all day and night long. It was a striking thing, leaning on the rail that Christmas Day, to see the sun and moon both above the horizon, each shedding its light. Our provisions were all but exhausted; our holiday repast had consisted of fish we'd caught, and of the supply of fresh water that one of our boats had managed to gather from a pool in one of the icebergs. Everyone was ready for the new land to the south; we had two sails set square to let the gentle north wind blow us thither.

During our three weeks' southward progress, the icebergs had become ever more huge and fantastic. Some were huge uniform rectangles, but others had sides that were smoothly carved by the water, with indentations that had become huge arching caves. The caves were at water level, so that the swell of the sea sloshed in and out of the ice mountains. In the fog, when it was the most dangerous, you'd hear the icebergs by the thundering of the water in their caves.

But Christmas Day was fair, and land was near. Eddie was up and about for the first time. I'd been bunking with Bulkington, leaving Eddie completely to Jeremiah's care. Eddie's quivering had gone, and his ghastly pallor had abated. As he and I stood leaning over the ship's rail, staring at the icebergs, I sought to engage him in conversation.

"Look how the sun lights one side of that ice mountain and the moon the other," I said to Eddie, hoping to stimulate his love of beauty. "And see the white petrels flying in and out of that cavern! It's like a ruined alabaster abbey, is it not?"

"It is like teeth," whispered Eddie. He had his hand shoved

deep into the pocket of his trousers. He looked at me oddly and then he drew his hand out of his pocket and showed the delicate ivory objects that lay in his palm. A chill crept down my spine.

"Virginia's teeth," said Eddie. His voice was fainter than the most distant cries of the birds.

I glared at Eddie till he put the teeth back in his pocket. "Tell me how she died," said I.

He stared out at the iceberg moving slowly toward our stern. His bulging white forehead was pathetically furrowed, and his mouth was pursed smaller than his little mustache. I felt some pity for him, and some rage. I nudged him. "I loved Virginia too, Eddie. You have to tell me."

He glanced over at me and shook his head. Still I insisted. "Why did you kill her, Eddie? Why?"

He shuddered and sighed, as if relieved I knew, and then at last he began to talk. His voice was weak and papery, but as he went on, some of its old melodious power returned. "The last night there, the Imp of the Perverse possessed me. What good were all our pawky careful plans? The end result of my machinations was that I'd alienated the affections of my beloved Virginia for an exploring expedition which I was not to make. Nothing waited for me back in Richmond but Mrs. Clemm's boardinghouse and the slow dungbeetle ball-rolling of my inevitable literary fame. The Imp of the Perverse, do you know him, Mason?"

"Not really," said I, eager to keep Eddie's voice flowing. "Go on."

"That last night I cheated a Lieutenant Bustler at cards and won a small fortune in gold. The Imp wished Bustler to be *sure* I'd diddled him, so I left an extra ace in the lieutenant's deck of cards. I made it back to my hotel in the early hours. I was out of opium. I could have waited till the shops opened, but the Imp would have it not. I took a crowbar from the toolshed behind the hotel and prized open the back door of the nearest apothecary. I found a ball of opium and a bottle of laudanum and stepped safely out. The Imp of the Perverse took it ill that things went so well.

At his bidding, I stood there smoking pipes till a constable happened by. When he asked me about the open door, I said he insulted me and then I bribed him with a Bank of Kentucky bill. 'Be sure to check if this is good,' I told him. 'And if not, seek Colonel Embry at the Hotel Norfolk.' "

A chunk fell off a cathedral-size iceberg nearby. The birds screamed, and the spreading circle of waves rocked our ship. "Go on, Eddie. Tell it all."

"I went back to the hotel and slept. When I woke it was midmorning. As soon as I remembered all that the Imp and I had wrought, I packed my bag and left the hotel by the back door. I hurried to the boatyard. Nobody was there but Virginia. She was sitting alone upstairs. I told her we had to depart immediately and that I didn't want to go back to Richmond. I told her we should go to Baltimore on the eleven o'clock packet, and then on to New York. She said I was hateful to her and that—"

Eddie stopped and gazed at me. His eyes were darker and more whirlpoollike than ever before. I was a bit frightened, for all that any threat he projected was not so much physical as it was spiritual. "She said she wished she had married you, Mason. You did it. I remember what you did. You and I and the Imp—we brought poor Virginia low."

"Go on, Eddie, go on."

"Virginia said she was not leaving the boatyard until she'd asked you what to do. She said she'd been scared to talk to you, but that now the time had come. I resolved to drug her and to bodily take her away. I made her some tea, dark and sweet and strong, and I laced it with two hundred drops of laudanum, four times my normal dose. I watched her drink it, and then I watched the rapid waning of her sweet moon face. She slumbered. I hurried downstairs with an eye to going out for a carriage—I would tell the driver Virginia was drunk, I would tell the packet-boat captain she was sick, I would lie our way to a new life. But as soon as I came downstairs, I heard a heavy wagon coming. I couldn't let you and Jeremiah find us!''

Arf appeared between us now, wriggling and cheerful. He was a great pet among the sailors and had gotten holiday scraps from almost everyone. In that strange half-human way he had sometimes, he put his feet up on the ship railing between Eddie and me. Eddie glanced distractedly at Arf and went on.

"I hurried upstairs. She was so still, so soft, so warm! I had the strength of a maniac, Mason, I picked her up and raced to the balloon box. We'd hide in there, sail out from Norfolk, announce ourselves, and be set ashore in Charleston or Savannah. I had money enough to ask the captain favors. I had gold!"

Arf licked Eddie's face, and for an instant it was as if Eddie mistook the dog for Virginia.

"Oh my darling," he moaned. "My dark new moon! Are you awake?" He clutched at Arf and then, suddenly realizing his mistake, grabbed tight hold and tried to throw Arf over the railing into the still, deep waters we were gliding through. Arf squealed; I stopped Eddie with a sharp blow to his shoulder; Arf dropped to the deck and hurriedly skulked away.

"We were quiet in the box. I had always loved it when Virginia lay very still with me. I was in paradise, pressed up against her in there, so still and quiet, with the satiny balloon cloth padding us all around like . . ."

"Like a coffin," I said. "Like a womb. You killed her with the opium?"

"They loaded us into the ship's hold and went away and came back with more boxes, and they *would* bustle about until the time for waking up had passed. I slept, and nestled against Virginia, and waited till the ship should sail." Eddie's voice had grown whispery again. There was a sudden cry from one of the mastheads.

"Land ho!"

I snapped my head to the left and, yes! There, beyond a long perspective of scattered icebergs, was a jagged line of white and, ah!, a line of green!

"When the ship moved, Virginia was stiff and cold." Eddie's hand crept into his pants pocket to fondle her teeth. "I meant to die with her. That's why I never cried out. But I was weak. I crawled to the provisions, and fed, and crawled back to her. Over and over. Jeremiah says six months have passed, yet for me . . ."

"Look, Eddie! Land!"

He swooned and fell to the deck. Eddie was guilty of Virginia's death, yet he was not, in any clear-cut way, a murderer. This set my mind at ease. Only God could decide if Eddie had suffered enough for his sins. I dragged him back to the bunk he'd taken over from me and joined the excited crew.

We picked our way among the icebergs and came into a bay of smooth water, filled with floating sea plants and fish. Bulkington stood in the bow, taking soundings. For the longest time, the bottom remained too deep to find, and then, a mere fifty yards from the grassy shore, we were over a shelf but three fathoms deep. This bottom was covered with thick ropes and sheets of an orange seaweed too tough to pull up. We dug in tight anchors fore and aft.

The view of the shore was as follows. There was a smooth beach of black sand, a meadow of grass and flowers, some green hillocks, rocks beyond them and, further back, a towering wall of ice. Beyond the wall of ice was a lifeless plain leading up to a range of jagged mountains. The beach curved around a half-mile to the right, eventually being pinched off by the wall of ice. The beach went on somewhat further to the left, ending in an area where a plumelike gray cloud hung over the water. Nothing could be seen beyond this smoky veil. As we anchored, several of us saw smooth black knobs sticking out of the ocean like seals' heads—but these objects failed to reappear. Though one might have expected to find seals and penguins in great numbers here, there were seemingly none.

Three boats were sent ashore; Otha, Arf, and I managed to get into the last one with Bulkington and the crewmen Sam Stretch, Isaac Green, and Jasper Cropsey. Jeremiah would have come too, yet at the last minute Dirk Peters shouldered him aside and jumped in.

We rowed like men possessed, then beached and jumped out. Otha ran across the beach and threw himself face down in the thick grass. I followed along and joined him. The grass blades were thin and wiry, with some stalks crowned by small, sweet-smelling yellow flowers. A hill lay ahead of us, and a stream trickled by on our left.

"Don't nebber want ter go back on no ship." Otha sighed, digging his fingers into the black soil. Arf danced around us sniffing wildly. Something like a mouse scurried into a hole, and Arf began to dig. "Could grow yams here," said Otha.

"I wonder what we should name it," I mused.

"Don' need ter name it no white name," said Otha. "It be."

The men still on the ship were crying out, so Captain Guy sent two of the boats back to pick up more. Soon all but a skeleton crew were on shore, scores of us, running and skipping and laughing with joy. Though there was of course no wood to be found, some men with spades dug up bricks of the thick grassy turf and made a brisk fire of them. Not that we needed the heat; Captain Guy ascertained the air temperature to be 54" F. The water was anomalously warm: 67° F! This unusual heat confirmed our suspicion that the bank of smoke or fog off to the east was of volcanic origin. It seemed that we had stumbled on a geothermal antarctic oasis.

Some large lobsterlike crustaceans were to be seen on the ocean bottom, which was covered right up to the shore with thick cables and mats of the ropy orange seaweed we'd seen before. Sam Stretch and a Feejee islander named Taggoo waded into the warm waters to try to catch some of the lobsters. The lobsters were fast and wary, but the men did catch hold of several melon-size creatures that they found swimming about. These curious animals were something like squid stuffed into snail shells. They had the surprising ability to either crawl on the bottom or to dart about through the water. They were carnivorous, preying on fish and on the nervous lobsters. Far from being afraid of men, the shellsquid (as we came to call them) swam right up to investigate anyone in the water and were exceedingly easy to catch. They pressed so close to us that it seemed they took us for edible carrion. The *Wasp*'s mate Joseph Couthouy, a conchologist, pronounced them to be a species of ammonoid, cousin to the nautilus, and told us something of their habits.

The shellsquid's eyes, feelers, scullers, and ninety tentacles jut out from its open end in a writhing orange bunch centered around a fleshy flap, which conceals a strong and razor-sharp beak (as Isaac Green would soon learn)!

A strong tubular nozzle projects from beneath the shellsquid's beakflap. This organ, Couthouy told us, performs a remarkable function: the creature propels itself horizontally by using the nozzle to slowly draw water into an inner pouch and to then forcibly squirt the water from out of the same nozzle.

The shellsquid has a separate, balloonistlike mode for vertical motion: There is just enough air sealed in the shell's chambers so that the shellsquid's net weight in water is but a fraction of an ounce. By filling its inner pouch with warm water or with air, it can tune its buoyancy to any desired degree. This means that the creatures can float on the surface, hover at any given thermocline, or contract their pouch to squeeze out all water and sink to the seafloor beneath. Once at the bottom, the shellsquid can swim back to the surface, squirting itself this way and that.

These were singular creatures—and far more sinister than we realized. But the most immediately striking thing about them was the incredible beauty of their silvery, logarithmically spiraling shells. It was immediately clear to all of us that these shells could make the ship's fortune. The shells were brilliant and rainbow-reflecting like thick mother of pearl yet possessing in certain lights a haunting, nacreous translucency. Every woman in the world would want a shellsquid brooch. The hunt was soon on, and the men caught nearly a hundred of them.

The easiest method for catching shellsquid was to wriggle

one's fingers wormlike in the water. Invariably, a shellsquid would jerkily squirt its way over and begin to attach its tentacles to one's hand. One then had but to snatch the shell from behind and fling the beast out of the water and onto shore. This was of course an operation that had to be done nimbly. Isaac Green was too slow about it, and one of the shellsquid managed to snip off the first joint of his forefinger with its powerful beak. Green screamed terribly, but the other sailors—hardened characters all—laughingly assured Green we could best revenge him by having a shellsquid "clambake." Our Christmas dinner of fish and water had left us quite hungry.

While a boat raced back to the ship to fetch a kettle, Otha and I wandered up to the top of the nearest hillock. Small, thick-furred rodents darted in and out of the flowery grasses underfoot, shying from our approach. At the top of the hill, Otha and I found a stand of bushy, thick-leaved plants that Otha thought looked like kale. Starved for any fresh vegetable, we sampled the leaves and found them edible though thistly. We gathered two bushels of them in our shirts and carried them down to steam with the shellsquid. Some other men had found potatolike tubers beneath the swampy stands of pink flowers that grew on the borders of the freshwater streams that trickled down from the wall of ice; still others had gathered baskets full of eggs from the nests that covered one of the hillsides.

Jeremiah and Eddie were ashore now too, and to complete our feast, Captain Guy sent one last boat back to the ship for the last of the crew and a barrel of rum. We ate and drank for hours. With the sun and moon rolling along the horizon face to face, there was no feeling of time past or time to come, there was only the joy of our feast at the end of the world, with no witnesses but the ammonoids and the wheeling flocks of birds.

The shellsquid's bodies were muscular and tough; though they were not large, a single one of the creatures was more than any man would normally feel like chewing down at one go. Yet the flesh was sweet and nourishing, and we all kept gnawing away at our victims. The scores of small orange tentacles were particularly easy to eat. Arf was partial to a rank congelation that was found in the furthest recesses of the ammonoids' large, translucent shells.

At Jeremiah's suggestion, we began drying the bodies of the uneaten shellsquid over the fire. They would make an excellent pemmican. Moreover, according to Bulkington, it was also true that there was a brisk Chinese market for exotic dried sea creatures of every kind. Captain Guy confirmed that members of the holothurian family—the sea cucumbers, the *bêches-de-mer*, and the trepang—fetched exceedingly high prices in Hong Kong. He expressed a hope that we might find *bêches-de-mer* in the waters that lay closer to the volcanic vent.

After eating and resting and eating some more, the members of our impending balloon expedition found themselves together: Eddie, Otha, Jeremiah, Arf and me. At the last minute, Dirk Peters attached himself to our group. We wandered slowly down the black sand beach toward the volcanic steam plume. The orange seaweed-covered shelf gave out quickly, and the water was very deep right off shore. Though as usual I had taken no rum, the others were in varying degrees of intoxication. Behind us were the crewmen, and their fire and their boats. It was midnight. Left to right we were the moon, the sea, Jeremiah, Eddie, myself, Otha, Dirk Peters, the antarctic land and, above its mountains, the sun, with Arf always somewhere in between.

"We'll set off from here," said Jeremiah. "We'll restock the cabin and leave as soon as tomorrow. Who knows how long this fine weather will last!"

"Whar we s'pose ter be goin' in dat balloon?" asked Otha.

"Over those mountains," said Jeremiah, pointing. "Or around them. Once past them, we'll most likely see the great South Hole."

"I see it," said Eddie slowly. "My imagination used to rebel at the great Hole. I was too frightened of it. But now . . ." Here he glanced around at us in search of forgiveness and comprehension. "What has a man who's been buried alive with a corpse have to fear of a Hole? My mind's eye can finally see it. After the mountains, we'll glimpse a miragelike far horizon above a near horizon. These will be the two limbs of the mighty circle that rounds the South Hole. If the Hole is clear, our eyes will trace the paths of the sun's rays pouring into the vast Hollow Earth-egg. Or, more likely, the Hole will be filled with a great vortex of golden gauzy mist. We'll float down through the haze; living in the sky like angels! Angels! And perhaps . . ."

"I took the trouble to stoke the stove and put all the lines in readiness," interrupted Jeremiah. "Just in case."

"Jest in case whut?" said Otha.

"Mutiny," said Dirk Peters. "Plague. Cannibals."

"There certainly don't seem to be any natives about," said I.

There was a sudden flash of white and a small, shrill scream. Arf was off like a shot and managed to head off the creature, which had just seized a mouse. It ran back toward us. With a slow, oiled motion, Dirk Peters threw his knife and nailed the creature to the turf. It shrieked once and died. It was all white, with hair that lay backward, hair pointing, that is, from back to front when patted flat. Its claws and teeth were a deep garnet in hue. This color was not the stain of mouse blood; the teeth and claws were a glassy red all the way through. More ornaments for the city women, thought I with a slight shudder of disgust. The creatures in this small volcanic bay were unique, and it was disturbing to think that two or three ships like the *Wasp* might wholly annihilate them.

Peters gutted the red-clawed beast with quick, efficient motions and threw the offal into the sea. There were fewer shellsquid here than near our landing site, but seemingly all that were present sped over to tear at the fresh guts Peter had thrown them. The water fairly boiled for a minute as several dozen ammonoids devoured the red-clawed beast's lights and liver.

Peters hung the cleaned animal from his belt, and we wandered on along the beach toward the volcanic plume. Staring at the animal's teeth, I remembered the mysterious Elijah. His teeth had been red, too.

As we walked on, Jeremiah told Otha more about the Hollow Earth, with Eddie adding fanciful word pictures and crackbrained hints that we might happen on the angel of Virginia. There seemed no special reason to go back to the crew; it was pleasant to be stretching our legs.

The seawater grew warmer and more choked with floating plants; there was no trace of the orange seaweed that so completely covered the shelf between our ship and our landing spot. The lobsters here were more plentiful, crawling about at the very edge of the sand and sunning themselves on clumps of seaweed. There were also great numbers of fish. Had we not been too full to care, we might easily have caught some.

Soon we were close enough to the volcano—a low cone jutting out from the edge of the land—that even the air was uncomfortably hot. An eerie flickering light filled the damp smoke that came out of the low, whispering vent. Fluffy ash and pumice covered the beach. The drifting sulfurous steam made it impossible to see more than a hundred feet in any direction.

"How do I get back?" asked Peters, interrupting our continuing discussion of the Hollow Earth.

"Just turn around and follow the sea," said Eddie. "We have no special need of you."

"No," said Peters, drawing his stiff lips a bit back from his heavy, crooked teeth. "How do I get back from the Hollow Earth?"

"I don't think you're coming," said I. "The balloon's lifting power isn't strong enough for five, is it, Jeremiah?"

"How to get back from the Hollow Earth was the gentleman's question," said politic Jeremiah. "I think it's likely there's wood enough growing inside the Hollow Earth to restock the balloon's supply of charcoal and float our way back. With any luck, we could make New Zealand, Cape Horn, or Tierra del

Fuego. Or mayhap there are folk in the Hollow Earth who know other ways out to the surface—perhaps there's spots where the ocean goes all the way through. Or could be it's so paradisiacal in there we'll want to stay forever. Those of us that come."

"This world's been up with me for years," said Dirk Peters. "I'm ready for your new one." His voice betrayed a longing that his hard, expressionless face concealed. He flipped his knife in the air and caught it by its handle, very near my neck. He did this several times.

"Maybe the balloon *can* lift five," said I presently. "Ah cain't decide which is wust," put in Otha, "gettin' back in dat ship, stayin' here wid no women, or flyin' up in de sky on some striped bag. Don' scare my man Mason dat way, Dirk."

"Peters can always take my place," said Eddie, making one of his unexpected swings. "I've been through the crucible; there's no longer any terror that can hobble my talent. My greatest works lie ahead of me, ripe golden fruits that will find place in the granary, nay the treasury, of American letters. Ought I not best sail back to New York?"

"Let's just wait and see if we can get the balloon full," said Jeremiah. "First things first."

# 8

---

# Antarctica

OUR DISCUSSION was broken off by a series of odd noises in the distance. First there was great splashing, as of whales breaching repeatedly, and then there were shrill sounds that I initially took to be cries of creatures like the white animal Dirk Peters had killed. The distant furor went on and on. We hurried back through the volcano smoke, straining our smarting eyes to see.

When we reached clear air, we saw that the empty *Wasp* was still there. The distance was as yet too great to make out anything of the men. The splashing and the shrieks had stopped. I ran down the beach. It seemed for an instant that I saw a series of humps, as of several men rapidly crawling back and forth near our distant kettle . . . but why would they do so? The waves near our little feast site were fiercely agitated. I ran all the way there, with Arf and Peters close behind.

The tipped-over kettle marked the spot where we had left our fellow crew members. The fire was splashed out. The men had stacked the marvelous shells we'd harvested into a square pyramid six tiers high. The bodies of half-dried shellsquid were lying about as well, also our three boats, the rum barrel, and a few scattered shoes and coats. But there was no other trace of the fifty-some men we'd celebrated with less than an hour before.

I halloed the ship, with no response. The ocean was bubbling violently in two spots, and the thick orange stalks of seaweed seemed to writhe with a purpose . . . writhe and splash closer.

Arf's ruff rose straight up. Sensing something truly evil, I ran with all my might for the same hillock Otha and I had climbed before. But Peters, savage Peters, grasped his knife and stepped to the ocean's edge to peer at the odd movements within the waves. And then suddenly—*a cablelike orange tentacle lashed out and wrapped around his neck!*

Like the stalk of a giant sea kelp, the suckerless tentacle was utterly smooth and flexible. It looked somehow familiar.

Unlike the fifty odd victims before him, Peters was a man of such brutal speed and craft that he was able to slice off the giant tentacle tip that held him, jump over the the next one that whipped out, and in one smooth gesture slash through a third, last, tentacle that wrapped around his waist. The feeler-things were everywhere up and down a thirty-yard stretch of beach, lashing about in snaky figure eights. Arf and I were already high up on the hillock. The three others were still well down the beach. Small, mighty Peters came running up the hillock toward me, whooping and triumphantly waving a ham-size piece of giant shellsquid . . . for that is what his attacker was.

From the hilltop we could see clearly. The very large patch of orange seaweed between us and the ship was in fact the facial squidbunches of two giant ammonoids that were most likely the parents of the small creatures whose shells we had been stockpiling! Of *course* I'd seen tentacles like that before; I'd eaten about eighty small copies of them for supper! If each of these giant shellsquid had, in this phase of its life, a shell like the small shellsquid's . . . what an incredibly valuable thing a shell like that would be. You could *live* in one! And that much meat . . .

But this kind of thinking was foolishness. How were we ever going to get back out to the ship? The most direct path lay right between the two giant ammonoids nestled against our shore. As it happened, each of our ship's two anchors was snagged into one of the creatures' flesh. They would part the cables or drag the ship under if they should swim down into the deep. I recalled that Bulkington's soundings had found no bottom nearby. Poor Bulkington!

Otha, Eddie, and Jeremiah joined Peters, Arf, and me on top of our hillock. I pointed out to them the way the orange "seaweed" patches formed two huge ammonoids. It seemed clear that they had temporarily moored themselves here to breed and that the small shellsquid were their offspring.

"Perhaps they are from the Hollow Earth," said Jeremiah, wonderingly. "Perhaps there is no ocean bottom here at all. Just think, we could be at the edge of a sinkhole that leads all the way through!"

"See," said Eddie, shuddering. "They see us."

Indeed, each of the creatures had lifted two vast eyestalks above the water. Thick and gray, the stalks stuck up like wharf pilings, and each of these slowly swaying columns was capped with a glistening black eyebulb two yards across. These were the same black knobs I'd seen briefly when we anchored. It was a horrible feeling to have them watch us.

"Ate all dose men, and wants ter eat us too," said Otha slowly. "Ah's gittin' out o' sight."

Beyond our hillock was a stream-crossed vale and, beyond the vale, a talus of loose rock leading up to a forbidding battlement of ice. We threw ourselves down by a stream and tried to think.

"The balloon's the only way out," said Jeremiah.

"Or the ship," said Eddie. "Couldn't we still sail back?"

"Five men sail the *Wasp*?" said Peters. "And three of us *gentlemen*? Not likely, Mr. Poe."

"We still have the boats," said I. "We'll row out around

the monsters and get on the *Wasp* from behind. We have to. That's where the balloon is.''

"Bravely spoken," said Jeremiah.

"Ah ain' goam back in no boat," said Otha.

"We have to stick with them, Otha," said Peters. "If they launch the balloon without us, they might not pick us up. Remember, we're just *coons.*"

"What about me?" said Eddie.

"You'll row with the rest of us," said Jeremiah. "It's high time you begin again to be of use, Edgar. Let us start at noon, when the sun is in the north. That's the time of day the ship landed. The monsters were quiet then.''

We slept a bit, and passed the rest of the time in killing four more of the red-clawed white beasts. Peters squatted in the bottom of the valley behind our hillock and the rest of us acted as beaters, shaking every bush and poking into every hole. We skinned the beasts and saved the meat, also the pelts with paws and heads intact.

Finally the sun was out over the ocean. We put Arf, our five redclaws, and ten of our hard-won shells in our chosen boat and eased it quietly into the sea two hundred yards up the beach from the monsters. With many a sideways glance toward the orange-glinting patch to port, Jeremiah, Peters, Otha, and I rowed with a will, while Eddie in the stern pointed out our course. Every second, I expected to see one of those huge eyestalks break the calm sea's surface, but for now all was still.

Once we were out past the *Wasp*, we turned and slowly stroked over to it, and then we were bumping up against its familiar wood flank. Our boat held a rope and a grappling hook, which we flipped ever so gently over the taffrail. Peters was up first, and I was last. Before I went up, I tied the rope around Arf's middle and Peters pulled him up, and then finally I was safe on board as well. Safe? I was too well aware that either of the ammonoids could pull our ship under or scour the decks with its tentacles.

"Peters, you must cut the anchor cables almost all the way through," hissed Jeremiah. "Mason, you and Otha go to the galley and take all the food and water you can carry. Eddie, you and I shall start the balloon's stove."

Otha and I went belowdecks and fetched a large sack of hardtack, a box of recently salted fish, and two demijohns of fresh water. Jeremiah filled our light brass stove with charcoal soaked in seal oil; it began to burn briskly. Now Eddie sprinkled his special salts from the jar we'd packed with the stove. The fire flared up and stank. Eddie snugged the stove's flue into the neck of our great rubberized silk balloon. Slowly, slowly, its flanks began to swell.

Peters busied himself charging and loading five muskets from the ship's supply. Seeing this, I remembered my pepperbox pistol and went back belowdecks privily to fetch it. I'd loaded it long before. If—horrible thought—the balloon was unable to lift all five of us, a hidden gun might stand me in good stead. Sensing that some great departure was imminent, Arf stuck close to my heels.

A half hour passed till the great balloon sluggishly lifted itself off the deck. A mild ocean breeze was blowing, so the balloon hung out over the ammonoids. Were they sleeping? Eddie and Jeremiah loaded more charcoal and salts onto the fire, and now the balloon began gently to tug its wicker cabin across the deck. We hurried on tiptoe this way and that, making sure none of the ropes fouled. A single thick rope attached the balloon cabin to a boss on the ship's deck.

The balloon grew strong and plump; the cabin jittered on and off the deck, its steel runners clattering. Jeremiah fetched a last few scientific instruments, and then Arf and we five men squeezed into the jiggling wicker box. For an anxious ten minutes we held it heavy on the deck. The crowded cabin was hot and close from the blazing stove, especially hot because our walls were padded with down-stuffed quilts in anticipation of the severe cold we would encounter over the antarctic ice. Outside the open window-holes we could see the sea, the patch of orange, the antarctic continent, and the mountains far away. I kept my hand on the pistol in my pocket. My pistol would be handier in these close quarters than the musket that each of us had, thought I, but now, finally, our box began to rise, slowly at first, and then in a quick rush of speed that stretched our tether to strumming tautness.

The sudden jolt snapped the ship's anchor cables, which Peters had weakened, and all at once our balloon was dragging the *Wasp* across the monstrous patch of orange tentacles. The giants awoke and lashed two, six, twenty thick feelers across the *Wasp*'s deck. Four horrible eyes lifted out of the water and gazed up.

Even as the orange tentacles began to stretch toward us, Peters reached out our cabin door and slashed through the rope that tethered us to the ship. Our balloon sprang into the air, racing up with a speed that pressed us against the cabin's creaking floor. We cheered until our throats cracked.

"My salts create a gas lighter than air," cried Eddie. "My theories are vindicated!"

The ocean breeze wafted us landward. As we drifted over the first great battlement of ice, the air temperature dropped and our balloon went even higher. I took what I thought was a last glance back at the giant ammonoids and saw something horrible. *One of them was still busy with the* Wasp, *but the other was floating up out of the water!* I screamed and pointed as the monstrous shell rose into the air, righted itself, and began—with thunderous spewings of gas and liquid—to speed toward us.

"The shell is full of naturally secreted hydrogen," said Eddie, his voice oddly calm. "Air is a fluid like water, you understand. We see a demonstration of the solution to a rather pretty problem in hydrostatics." He sank slowly to a corner of the box and curled himself up there next to Arf. "Virginia," he said, stroking the dog. "Virginia."

"We'll shoot the damned mollusk down," said Peters,

grimly shouldering his musket. "Aim carefully, men, and wait until it's close by."

We were a thousand feet up in the air now, with the icy antarctic waste sweeping by beneath us. It was easy to see down through the wicker cracks of our cabin floor. Otha and I aimed our muskets out one window, Peters and Jeremiah out the other.

"How do dis thang work?" Otha murmured to me. As a slave, he'd never been allowed to handle a gun.

"Look down along it and squeeze the trigger when I do," I told him. "Hold your shoulder loose for the kick. Use your arms like a spring to gentle it." The vengeful ammonoid surged suddenly closer, its vast shell shining like a polished cloud. Still closer it came . . . and then with a great crash we all fired.

The guns kicked very powerfully. The cabin rocked so sharply that Arf and Eddie skidded across the floor. Arf hit a wall, but Eddie slid out the door. His frantic cries were drowned by the high shrieking of gas rushing from the giant ammonoid's punctured shell; it zigzagged wildly and went screaming down to smash into a smudge of orange and mother-of-pearl on the undulating white plain far below. There was no sign of Eddie.

Otha held my legs, and I leaned out the door to see beneath the balloon box. Sure enough, Eddie was there, dangling upside down, with one foot caught in a bight of rope. He gazed silently up at me, his face gone bright red. I was so shocked by the last few minutes' rapid changes that I burst out laughing at his awkward plight. I laughed so hard—if laughter it was—that I wet my pants.

Presently, Peters contrived to pull Eddie in. We battened the door's shutter closed and then, finally, we were fairly launched. The other giant shellsquid showed no signs of coming after us. Still speechless, Eddie produced a flask and drank all but the single gulp of it that Peters was able to claim. Meanwhile, Jeremiah got out a sextant and took a reading.

"How long do you think it will take?" I asked him.

"We're at seventy-seven degrees latitude," said he. "I think it likely that the South Hole's rim lies all along the eighty-five-degree latitude line. A degree of latitude is sixty miles, which makes it four hundred eighty miles due south to eighty-five degrees, and seven hundred eighty to the Pole. I measure our present speed some twenty miles an hour; that makes four hundred eighty miles in a day, and seven hundred eighty in a day and a half. It's one P.M. now. If the wind keeps up from the north, we should see the Hole sometime between noon and midnight tomorrow. Maybe sooner, if the wind increases.''

"How you know dey *is* a hole?'' asked Otha.

"I'd wondered that myself,'' said Peters.

"Every animal has a hole at each end,'' said Eddie, once again in the corner where Virginia had died. "And is not Earth a creature that lives and moves?''

"Mr. Symmes had many arguments for the Hollow Earth,'' said Jeremiah. "But the time for argument is long past. Right now we need to stoke the stove powerfully enough to lift our craft over the mountains.''

As no one else offered to, I took charge of the stove first. We had two big burlap sacks of charcoal aboard, and every few minutes I eased another piece of it in through the stove's grating. After about an hour had passed, I was hot from the fire, but the others—who had been resting or sleeping—were cold in the thin high-altitude antarctic air. Otha was only too glad to spell me at the stove. I stood up and looked out the cabin window to the south.

For a moment I had trouble making sense of what I saw. The upper half of the window showed deep blue sky with a full moon in it, but the lower half of the window was simply white. For a second I thought it was glassed in and frosted over. But the window was a hole, and the white I saw was the inhuman landscape below. Refocusing my eyes, I could make out crevasses and wind-carved mounds—so prominent that for a moment I thought the ground was quite close below. Had I stoked the oven for nothing? Just then I glimpsed far ahead of us a small blue blot racing across the snow—our shadow, impossibly elongated, impossibly far. The space around me began to stretch and tremble as my mind labored to understand. I held tight to the wicker windowsill, fearing the great empty whiteness would somehow suck me out. We were over a thousand feet high, and those mounds and cracks I saw were mighty hills and canyons!

For half an hour I watched our distant shadow race and ripple ever higher—the foothills beneath us were piling up to a turreted mountain range ahead. With luck we would clear it.

Now Dirk Peters took his turn at stoking the stove, while Otha came to look out the window with me. Eddie was unconscious from the liquor he'd guzzled, and Jeremiah was constantly busy taking sightings, making notes, and adjusting the balloon bag.

"Whar de jungle?" Otha asked me.

"What jungle?"

" 'Lijah talk 'bout a big wet jungle down in Mama Earth's genitive parts. He say dass whar he come from."

"He said that? Why didn't you tell me?"

"Maybe 'Lijah from de Hollow Earth, Mason. Maybe black folks is king ob dat world."

"Elijah wasn't really black. He was white. He was an albino."

"White *color*, but he were a slave. If he a slave, he *black*."

Peters glanced up at Jeremiah. "Are we going to make it?"

"It's hard to get a steady sighting," said old Reynolds, lowering his telescope with a sigh. "But since the sun is virtually on the horizon, our shadow on any vertical wall must be at the same altitude we are. One might think of the mountain ahead as an eroded wall. If our shadow gets over it, then we will. If not, then not."

We four watched as our shadow moved up the great slope ahead. We were close enough that we could see shadings in the ice, see caves and overhangs fit for beast or hermit, but all was empty. Our shadow was like a footprint—the big ellipse of balloon over the trapezoid of basket—man's first footprint here, wriggling toward the sky.

But not fast enough. We were still well below the great white mountain's ragged upper rim. I took it on myself to go through Eddie's clothes and find his jar of salts. The jar was wedged into his trouser pocket, and beneath it was a rattling clutch of small pebbles that only belatedly did I understand to be Virginia's teeth. I snatched the jar out, Jeremiah prized the stove's top plate off, and I emptied in all the crystals that would come loose. The fire consumed them in bursts of color, and dizzying fumes filled the cabin. The fire sang, our great balloon bag creaked and swelled, and just as we were about to meet our shadow footprint, it slid over the mountain ridge and sprang away. We followed after; I turned and stared back.

I will not soon forget the sight of that eroded razor ridge. The others were looking ahead, so only I saw it—only I, of all men ever to live, have seen that ridge, its bare gray rocks painted by the western sun's gold glints and blue shadows, painted as so many million times before. This one time in all history I was there to see it for all mankind, and I felt that the ridge knew—knew me as a human, and knew me as motherless Mason from Virginia—sensing my passage, the ridge sent out long wind-blown streamers of snow, icedust fingers calling me back to the world of my birth. But no return is possible. That scoured antarctic spine was the final edge of a world I shall never see again.

The high mountain wind caught us, filling the flanks of our swollen black-and-white balloon with chaotic thrumming. For a few minutes, it was all we could do to hang tight and to keep our instruments and provisions from shifting too wildly. Eddie woke, stood up, fell down.

Finally, we gained our feet and stared southward. There was nothing but an endless expanse of white ahead of us as far as the eye could see.

"Whar de hole?" said Otha. "An' de jungle?"

"Where is it?" echoed Peters.

Eddie, still sitting on the floor, gazed up at us, an odd grin on his face. "Let me describe what you should see," he said slowly. "Undoubtedly you do *see* but are too narrow-visioned to *know*. The near edge of the great Hole is like a depression in the horizon. Above the depression are swirling fogbanks crowned by Jovian thunderheads flickering with planetary energies. Arching above the great atmospheric maelstrom is a second horizon line, the Hole's far lip. Surely you do make it out! Mason! Jeremiah?''

"Not yet," said Jeremiah softly. "Calm yourself. I said it would take at least twenty-four hours. Wait until the sun has gone full circle. We'll see the Hole soon.''

But we did not. The wind held from the north, driving us along at a ground speed nearing thirty miles per hour, yet we continued to see nothing but unbroken white waste. We slept in shifts, keeping the stove stoked with our ominously diminishing stock of fuel. The sun rolled past the west to glare at us from the south at midnight; it arced east to the north and noon again and still we saw nothing; and still the sun rolled; and then it was three in the afternoon of our second day in the balloon.

The air temperature was thirty degrees below zero. Blessedly, the skies were clear and the wind was still from the north. Arf and we five men sat huddled together for warmth near our stove. We had pulled the quilts off the walls to wrap around ourselves, but it was not enough.

"Eighty-nine degrees and forty minutes of latitude," said Jeremiah, peering up through his sextant at the sky. "Twenty miles to the South Pole." He fell silent and began fiddling with his two delicate clocks, one run by a spring, one run by a pendulum. He expected the presence of Earth's Hole to show itself as a difference in the clocks' rates.

"There's no more charcoal," announced Peters. His voice was muffled because his mouth was full of dried shellsquid. We were eating almost continuously in an effort to keep up our body temperatures in the face of the nightmarish cold.

"We can break off pieces of the cabin to burn," said Jeremiah, trying to keep his voice calm. "Mason!"

I felt dumb and tired. Pretty soon we would all be dead. I hugged Arf and pressed against Otha.

"Do you hear, Mason?" said Eddie. "You and Otha break up the shutters and put them in the stove."

He was glaring at me imperiously from beneath his high, pale brow. A spasm of hatred went through me. Eddie Poe's mad notions were to be the death of us all, and still he struck his charlatan poses. I wanted to smite him, but any movement would let in more cold, so I tried to spit at him. The spit froze to my face. "Go to hell," I hissed. "You damned crazy hoaxing killer."

"Come, come, Mason," said Jeremiah, struggling to his feet. "Perhaps the Hole is very small! In less than an hour we'll be at the Pole! And the clocks . . . it's hard to be sure with the cabin's motion, but my clocks show certain—"

"In less than an hour the balloon will crash," said Peters. "Look how soft and wrinkled the bag is. Look how near we are to the ground."

"Ah's *cold*," said Otha. "Do somethin', Mason!"

I moved Arf to Otha's lap and wrapped my arms around them. The cold was astonishing. Jeremiah and Peters broke up the balloon box's shutters and began feeding the scraps into the little brass stove. Out the door I could see the ground, only a hundred feet below. Once we landed, it would be all over.

"Where are my salts?" demanded Eddie.

The jar was in my pocket, but I didn't want to give him the satisfaction of an answer. Instead I lurched over to the stove, loosened the few remaining crystals with my finger, and tossed them onto the flaming wicker. The balloon puffed up feebly, and we limped a little higher.

Before four o'clock we'd fed the stove the cabin's ceiling and most of the wall that held our door. We hoped the door's joists and the other walls would hold our floor in place. But this was not to be. Three walls' connections to our floor gave way, and the floor began to creak out from under us like a slow-opening trapdoor.

"We're landing now!" cried Jeremiah, yanking on the cord

that led to our balloon's upper vent. If I hadn't held Arf under one arm, he would have skidded out through the gaping crack between the partially demolished wall and our sloping floor. We men clung to the window and doorframes like monkeys, peering and jabbering as the ever-blank white ground came up at us too fast.

We landed with such a jolt that the cabin fell over onto one side. The stiff wind plucked at the half-empty balloon, dragging us across the wind-polished snow and ice. Now the hot stove came into contact with one of the quilts and the cabin filled with smoke. To make things worse, it was the open-door side of the cabin that was facedown. We left the cabin in chaos, fighting our way out of the three windows. Peters and Otha were out first, I believe, then Jeremiah, and finally it was my turn. I thrust Arf out; he thudded to the ground with a yelp; we were really gathering speed. In the dense smoke I could see next to nothing, but when I lunged forward to roll out the window, something caught my ankle. Eddie.

I kicked out at him, but he clung with the strength of the damned. There was nothing for it but to reach down, get hold of him, and push him out the window before me. I followed close after. The rushing ice slapped my face violently. I rolled twenty yards and came to a rest, aware again of how very cold it was.

The sun and moon gazed down blankly. The wind whistled, and from downwind came the crashing and bumping of our cabin being dragged further by the nearly flat balloon. Dotted out behind me were Arf and my four fellow explorers. I called Arf, and he ran to me, glad and barking to be on firm ground. When he got to me he shook vigorously, his way of punctuating a new paragraph of activity.

All the others, save Eddie, were standing and straggling toward me, drawn by our cabin. A number of our possessions had been scattered about. Jeremiah and Peters were gathering things up as they came. Noticing Jeremiah wrap some rope around his waist, I picked up a nearby coil of strong silk cord and did the same. Arf shook again and stood there panting, fully at ease with the few hours of life that were left us. I wished I could share his sense of the eternal now.

The three others leaned over Eddie. Loud words and gesticulations, then finally the great man rose to his feet as well. Perhaps he'd hoped they'd carry him.

How strange it was to be here, so far from everything, beneath a sky so big and empty. There were no birds, no clouds. I felt this oddly wrong: Earth's farthest corner should be dark and packed, not bright and blank.

". . . the pendulum clock was running noticeably slower than the spring clock towards the end," Jeremiah was saying as they approached. "That implies there is less gravity here, which means the Earth's crust is quite thin."

Otha and Peters said nothing, simply slogged along unlistening. But where Peters was grim, Otha was solemnly gay. I think he was very happy to be out of the balloon alive. Eddie seemed dazzled by the fantastic vast waste around us. His lips worked silently, as if he were framing verses. He kept his hands shoved deep into his trouser pockets.

"Are we at the Pole, Jeremiah?" asked I.

He drew his sextant; sighted the sun, the moon. "To a hair."

"Whar is it?" said Otha. "I don' see no pole stickin' up."

"It's just a spot like any other," said Peters bitterly. "Just a spot to die."

The wind dropped. Far ahead, the cabin and balloon stopped moving. The cabin was marked by a plume of fire and smoke.

"Let's go there and get warm," said I.

We walked slowly, for we knew that once we reached the burning cabin, there'd be nothing else to do. Each time I took my eyes off the smoke plume, I got dizzy and confused from the blank white everywhere. Then, seeing something red in the snow, I thought it was the stableboy I'd killed, sent by God to haunt me. But it was only one of our redclaw carcasses. I picked it up and shoved it in my pocket.

Eddie was a killer too, and certainly Peters as well. Probably, Jeremiah had done in an islander or two during his travels, which left only Otha and Arf as the innocent ones.

"I'm sorry, Otha."

He was right beside me, with Arf at our heels. Unlike me, he still had his quilt; he had it wrapped tight around him. King Otha of the South Pole. He glanced down. "You not as sorry as ah is. You de same color as de snow. Gwine be whited to death here. You wish we was back on de farm?"

"We had some fun on the way."

"I had me a gal called Juicita in Richmond. Effen she wif chile, den I left somethin' back dere. I guess dass de most a man kin hope to do."

When we got to the cabin, it was burning pretty briskly. I'd had some thoughts of wrapping myself up in the balloon silk, but now, as we stood there warming our hands, the silk caught fire too. The liquid caoutchouc rubber we'd varnished it with was quite flammable; Jeremiah had been careful to put several layers of spark screens in the stove's chimney. But now a piece of flaming wicker fell onto the balloon and the whole thing flared up at once in a quick puffball of heat. It swelled like an earthbound sun, rose a bit, then burst and fluttered down in ashes on the dampened snow.

The contents of our cabin were pretty much gone, including our stores of saltfish, shellsquid, and biscuits. We drank from the puddles the fire had made, privily nibbled up whatever food scraps we had in our pockets, and then there was nothing left to eat at all. Peters seemed the most desperate, and began to talk of eating Arf. To placate him, I stripped the meat out of the redclaw pelt I'd found and shared that around for each of us to roast in strips over the dwindling fire. The meat tasted so odd that I let Peters have my share as well. By six in the evening, the cabin fire was down to ashes. The wind rose and began to blow the ashes away.

"I *will* have that dog!" cried Peters suddenly. He drew out his knife and lunged toward Arf. Arf yelped and took off to the other side of the embers. Peters circled after him, and I started after Peters. Now the three of us were running circles around the wreck of the cabin—Arf in front, his eyes rolling, followed by Peters with knife held high, followed by me not really wanting to catch him. I called to Otha, and he joined with me. Eddie had been sunk in thought but then, on our third circuit around the hot ashes, he noticed Peters and the dog, felt threatened, and began running too, just in front of Arf. Jeremiah, feeling a need to calm our mad antics, leaped up and began chasing after me and Otha.

I think we all felt it was nice to be doing something, utterly pointless though it was. Ten, twenty, perhaps a hundred times, we circled the dully glowing cabin ashes, speeding up, slowing down, stamping our feet and yelling. Only Peters seemed serious about it. Over and over he lunged at Arf, over and over Arf pranced away. The rhythm of our running began to set off a kind of cracking noise in the ice; we ran harder. More cracking.

"Keep it up," called Jeremiah. "Something's happening!"

Three more circuits we ran, with more and more noise from the ground below, and then, all at once, the ice gave way and we fell through.

# 9

# Symmes's Hole

AT FIRST I thought we were falling into a crevasse. The ice gnashed, and big blocks and chunks fell every which way. Our screams were faint in the cracking roar. I was yelling, "Mother," and Otha was crying for Turl. Each instant I expected to be dashed senseless. The strong light through the ice and snow bathed everything in brilliant blue—all was bright confusion.

Arf and the men were near me, though I could only see bits and pieces of them. We were packed all around by a free-falling clutter of ice fragments. Above us were great creakings and thunderings; more and more of the ice was breaking free—monstrous tumbling chunks larger than the biggest icebergs seen at sea. We had started an ice avalanche into some incredibly vast cave or crevasse and—

Now there came a hideous shriek. "Help me, for the love of God!"

It was Peters. His body had gotten pinned between two flat-faced ice boulders. Peters's head and feet stuck out like the head and tail of a steamed catfish on one of the loaves the James

150

River ferrywoman had given us. Now a small, dense chunk of ice caromed off several others and cracked spinning into the boulders squeezing Peters. There was a shriek beyond anything that had gone before. Peters was crushed and mangled like a beetle in a mill, like a grape in a winepress. The whole blood of his body stained the giant crystal masses, and he was quite still.

Arf and Otha were somewhere above me; Jeremiah and Eddie, somewhere below. Still we fell. The light remained strong. There seemed to be no walls enclosing us at all. Bit by bit, the jostling ice chunks dispersed themselves. Even though more ice was still coming loose high above us, we were falling at the leading edge of the onrushing masses. There seemed no reason we could not safely fall onward in this wise—until, that is, such a time as we hit bottom, if bottom there was. We were falling at speeds no humans had ever known before, perhaps as much as a hundred and ten miles per hour. The buffeting air had turned me so I was falling on my back, facing up toward the ice.

What lay behind me, down toward the Earth's center? I knew better than to crane my head back and have my neck broken by the wind's savage force. Instead, I rolled sideways so I was falling facedown. This was a bad position, for now my legs tipped up and I began planing rapidly to one side, moving so fast that I couldn't breathe. The air at my mouth was a heavy stone pillow smothering me. Instinctively, I spread my legs and dug in my feet, making an air anchor. This slowed me and pitched me backward, and now I was able to move my forearms enough to mask my face with my hands. I gulped air and stared down through slit fingers into the dim pit.

Even had the wind not hindered me, my eyes were all but blinded from the pitiless light of our thirty hours on the iceplain. Yet I could see something below, a green disk with blue spots and washes of pink light. An inner orb? The tunnel's other end? Far away, but not infinitely so. Holding my breath and squinting, I stretched out my arms toward the disk. My fists held some eight inches apart spanned it. It was the size of a woman's round face.

Tired of fighting the wind, I rolled back over to stare at the spreading avalanche behind us.

The falling ice islands had spaced themselves out nicely, and I could get a good clear view of the land overhead. It was an immense blue and white glazed boss of ice; the central antarctic plain, with the sun and moon on the other side of it. It was a bumpy gelid landscape, and we were flying "up" into the air away from it.

It wasn't quite like we were *flying,* though. With all the ice tumbling right behind us, it was more as if we were riding the crest of a black powder explosion. I remembered once Ma's brother, Tuck Tingley, had packed black powder under a big stump at the edge of our barnyard. The stump had ridden skyward on a spreading dome of dust and rubble till all collapsed.

But we weren't going to fall back. With luck, we would fall all the way to the Hollow Earth. The air was thick but breathable, and as the time passed, we seemed to be falling slightly slower than before. The air temperature was becoming more comfortable every minute. It occurred to me the ice avalanche would melt and turn into friendly water before it could ever reach us. I spotted Otha crouched on a huge iceberg far above me. I wouldn't have wanted to be so near that mass, but I suppose he found it soothing, with his love of solid ground. I waved, and he waved back almost cheerfully. Arf was a wriggling black dot in the bright blue distance. This was working out wonderfully.

The farther we fell, the more of the underside of the antarctic icescape became visible, its distant stretches fading into dim hallucinatory curved crests of antediluvian ice. By this vast icedome we were as dust motes and the greatest of the ice islands were as fretful gnats.

Perhaps the ridge we'd flown over yesterday had been the outflung upper lip of this vast shaft. If so, the whole central antarctic iceshield was a plug, an accretion whose irregular eonslong growth had filled in the upper end of Symmes's Hole!

Like a lever whose movement sets off the linked workings of

some vast mechanism, the jarring of our footsteps was causing the great plug to break up completely. The huge iceplain was shattering and falling after us, but the tumbling ice was slowly melting. A few fat water globs were starting to rain down past us. I caught a gout of water in my cupped hands and sucked at it. The water was fresh, it was clean, it was millions of years old.

Yes, Symmes was right. Mother Earth had a big South Hole, a shaft that tunneled straight down from the surface to . . . to what? I covered my eyes for ten minutes to drive the light from them, and then I got into facedown position to stare down again.

A quarter mile ahead were Eddie and Jeremiah, falling arm in arm. At the edges of my vision I saw dim hints of the shaft's incredibly distant walls, perhaps a hundred miles away from us on every side. The walls glowed faintly nearby, and more brightly further down. The far end of the shaft had waxed to something like the size of a porthole or a dinner plate held at arm's length. The disk was mostly green, but in its center was a bright pink spot, and flowing out from the bright spot were shifting pink lines. Clustered around the central spot were tiny blue-green jewels. I was looking out our great tunnel's other end, out into the Hollow Earth. It seemed we must fall many more hours to get there. The air was so thick and heavy that I felt giddy. I stared down, musing, for quite some time.

Something thudded into me. I screamed, but it was only Arf. Last time I'd noticed him he'd been a dot far above me. Apparently, he'd tucked his legs up and pointed his nose out to fall fast enough to catch me. I spreadeagled myself on my back so I could put Arf on my chest and pet him and talk to him.

"Yes, Arfie. *Poor* Arfie. Peters want eat Arf and Arf run away! Arf break through! Good boy. Good smart Arfie baby. Him sooo fluffy!"

Arf smacked his lips a few times as he did when uncertain, and then he attempted one of his new-paragraph ear-flapping body shakes.

He lost his footing, and the rushing wind tore him back

away from me. Seized with a spirit of hilarious deviltry, I rolled facedown and began moving my arms and legs to dart this way and that. Our overall speed was less than it had been, and I was able to breathe, though each slow thick breath made me dizzier. Arf flew after me, steering himself with small movements of his head and tail. We played tag for about ten minutes, finally coming together in a crash that dazed both of us.

We fell quietly through the heavy, stupefying air for an hour or more. Finally the air began to thin, and with the lessening of the atmospheric pressure, my alertness returned. It was getting very hot, and there was rain all around us. Our speed had diminished to less than half of what it had been before. Peering through the rain, I could see the distant cliffs glowing dark red. Down below, there were white-hot seams and patches in the cliffs and shapes like huge stone terraces jutting out from the shaft's walls. Half a mile behind us was Otha on his big iceberg. I resolved to fly up there with Arf to escape the increasing heat. I hoped Jeremiah and Eddie would have the sense to do likewise.

By dint of much flapping of my arms and legs, I was able to make my way slowly up to Otha's great ice island. It was a strange experience to see the huge white mass looming closer and closer. I kept hold of Arf's leg to make sure he came too. His hair was very fluffy from the hot breeze, and the spiral tattoo Peters had put on his belly showed clearly.

Otha was squatting in the middle of a soggy icefield about the size of our Hardware farm. He looked cold and wary, reminding me all at once of the Christmas three or four years ago when Pa had gotten drunk and raped Turl. I hadn't thought about that night in a long time.

All five of us had been in the house that Christmas Day—I guess it was 1832—eating and drinking, white just the same as black, or so it seemed. Luke polished off a half a ham and a jug of whiskey and fell blissfully asleep on the rag rug on the smooth boards before the hearth. Otha and I were happily playing with a polished beechwood skittles game Uncle Tuck had made for me. He'd dropped it off Christmas morning on his way in to the

annual party at the Perrows'. Otha and I had never seen a game
like it before and we were enthralled. To complete our joy, Uncle
Tuck had brought us a whole bushel of oranges!

A skittles game, I should explain, is a hollow box six inches
deep with a bottom two foot by four. There are slender pins
standing inside the box. The box has wooden baffles in it; it's like
a roofless house with walls breaking it up into rooms, and the
pins are like people in the house, with the more isolated pins
counting more. The player whose turn it is winds a string around
a tall wooden top and sets the top spinning inside the box, and the
score is based on which pins are knocked down. The skittles-top
is a spindle-shaped piece of wood consisting of a five-inch shaft
with a thin disk at one end. Balancing on its long narrow shaft,
the top must spin rapidly to remain upright. It moves about the
skittles-house slowly, tremblingly, feelingly—until it hits a wall
or a pin and trips or darts off on a tangent. The top's motions are
quite unpredictable, and therein lies the fascination of the game.

The rape—if rape it really was—took place silently in the
kitchen, where Pa and Turl had been drinking and playing dom-
inoes, and we never looked up from our skittles or even knew,
until 'round midnight Turl came into the big room with her face
crooked and told Otha he ought to go in there and kill Pa. She
started shaking Luke and screaming. Pa got his arm under mum-
bling Luke's armpit and waltzed him out to the slave cabin, with
Turl behind them railing. Otha jumped on Pa's back and started
choking him. I pulled him off, and Pa slapped him. Otha ran back
in our house and broke up my skittles game—snapped the top and
jumped up and down on the box till it was kindling—and then he
ran off into the pasture. It was a warm Christmas, with a few
inches of rained-on snow. Pa passed out, and I lay in bed crying
over the broken game. Finally, I went out to find Otha. He was
squatting in the pasture holding the broken skittles-top and looking like he wanted to freeze to death. I told him it was safe to
come home; he said it wasn't safe anywhere. I said we'd make a
new skittles game; he said he wanted a new ma.

It took the better part of a year till things settled down. At first Turl acted like it was forgotten, and then that spring she started flaring up and crying and yelling all the time. She wore more clothes than usual. I remember her standing in rags in the rain outside the farmhouse yelling one April day. I didn't make out what she said, but Pa agreed to let her return to visit with her sister in Lynchburg for as many months as she wanted. Her sister belonged to the Perrows. Turl hadn't returned till harvest time, and from then on she'd chattered about her nice little nephew down to the Perrows' and how he 'minded her of Mason.

Now I touched down from the air right in front of Otha. I was holding Arf under one arm. My feet dug into the iceberg's slush and held me still against the wind. Otha stared at me blankly. The chill of the ice and the nitrogen narcosis of the high-pressure region we'd been through had quite numbed him. I talked to him and shook him till he stood up. It was cold next to the ice, but as soon as you stood up, you could feel the heat of the scorching wind. Otha looked around, slowly coming to his senses.

"Is we daid in hell, Mason?"

The cliffs were yellow-hot, and closer than before. Even though there was rain all around us, we could see pretty clearly. Vast cataracts of lava were gushing out of holes in the cliffsides and drizzling down into lakes of fire. There were a few falls of water, too, huge surging gushers that issued, I supposed, from maelstroms or from undersea caves. As the water hit the lava, it would steam up, with most of the vapor being sucked back up into other holes in the giant honeycomb structure of Mother Earth's steaming innermost flesh.

A distant iceberg tumbled into one of the lava lakes, making a huge puff of steam. As more ice and rain bumped into the hot cliffs, the tunnel grew filled with clouds. Just before the fog grew too dense to see, Otha pointed out something moving out of one of the distant waterfalls: a giant spiral shell with a trembling fringe—a shellsquid!

There were great roars and cracks as more and more ice

crashed into the hot cliffs, chipping chattering chunks off them. Now the clouds grew quite black, and bolts of lightning began to flicker. The walls gleamed white-hot through the building storm. The air was witheringly hot, and all the rain had been turned into vapor. We crouched down against the surface of the iceberg.

"Can you see the others, Otha? Can you see Eddie and Jeremiah?"

Just as I asked, Eddie came planing up toward us, riding piggyback on unconscious Jeremiah's back. I signaled to him, and he managed to land near us. Eddie's eyes were blazing with excitement; he said that he'd seen shapes moving in the fire of the cliffs, great demons of the molten core. Though there were no signs of Virginia's ghost, this once the waking world had trumped Eddie's wildest dreams.

We dragged Jeremiah over and revived him from his heat prostration. He was feeble and confused. Arf and we four men laid ourselves down in a hollow of melted icewater like hogs in a wallow. As fast as the wind could evaporate the water from around us, the ice melted more. A full-blown squall was raging, and the hellish cliffs were racing past—though not nearly as rapidly as I would have wished them to. Every now and then, a lightning bolt would flash into our dwindling ice island and a tingle would surge into me. Jeremiah was moaning, and Eddie was chanting blank-verse descriptions of the fiery beings he thought he'd seen.

Finally, the air began to cool. The cliffs dimmed to red and then to black. We were falling much slower than before. Our vast ice island was shrunken to the size of a drifting, creaky ship.

"How far we've come!" exclaimed Jeremiah, fully recovered. With our reduced speed, we no longer had to yell to be heard over the beating wind. "The pressure, the heat—did you save me, Eddie?"

"I am not wholly a villain and a wretch," said Eddie. "And our Symmes was not utterly a fool. But why do we fall so slowly?"

"It's as I told Mason," said Jeremiah. "Newton's calculus demonstrates that there is no net gravitational force within a spherical shell. Although the matter below us still draws us down, all the matter above us is pulling us up. When we reach this tunnel's end, the forces will balance."

"Ah, but what of the masses at the Earth's very center?" said Eddie. "See them, pink and blue? They will pull us further."

"So they may," said Jeremiah. "I wonder—"

There was a great shuddering crack, and the ice island we were on broke in two, with Eddie and Jeremiah on one half and Arf, Otha, and me on the other.

"Jump free!" I urged Otha. "Remember Peters!"

"When we goam see real solid ground?" demanded Otha. "Ah done had it wid water an' air."

"You can help me look for some," I told him. "Come on, we'll fly arm in arm." Eddie and Jeremiah had already launched themselves together; Otha and I followed suit. Agile Arf flew alone, darting among us.

Glancing back at our shattering iceberg, I saw something extraordinary: A large flattened ball—really a hemisphere—had been frozen into the ice's core, and now the half-ball was tumbling back toward the clouds and cliffs. It was of shiny metal, some thirty feet in diameter, and with a slanting flange or ring projecting out along its base, giving it a shape something like a fried egg. Before I could point it out to Otha, the metal object had vanished into the glowing haze behind us. Months later, at the very center of the Hollow Earth, we would find another artifact like it, but just now, not knowing what to think of it, I put it out of my mind.

Soon we were falling much more slowly than before. As we drifted further, the air grew caressingly pleasant. The disk of the tunnel's lower end was bright and big—when I stretched out my arms and held my hands on either side of the disk, my hands were four feet apart. Behind us I could see nothing of the tunnel's upper end, nothing but the continuing storm of fire and ice. We were ahead of what little rain made it through the hot storm zone, and there were only a few chunks of ice remaining. More worrisome were the numerous rocks that were falling after us.

"Dis be some wild ride, Mase! Smell de jungle?" Though Otha kept cautious hold of some part of me at all times, he was beginning to enjoy himself. I sniffed the gentle breeze; there was indeed a faint rank smell of vegetation.

I gestured at the disk ahead of us. "The Hollow Earth!"

"We goam walk aroun' on de inside?"

"Or fall clear to the middle. Can you make out what's there?" I knew his eyes were keener than mine. Otha put his hand to his brow and peered ahead.

"It be a spider," he said. "A pink light spider wid blue-green aigs shiverin' all aroun' it, 'bout to hatch. We don' wanna go way down dere, Mason!"

"Can you see anything at the edge? At the lip of the tunnel? The edge looks fuzzy to me. Do you see trees?"

As we peered downward, a huge irregular triangle of pink light came swelling out of the disk's tangled central "spider." The triangle's nebulous base grew wider and the central vertex grew more obtuse. In a minute, the brightening sheet of pink light reached past the edges of our disk of vision. The bright pink made it easier to see.

"There do be a tree line," said Otha. "Wif vines." The miles-distant lip outline had the roughness of a wooded mountain ridge in the blue hills of Virginia. And here and there you could see twinkles of pink light through the lip, like seeing through bushes.

Suddenly, the pink light filled the whole tunnel around us. There was a throbbing and a hum. All my hair stood on end. Windblown Arf looked like a dandelion seed. The pink energy bath brought no extra heat. It lingered and buzzed, and then it moved on. While it was filling our tunnel, I got a good look at the walls. The tunnel sides were of mixed stone and soil, glinting with streams and bedecked with verdure. A few miles farther ahead, the walls ended, giving way to a vast tangle of giant plants.

That we were quite near the tunnel's end was evidenced by the fact that the mouth's apparent size was growing so rapidly, even though by now we could not have been falling more than thirty miles per hour. We folded in our arms and caught up with Jeremiah and Eddie. I latched on to Jeremiah, and we all bounced around awkwardly as if we were playing crack the whip. Then Arf slammed into us and made it worse. Finally, we settled down: Otha, me, Jeremiah, and Eddie Poe falling arm in arm.

"Let's plane over to the side while we're still moving fast enough," I suggested. "Otherwise we'll be stuck in the middle."

"We wants somethin' ter eat," put in Otha. "Wants some solid ground."

"Faint heart," said Eddie. "Would it not be nobler to fall on and on towards the light?"

"Not without provisions," said Jeremiah. "And who knows how long it would take? We didn't come all this way just to die, Eddie."

We angled ourselves like a great wing, and slowly, the nearer side of the shaft approached. So fissured and overgrown was the wall that it soon took on the appearance of a rural landscape and it was hard to remember it was the wall of a huge well we were slowly rising from. What with our sideways motion, many of the lava rocks were passing us, and other debris as well—clods of dirt, loose tree branches, a few dead birds, and some shattered bits of shellsquid shells. I kept glancing back to make sure nothing would hit us, not that a simple collision would have mattered at the slow speed we were moving. Once, a rock came close enough for me to touch. I caught hold of it and hefted it. It was very much more massive than any stone I'd ever held; it was at least as dense as gold. Ordinarily I would have kept it, but now I threw it as hard as I could, in the hope it would drive us closer to the cliff. This helped a bit, but the slight impetus was soon vitiated by the natural friction of the air. We were still a few miles from land.

The appearance of the sphere's very center was as puzzling as before. All lines of sight near the center were warped and distorted, surrounding the center's blobs of blue with weird halos and mirages. The light there was bright and chaotic and lacked all coherence. Central Sun? Perhaps not. I resolved to call it the Central Anomaly. Earth's interior was illuminated not so much by the Anomaly proper as by the branching pink streamers of light that stretched from the Anomaly to the inner surface of the great planetary rind we'd fallen through.

Slower and slower we fell, and then we were wholly becalmed. The great Hole stretched around us on every side, the nearest edge at least two miles away. Though we were dead even with the bottom end of the hole, the giant trees which clung to Earth's inner surface reached three or four miles farther inward. Was our long voyage to end with us slowly dessicating in this balmy pinklit air? We waved our arms and legs till we were exhausted, but no closer to solid ground did we get. One by one, we dropped off to sleep.

I woke with a start. Had I heard the cries of birds? It felt like hours later, but we were in the same spot, utterly and totally motionless. When our fall ended, we'd fetched up in midair, on a level with the inner edge of Earth's crust. Except for the dryness, it was like floating in water near land.

The tangled green band of the miles thick jungle framed my view down into the Earth's vast interior. It was pinklit and teeming with life, shading into mist in the distance. Flying creatures filled the air like schools of fish; here and there, larger creatures preyed on them. I could see three huge shellsquid in the distance, also a large, flapping animal resembling a skate or a ray. Despite the mist, I could see a good way up the sides of the interior surface around me—perhaps two hundred miles. If the outside surface of the thick rind we'd fallen through was Earth, thought I, the inner surface might be called Htrae.

The part of Htrae near our Hole was covered with bright

green jungle several miles deep. The jungle was dotted with great jiggling ponds of water like giant dewdrops. Here and there, drops were breaking free. Those drops nearer to our level at the base of the jungle and the shell of Earth proper hung more or less motionless. But those drops near the top of the jungle inevitably tended, if let wholly free, to fall in toward the center. The farther the drops got from us, the faster they fell. Newton or no, there was some force that drew matter past the Rind and on toward the center. The Central Anomaly drew things to it more powerfully the closer they got.

In any case, I repeat that there was no gravitational push or pull whatsoever to be felt in the aerial Sargasso sea where we now languished. This region was a kind of gravitational shelf between the zone of Earth's influence and the zone influenced by the Central Anomaly.

In the distance, above the trees, the Htrae landscape rose higher and higher, growing ever paler, till it was lost in distant mists. The landscape was all in patches. Parts of it were nubby deep green jungle, parts of it were smooth and a lighter green, and here and there were bare gray rocks. One small region was a charred dead black—the site of a fire, I assumed, noticing a glowing line along the black patch's edge. Beyond the nearest part of the jungle, I could make out a pale blue sea that shaded to green and blue-black. Perhaps there were deep marine holes in the Hollow Earth, places where Earth's oceans connected to those of Htrae.

The nearest bit of the land about the tunnel mouth was still at least two miles away. Rocks from the tunnel and various-size drops of water floated around us. Though Arf had clung to my pant leg by his teeth while I slept, vagrant breezes had wafted the others away. We were situated at the vertices of a rough equilateral triangle fifty feet on an edge; Arf and I at one vertex, Eddie and Otha at another, and Jeremiah at a third.

Raucous cracking cries broke out. Quite near us were two stub-winged white birds tearing at a piece of food. At first I did not realize how large they were. I thought them near us, and I took the disputed morsel to be something like a fish or a rat. But then a human leg came loose, and I realized their food was the mangled corpse of poor Peters. Each of the birds was as big as two horses. The one holding Peters's severed leg flew off toward the cliff, and the one with the bulk of Peters shook its head briskly, working at tearing the body into bits.

The bird was roughly the shape of a penguin, though its small wings moved in a blur like those of a hummingbird. The bird's yellow, tapering beak was disproportionately large in comparison with its snowy head. The eyes were bright blue beads set into protective feather ruffs. Its claws were rather small—more like a songbird's than like the talons of a predator. Perhaps it was but a scavenger and we were safe.

More squawks rang out in the distance. Three more of the beasts were winging from Htrae toward us. Arf pressed against me in fear. I took out my pistol and examined it. The powder was wet; it would not fire. What else did I have on my person? A tinderbox, a handkerchief, fifty feet of silk rope around my waist, and the pelt and head of a redclaw. The birds drew closer. I resolved to sacrifice the redclaw, and then Arf, if need be.

The bird with Peters shook its head sharply, still not quite able to get its own piece of meat free. It was horrible to see the corpse dance to the rapid vibrations of the bird's head.

Now something shone and flew toward me—Peters's knife! I stretched my arm to the limit, and the big knife's haft plopped into my open hand—a tangible sign of good fortune. I slid the long strong blade into my boot top. Arf had brought me luck; I'd been mad to think of buying time by feeding him to the birds. A better plan formed in my mind. The other men were awake and yelling to each other; for now, I paid them no mind.

"Good boy, Arfie!" I unwound the rope from my waist and put a tight loop of it around Arf's chest, right behind his front legs. One of the dense boulders was near us, a big one the size of a slave cabin. I wrapped the free end of the rope tightly around my wrist and paid out the rest of the rope into loose bights. I threw Arf away from the boulder, and the reaction sent me tumbling toward it. But before I could reach the rock, the rope reached its end, twanged, and pulled me and Arf tumbling back together.

"Sorry, boy. Let's try again." There were four of the monster birds pulling at Peters's corpse now; unless they were solely carrion feeders, it would not be long until they set upon us. I threw Arf again, at a slightly better angle, and this time I caught hold of a ledge of the heavy boulder before the rope reached full extension. Arf yelped, the snap jolted my arm in its socket, but I hung fast. Arf tumbled back to me and the boulder. Now I had bait, and I had something to hide behind.

"All right, Arfie, pretty soon now we're going to fish for a bird."

"Mase! Hey, Mason, here ah comes!" It was Otha. While I had been busy with Arf, Jeremiah had thrown his own rope to Eddie and Otha. The three of them were together, and now Otha braced himself against the two men's chests and sprang toward me, Jeremiah's rope uncoiling behind him. I held tight to my rock and reached out to catch Otha's hand. We connected on the first try. We four men hauled on the rope till we were all clustered together on one side of the massive cabin-size boulder.

"What a vista." Jeremiah puffed. "See how the land tilts up and away—I feel like we're in the Garden of Eden! And see the glints of water everywhere! Surely we will find men in these plains and jungles. Kind men and lovely women."

"How we gone git over dar?" asked Otha.

"What of those birds nearby?" exclaimed Eddie, peeking around our rock's edge. "Do they feed on—"

"It is the corpse of Peters," said I, drawing his knife out of my boot top. "See."

"Hideous," murmured Eddie, his eyes glinting. "Those small claws—almost like hands. I dub them *harpies*."

We all peeped around the rock's edges, staring at the harpies. Now a harpy flew close by, carrying one of Peters's arms away. Its small, active wings made a deep buzz. Three other harpies remained, wielding their beaks to open up the corpse's abdomen. Three more approached.

"Here is my plan," I told the others. "I throw Arf out as bait. When one of the harpies comes for him, I pull him back to us. We grab hold of the harpy, and in its fear it flies back to land, towing us with it."

"How 'bout dat beak?" said Otha. "How 'bout dem claws?" He had taken out his bowie knife. "We gwine cut 'em off?"

"Better not to injure it," said Jeremiah. "Lest its fellows attack it." His hands were nimbly working at his coil of cord. "Here is a noose to hold the beak," he said, holding it up. "And two others to bunch the claws."

"What if someone gets left behind?" asked Eddie.

"We'll bind together like mountaineers," said Jeremiah, fashioning four firm loops into the rest of his rope. Each of us slipped a loop around his waist.

There was a flurry of squawking around the grisly remains of Peters, and then one of the harpies came buzzing our way. The others had driven it off.

"All right, Arfie," I said. "Play dead." I gave him a gentle push, and he went drifting out to the rope's full extent. The harpy spotted him. Arf began to struggle fruitlessly; the harpy buzzed closer, darting its head this way and that.

I began slowly reeling Arf back, and when I saw the harpy cock its head for a deathblow, I gave the cord a sharp jerk. The huge white bird zipped around the rock's edge after Arf, and then we four men were upon it. I stunned it by slamming the butt of Peters's knife into its head. Jeremiah got his noose tight around its beak and then helped Otha fasten the two other loops around its claws. Eddie scrambled onto its back and sank his hands into its feathers. I snugged Arf under Eddie's arm. The next instant the beast was struggling and striking out at us. Finding myself at its breast, I locked my arms around its neck to hold it still. Otha and Jeremiah had tight hold of its bound feet down below. My knife was still in one hand. I pressed the blade tip against the creature's throat, ready to kill. Sensing the danger, it stopped trying to peck me. One of its huge blue eyes was inches from my face.

"Don't fight," I said. "Just fly home. Over there." I jerked my head toward the jungle.

The harpy's wings had been beating in fury all this time, and we were already a hundred feet away from the rock.

"Land," I said soothingly, though not letting up the pressure of my knife. "Fly us to land, big bird."

Slowly, erratically, it did. First it flew perhaps two miles in toward the Earth's center—and then it angled over toward the middle of the giant jungle wall. At first it felt to me as if the bird were flying up toward a huge green ceiling; and then my sense of up and down shifted, and I felt the bird to be flying upside down toward a wooded floor. Both impressions were of course wrong, as we were moving crossways. The jungle was a tangle of vines and branches, brightened with the shimmer of huge globules of water trapped here and there. Some immense flowers bloomed. Two harpies flew out to greet our carrier and then, seeing us, flew off uttering harsh caws of fear.

We circled a huge leafless tree trunk with branches stained white from bird droppings. The harpies' roost. A dozen of them flew off as we landed—or tried to land. I heard thuds and a curse as Jeremiah and Otha smacked into one of the tree branches, and then came Jeremiah's cry, "Let go!"

I unclasped my arms, slipped the noose off the bird's beak, and pushed my feet hard against its chest to get free. There was a jerk at my waist as my ropes pulled Arf and Eddie off its back. And then our harpy screamed and flew away, leaving us five and our ropes tangled in the branches of the harpies' home tree. Slowly, Jeremiah and I got our ropes unknotted and fastened them back around our waists.

"Let's climb down," said Otha. "Fore dey comes back."

"Up," said Eddie. "You mean climb *up*. See the loose twigs out there, see them falling towards the center? The center is down, the land is up."

"Ah ain' no fly on no ceilin'," said Otha. "When ah climbs outten a tree, ah climbs *down*. Come on, Mase, let's find us somethin' to eat."

"I'll come, Otha, but I think Eddie is right. *Down* is toward the center; it's the way things fall. And *up* is the other way. We have to keep a common tongue."

"Sho'," said Otha. "Den tell me which way be north." He gave himself a shove that sent him up—or down—to the tree's next branch.

"Let's call it *out*," said Jeremiah. "*In* is toward the center, and *out* is back towards where we came from. Towards the crust. Agreed?"

"Agreed."

I pushed off after Otha. I floated easily through the empty air, steadied myself on the next branch, and pushed farther. Jeremiah was behind me, and Eddie took up the rear—most *inward* of all.

Our progress was easy. Rather than heading straight back out toward Earth's crust, we chose to go deeper into the jungle, angling crossways. In the all but weightless surroundings, we could hop from branch to branch like squirrels—though it took some bone-shaking crashes till we learned not to jump too hard. It was so strange to be living with practically no gravity. How odd and how wonderful that the attraction of the great domed planet crust behind us exactly balanced the pull of the land close ahead.

Soon we were in the midst of foliage. Although no solid ground was visible, the fluttering pink light from the "sky" provided a steady reminder of which way was which. Birdsong sounded on every side of us, also the rustlings and cries of other animals.

There were large droplets of water everywhere—some as big as peaches, some as big as pumpkins. In the moist air, they condensed like dew. But in these near-weightless conditions, the water drops were free to merge and grow to unearthly size. I drank several of the smaller ones. The bigger, head-size drops held tiny fish with stubby fins like legs. Our passage knocked the drops loose, and they slid down to merge with drops closer to the jungle's inward edge, the larger drops sliding into the sky and falling all the way to the center, there—I supposed—to be cooked to vapor and sent back Htraeward.

All the trees and vines had extra tendrils at their forks, tendrils designed to hold the waterglobs. Additionally, small parasitic plants had taken root in each of the tree trunks' crotches and flaws; these orchidlike plants bore flowers of an overwhelming intricacy. Small-winged dragonflies darted from plant to plant; there were also gnats, june bugs, oversize aphids, and enormous ants that would never have been able to get around in normal gravity. Mist and fine rain from our great icefall was drifting through the trees, swelling the big drops, which bulged everywhere.

After ten minutes of swinging through the wet branches, we found our first food: a vine covered with red berries the size of apples. Otha bit into one and smiled; the rest of us followed suit. The berries were sweet and juicy, each holding a single big seed. I ate three of them. Dragonflies buzzed around our discarded seeds; a thing like a thick eel stuck its head out of a hole in a tree branch and caught one of them. I wondered if the eel would be good to eat, but then it had writhed back into hiding.

A bit further on we found some fruits like bananas; these were filling, though somewhat bitter. A large, hairy spider leaped from one of the banana plant's white flowers and hurried away. A green-throated bird the size of a partridge caught the spider and began to devour it. Otha drew out his knife and threw it Peters-style, pinning the plump bird to a branch. It screamed terribly till Otha cut its throat and gutted it. Great scuttlings filled the branches where Otha threw the innards.

"Let's keep moving," I said. I was in no rush to meet this jungle's scavengers.

"Oncet we gits 'nuff food, we kin build a fire an' cook," said Otha. "You kill somethin', too, Mason. You got a knife, Eddie?"

"I do not," said Eddie. "I think it unwise to inaugurate our stay with wholesale slaughter."

As we went deeper into the Htrae jungle, the light grew dimmer and the chatter of animal life swelled. I saw several small, furry creatures with long arms, but they were too fast to kill—not that I really wanted to. Something like a pig was more what I was hungry for, or a fish.

My wishes were answered when all at once we came on the biggest waterball yet—a monstrous trembling sphere the size of a barn, hemmed in on the upward side by vines and tendrils and cradled on the inward side by the crotch where a huge dead branch stuck out of a living tree. Peering into the water, I could make out some of those stubby-legged fish I'd seen before, only these fish were plump and a foot long. I slipped out of my clothes and pushed into the water, my new knife in one hand. The fish scattered. I swam across the waterball, stuck my head out for air, then swam back. One of the fish got right in front of me. I swam at it, trapping it against the surface, but just as I lunged with my knife, the fish jumped out of the water. I came out after it only to see the fish flopping its way up through the air, using its little finlegs to push off from every branch it passed. Maybe later it would creep back into this big glob, or maybe it would find another. Let it be. I rested.

The warm, humid air felt good on my bare skin. I sat on the dead branch's outward side, lightly anchored down by the faint gravitational tug. Arf was near me, now and then starting into midair and bouncing from vine to vine, propelled by the beating of his tail. The others poked around, looking at this and that. We all agreed that if we could catch some more food, this would be a good spot to camp. The ground or crust was at least a half mile further out, but there seemed no special reason to push that far;

the jungle would only get darker and wetter and more filled with death.

"Let's try this," said Jeremiah, producing a fishhook and line from inside his coat. He pried some loose bark off the dead branch and found a fat grubworm to bait his hook with. My direct attack had left the fish too skittish to take the bait immediately, but after ten minutes' time, Jeremiah caught one, and then another. I found a strong hollow stick like a bamboo shoot and used a few feet of rope to lash my new knife to it. I'd planned to spear a fish, but just then another bird chanced past and I managed to hit it with my first throw. Otha and I set to work plucking feathers.

"How 'bout a fire, Mason?"

"A fire by all means," said Eddie. "This jungle gloom oppresses my spirit. Why are we here? How will we ever get back? I should be busy *writing* about strange worlds, not exploring them. This is entirely too much!"

"We can build a new balloon," suggested Jeremiah. "Thanks to us, the Symmes Hole is wide open. We can balloon out and return to America. Once you've written the expedition report, Eddie, I can organize a really well equipped—" There was a coughing roar in the distance.

"Build dat fire," repeated Otha.

I took out my tinderbox. The branch whose outer side we rested on was perhaps ten yards in diameter, and the verdant tree it connected to was easily fifty yards through. Though our dead branch was rather damp on the surface, its pithy inner layers were dry and corky. I used my knife to chip out a pile of the punky stuff. There was no obvious place to put a fire, so I tried building it in midair. The pith caught fire properly, but the flames didn't seem to know which way to go, and soon the scraps I'd assembled drifted apart and died into sparks. I tried again, this time starting my fire right inside the depression I'd chipped out in the branch. With no real down or up, the flames couldn't rise properly, but eventually I had ignited a stable, good-size glow.

Each of us skewered a fish or a bird on a green branch and held it to the coals. The hanging, weightless smoke made our eyes smart, but the sizzling of the meat was wonderful to hear. As we cooked, I poked and stoked the fire until it had spread all the way to the inside of the branch, which seemed to be hollow. We could see wisps of smoke coming out of knotholes for quite some distance away, and the huge tree stem was filled with the scrabblings of small creatures fleeing the fumes. A family of disgustingly jiggly flesh-colored salamanders squirmed out of a knothole nearby and flopped themselves away. One of them brushed against my neck, and I shuddered. What if some really big creatures showed up?

We crouched over the fire, turning our sticks till our food was ready. Otha and Eddie each ate a bird, Jeremiah and I a fish. We traded off bits of our meats; they were all quite good, though the fowl were somewhat bloody. By the time we were through, the fire had opened a three-foot-wide hole in the tree. The bright blaze heartened us.

Numerous grubworms and small transparent scorpions were squirming out of the hot wood; we used them to bait the fishhook and catch four more of the legfins. Once we'd roasted these and had eaten some juicy purple fruits, we were full and ready for sleep—but by now our fire had spread so much smoke that the air was not easily breathable. By judiciously cutting a few vines, we managed to tease the great trapped waterball over a few yards and quench the flames. As the air cleared, we tethered ourselves to a thick vine that embraced the tree trunk some small distance further up. Hanging there like strange fruits, we chatted softly, drifting toward sleep.

"A balloon's the thing," said Eddie. "We can make one of gum and giant leaves."

"But how to heat it?" I queried. "We have no stove."

"How 'bout dem giant shellsquid," put in Otha. "We could catch one of dem and ride it away. I seen some of 'em in de tunnel and more of 'em down dere in de sky."

"Surely there are people here," said Jeremiah. "If not in this jungle, then out above us, in the rock, or at the jungle's edge where it meets the sea."

"I saw something like a metal ship in the tunnel," I said. "It was frozen inside Otha's ice island till it broke up. I think it was an airship."

"Infernal machines," said Eddie drowsily. "Can we trust hell-creatures for aid? No, no, we must press inward, down through the sky to the center. Angels may live there, sweet white angels with wings . . ."

# 10
## Seela

IT TOOK ME a while to fall asleep. Down in the center of the planet, huge vague fingers of energy wandered and branched, filling our deep jungle with shaking light. To my solitary fancy, the flickers came in rhythm with the sounds: the buzzings of insects, the stealthy rustles of unseen crawling things, and—most unsettling of all—the plops and wallowings of great creatures slipping in and out of the ponds. Now and then would come a distant howl or shriek to set my hair on end. So wet was the air that jiggling gobbets of water kept landing on my face and oozing into my nose. I tossed this way and that, fretting at my tether while Arf and the three men snored.

I thought of Virginia. It was incredible that Eddie's possessiveness and folly had killed her. Sis had been an odd duck, but I felt I'd loved her. The remembered feel of her chalky flesh up in Mrs. Clemm's dark garret haunted me in complex ways. More purely pleasant were my memories of Sukie, and of my two visits to a woman named Lupe in Rio. Sukie, Virginia, Lupe. Would I ever meet a girl to truly love? Love . . . love was a maze, a heavenly city . . .

Otha woke me, who knows how many hours later. "Hsst, Mason! Ah hears somethin'!" I rubbed the sleep out of my eyes and tried to listen. The cries and rustles of the jungle beasts were unchanged but, yes, there was something new—a roaring, almost human sound, oddly warped and amplified.

"You think dar be giants here?" asked Otha. The faroff garbled yelling went on and on. "Sound like he hungry, too!"

Flesh-eating giants? I woke Eddie and Jeremiah. "There's some kind of monster," I told them. "Over there!"

Jeremiah cocked his head as alertly as Arf. "Let's go investigate!" said he.

"What if he eats us?"

"We'll sneak and mayhap steal his treasures. Stout heart now, Mason!"

So sneak we did. The direction of our travel lay crosswise rather than inward or outward. Now and then the giant voice—for a human voice it surely was—stopped its droning blabber, but never for long, and as we drew closer it got ever louder. As the end of an hour approached, the light became brighter, and then we found ourselves at the jungle's far edge, peeping out of the immense thicket like anxious wrens.

A huge ocean spread across the Earth's inner curve, hanging in the distance like a great, never-breaking wave. The jungle's limit was as a huge wall that stretched miles outward to the edge of the sea and mounted miles inward toward the center of the Hollow Earth. Great vines thrust immense flowers out into the free, light-filled air above the sea. Rather than facing inward toward the Earth's center, the flowers pointed toward the sea, and each of them cradled a huge central glob of water. The voice was clear enough so that we could make out individual nonsense words—yet no giant was to be seen.

Turning our heads this way and that we finally determined that the voice came from the nearest flower, just inward from us. This vast blossom was like a half-mile-wide sunflower, with a great yellow center and a ruff of lazily undulating white petals.

There was a dark green flaw near one edge of the flower's surface, and lying near the flaw was a long, straight tube—seemingly a bit of plant-stem. Otha, whose hearing was the sharpest, reckoned that the giant voice was coming from the tube. Some pale figures—people, insects, worms?—moved about in the flaw near the tube.

Jeremiah tossed a fat berry toward the flower. The berry coasted inward and dwindled to a speck that landed near the jewel-like lake that rested in the flower's center. After a brief consultation, we jumped after the berry. Midway during our approach, the owner of the giant voice noticed us and cried out an alarm. The green spot's infestation of pale figures dispersed, and all was silent. I prayed that we weren't making a fatal mistake.

The yellow field of the flower's surface was smooth and leathery, filled with the buzz of large insects and the cries of the small animals that preyed on them. A regular pattern of raised welts marked the surface, dividing it into hexagonal plots. Each plot was roughly the size of our barnyard; each of them formed a smooth depression with a hole in its center. The air near the surface was filled with a sweet smell. The lake's near-weightless waterball bulged out sharply. All was calm as, ever so gently, we touched down.

I tore off a piece of the yellow flower and chewed it. It was good, like a sun-dried peach or apple. A jewellike beetle with small wings landed to gnaw at the hole I'd made in the flower; I shooed it, and it flew off, glinting gorgeously in the light. After the dank, thicketed jungle, this was paradise. Slowly we gathered around a small pool of water which had collected in the center of one of the hexagons. The hexagons' central holes were ringed by stubby tubular petals of an especial toughness. There was still no sign of the pale figures, and no hint of the giant voice. We ate and drank and rested, Otha yodeled, and poor drawn Eddie's limbs began gaily to wave.

We'd all been eating at the same part of the flower, and now there was a hole big enough for me to stick my head in through the surface and look. It was like looking into a yellow room the size of a house. A thick central column was in the room's center, stretching from floor to ceiling—terminating in the hexagon's central hole. Three embryonic seeds nestled against the central tube, connected to it by thick tendrils. Each of the big flower-cell's six walls had a triangular gap in its bottom, a kind of door through which I could see into neighboring cells, each with its own central pillar and three seed embryos. For a moment I saw a pale shape moving in the next cell over—who lived here?

Suddenly, my legs and arms were seized from behind and I was yanked out of my peephole. A horde of pale-skinned men and women surrounded us. Their clothing was of bright-colored petals, and for weapons they bore sharp rapiers fashioned from thorns. Their hair was red and blond; their eyes were green and blue. Many of them wore necklaces of heavy trinkets. My three companions had already been overcome, and one of the pale attackers held Arf tight in his arms. Before I could think of struggling, my hands were lashed behind me and my ankles were bound together. My captors, two pink-clad women, picked me up bodily. As they carried me, they chattered excitedly to each other and to me, but I could understand nothing of what they said—it might as well have been birdsong. Now they laid me down next to my companions, also bound.

"Yes, we are your friends!" Jeremiah was shouting in hearty tones. This having no effect, he switched to one of the Polynesian tongues he knew. "*Nui-nui lama-lama papeete nami-lo!*"

"They're angels!" raved Eddie. "They flew from the sky!"

Our captors—there were perhaps thirty of them—paid little attention to our expostulations. Most of the pale people clustered around Otha, staring at him in solemn wonder, haltingly reaching out to touch his skin. One of them put her necklace around Otha's neck. Several of them made as if to kiss Otha's hands and feet; others began to chant.

Had they never seen a Negro before? Even more ridiculous,

those few not worshiping Otha were enthralled by Arf. Ever accepting the moment, Arf had stopped barking and was now wagging his tail and licking the face of the youth who held him. The youth simpered and began to lick Arf back. Several others pressed forward and licked Arf's nose as well.

While these odd displays continued. I had ample opportunity to examine our captors. They were so pale-skinned that their veins showed. Each of them had a thick shock of fair hair cut bowl-style. Their features were delicate, even beautiful. They were short and slender, with the exception of their legs, which were thick and heavily muscled. Their necklaces held crystals, shells, and carved bits of wood. Some were also clothed in bright fluttering togas made of fresh flower petals, and each of them had oddly trimmed petalbases strapped to their legs. The leathery, tubular petalbases were like spats—I grasped their purpose when I saw a girl hop up into the air and kick her way outward from the giant flower. Each time she kicked backward, her leggings filled out and caught the air, driving her forward. Airfins! Wings!

"*Ahnaa bogbog du smeeepy flan? Mii'iim doc janjee?*" One of the pink-dressed girls was standing over me.

"Set me free," I begged her, holding up my bound ankles.

She laughed and made a dismissive gesture. "*Ah'mbaa na toloo klick gorwaay,*" said she. Her voice was calm and musical, and she lingered over the long vowels, singing them each through a tone or two. She and her companion took hold of my arms and, with a sudden spring, launched us into the sky. They kicked their legs in steady rhythm, popping the strong petalparts against the air. The rest of them followed us, bearing Otha, Eddie, Jeremiah, and Arf.

We worked our way around the giant waterdrop that occupied our flower's center and flew out toward the great yellow disk's edge. There, in the surface of the flower, was a large ragged hole, and lying next to it was the great noise-tube we'd seen from afar. All the yellow cells with their seeds had been cleared away here—perhaps for food—leaving an open hexagon a hundred yards wide. My bearers kickpopped down to land us in the hexagon. The ground here was tough dark green vegetable matter, presumably the same material as our great flower's vines and leaves. The wall openings in the cells facing the open space had been widened, so that the effect was of a village green surrounded by stores and houses. Numerous faces peeped out from the cells.

Seeing their defenders land with all intruders tightly bound, the fair flowerpeople came surging out into the green. When they glimpsed black Otha and hairy Arf, their excitement knew no limits. It was only a moment till they were all around us, shouting in nasal singsong. Everyone wore the petal leggings; many wore nothing else. Several of them began to beat on big hollow seedpods, someone else produced a trumpetlike hollow plantstem and began to play, and now a slight youth flew to the big tube that had attracted us and began yelling into one end. The tube's ends were covered over with tight-stretched membranes (one with a small central hole), thus turning the tube into a huge reverberator. Giants indeed! Moist slices of what seemed to be flowerseeds appeared, and the flowerpeople began celebrating in earnest.

As always here, the sky was filled with pink flickers; it was perhaps as bright as early dusk. We four were propped up sitting back to back in the green's center. Otha and I were side to side, with Eddie and Jeremiah behind us. Arf, who'd been set free, lay at my side, alertly watching the noisy crowd.

"Maybe dey cannibals, Mase? Some do have a nasty look."

"You're right. See how that one has his teeth sharpened? And the woman over there . . . see the way she's painted her body? These are real savages, Otha. It's strange because they're so—"

"Dey be so white. Dey look too good to talk to de like ob me, Mase, dey look like de first families ob Virginia. And den dey carry on dis-a-way. Looky dere!"

As the drumming grew wilder, the dancers threw themselves around more and more wildly, emitting fearful whoops and making hideous grimaces. Several couples even progressed to public embraces of an ultimate intimacy. Those who had to relieve themselves did so quite openly. It was unpleasant and singular to see such fine-looking people exhibit this bestial behavior.

Just when the orgy had reached fever pitch, the drumming stopped and all began crooning a single utterance: *Quaihlaihlo*! They pronounced the barbaric name much as we would say "*quite likely*."

A lone figure appeared from one of the empty seedcells: a tall bejeweled woman, with skin as white as the inside of a puffball mushroom. Her scalp was shaved and painted black. This was Quaihlaihle, the queen of the flowerpeople. She walked slowly toward us, ignoring the filth that had been scattered by the dancers. She was clothed in dyed and laquered plantparts that fit her like armor. The bright plates of her plantarmor were spangled with glittering bits of stone and shell. Unlike the other flower-people, Quaihlaihle had the thick lips and dark eyes of a Negro. Yet her skin was, as I say, utterly white. When her gaze lighted on Otha, her face split in a fierce smile. Her glistening teeth were a bloody ruby-red.

"She look jus' like 'Lijah," Otha breathed.

"And like the redclaws," I added. I still had the head and pelt of one of the red-toothed antarctic beasts—not to mention my gun and Peter's knife. Our savage captors had not thought to search us.

"*Lamalama tekelili?*" said Quaihlaihle to Otha. Noticing Arf, she stooped to pet him, long and slow.

"Yazzum," said Otha. "I'se de boss ob dis party, sho' 'nuff. Dass my dog, too. I hopes you treat us nice. How 'bout you unties us to start wid, Quaihlaihle?" He raised up his bound feet and hands.

"*Bogbog doc janjee!*" exclaimed Quaihlaihle. "*Ombon-doohoo!*" One of the men nearby sprang forward and used a dagger of sharpened shell to cut Otha's bonds.

"Me, too," I urged, holding up my hands. "Untie me, too."

"Yes," said Otha, standing and rubbing his wrists. "Untie all of us, Quaihlaihle."

She stepped forward, took Otha's head in her hands, and licked him all over his face. Though Otha was tall, she was every bit as big as him. As she greeted Otha in this barbaric fashion, the flowerpeople began again to chant. She gave another command, and the man with the shellknife moved around the three of us, cutting the tight vines that had bound our hands and feet.

"That's a relief," said Jeremiah. "We should present them with a gift. What do you have in your pockets, Eddie?"

"An empty flask," said Eddie. "A pocketknife. A twist of tobacco. Virginia's tee—" He cut the word short and hastily continued. "Paper with a few verses and—deuce take it! My pen and ink are lost."

"What do you have, Mason?"

I didn't want to tell them of my gun. "How about a redclaw pelt? I've still got one. The queen should like that; it has red teeth like hers. Maybe she can wear it for a hat."

"Excellent," said Jeremiah. "Give it to me."

"To you?"

"I'm the leader, Mason. I've dealt with savages before. Trust me."

So I pulled the wadded up redclaw pelt out of my pocket and slipped it to Jeremiah. The scabby pelt was wrapped around the red-toothed head. With a flourish, Jeremiah spread the skin and head out on his two flattened hands, stepped forward, and crouched before Queen Quaihlaihle, making his offering. He was the very image of a humble subject.

The turmoil that ensued is hard to describe. The queen began to scream most terribly, and a second later a woman with a long thorn-rapier had darted forward and plunged her point through Jeremiah's heart. He gave a terrible groan and fell sideways. The man with the shellknife darted forward and sawed open the dying Jeremiah's throat, sawed as if to cut his head off. Great quantities of blood gushed forth, some of it floating off in bright globules. Still screaming, Quaihlaihle snatched up the offending redclaw and crammed it down into the yawning hole that the man had cut in Jeremiah's neck.

I drew out the big knife I'd gotten from Peters and took off running, making ten or twenty feet with each bound. I heard someone close behind me. If I went to the flower's surface or the sky, I wouldn't have a chance. Instead, I dove into one of the open cell doors and raced through to the next and the next and the next. All the cells I entered were empty save for seeds and central pillars. Most of the seeds were dry, juiceless husks. Someone was still close behind me. I blundered on for ages and finally, out of breath, I caught hold of a cell's central tube and hid behind it. When my follower entered the cell, I leaped out roaring with my blade raised high.

"Don't, Mason, don't kill me!" shrieked Eddie, for it was only he.

"Thank God it's you, Eddie." I could have kissed him. "Let's go deeper into the maze until they calm down. We'll escape when . . ."

"When it gets dark?" Eddie smiled.

"Some way. What happened just now?"

"I surmise that the redclaws are viewed as sacred beasts and that Jeremiah has borne Peter's punishment for having killed one. The queen had red teeth as well. Did you see how quick she was to push the redclaw into Jeremiah's gullet?"

"I saw it."

"Quite extraordinary. It was as if she meant to plant the slain beast's *mana* in poor Reynolds's hale frame. As if he were a sarcophagus and the pelt a pharaoh. I wish I had my pen! I need to write! So many choice happenings are flitting by. We must find a way back to Earth, Mason. My narrative of this trip could make my fortune. Make *our* fortune. Promise me that you will cast your lot with mine, Mason. I . . ." Eddie's voice faltered. "I know that you think ill of me. No man is a hero to his valet, but—"

"I'm not your valet, Eddie."

"If Otha is your slave, then you are my valet and Arf is Otha's dog. Arf and Otha are ensconced in the camp of the flowerpeople. You and I must stand together or die, young Reynolds. You know this, yet you find our union a heavy duty. You despise me, do you not? You think me a cold-blooded murderer. You do not forgive me for the death of Virginia."

"You poisoned her, and I do not doubt that you violated her dead body. It is a certainty that you pulled out her teeth; you bear the teeth with you still. You killed Virginia and you defiled her corpse. She deserved better, Eddie. She was only a child."

We were wandering side by side through the cells. Each cell was a hexagon in floor plan, with six rectangular walls ten to fifteen feet in height. As we moved away from the flower's edge and toward its center, the cells grew larger. Every wall had a small tentlike rent at its base. Wishing to ensure that Quaihlaihle's folk did not follow us, we moved rapidly through the rooms as we argued. At the moment I threw my indictment at Eddie, we were near the center of a cell.

The sky sputtered to bright; Eddie blanched pale and dour. "Forgive me, Mason. I am three parts mad, this is no secret— but, pray, I am no fiend! The teeth . . . the teeth were my only violation. I had no thought of killing Sis. Truly, Mason, you do me grave dishonor. Were we in the real world and I in my right mind, I would horsewhip you or challenge you to a duel! But this is not Earth but Htrae or, better yet, Thur . . . or Ruht or MirrorHtrae. . . . I've had visions of the rest of our journey, Mason. We'll travel on through the center—"

"The Anomaly, I call it," said I as we pushed on into another cell. The three seeds in this cell were full and turgid.

"How apt, my boy, how scientific! Through the Anomaly we shall go, and then—I do not quite grasp what I have forseen— into an antiworld which has its own MirrorHtrae and its own MirrorEarth surface to tunnel up to. . . . Believe of me what you will, I do not trouble to deny it. I am marked for torment and death, but also am I marked for greatness. I am not like other men! Do say now that you throw in your lot with mine.''

"Eddie, I—"

"Hsst!"

He cut me off with a quick light touch. There was someone in the next cell! Once again, I drew my knife and crouched behind the room's central pillar. Eddie got close behind me. The plantparts whispered as the person pushed through the wall rent. Delicate footfalls. A light rasping noise and then faint slurping. Ever so slowly, I eased my head out from around the pillar. A beautiful blond maiden was there, pressing her mouth to one of the seeds. She was naked save for her legfins and an elaborately patterned necklace.

"Seize her," hissed Eddie, peering out from behind me. Even as she looked up, I sprang forward and clamped my left arm around her waist. She screamed but struggled little. I sheathed my knife and pressed my right hand gently to her mouth. Her mouth was slick with the seed's albuminous juices.

"Don't be frightened. I'm Mason, and that's Eddie. We want to be friends. Yes, we want to be friends." Her rolling eyes fastened on my face. Such bright, intelligent features she had. Her eyes were hazel. Her nose was small and gently curved. Her upper lip was fuller than her lower lip; this upper lip was a smooth, kissable band, with only the smallest of indentations at its center. I smiled and nodded. "If I let you go, do you promise not to scream?"

She regarded me calmly. I smiled once more, and slowly I took my hand off her mouth. Her mouth moved slightly—I made a small cry and cut it off by slapping my hand over my own mouth. The smell of her saliva was wonderful. My arm around her waist held her body tight against me. She was marvelously supple and alive. I pretended to struggle at the hand over my mouth, popping my eyes and blowing my cheeks out. She stared, understood, giggled. I dropped my hand from my mouth and put it around her waist to meet my other. Everything about her looked and felt right. I almost blurted out that I loved her, but instead I just stared in her light brown eyes.

"*Emthonjeni womculo,*" she said. "*Thul'ulale.*"

"Dear girl," put in Eddie, striding forward and startling her. "Be assured that Mason and Eddie are kind and funny men. I am Mason's master." Fixing an impudent simper on his face, he drew out a handkerchief and deftly knotted it into the shape of a rabbit. The girl stared at him in puzzlement that changed to fear as Eddie waggled the rabbit's ears and began to dart the head oddly.

"Stop it, Eddie," said I. "Sit down and be quiet or, better yet, go away for an hour. I saw this girl first. She's mine."

For a wonder, he left quietly.

"*Sini lindile,*" said the girl. "*Nansi* Seela." She made a graceful gesture at herself and then at me. "*Goobaam?*"

"*Mason,*" said I, tapping my chest. I was wearing trousers, boots, a collarless shirt, and a jacket. She was wearing a kind of diaper or breechcloth of white flowerpetal. "I'm Mason and you are Seela?"

"Seeylaaah," she said, imitating my voice. "*Nansi* Seela. Ma'aassong?"

"Mason," I said, correcting her. After a few more tries, I could say her name the way she wanted me to. She taught me that the embryonic seeds were called *juube*, and she showed me how to bite off a piece of a *juube*'s rind and lap up the thick clear juice. The juice was something like sweetened eggwhite, with a bitter aftertaste. It was invigorating, and a bit dizzying. As we taught each other our names for this and that, I grew warmer and warmer. My feet were uncomfortable in my wet boots, so I took them off, also my jacket, also my shirt.

Seela plucked at my trousers. "*Nicabange orlooah?*" She stood and fluttered her legs. Her petal leggings popped against the air and drove her up the cell's leathery yellow ceiling. She drifted back down. "*Goobaam?*"

I kicked my legs, but of course my trousers did nothing for me. Seela plucked at my trousers again, talking volubly. I went ahead and took them off. I was not to wear a full suit of clothes again for six months.

So there we were, nearly naked in our yellow cell, Seela and I. Her hair was yellow-blond. Her face was neat and fine, with a firm round jaw. Her eyes were greenish brown. Her limbs were pleasingly proportioned, and her body a wonderland of young womanly curves. Did she mean for us to make love? Suddenly, she picked up my big knife, lying by my boot. From everything I'd seen so far, metal was unknown to the flowerpeople.

I took the knife from her and stabbed it into one of the *juube* seeds, showing her how sharp it was. Then I turned it sideways and let her look into it as if into a mirror. She was briefly fascinated. She stared at her own eyes for a minute, then put the knife between us and moved it up and down, swapping her view of my eyes with her view of her own reflected eyes. Our eyes were remarkably similar. More and more, I felt that this woman was meant for me.

Just as I was about to kiss her, she leaped up the ceiling and made a big slash in it. She did this two more times till she'd cut out a triangular hole. She pulled herself out through the hole and beckoned to me. Before following, I rolled all my clothes together into a bundle and stashed them under the curve of a *juube*. Seela called to me from above; I crouched, then leaped with all my strength. In the low gravity, my leap was enough to shoot me right through the hole. Seela caught hold of my bare foot as I flew past her.

"*Nicabange smeeepy doolango,*" she said.

I sat on the flower's cut edge and peered around. The village hexagon was far off, though closer to us than I had hoped. I could make a out a few figures moving in the air over the hexagon. At this distance they looked like large insects. Seeing them, I instinctively flattened myself against the flower's surface. Seela looked at me curiously. I pointed over to the hexagon and made a stabbing gesture at my throat. "They don't like me," I told her. "Quaihlaihle killed one of us already."

"*Quaihlaihle shange yejazi,*" said Seela, making a sour

face. Now she turned her attention to the center of the hexagonal flower dimple we were in. The big flower-cell's central column met the surface here in a hole which was surrounded by a cluster of tubular petals. Using my knife with growing skill, Seela cut off two of the tubular petals and trimmed away most of the material from one side of each, leaving a big concave fin with a ring at one end. She slipped the rings over my feet and then I was wearing petal flightfins like her. She called them *pulpul*. She was eager to give me a flight lesson. I hesitated; she grabbed my hand and kicked us up into the air.

When I tried a kick, the *pulpuls* fluttered uselessly. Seela turned around and showed me how to slip my toes and the front of my foot through a slit she'd made near the petal's end. Now, with the *pulpul* held by the ring around my shin and by the slit at the end, I could kick and catch the air just as Seela did. Even so, my first attempts at flight were anything but smooth. I kept kicking too hard or too soft and sending myself cartwheeling. Every so often my toes would slip out of one of the slits and the *pulpul* would go flapping. Seela was all around me, laughing and helping, and finally we managed to fly all the way to the great central waterglob and back.

There were other isolated fliers here and there on the flower-surface, so there really was not so much to fear from the villagers' seeing us. As we came back near our starting point, Seela began kicking outward toward the Earth's inner rind. I flew at her side. Now that we were farther from the flower, I could see the Central Anomaly again, with the soft pink lightning that pulsed and branched out to fill this whole huge hollow world. We stopped kicking and began to drift back inward to the flower, and now Seela's arms were around me and we kissed.

This was a moment I shall never forget—the two of us drifting through the mild, sweetly scented pinklit air, only we two, nearly naked, clasped tight to each other, Seela and Mason, our mouths pressed together—ah, the feel of her bold tongue, the taste of her smooth lips—it was then, at that moment, that Seela became forever my bride. All my nearly sixteen years of life I'd felt incomplete, not fully real, but now, with Seela, some profound lack in me was filled, some parched longing was finally watered.

"Seela."

"Mason."

We kissed most of the way back down and then landed on the cell where Seela had cut out the triangular hole. My knife was still lying there, stuck into the flowerstuff. It occurred to me to wonder what Eddie was up to.

There was no sign of him in our cell or in any of the six neighboring cells. We circled out to search the ring of twelve next-closer cells and the ring of eighteen next-closer cells after that. Halfway through the third ring, I noticed something: There was a pool of juice by one of the *juubes*, and scratched on to the cellwall near it were words. I recognized Eddie's writing. He'd been here, drinking *juube* juice and cutting words into the flower.

"Ichor. An ant I. Sweet confusion. Angels crowd about my head." There was more, not all legible. Evidently, he'd drunk enough of the *juube* juice to become intoxicated. The last words were, "I FEAR NOT!" Heartened by the *juube*, he'd gone to rejoin the flowerpeople.

Seela gave me a calming pat and motioned for me to follow her. First we went back to the starting cell and got my clothes. Seela used my knife to cut out a quarter of the *juube* seed she'd been drinking from earlier and gave me the huge slippery thing to carry. Then we set off away from the flower's center, but not in the direction of the village.

Within half an hour we'd reached a cell that seemingly she used for her home. This cell was out on the flower's very edge. It had a round window cut in one wall. I was frightened to hear someone in the next cell over, but she drew me in there and introduced me to an old man. Although I initially assumed he was her father, I would later learn that the flowerpeople had no concept of paternity. The old man was simply someone who'd grouped himself with Seela. She cut him a slice of *juube* seed; he wolfed it down and fell into a reverie. I realized how very tired I myself was. I followed Seela back into her own room, with its view out into the Hollow Earth. I ate some *juube*, too, and, soothed by its intoxication, dropped off to sleep.

# 11

## Inward!

MUCH LATER, I woke alone, feeling wonderfully rested. From where I lay, I could see out the window to the sea. Seela's room was the first safe haven I'd known since debarking the *Wasp* for the antarctic coast on Christmas Day . . . how many days ago? I'd passed a day on the beach and a day in the balloon, nearly two more days falling through the hole, another day getting down into the jungle, and a day getting out to the edge of this flower. If I'd slept as long as it felt like, today was likely New Year's Day, 1837.

Here in Baltimore, as I write this narrative in a rented room, it is my birthday, the second of February, 1850. We've had a bitter cold winter of it, Seela and I. We are very much in love. It is dawn; quite soon I must go to Ben's Good Eats to wait the breakfast shift. I'll be on duty till after dark. I long for a better life. My skin is paling steadily, so there is hope.

Though I was born in 1821, I am seventeen today, not twenty-nine. The cause of this discrepancy is that twelve years passed during the single hour that Seela and I were in the heart of

189

the Central Anomaly. Looking out from that frenzied zone, I saw the South Hole dim and brighten a full dozen times. For me, the New Year's Day of 1837 is as one month and *one* year ago, not *thirteen*.

When I woke that day, a melonlike drop of water, a square of flowerleather, and a slice of *juube* lay nearby. I drank the water and ate the flowerleather but forbore from eating of the jellylike *juube*. Its effects were too enervating. Instead, I took advantage of my isolation to get out my pistol and unload its four chambers, crumbling up the caked powder and spreading it out so that it might thoroughly dry. If I was to free Otha and Eddie, I might have to kill someone. While the powder dried, I leaned out the room's round window, looking things over.

I had a clear view down inward. I could see the green curve of our flower's underside, tesselated with rhomboidal green plates. Several miles off was a different vine, with a flower that was blue and orange where ours was white and yellow. Like ours did, it faced outward toward the Rind, and held a vast waterball cupped in its center. I wondered if people lived in that one, too.

Beyond the other flower, the jungle wall stretched further inward, finally giving way to sky. The air was so cluttered here that I could barely see the Central Anomaly, let alone the Hollow Earth's other side. This land's essential concavity was, however, apparent if I turned my gaze away from the jungle and gazed out across the sea.

Fruits, leaves, and debris drifted steadily inward from the jungle. Clouds drifted outward to sink into the sea—parts of it were covered by great fogbanks—while various-size drops of water came loose from the sea and the jungle and fell inward. Looking outward toward the ocean, I saw something that, by its very familiarity, surprised me most of all: a whale breaching.

Due to the distance, I was not at first sure that was what I really saw. But yes, it was a whole pod of whales, four huge right whales like the ones we'd seen cavorting south of Bouvet Island. Instead of falling back into the ocean, the whales beat their flukes against the air and made a slow progress inward, their great mouths spread wide to take in whatever fry they met. They were perfectly comfortable in the Hollow Earth's low gravity, and as mammals, they had no pressing need for water. I watched fascinated as the whales cleared out a volume of air that had earlier been dark with life. They ventured inward almost as far as I was—the zone where the Anomaly's slight attraction began to be somewhat too insistent—and then they turned flukes and beat their way back to sea.

My powder being now quite dry, I reloaded my gun and stuck it in my jacket, which I donned. I decided not to bother with my shirt, boots, or trousers, pulling on instead my *pulpuls*. I had underwear, I may add, to cover my privates. Seela had made off with my knife. Yesterday she'd been deeply impressed by the ease with which the steel blade could cut the *juube* seeds into managcable picccs.

I poked my head into the next cell to see what the old man who lived with Seela was doing, but he too was gone. Neatly arranged in one corner were the sum total of the pair's possessions: a few dozen small seashells, some gnarled bits of wood, a crystal, and the domed carapace of what might have been a tiny lobster. Each of these trinkets had a hole in it, natural or drilled, and they were threaded onto limp slender cords woven of plant fibers. The fibers crossed each other to form a mesh that held one of the baubles at each vertex. The joint treasury was like a net knotted out of the necklaces the flowerpeople wore. With the soft cell floor to sit or lie on, there was no need of furniture; with food all around, no eating utensils were required. I'd noticed two thorn-rapiers in here yesterday, but those were gone. Perhaps the two had gone to the village together. I resolved to follow. Rather than blundering through the cells again, I would fly. Not letting myself worry about it too much, I pushed out through the round window in Seela's room. My legs were sore from yesterday's exertions, but after a few kicks they felt all right.

I flew out along the vast curve of our flower's outer white

petals, over the petals, and across the flower's yellow center to the village. Striving to be inconspicuous without actively skulking, I landed a hundred feet from the village hexagon's edge and crept forward to peer down.

Blessedly, Jeremiah's corpse was gone. The villagers were wandering around sluggishly and at random, feeding on big slices of *juube* they had gotten from . . . Seela. She and the old man had set up a business at the edge of the hexagon; using my knife, she'd sectioned and brought in a number of quartered *juubes,* and now she was providing villagers with unlimited *juube* in exchange for the kinds of shells, crystals, and wood bits that the flowerpeople seemed to treasure. As I watched, a grinning man clumsily unknotted his necklace and drew off a large seed—bright red in color—which he gave Seela in exchange for a fresh slice. The old man's fingers busied themselves knotting the profits into the nodes of an intricate money net like the one I'd seen in his bedroom.

The powerful *juube* intoxication had calmed the villagers, and they seemed nowhere so fearsome as yesterday. Yet the memory of Jeremiah made their calm all the more terrible. Across the hexagon, I could see Quaihlaihle and Otha sitting face to face in a decorated cell. Eddie mingled freely with the villagers. He was reeling drunk. Arf was sleeping on the ground near where I lay. The flowerpeople were terrible, but could there not be a place among them for me?

"Ssst. Arfie!"

He sat up, sniffed, and looked my way. It was a joy to see his long, toothy grin. I hopped down and embraced him. If I stuck close to Arf, then surely the flowerpeople would do me no harm.

This hope proved all too true. For the next four months I became, in effect, Arf's servant. I was expected always to be near him, and if I were seen to neglect petting and cozening him for any significant length of time, I would be bullied and poked. I came to know his body as well as my own, and his smell became so much a part of my hands that it was unpleasant to bring them near my face. The noise Arf made when drinking water was a particular wonder to the flowerpeople. During their frequent feasts, they would serve Arf water that was set on a stretched petal, it being my job to keep the petal tight. The taut membrane amplified the sound of his slurping. Everyone would listen raptly. When Arf finished drinking, Quaihlaihle would drink, and then Otha, and then the rest of us.

Otha of course found our role reversal vastly amusing. "Curry dat dog dere, Marse Mase," he'd call to me with a chuckle. "An' be quick about it. Seem like dere a speck down dar on his toe, boy. Shine dat right off!" He was prince consort; I was a dog's groom. The sheer absurdity of the situation kept me from taking it very much to heart. The overriding fact that I was living with the woman I loved made everything easy.

For his part, Eddie got on well enough. Now and then some of the women would force him to engage in sex with them, though he misliked it greatly. His very reluctance served to goad these savage women to take ever more scandalous liberties. Aside from that, Eddie's life was peaceful. Like me, he abandoned all clothing but jacket and breechcloth, using the jacket to hold those few possessions he still had—paramount among them Virginia's teeth.

He drugged himself regularly with *juube* and, sober or not, passed much of his time writing. Ink and paper had he none: He wrote by scratching with a thorn on the flower walls. The impermanence of this medium troubled him not, for once he'd achieved some lines that he deemed acceptable, he memorized them. His work in progress was an epic poem describing our journey, metered and rhymed for ease of recall. He recited it to me from the start once every few days, and indeed many of his felicitous phrasings have found their way into this, my own narrative.

I found myself getting to like Eddie as a friend. Eddie, Otha, and I were all learning a few words of the flowerpeople's tongue, but anything like a long conversation with, say, Seela was impossible. Instead of an elegant flow, communication with a flowerperson was like the passing back and forth of small smudged tokens. Water, Arf, Shellsquid, Me, Flowerleather, *Juube,* You, Fly, Hungry, Queen, Love . . . the same simple images over and over. In contrast to this, Eddie's speech was, as always, a fount of elegant expression and bold ideas.

He spoke to me often of his distress that he was not back on Earth's surface consolidating his literary reputation. The theme of the double obsessed him, and he had a notion (quite accurately prescient, as events would prove) that there existed some MirrorEddie or AntiEddie who even now was taking advantage of all the groundwork Eddie had laid. "My style is his," Eddie said. "And more than that, my myth and my legend. After my work at *The Southern Literary Messenger,* are not my name and character familiar to every cultured American? Have I not made myself into an elemental force of our national literature? And now here am I, living among analphabetic savages with no intellectual companion but a farmboy!"

I attacked him on the last point, and he grudgingly allowed that due to my innate literary gifts and to my habit of wide reading from earliest childhood on, I am nothing like what the word *farmboy* suggests. To lift his spirits, I suggested flatteringly that due to my association with him, I was in fact becoming an ever more highly educated man.

Eddie was above all interested in what lay inside the Central Anomaly. The more we stared at it, the more confusing it became. The huge pink sparks or discharges that lit up the Hollow Earth all ran through the Anomaly, and the air there was filled with glinting blue lights. Otha told us that Quaihlaihle said that she had come from the Anomaly. This was one of the reasons the flowerpeople honored her so. For them, the Hollow Earth's vast center was a region of terrible awe, a land for the gods and the dead. Quaihlaihle said she'd come from a black tribe of the "gods" near the center; she said she'd been carried outward to us by some huge creature, which she called a *koladull*. Supposedly, she'd originally been black-skinned, but out here she'd faded to white. Otha was eager to meet the black tribe in the Hollow Earth's sky, and he supported Eddie's plans to go to the Anomaly.

The flowerpeople's fears of the sky were not unfounded. A major sticking point in any plan to go further inward was the great danger of being eaten by a shellsquid during the long fall to the center. During the four months we spent on the flower, several flowerpeople fell prey to the marauding ammonoids, or *ballula*, as they called them. At unpredictable intervals, one of the creatures would appear and drag its tentacles over the flower, feeling for prey. As it was easy to see and hear the monsters coming, those who fell prey were generally ill or intoxicated. Of course, one always took care not to sleep in the open. But what could we do if a shellsquid appeared during our proposed tumble to the Anomaly? No immediate answer presented itself, and we lingered on.

Other than chanting and drumming, the only creative activity the flowerpeople engaged in was the weaving of nets. Some of these creations were quite remarkable. Made of long fibers from the stem of our flower, they grew irregularly to immense size, with individually designed patches branching off here and there like rigging. Sometimes these nets were left undecorated, to be used as seines to trap a school of airshrimp, which were then eaten raw. Other times the giant weaves were decorated with various organic trinkets and set floating as airy ballrooms in which the tribe could dance about. As well as the communally made nets, each individual or living group had its own treasure net, to which they attached the bits of shell, bone, plant, or mineral that they particularly valued.

As on Earth, the most acute source of danger was other people.

The nearest tribe to ours lived on the blue-petaled flower that I'd noticed New Year's Day. These flowerpeople were in every respect similar to ours, save that their garments were blue and orange rather than white and yellow. Now and then, a few people would fly from one flower to the other for a change in flowerleather and *juube,* also to swap baubles and to look for mates. Generally, only the unhappiest and least attractive members of our tribe consented to join the blueflowers. Our tribe took great pride in having Quaihlaihle as queen, Otha as king, and Arf as mascot. The blueflowers had nothing so grand, so I suppose that a conflict was inevitable.

The war started quite suddenly. We were sitting around the hexagon talking and eating. I'd just held the taut petal for Arf to drink, and Quaihlaihle was feeding him some airshrimp. There was a noise from above, and suddenly a party of twenty blue-clad men and women flew down, long thorns at the ready. Before I could really do anything, someone had kicked me in the head and seized Arf. Two others got hold of Otha, who was sluggish from *juube.* Quaihlaihle quickly killed one of her attackers, but then, terribly, someone stabbed her in the neck.

"Run!" screamed Eddie, tugging at me. I hesitated, but Seela was running too, so I followed them into the cells. A minute later the raid was over. Arf and Otha were gone; Quaihlaihle lay dead.

Our flowerpeople began a feverish process of mummification and sky burial. They wrapped Quaihlaihle from head to toe in a money net, and then in petals, sealing them tight with a strong-smelling mixture of nectar and sap. The idea seemed to be that by working quickly enough, they could pass her body off as some kind of seedpod; the plant juices would cover any carrion smell that might lead the harpies or shellsquid to eat her. Two hours after Quaihlaihle died, she was launched. Four of her most faithful subjects flew her so far inward that they shrank to dots; they released her and flew slowly back, a tribal member chanting through the great reverberator tube all the while.

*"Ahmani tekelili embogolo,"* said Seela. She is returning to the black gods.

The funeral over, it was time for revenge. We cut ourselves

strong fresh *pulpul* fins and picked out the sharpest thorn-rapiers we could find. I drew my gun and checked my powder by firing a test shot off into the air. Seela and the flowerpeople were mightily impressed; I would be an important member of our war party.

The reader may wonder at my willingness to risk my life in a dispute among savages, but you must realize how deeply the life on the flower had begun to bore me. *Juube* intoxication was an ever-present temptation, and I had to struggle to keep from falling into the bad habits of Eddie and Pa. I'd already examined and categorized all the dozens of creatures that lived here; I'd tasted the delights of love to satiation; and I'd worn out my brain with facts from Eddie. Now I was happy to have something exciting to do.

As one of the more agile flowerpeople, Seela was in the war party, too. I was surprised when Eddie insisted he come as well. Was it his hunger for experience to write about? In a way, yes: I would soon see that Eddie's aim was to turn our attack on the blueflowers into a safe passage to the Central Anomaly. But for the moment he told us only that he had an idea for an ingenious engine of war.

At Eddie's direction, we gathered fifty of the flowerpeople's sharpened shellknives and knotted them into one of our precious silk ropes. The flowerpeople were clever at weaving; in a short time, the knives were arranged in a tight spiral along the rope's axis, blades angling out. Eddie now revealed the elegance of his plan, and we cheered.

Twoscore flowerpeople set off with Seela, Eddie, and me, kicking across the sky toward the hated blue petals. Everyone seemed more animated than ever before. I had a moment of vertigo when we were midway between flowers—what if a shell-squid should come for us here? But I had little time to worry, for the blueflowers saw us coming and a squad of them came rapidly kicking out to meet us.

I fired a gunshot to frighten them, and then, while our rapiers engaged theirs, Eddie, Seela, and I flew inward past the blue petals and lighted on the vine on which the flower grew. No one bothered us. We found the thinnest part of the flower's stem and set to work pulling our bladed rope back and forth like a team of loggers manning a double-handled saw. The plant stuff was tough, but slowly we made progress. Great quantities of sap oozed forth, lubricating our cut. In the distance, the airbattle raged on with screams and savage yells. As the stem weakened, the great blue flower gradually nodded away from the ocean and toward the planet's attractive center. We sawed like possessed souls. The flower turned more and then, with a great, leisurely rending, tore free. Slowly, slowly, it began drifting away from the vine and inward!

We caught our breath, rolled up the bladed rope, and flew out to where the battle had been. Disheartened by seeing disaster overcome their home, the blueflower warriors were in full rout. Our rapiers surged after them, stabbing and killing, and taking the dead warriors' necklaces. Figure after figure came swarming out of the blue flower, looking for a place to go. Back on our flower, a batallion of defenders stood ready to demand fealty of all who came to beg for mercy.

"Quick," said Eddie to me. "Let's get inside the blue flower and ride it all the way to the center of the Earth!"

"That's why you had us saw it off!" I gasped.

"Of course. We can't hang here forever, Mason. We've got to press on! My dreams have told me. We'll go through the Central Anomaly and back to Earth . . . or MirrorEarth. Come!"

"All right," I assented. In the fever of the moment, I was ready for any adventure. "Let's get aboard."

The open skies of the Hollow Earth held such terror for the flowerpeople that none of them wanted to stay on the falling blue flower. Scores of the blueflower tribespeople kicked up past us as we made for their home. Seela seemed unsure what we were doing, but I urged her on. We wriggled through the falling flower's blue petals and kicked across its orange face. A last few stragglers were leaving the face. The flower would have been wholly deserted, but there, tied to the ground of the empty village hexagon, were two lone figures: Otha and Arf.

We touched down next to them. With the flower in free fall, there was no force to hold one to it; indeed, given that the fluttering blue flower fell more slowly than a person, one had to keep kicking upward to stay at its surface. Once we'd cut Arf and Otha free, we made our way into one of the flower's cells. As the flower was pointing inward, we came to rest on the soft leathery ceiling of the cell. Arf had grown very fond of me during my period of servitude to him, and he was inordinately glad to see me.

Otha immediately understood Eddie's plan: We'd ride the flower all the way to the center, the flower a ship to keep us safe from shellsquid. Otha was eager to meet the fabled black folk who lived in the Htraean sky. But Seela was in a frenzy to be out of the falling flower and back up to the zone she came from. The falling and the sky filled her with a terror as great as what we'd felt when the antarctic plain gave way beneath us. I held her tight, trying to calm her. She clawed my face and got loose. Before she was out of reach, I tore off her *pulpuls* to keep her from flying away. She ripped a sheet of petal out of the wall that separated our cell from the hexagon, wriggled out the hole, and tried to flap her way into the sky with the scrap of flowerleather she held. All she managed to do was to fall a small distance inward from us. I stuck my head out the hole she'd made and stared up at her. Her smooth face was wet with tears, and she was screaming about *ballula*.

After we'd fallen another half hour, Seela accepted that there could be no escaping, though she was still furious at Eddie and me. Otha kicked out and brought her back aboard. The flower fell and fell, the air beating hard against us. Eddie above all found our plight romantic and wandered feverishly among the blueflowers' deserted dwelling cells. He told us a long tale about the legendary abandoned ship *The Flying Dutchman*, taking a ghoulish necrophiliac pleasure in his detailed evocation of a lifeless, floating ship. We each ate several big slices of a *juube* that Seela found. I tried to interest her in sex, but she spurned me. Depressed and worried, I ate more *juube* and sank into a daze.

Quite some time later I was brought to sensibility by Seela's cries of warning. A giant *ballula* shellsquid was about to attack. The *ballula* was a large one, easily a quarter the size of the blue blossom we hid in. Having expelled enough hydrogen to ballast itself to our speed, it rapidly fastened its whole mass of tentacles to our hexagon. I should have fled with the others into the flower's far recesses, but the *ballula* so terrified and fascinated me that I stayed glued to my spot on the ceiling of the ripped cell at the hexagon's edge, air whistling in at me. The treacherous *juube* made my plight comfortable and interesting, and to be honest, it gave me a perverse, fatalistic delight to have refused Seela's tearful entreaties that I come away to safety.

I could see the *ballula*'s basilisk eye not ten yards distant, but it didn't seem to see me. Between its eyestalks was a long, tapering fleshflap, a kind of nose one might say. Beneath the noseflap was the inhuman beak. Quantities of saliva streamed from the beak's serrations. Ranged tight around the beak were ruffled palps, and beyond the palps were the ninety-odd orange tentacles, smooth as kelpstems, some of them two hundred feet long. The sensitive tentacles whipped and fumbled, forcing their way into cell after cell, feeling and tasting for human flesh. Ultimately, a tentacle entered my cell. I lay motionless staring as the tapering fleshy limb palpated floor, walls, and finally ceiling. When the feeler slapped across my face my trance broke. The grooves and ridges of the limb sensed me immediately, and the tip of the feeler began to wrap around my neck. Remembering Peters, I took out his knife and cut a yard of the feeler tip off. The whole tentacle jerked back sharply, and there was a greedy, rapid beating as the *ballula* fastened its face to my cell. The beak tore through the thin flowerleather; a cruel gray eye appeared. Finally galvanized, I screamed floridly and dove for one of the cell's exit holes. A tentacle caught my ankle, but I cut that one off too.

Moving as fast as I could, I hurried through a random succession of two dozen cells, only to find myself with Eddie, Otha, Seela, and Arf. Seela grabbed me and gave me a kiss.

"Mason done made dat *ballula* hungry," said Otha.

"Hssst," said Eddie, white with fear. "The utmost silence is required."

The *ballula* tore at our flower for a few more minutes, ripping out the ceilings of many of the cells. Not finding us, it backed off and sped at our flower, ramming it heavily. The shock split our cell's ceiling and the wind sent us flying out like salt crystals from a shaker, one dog and four people, tumbling down with the huge blue flower. There would be no time to kick back to safety. The great nautilus was too close. Otha flung his bowie knife at the creature—to no effect. Remembering my gun, I drew it and fired its last two shots at the *ballula,* but managed neither to puncture its shell nor to hit any spot that was vital. The bullets disappeared into its furious orange flesh like stones into water. My mind raced as the great beak approached.

I'd stolen the pistol from Lucy Perrow's father in Lynchburg, shot the stableboy with it at the Liberty Hotel, pawned and redeemed it with Abner Levy in Richmond, threatened Eddie with it in Norfolk, recharged it on the *Wasp,* dried the powder in Seela's flowercell, and now all in one day I'd used up its last four shots . . . for nothing. Cursed weapon!

I flung it into the *ballula*'s maw with all my strength, giving the beast a moment's pause. And that would have been the end of me, only now there came a roaring noise as of a huge bonfire. By the time I'd turned to look for the source of the noise, it was upon us, a huge dark shape with flame trailing from it. A beast of some kind, with an upturned mouth wide open in rage. The vast *ballula* twitched galvanically at the sight of the thing and drew in its tentacles preparatory to jetting away. But before it could escape, its giant enemy was upon it. Borne on a flaming jet of gas, the intruding creature flashed forward, seized the *ballula*'s bunched soft parts, and yanked the struggling squid right out of its shell.

A moment later the flaming beast was gone. The fleeting glance I had of the furious creature gave me the impression of a giant pig's head mounted on a body curved and segmented like a shrimp's. To have a name for it, I called it a shrig, even after Seela told me that her tribe called it a *koladull*. I would have liked to examine the empty *ballula* shell, but it was quite some distance from us, propelled by leaking gas. We got back into the shelter of our battered blossom and fell uneventfully for another few hours, now and then sticking our heads out to look around.

And what did we see? Though the air of the Hollow Earth is thick and cloudy in spots, we could see a great deal. Outward from us was the hole we'd come through and the hole's surrounding jungle. Hard by the jungle was a great inner sea stretching nearly a third of the way around the inner Htraean surface. At the edges of the sea were two huge continents, and beyond these continents another ocean. All lines of sight that passed too close to the center were confused, but by and large the arrangement of land and water bore a rough resemblence to the patterning of Earth's outer surface.

As we were off to one side, we couldn't see through the South Hole. It occurred to me to try and see if there was a North Hole, but the confusion at the planet's center obstructed my view.

As we neared the twentieth hour of our fall, the appearance of the planet's center changed drastically. Though we were falling more slowly than before, the center seemed to grow faster than ever, swollen by some miragelike trick of space and light. The blue dots near the center could soon be seen to be immense floating waterglobs, jiggling irregularly. Otha dubbed them the Umpteen Seas. The seas were arranged upon a spherical shell of space in which gravitational equilibrium apparently obtained. There were about fifteen of them. I suppose the average Umpteen Sea held the volume of one of our Great Lakes or of Lake Geneva. The region within the spherical shell occupied by the Umpteen Seas remained visually indecipherable. It was brightly lit, with some stable dark objects and a curious lensing effect about the center, as if a spherical mirror were located there. This was the region whence the continual pink light-tendrils emanated. Something in the tight wrapping of space near here made me think of a skittles spindle. Out near the Htraean surface all was flat and comprehensible, yet here, near the Anomaly, things were tight and warped as on the girth of a spinning spindle's stuttering tip. As we fell closer to the Umpteen Seas, the inner anomalous zone began looming so insanely large that most of the Htraean surface was eclipsed. Whichever way I looked, save directly outward, I saw nothing but the jiggling seas, the blotched inner sphere, and the rubbish around us.

So near their source, the pink lightstreamers were as all-pervasive as waves in the sea. Each of the streamers heated its own river of air, creating winds that buffeted our blossom this way and that. The air around was filled with other items that had fallen inward from Htrae—stones, twigs, bits of earth, dead animals, excrement. There were flocks of birds feeding indiscriminately on the objects that fell in. Most of the birds were like fist-size hummingbirds, pretty and quite harmless. There were also a few larger creatures that were not quite birds. These beasts, which Eddie told me resembled Earth's extinct pterodactyls, had scaly skin instead of feathers and huge serrated beaks that were balanced by conelike projections from the back of their heads.

Largest of all were the shrigs, present in great numbers. They ranged in size from cow to whale. Small shrigbirds hopped around on their hides, eating parasites. Beating their fantails and their tiny winged legs, the shrigs fed continually, not hesitating to gulp in boulders as well. Their mouths were long lipless slits, edentate snouts that seemed always to be smiling. It was hard to identify these pacific feeders with the creature who'd so savagely handled the *ballula*. Their segmented, hollow bodies grew more distended as they ate. They ate not by chewing but by engulfing and swallowing whole. They made a resonant grunting sound as they swallowed. I later learned that when a shrig was quite full, it would convert much of its food to flaming methane, which it would spew forth in order to fly, cometlike, up to one of the Htraean colonies where it roosted.

A horde of shrigs fell upon our flower and began chewing it to bits. Inevitably, one of their snouts appeared in our cell. Seela poked it with her thorn and it moved away. Even so, after another half hour, they had so eaten into our flower that they became a real nuisance. A large shrig actually bit onto Eddie's legs, but we were able to pull him from the shrig's toothless maw before its powerful peristalsis had moved Eddie into the shrigian gut.

We decided to abandon the blue flower and kick off for the Umpteen Seas on our own. We checked our *pulpuls* and flew out into the air. As long as we remained quite strenuously active, the grazing shrigs were unlikely to eat us. As omnivores, they preferred the simplicity of ingesting motionless things. But this meant that if we were to sleep while falling through their zone, they would surely eat us. The lion-size pterodactyls were also a cause for some worry. We turned ourselves head inward and began kicking in gravity's aid.

A particularly powerful lightriver flowed past, bouncing me off the parasite-ridden hairy hide of a nearby shrig. The creature twitched irritably and snapped its tail to move away. Eddie and Seela were nearby, as was Otha, who carried Arf in his arms. We moved steadily inward toward the Umpteen Seas. The gravity gradient was gentle as it had been in the stagnant zone near the end of the South Hole. It took real work to keep moving inward, but at least the shrigs were thinning out.

As we progressed the air grew brighter and clearer, and I began to feel a rising sense of joy, coupled with an intense sense of affection for my companions. Quite spontaneously we broke into song—a familiar song of the flowerpeople. I'd never been able to get the words straight, but now, all of a sudden, the lyrics poured out of my mouth as if Seela herself were moving my lips. Singing her words, I understood Seela better than ever before. She was more than a beautiful exotic female, she was a person just like me. We sang on, and now our words were Otha's; we were singing a lullaby that Turl had used to sing. I felt such union with Otha, and then, as the song changed into Eddie's poem, I felt an acceptance and love for Eddie that I'd never had before. I could tell him anything, and indeed I did, letting my thoughts race out into my own song that somehow all the others could sing just as fast and as feelingly as I. Even Arf shared in this mysterious mental union; looking at him, I could actually sense the thoughts and emotions of Arf—the worshipful friendliness he felt toward me, his interest in our flight, his hunger for the meat of a shrig, and under it all, a boundless volume of what can only be called *slack*. No carking, swinking workaday worries for Arf the slacker, most truly himself when asleep in a patch of sun.

The streamers coming out from behind the seas were narrow and strong, leaving sharp wakes of heated air. The nearest sea had a big island in it, a turfy ball of dirt whose volume was perhaps one fourth that of the water. Small black human figures moved where the island met its sea. They spotted us, and one of the black gods came moving up.

He had *pulpuls*, but he also had a shiny platform to stand upon. It was like a rounded-off plank or board. The purpose of the board became clear when he managed to station himself in the moving forked crotch of one of the pink lightstreamers passing by. The slightly cupped underside of his board caught the hot airwave, and he rode up at us like a man in a lift. He leaned back on his board to deftly exit the wave a hundred feet off from us. It was easy to identify with his movements; it was as if his mind grew clearer to me as he approached. There were to be none of the communication difficulties we'd had with Seela's flowerpeople—for the boardrider seemed to address us in perfect English.

"Greetings," he said civilly, kicking his way over to us. His *pulpuls* were wider than ours and seemed to be made of leather. The lightriding board, which he now carried like a shield, was of polished shell. "Congratulations for completing your journey! We are honored to have so brilliant a guest as an Edgar Allan Poe. Mason Reynolds, we salute your efforts in bringing your party here. Seela, *dmbagolo laaa nuinullee orbaahm*. And, Otha, bro', we be hopin' you stay here fo' good.''

It was peculiar how understandably he could speak to each of us—even more peculiar was the fact that when he talked, his face and lips did not move.

"Yes, Mason," said he, catching my thought. "We black gods are mindreaders. The Great Old Ones have provided us with this and many other skills. Come down to our land and share our blessings." The words came as a silent torrent borne on his gaze.

"Do you hear too, Eddie?" I asked.

Eddie nodded. "What do you call yourself?" he called to the black figure.

The answering syllables formed themselves full-grown in my mind. "We are all one. We are tekelili."

# 12

## Tekelili

WE ARE TEKELILI. This was the constant theme of our time in the region of the Umptccn Seas. So long as any person is there, that person is tekelili.

Most simply, Tekelili is the name used by the black gods for themselves as a tribe—a tribe to which any fortunate visitor to Earth's center belongs. But *tekelili* has a more specific denotation.

The true Tekelili are the awesome beings who live in the heart of the Central Anomaly. It is in honor of these wondrous creatures, also known as the Great Old Ones, that the black gods call themselves Tekelili. They do this in the same heraldic way that a tribe of snakehandlers might call itself Cobra.

The Great Old Ones are, by virtue of their habitat and nature, deeply connected with the third meaning of *tekelili*, this being "imbued with a mental and emotional state of the utmost compassion and understanding." If I can tell you truly I am tekelili, then I can read your mind.

While I was tekelili, I could sense directly the thoughts of all beings around me—aphids, shrigs, people, black gods, Arf, the

Great Old Ones themselves. In immediate practice it meant that
I was ever aware of each nuance of everyone's feelings. Note
well that this tekelili sensitivity worked not merely on the emo-
tive level but also on the abstract and purely intellectual levels,
even to the point where is someone happened to think of a number, I would know what the number was . . . and they would
know that I knew, and I would know *this,* on and on to the point
where, as the black gods said, *"We are all one."* We were all
tekelili, living there at the very throat of the maelstrom, between
the twin worlds, surrounded by the vasty mentation of the mighty
Tekelili beings whose cosmic thoughtstream flowed profound
and unquenchable as a river upon which our thoughts were small
eddies.

Our Eddie Poe talked to them most of all; it is thanks only
to having absorbed the conversations between him and the Tekelili that I understand the geography of the region of the Umpteen
Seas and the Central Anomaly sufficiently well to attempt describing it here.

Suppose that at the Hollow Earth's center there were a large
shiny ball. Outside this mirrorball would be the Umpteen Seas,
the Inner Sky, then Htrae, the thick planetary Rind, and, beyond
the Rind, the Earth I came from and its outer sky with Sun,
Moon, and Stars. Suppose that all of this were reflected in the
central mirrorball, so that staring into the mirror one could see
Umpteen MirrorSeas, an Inner MirrorSky, a MirrorHtrae, a MirrorRind and, beyond the MirrorRind (were the MirrorRind
transparent), a MirrorEarth beneath an outer MirrorSky with Mir-
rorSun, MirrorMoon, and MirrorStars. Imagine all this and then
imagine that the central ball is no mirror at all but simply a
window between two worlds—an open airy window. This is what
is true.

Or again, compare the human race to a race of waterstriders
darting about on the surface of a sea that they take to be the
World. Suppose that the striders cannot dive; nor can they jump
off the surface any more than we can leave our space. Now

suppose that on the sea's surface is a floating wooden ring. Hydrologic tension makes it easy for the striders to cling to the ring's outer edge. They find food on the ring; also do they lay their eggs there—they call it Home. We are like them, living in comfort on Earth, the outer part of the hollow shell that is our planet. Drawing the simile further, suppose that a group of striders finds a small gap in the ring; they wriggle through and explore the ring's inner edge, Emoh. Understand that these striders are like our party, pushing through Symmes's Hole to reach Htrae.

Were our Hollow Earth to hold nothing but empty air, it would be as if the waterstriders' Home ring held simple flat water. But what if the ring's center holds a maelstrom—a cylindrical tapering vortex tube on whose walls the spiders can move about? And what if, like a cake of ice, the worldsea has a lower surface as well as an upper surface; that is, what if our space has two sides? And be these hypotheses allowed, what follows?

For the waterstriders, the lower surface is an unattainable MirrorWorld parallel and distinct from their own World. I say unattainable? Not quite. It is a law of nature that any vortex pushes on till it meets a boundary. Therefore, the smooth, airy throat of the ring's central maelstrom leads down through the cosmic waters, opening out to blend smoothly with the lower surface known as MirrorWorld. To complete the analogy, one must only imagine that on the mirrorsurface there floats a mirror ring on whose inner MirrorEmohan edge our intrepid waterstriders may rest themselves before finding their way out through the mirror ring to a MirrorHome.

I fix the image and draw a first conclusion. The waterstriders live as two-dimensional beings; for them the world is a surface; and the boundary between their World and MirrorWorld is a circle around the narrowest point of the connecting vortex's throat. Therefore for us, who live as three-dimensional beings in a world of space, the boundary between World and MirrorWorld is a sphere. And it is this Central Sphere's surface that comprises the Central Anomaly to be found at the core of the Hollow Earth.

The Earth is hollow. Inside it, about its geographical center, there is a small spherical zone: the Anomaly. Inside this sphere is another universe, by and large a mirror image of Earth's. Though seemingly squeezed, the mirroruniverse does not feel cramped. Indeed, the citizens of MirrorEarth believe that they are outside the Anomalous sphere and that *Earth* is inside. Who is correct? Both and neither.

The reconciliation of the paradox lies in the fact that, for a person directly on the surface of the spherical Anomaly, the sphere looks flat, like a plane, with jiggling Umpteen Seas and MirrorSeas all around, and with, if one looks out of the plane, Htrae on one side and MirrorHtrae on the other. I know, for I was there. Let me give off theorizing and tell how I got there.

As I said, we were greeted by a black god who rode a lighttube's energywave up to us, and when Eddie asked him what he called himself, he replied, "We are all one. We are tekelili."

"Sho'," said Otha. "But whut you *name*?"

Instead of giving us a word, the man gave us a personal totem image, a stylized picture of himself on his board riding a giant forked lightstream. From then on, when I wanted to refer to him, I had only to think of this image and all the tekelili people there would know what I meant. To write of him here, I'll say his name was Lightrider.

Lightrider came closer to us, radiating interest and goodwill. He was naked, save for his leather *pulpuls* and a woven leather thong wound around his narrow waist. A dagger of polished shell was clipped to the plait. He had long limbs, and his skin was coal-black from head to toe. He had a straight nose, thin lips, and large gleaming eyes. His teeth were red, like Elijah's and Quaihlaihle's. He reached out and touched each of us in turn: Eddie, Otha, Seela, Arf, and me. He wanted to know our names. Feeling his query, each of us said our name and thought an image that, thanks to tekelili, all could perceive.

Eddie's picture was of himself standing, holding a sheaf of handwritten papers and reading aloud. Writer.

Otha's image was of himself in good clothes with an admiring woman (Juicita?) pressed up against him. Lover.

Seela's picture showed her back home, getting the flowerpeople to give her trinkets for *juube*. Trader.

Arf's image was nonvisual; it was a simple distillation of his smell and his bark. Arf!

I hesitated before saying my name and forming a picture of myself. What, after all, was I? A bookworm? A farmboy? An explorer? Seela's man? As I said, "Mason," a terrible image appeared quite unbidden: the image of me in Lynchburg, gold in one hand, gun in the other, turning to fire back toward the stableboy. Killer-thief.

There was no use to try and change it, and no need to apologize. The whole story was written on my brain for all to see. While I still agonized, Lightrider showed us an image of his home, a green land mass stuck to one of the Umpteen Seas. He set off toward it, bidding us follow him. Kicking with a will, the others flew after him, silently chattering and marveling at the portals that tekelili had opened. Sensing my hesitation, Seela beamed love and forgiveness back to me. I followed.

The closer we got to the Umpteen Seas, the deeper did we venture into the spindle or throat of the spacebridge that stretches between the worlds. Earlier I'd been able to see Htrae in every direction, but now, unless I looked back outward over my shoulder, most lines of sight led to a jiggling sea. The seas danced like slowed-down versions of the bucketsful of water that, on idle boyhood afternoons, Otha and I sometimes used to slop high into the sunny air to watch. Straight inward, past the seas, was the Central Anomaly, a mystery of dark shapes and pink light.

The sea that Lightrider steered us toward must have been fifteen miles long. Just now it was shaped more or less like a giant foot, oblong and somewhat flattened, with a round grassy chunk of island stuck to one end like a heel. But no configuration of an Umpteen Sea lasted long. As we approached, the watery foot stretched, pinched off a toeglob as big as a city, and then rebounded, forming a kind of huge eyeball with the island as pupil. A little later, another sea's cast-off waterglob splashed into Lightrider's sea and set it shivering from side to side. Washes of water swept across the green island.

"How can you live there without drowning?" Eddie asked Lightrider.

"We sleep in the air, mostly," he said (or thought), forming an image of black gods hanging in midair with their slack arms out in front of them like rabbits' paws. "Land's just a place to meet."

The closer to the island we got, the harder we had to kick. Though the gravitational gradient still pointed inward, it was weakening greatly. Evidently, the seas rolled about in a gravitational trough just this side of the Central Anomaly, or Central Sphere. The Sphere was clearer now, by the way. It was tiled with huge, slipperlike dark shapes dotted with points from whence the pink lightstreamers issued. Streamers must have extended to the Sphere's interior as well, because the cracks between the dark shapes were very bright.

But again, unless I looked directly inward or directly outward, I saw nothing but Umpteen Seas, the real ones nearby and mirages of them more distant. Two black figures flew up from Lightrider's home island. Like him, they were naked and tekelili, and like him they were glad to see us. One, a woman, imaged herself as Shrighunter. Her totem showed her grinning by the huge dead body of a throatless shrig.

Answering our questioning thoughts, she explained that when searching for meat and skins, the black gods would fly or lightride out to the zone of the shrigs and kill one. There was no tekelili so far from the Central Sphere, so killing a shrig did not cause the intense mental agony that it might down in the Umpteen Seas, where catching and killing even a fish was rackingly unpleasant. Shrighunter's method for killing a shrig was ingenious. Holding her knife at the ready, she would draw a big breath and lie still in the path of one of the indiscriminately omnivorous beasts. Likely as not, the creature would gum her down into its maw. Once she was there, she'd cut her way out, severing the shrig's throat as she did so. Shrig meat was very good, she assured us, and all the black gods' *pulpuls* and braided ropes were made of shrigskin.

The second black god was a man whose personal totem was hard to decipher. It showed him surrounded by pink light and by irregular green-brown bulks, still and calm, with the distant Umpteen Seas whirling around at insane speed. One might call him Watcher. He was an imposing man. In strong gravity he might have seemed stubby-limbed and overly fat, but floating here, he looked solid and magnificent. He asserted that he'd been living in this region for three thousand years.

Year was, of course, not the exact concept that he used, tied as it is to our surfacedwellers' image of a planet circling a distant sun. The expression he used meant something more like summer or shrig-feeding season. But peering deeper into Watcher's mind, I could discern that the black gods' operative definition of a year was equivalent to our own, as I will explain later. Lightrider and Shrighunter were in awe of Watcher—he was a mythical figure, with them but rarely, bearing firsthand knowledge of the history of the black gods' race. He'd achieved his great age by periodically entering a curious zone of slow time near the Central Anomaly. Each generation of black gods had the Watcher among them for but a few days. Somehow he'd known we were coming, and he'd emerged to see our arrival.

Shrighunter was well proportioned, and as we kicked along behind her, Otha stared at her buttocks and formed lustful thoughts that all of us could see. Here was an embarrassing aspect of mindreading. As if Otha had said something rude, I began thinking apology thoughts over Otha's passionate ones, even though I myself kept shooting glances at Shrighunter as well. Eddie's reaction to these emotions was curiosity and a kind of contempt at the idea of Negro sex. Seela wondered why I wasn't looking at her. The black gods laughed.

"Maybe later," Shrighunter thought to Otha. "You looks long and strong."

"Relax," Lightrider seemed to say to me. "There's no use trying to cover things up."

"What's wrong with black?" Watcher said to Eddie. "If you stay here awhile you'll be black, too."

Their sea was slowly stretching back into a footshape, leaving the grassy ball they called home mostly uncovered. We touched down on it where a flock of other black gods rested. A few of the region's iridescent hummingbirds hovered nearby. The island grass was waist-high and tangled, and bore small kernels of grain. It was relaxing to jam oneself into the grass and not always be floating away. The air was perpetually filled with pink streamers here, and their breezes dried the grass where the sea had wet it. Just as I landed, a lightstreamer ran right into me. Although it buffeted me about and made me feel hot and tingly, it did me no harm. The black gods thought welcoming thoughts and said that the light was a good omen.

Within five minutes of landing, I knew the members of the tribe of black gods a hundred times better than I'd gotten to know the flowerpeople during four months. How crude and brutal that old life seemed. I tried to keep this thought from Seela, but of course she saw it. Trying to cover a thought never had any effect but calling attention to it.

Coming to sit by me, Seela explained that I had never gotten to understand the flowerpeople's culture. Looking from inside her mind, I could now see that their language had myriads of poetic nuances I'd been deaf to. And the huge, useless trinket-bedecked nets they were forever knotting together—these, I suddenly grasped, these were the flowerpeople's art and literature! To my shock I next learned that till now, for her part, Seela had thought me a poor deprived savage from a distant small flower. Why else would I have known so little of knotting nets? All her friends had mocked her, she now told me, for taking a lowly captive slave as lover simply because she liked my looks. Yet all along she'd known I was good. And now she knew that I was smart. Her only surprise, she told me, was that Arf was so much less intelligent than I. Finally she could see the oddity of my four months' indenture to Arf, which all the flowerpeople had taken as being so obviously a matter of course.

"Dear Mason, you were very patient!"

"It was worth it, Seela, to be near you. Anyway, I like Arf."

Wedged into the grass at our feet, Arf grinned up at me, his light brown eyes mild and lively. "This is fun," he thought to me. "I'm glad. Is there food?"

The black gods had been listening in with interest, and now one of them sent Arf the image of a meaty baglike creature in the grass beneath his paws. Now that it was brought to our attention, we all could sense the thing. Seela called it a *woomo*. The *woomo* sensed us sensing it. Arf began to dig, and soon he had it. The tiny terror the dripping leather bag gave off was no worse, I suppose, than the screeches of a chicken on the chopping block. Yet the new tekelili intimacy of the sensation was unnerving. Arf dropped the *woomo* and took a step back.

"Here," called a black god who lounged near us. I'd already noticed his intense interest in Seela. His icon image showed him riding a lighttube and dipping a rack full of dead creatures' flesh into the heat. Smoker. He had a woven basket filled with dried meat, some of it shrig and some of it *woomo*. He gave Arf several pieces, laughing to share in Arf's doggy joy. Seela and I received some of the meat as well, as did Eddie and Otha. The shrig was like sweet pemmican, with the *woomo* both tougher and more jellylike. *"Woomo koladull tana'a goobaam!"* exulted Seela. She recognized both foods, from legend if not from actual contact. She said that the flowerpeople regarded them as the highest and rarest of delicacies: the equivalent, if you will, of our ambrosia. We ate the meats with the grasses' ripe grain, now and then tossing a scrap to the greedy hummingbirds.

I felt like a hero in heaven there, sitting with my loved one. The Sphere of the Central Anomaly loomed nearby like a giant sun. Oddly enough, it no longer pulled at us; we were in a gravitational equilibrium whence every direction was up. Here at this balance point I began to feel as if I could sense the very mind of God: busy, calm, and all-loving.

How was Eddie taking all this? He was overcome with a profound joy far beyond any mad ecstasy he'd ever dreamed to attain. By the time I contacted him, he knew so very much already. It was he who showed me the vast organ-chords of thought streaming from the Tekelili beings who made their home on the Central Anomaly. Sensing his appreciation, the great beings had directed a blazing bright river of pink light directly onto him. Of us explorers, only Eddie had the black gods' ability to channel the Great Old Ones' output into imaginable dimensions. Unaided, the complexity of their reality would have left me looking at my hand or wondering what there was to eat. With Eddie I could *see,* I could draw mentally near to the beings on the Anomaly, all the while taking in Eddie's commentary as directly as if he were whispering in my ear.

So what are they like, those buried Titans, those gods within the Earth? The answer is at first a surprise, almost cynically ridiculous, though Eddie explained to me that their appearance is a confirmation of what modern paleontological science might have predicted.

In fine, the Great Old Ones are huge *woomo,* watery bags similar to the creatures that sailors call *bêche-de-mer,* trepang, or sea cucumber. A zoologist would place them in the class Holothurioidea of the phylum Echinodermata, which means that the barrel-shaped holuthurians are cousin to such echinoderms as the starfish and the sea urchin.

So humble to see are the Lords of Creation.

I remembered hearing Bulkington and Captain Guy talk of *bêche-de-mer,* telling of how the earliest cruises to the Feejees had gathered hundreds of the creatures, which had then been dried in the sun or smoked over open fires on the beach. Sold in Canton, the best quality *bêche-de-mer* fetches ninety dollars a hundredweight. Their purchasers are voluptuaries who use the *bêche-de-mer* as a tonic and as an exotic delicacy, akin to birds'-nest soup. Bulkington had asserted that when set into hot water, a dried *bêche-de-mer* will permeate the fluid with so marvelous and slippery an edibility that a woman treated to a private dinner of such wonder will surely—but I lose my train of thought, I shy away from our universe's humble mystery: the Titans at world's end are graven not in Man's image, nay, nay, the Great Old Ones are ludicrous slippery sacks. Even so, let me now stress, their minds are clear, wise, and beautiful. Indeed, it was their minds whose emanations I had thought to be from God Almighty!

Examining three Great Old Ones in detail with Eddie, I found them to be enormous thick-walled meatbags proportioned, severally, like a rolling pin, like a Turkish hassock, and like a gourd. All three had flexible bodies that were deeply striated as a sea urchin's shell. The five longitudinal stripes that run along their bodies consist of warty bumps in double rows, the warts the size of small mountains. These warts resemble a starfish's tube-feet and are flexible and roughly cylindrical, with somewhat concave tops. The extremities of the great sea cucumbers' bodies are as two poles: cloacal and ingestive. The cloaca is a thick turned-in pucker, but from their ingestive ends the trepangs evert ten branching treelike limbs of enormous intricacy. The flexible branchings give them an appearance like sprouting yams. The oral fans are used for seining food from the air; each *bêche-de-mer* periodically drawing its branchings back into its mouth, there to consume what has accreted. The ten fans are taken in turn—as a child would suck its fingers.

The rows of warts are used for sensing and for communication. The Great Old Ones' major sensory mode, other than tekelili union, is *electric*. Each of the tubes of light that flows out in any direction from the Central Anomaly emanates from one of the swaying mesas on their hides. When I watched attentively, I could see how the skeins of light darting through the inner sky were like giant ghostly versions of the Tekelili beings' fans.

Apparently, the dual, mirrored spinning of Earth and MirrorEarth makes the Central Anomaly an endless source of electric fluid, and the giant holothurians use their tube feet to manipulate the continual discharge. Before he changed his mind about the Great Old Ones, Eddie took this to mean that our planet is a giant body, with the trepangs comprising a galvanically active central brain benevolently working for the greater union of the whole.

Of the Great Old Ones' inner nature I can give little more than my initial impression: They were calm, busy, and filled, I would say, with love for the world and for all the living things in it. The tekelili mindreading ability is an effect that seems to take its physical cause from the spatial constriction at the Central Anomaly. An equally odd physical effect obtaining at the throat of the bridge between the worlds is *timelessness*. Relative to a mind on the Central Anomaly, Earth and Htrae are moving with immense speed, yet so strong is the central tekelili that nothing goes unnoticed. I recall the words of a hymn—"A thousand ages in Thy sight, are like an evening gone." How to fit something so majestically great into my small mind . . . and how to tell it?

At the very peak of our first union with the Tekelili, Eddie and I were able to see out through them. I could see out through the Tekelili's all-probing eyes of light and into all of Earth, Htrae, MirrorEarth, and MirrorHtrae. I could sense each sentient creature, and as I felt for one who thought of me, I came in contact with dear Pa.

Pa was drunk. It was evening; he was standing in a hilltop graveyard, very sad. Through his eyes I could see the Lynchburg hills that held the Perrows' house, St. Paul's spire, and Sloat's Liberty Hotel. That was in the background, but in the foreground was a gravestone that said

Mason Algiers Reynolds
February 2, 1821 – May 1, 1836
"What Laughing Heart Has Died in Vain?"

Before the picture wholly dissolved in Pa's helpless tears, I called Eddie to share and verify the melancholy lines. Me dead on May 1, 1836, the very night I'd robbed Sloat and shot the stableboy?

Another mystery followed right away, for now Eddie drew me to a vision of his own: of himself and Virginia settled in New York City in a small house with Mrs. Clemm and two boarders. We saw through Eddie's eyes, we saw his delicate, ink-stained hands working at the ending of his novel-length sea-adventure. Now he squared together the manuscript and we could see the title page, which read: *The Narrative of Arthur Gordon Pym of Nantucket*. This other Eddie's gaze lifted from the paper to rest on happy Virginia, sitting by the window singing a lullaby to a kitten in her lap. A gentle spring sunset was in progress outside.

Me dead and Virginia alive? Yes, yes, but it was MirrorPa at MirrorMason's grave and MirrorEddie dreamily admiring his MirrorVirginia. These images came not from Earth but from MirrorEarth! Working together, Eddie and I moved our concentration to the line of force in the lightstream issuing from the tubefoot radially opposite from the one that had led us to MirrorLynchburg and MirrorGotham. Back, back, back to Earth.

Here things were very different. Pa thought of me still, but with disappointment and loathing. I was the killer-thief ne'er-do-well who had forever left town. After stealing the gold, murdering the stableboy, and becoming involved in a slave rebellion, I had gone on to counterfeit bank notes and take refuge on the high seas. Pa was drinking water on his porch at home. It was dusk, Luke and Turl were with him, and they were slowly talking about the lien on Pa's property and about the good times before the boys had gone.

I showed this to Eddie, too, and he showed me how on his Earth Mrs. Clemm was back in Baltimore, alone to wonder and to grieve.

While the Tekelili showed us all this, I was still sitting on the grass with Seela. Following my thread of attention, she could see the Great Old Ones too. She found them grotesque and menacing. Giving me a poke and a shake, she brought my attention back to the grassy field we sat in. Out of sight over a hillock was Eddie, a river of light flowing down on him. Arf was at my feet, still grinning—in his own way just as wise as any giant holothurian.

Before retrieving me, Seela had been in contact with a black god. This woman—we called her Jewel—bore the mental icon of a glittering crystal floating in black night. She wore numerous lovely necklaces beset with gems like diamonds, and she was interested in trading one of her necklaces. Seela's necklace was not all that Jewel was after, but here modesty must draw a veil.

"Dis be de best, huh, Mason?"

"It's very nice indeed. Do you miss Quaihlaihle?" We were lying on our backs side to side: Shrighunter, Otha, Jewel, Mason, Seela, and Smoker. Seela now wore one of Jewel's necklaces in place of hers. Arf had wandered off, and Eddie was still in mystic communion with the giant sea cucumbers.

"Quaihlaihle bossy and she too white. Gib me a black woman any day. Say black—you lookin' kind o dusky, Mason. You an' Seela bof."

Until now my skin had looked pale, even paper-white in the bright pink light, but now, all at once, it did seem . . . dusky. I held up my arm and stared at it. Could Jewel's color have rubbed off on me? Of course not. Was it just that my eyes were tired from the glare? Why *must* the trepangs train the lightstream on us so?

"The Tekelili always shine the light on us when we fuck," Jewel told me. "Be glad. The light is good; it makes your skin dark and strong. You look better already."

Now I understood why Elijah and Quaihlaihle had been white! The black gods were, strictly speaking, as white a race as the flowerpeople! It was only their constant exposure to the intense light of the Central Anomaly that kept them black! In which case . . .

"Eddie!" I called. "Are you nearby? Come here so I can see you."

The grasses shook, and a small man appeared, black as a raisin. A steady stream of pink light was cascading down over him, fluttering his fine hair. Eddie Poe! With his delicate features, he looked for all the world like a gentleman's personal manservant.

Seeing me see him, Eddie saw himself and screamed in horror. "Oh no!" cried he. "I won't be made into a damned nigger! We've got to get out of here, Mason! We've got to get white!" The depth of his anguish was easily apparent. Edgar Poe feared entombment and heights and women's genitals—all these he'd had to face during our journey, and he'd borne it. But his fear of blackness and of slavery was even greater, and being turned black drove him into a frenzy unlike any I'd seen before. Seela and the black gods were wholly unable to understand Eddie's passionate aversion to what they considered a simple state of good health. I could understand, but—to tell the truth—as a farmboy I'd never felt as fully white as city folk like Eddie. If being in heaven meant being black, then so what? At least we were here. Rather than gloating extravagantly, Otha contented himself with a few simple witticisms at Eddie's expense.

"Now you black, you be dumb too, hey Mist Poe? Gwine fogit how to write? Gwine hab white folks read you de Bible?"

"Don't, Otha."

Eddie screamed curses at the Great Old Ones till they took the light off him, and then he floundered past us and dove into the Umpteen Seas. He stayed in the water a long time, swimming about and rubbing himself, his mind a frozen blank. The black gods giggled and began to chat.

Smoker and Shrighunter told Otha about how they'd caught their last shrig, while Seela and Jewel discussed their new necklaces. Seela explained what each of her threaded trinkets denoted—each stood for a state of mind or for a historical moment. Jewel began showing Seela how she wove plant fibers into little nets to hold her gems to the necklace cord without having to drill holes in them.

"Where do the crystals come from?" I asked Jewel.

"They're shit from the Tekelili eating shrigshit after they eat our shit," she responded—an answer rude and confusing until she showed me the images to explain.

The explanation involved another geography lesson.

The Central Anomaly is gravitationally "uphill" from the Umpteen Seas, as is Htrae. The Seas form a kind of gutter around the Central Anomaly; they lie at the very bottom of every unimpeded fall. Therefore nature would seem to dictate that it is the Seas' natural state to be choked with crustal debris. But in fact the Seas are as clear as springwater. This is due partly to the alchemy of the Seas' delicate plant and animal life, partly to the Tekelili's judicious aiming of their lightrays, and in no small measure to the efforts of the black gods, who haul debris from their seas as punctiliously as any farmer expunges stones and brush from his laboriously fructified terrain. If it had not been for the traditionally practiced custom of shrigshitting, as Jewel called it, the Umpteen Seas would have been foul puddles, dangerously jostling with muddy rocks.

For untold thousands of years, the black gods and their progenitors have been hauling rubbish out of the Umpteen Seas. A few choice tidbits are carried in to the Great Old Ones, but most of the debris is ported back outward to the zone of the shrigs. The omnivorous shrigs, who appear in this zone seasonally—from March to August—will eat anything they can swallow: animal, mineral, or vegetable, living or dead. This active season is the summer of the Umpteen Seas, and during the winter—September through February—the shrigs are in their roosts on Htrae, mating and raising their young. Their only natural enemies are the black gods and the *ballula*.

As a shrig eats, its gut cooks some of the food into methane gas. When the beast is full, it releases the gas, striking flints to set the gas aflame. The flints are gripped by prehensile extrusions of the shrig's muscular anus. As the shrig rides its flaming jet back outward to its nest, a certain amount of debris escapes with the gas, though the bulk of what the shrig has eaten is carried back out with it to Htrae. Seela interrupted to remark that among the flowerpeople, shrigs are known to live communally in huge hives along the Htraean Equator. Their castlelike roosts have walls molded from their solid waste.

"So the jewels fly out of the shrigs with the flaming gas?" I asked. It was wonderful to be sharing thoughts with these two beautiful women, even though the thoughts be of excrement. A huge Umpteen Sea hovered near ours, and the light from the Central Anomaly was strong and pleasant.

"No, no," said Jewel, and showed us more. A certain proportion of the particles that leave the shrig have sufficient velocity to shoot past the zone of the Umpteen Seas and into the Central Anomaly. It is primarily for these nuggets that the Great Old Ones comb the air with their vast fans. And when their huge, slow light-energized guts have fully digested the nuggets, the substance that remains for the Tekelili to excrete is like jewels. The process is perhaps analagous to the way in which geological forces squeeze jungle wrack into coal and coal into diamonds.

"So you fly near the Central Anomaly and look for falling gems?" I asked Jewel. "Is it dangerous? Do the Great Old Ones eat people?"

Jewel smiled. "We don't call it Anomaly. We call it InOut. Some people who've gone there haven't come back yet. Maybe they're on the other side. I don't think the Great Old Ones would eat a person. I eat *woomo,* but it would hurt a Tekelili too much to eat me. They're more sensitive than we are, because the tekelili is stronger near the InOut. We carry some dead things up to them. They like the food, but they don't like us to stay in there. They grab you with their branches and throw you out. A person can get confused around the InOut. I use tekelili to know when to go to fetch jewels, and I move *fast*. But no matter how fast I go, my friends out here think I'm gone five or ten years. Watcher likes doing that. He goes in and balances on the light-tubes until the Great Old Ones throw him out. He was born more than a thousand years ago.''

"What is a year?'' asked Seela.

"Look,'' said Jewel, pointing out toward Htrae. Due to the odd spindling of space near the Central Anomaly, our view of the planet's inner surface was quite distorted. It was as if I was looking out through a large lens that squeezed the whole planetary surface into a broad disk over my head. The edges of the disk were fuzzy, with faint mirage images beyond them. What we saw was like a round flat map of the Earth's interior. I'd had occasion to look at it earlier, of course, and I noticed now that the disk had rotated from its original position. Listening in on my thoughts, Jewel explained that the Htrae disk rotated roughly once per full period of sleep and wakefulness, that is, once per day.

Seela had the flowerpeople's wholly chaotic notion of time and found even the idea of a day confusing. Jewel went on to explain that a year was made of 365 days and that one could tell what time of year it was by looking at the North or the South Hole.

The North Hole! Though I'd often wondered if such a thing existed, till now I'd been unable to look for it, what with the Central Anomaly being in the way. But now, down in this space spindle that bent light rays like a lens, I could see the whole Htraean surface, and sure enough, it had two holes in it, each about the size of a silver dollar held at arm's length.

The South Hole was a clearly demarcated circle set into a big patch of green jungle. As the time of year was now, so far as I could reckon, early May (I believe now that the date must have been May 1, 1837, the anniversary of MirrorMason's death on MirrorEarth), this meant that the antarctic day had shrunk to only a few hours of sunlight. It was not surprising therefore that the South Hole was quite dark, with only a faint reddish glow from its walls' molten falls of lava.

The North Hole was to be found in the midst of a great blue sea. It was near midsummer in the north now, so the hole was lit with bluish light—seemingly from the open sky. The water around the hole glowed blue-green with light as well. The North Hole was a vast maelstrom! I strained my eyes, trying to make out if one really could see clear through. Was that not a bit of the sun's disk that I saw through the North Hole? With the hole wide open, our trip would have been easier had we taken our balloon north instead of south . . . were we willing to endure the terror of floating down the wind-torn throat of such a vortex.

Making out the details was complicated by the fact that at all times the Tekelili kept a steady barrage of pink lightstreamers going, with a special concentration of the streamers precisely at the North Hole. I am sure that some of the streamers went clear through to join the shimmering curtain of celestial light that the Esquimeaux term Oomoora's Veil. By sending lightstreams out through the North Hole (and, now that my party has reopened it, the South Hole), the Hollow Earth's Tekelili beings do put themselves in touch with the solar system at large.

By way of answering Seela's question of what is a year, Jewel now spoke of how brightness moved back and forth between the two great holes and how these changes were linked to the migrations of the shrig. Seela, who had never seen either hole from her flower, found this quite amazing and wondered what lay outside the holes.

"My friends and I come from the outside," I announced. Perhaps with the North and South holes visible before us, Seela could now understand what I'd unsuccessfully tried to tell her several times before. There was some kelplike seaweed stuck in the grass near us, and the leaves bore hollow, round flotation bladders. I fetched one of the pods and showed it to my two female friends. "The planet is like this hollow ball," I said. "I come from the outside, and now we are inside." Using the tip of Peters's knife, I cut north and south holes in the bladder. "This is where we came in." Holding the ball in one hand, I made a fist of my other hand and put it out at arm's length. "Imagine light coming from this hand. Sometimes the hole points toward the light, and sometimes it tilts away. Back and forth. That's what makes a year."

Neither of them truly understood, but before I could go on, we were interrupted by the return of Eddie Poe, naked save for a breechcloth and still completely black.

"It won't wash off," he complained. "I half hoped to drown myself, but I am too exceptional a swimmer to stay under. I am quite black. And with those evil giant trepangs gloating over us—no, it cannot be endured. Mason, we must press *onward*." I knew that *onward to MirrorEarth* was what he meant.

"I likes it here," said Otha. "I plannin' to stay. Gwine go hunt us some shrig."

"I like it too," I told Eddie. "Can't you see that this is heaven? Even if I were willing to leave, which I'm not, I don't see how we could ever fight the gravity all the way back out. It's at least three thousand miles back up. And even if we were going to try to go to MirrorEarth, which we aren't going to, we'd have to start by finding a way through the Central Anomaly." Poor MirrorPa. I wondered how MirrorMason had died. Nobly, no doubt. They'd welcome me like a king if we made it there! And what a thing it would be to see Virginia again and to watch Eddie hatch schemes with his double!

"Aha! Let me show you what I found!" Eddie fed me an image of a metal object, shaped like a fried egg, drifting beneath the waters of our Umpteen Sea. The entire disk-shaped object was no more than forty feet across. The egg's central "yolk" was a hemisphere some fifteen feet across, and the surrounding disk of "eggwhite" added perhaps twelve feet on every side. It was in every way like the object I'd seen when our iceberg broke up as we fell through the hot center of Symmes's Hole—so much so that I wondered if Eddie had really seen a second one. Now that he and I had shared tekelili, many of my memories were his. I knew from experience that Eddie would not be above the hoax of

appropriating my image and passing it off as his own. Perhaps
he'd been driven into a fugue state by the shock of his mad mood
swing—from the pantheistic ecstasy of union with the Great Old
Ones to the shocked despair of learning he was black. But when
I peered deeper into his mind, I found only a voice slowly chanting verses from a poem he called "The City in the Sea."

No rays from the holy Heaven come down
On the long night-time of that town;
But light from out the lurid sea
Streams up the turrets silently—

Despite my doubts, the black gods recognized Eddie's image of a skirted metal hemisphere; they knew it well. Cheerfully
acquiescent to Eddie's desire to salvage the great metal fried egg,
they accompanied Eddie, Seela, Otha, and me as we flew out
over their sea and dove into the water some distance from their
island. I made sure I knew which way the surface was, and then
I kicked down into the clear water, keeping my eyes wide open.
Retracted pink light filled the water; fish swam this way and that.
Further down I could see something glinting—a metal ship
shaped like a round cup turned over on a saucer. Then I was out
of breath and had to kick for the surface.

Due to its weight, the object tended to drift to the sea's
center, but it developed that the black gods occasionally made a
sport of hauling it up. It was of an alloy utterly impervious to
erosion. The black gods said that each time they fetched it out of
the water, it was as bright as ever before. Seeing our interest in
it, they contrived to get some of their braided ropes fastened to
holes in the "white" of the fried egg, and they pulled it to the
water's surface.

As the fried egg rose, Eddie told me it was his opinion that
the Great Old Ones had ridden the egg here from some distant
star. Now that they'd turned him black, he thought of them as
malign and evil, so it was therefore comfortable for him to regard

them as something external to the order of nature as it should be. The egg broke free of the water.

Eddie and I splashed over and tied my silk rope through holes in the egg's rim to help the black gods pull it free of hydrologic tension. Though it had the gleam of metal, the rim's substance had the slippery feel of oilcloth. Etched into the rim was a filigree of hieroglyphs too odd to decipher. The whole group of us pulled the gleaming fried egg through the air to a spot comfortably near the island's grassy ground. The craft had thickly glassed portholes and a hatch that stood open. The hatch had straight sides and a rounded top, like the arched entrance to a companionway. There was no door or hatch-cover to be seen. A great amount of water was still lodged within the egg. The black gods showed us how to coax the water out and how to tether the thing to the grasses. They did this once or twice a year as a kind of entertainment.

The inside of the ship was quite gutted. There were three shattered stands that must have held seats; also, there was an alcove that could have housed bunk beds like those on the *Wasp*. Behind the alcove was a bulkhead sealing off a third of the craft's hemispherical bulge—I imagined that within the sealed compartment there might be a stove to produce lifting gas. The craft had a porthole on either side and a long, thick-glassed view port right in front of where the seats had been. Beneath the view port was a slanting panel with the broken-off stubs of what must once have been controls. Watcher said that the black gods' ancestors had broken off all the pieces they could use for ornaments. There were numerous hieroglyphs within the cabin: a circular frieze of them wound around the walls, and hieroglyphs in oval cartouches were engraved near each of the vandalized controls. Some of the hieroglyphs seemed to show the fan-capped barrels of the Great Old Ones; others looked like that poor forked radish, Man. Had Man and the Great Old Ones used the fried egg together?

Eddie was enchanted. "What an incredible sense of antiquity," he mused, running his black finger over the slippery metal—if metal it was. "Do you feel the hush, Mason? It's like the crypt of a cathedral or a tomb in the heart of the great pyramid. The profaned temple of an unknown, raving god. Plato's myth of Atlantis—perhaps it is no myth at all."

In a fever of curiosity, Eddie began peering at the hieroglyphs and muttering to himself, his mind seething with symbols and theories. After a half hour of this, the black gods grew bored and drifted away. I stayed with Eddie, curious to see where his investigations would lead. Arf was here too, though Seela was off with the gods.

I dozed off, and when I awoke, Eddie was on tiptoes by the open hatch.

"See, Mason, see!" He dragged his fingers along the ceiling with a swift, hooking motion and the walls around the hatch grew together, covering over the hole. Another movement of Eddie's hand, and the door was back open.

"I triumph!" cried Eddie. "I care not whether my impostor's work be read instead of mine. I have stolen the golden secret of the Egyptians. This door shall take us to the MirrorEarth and to the charlatan MirrorPoe. I will indulge my sacred fury!"

# 13

# Through the Spindle

EDDIE SPENT the next six weeks in the fried egg. Not only was he fascinated by the continuing puzzle of the hieroglyphs, he liked being set apart from the rest of us. Initially he might have had the notion that staying in there would help him get white again, but in fact the pink light could always find its way in through the ship's windows and branch into every crevice of the cabin. Tired of having to drift off into the sky and be brought back to ground, Arf spent much of his time in Eddie's egg or in the tangled grasses beneath it. Now and then an unexpected surge of water would wash over the land, and Eddie and Arf would dog-paddle above their home until the water sloshed away. So far the egg's tethers had held.

Occasionally I visited with Eddie, but most of the time Seela, Otha, and I were having fun playing with the black gods. We shared thoughts, we made love, we dove and swam in the lovely clear seas, Lightrider gave us lessons in riding the heated lighttubes, and we helped with the endless task of hauling debris up to feed to the shrigs. The next stage of my journey began late in the month of June 1837.

Seela and I had just shared a particularly romantic interlude, and had then fallen into that delicious slumber that is the consequence of passion well spent. We woke to find that as a result of a tekelili agreement, our close friends among the black gods had gathered to take us shrighunting. As the supplies of leather and dried meat were down, it was decided that we'd try to kill two shrigs if we could—though killing more than one per day was difficult. Usually, the first scent of blood sent the herd fleeing halfway around the Umpteen Seas.

We gathered to bathe ourselves and to eat some of the sweet, chewy grain from the grasses. Shrighunter had been schooling Otha in her craft's minor arcana, and he was ready to put his new knowledge to the test. He asked for the loan of the big knife I'd gotten from Peters, and I gave it. We all joined hands then, and Watcher put himself in contact with the network of the Great Old Ones. More so than the other black gods, Watcher had Eddie's heightened ability to channel the thoughts of the Tekelili. Sputtery pink light played over his patrician features, and the knowledge flowed among us. There was a herd of twenty shrig fifteen miles out from us in the direction of the North Hole.

As well as shrigskin *pulpuls*, we each had a thorn-rapier and a polished piece of *ballula* shell. During the winter months, when the shrigs are off in their nests, all kinds of debris falls into the seas. *Ballula* shells are deemed to be the best material for making what the black gods call lightboards, these being the little platforms on which they ride the spreading heat of the branching tubes of pink light. The cupped, pearly inner surface of a *ballula* shell is ideal for catching the pressure of the heated air. Each lightboard has a footstrap and is shaped like a lozenge bounded by two circular arcs. Even a small *ballula* shell can be cut up into as many as fifty lightboards.

Usually, it took a little time for each member of a hunting party to catch a good lightstream, but with Watcher here, the Tekelili were unusually helpful. Tube after tube of hot, forking light washed past our island, strong and steady as ocean waves.

Seela and I kicked up and caught a tube together. Under

Lightrider and Smoker's tutelage, we'd gotten pretty good,
though I still knelt on my lightboard rather than standing on it.
Seela hooked her foot into her strap and slid this way and that,
carving airy curlicues around me.

Soon the shrigs were visible in the distance as distended
larval forms with busy heads. We rode a little closer and joined
the other hunters waiting there. Shrighunter and Otha had swathed
their bodies in thick layers of damp kelp. Our hunting strategy
was simply to kick our way close to the shrigs and there to leave
Otha and Shrighunter like ordinary rubbish bundles. If all went
well, two shrigs would swallow them whole and they'd simulta-
neously cut their way out.

"Ah knows where, but how do ah knows *when* to cut de
shrig's neck?" Otha was asking Shrighunter when I arrived. At
this distance from the Central Anomaly, the tekelili mindreading
ability was terribly weak. We had to put our heads right by the
black gods' heads to be able to understand them.

"Do it as soon as you can," said Shrighunter. "If you wait
and I cut first, your shrig will panic and fly away. Some of us
have disappeared that way. If you get swallowed down past the
throat, cut yourself an airhole in the shrig's bodywall as soon as
you can. Make sure it's a small hole. Once you catch your breath,
squeeze out quickly."

Seela, Watcher, and I bore the wrapped Shrighunter while
Lightrider, Jewel, and Smoker handled Otha. Watcher was in
rollicking good spirits; it was rare for him to spend this much
time outside of the Central Anomaly.

"It's good you came," he said, pushing his head against mine.
"You break the symmetry and foment chaos." I caught an
image of the MirrorWorld as a boring repetition of this World.
Like a vampire, I had no reflection.

"Are there two of you?" I asked Watcher.

"Yes," he answered. "And my other self is out hunting
today, too. But he doesn't have you and Seela." He ran his thick,
stubby hand caressingly along Seela's back. "The Tekelili agree

with Eddie. You should go on to the MirrorWorld. The Mirror-World needs strangeness. MirrorEarth doesn't even have a North and South Hole."

By then the tekelili had faded too much for me to query further. This far from the Central Anomaly's influence, space opened back up, and I could see out toward Htrae in every direction except the inward one. It was a marvelous thing to be floating in this huge round sky, the great North Hole maelstrom high above me like a distant navel of the world and the gleaming Umpteen Seas beneath my feet.

Three shrigs were nearby, watching us like cows waiting for crabapples. From long habit, they were eager for the tasty dense waste the black gods brought them. One of them beat its tail to come closer, all the while eying our heavy kelp bundle with interest.

Watcher said something to Shrighunter in their own tongue, and then we flung her free.

Off to my right, the other party released Otha. We kicked back a few hundred yards; a shrig's death throes were said to be dangerously violent, similar in nature, I presumed, to a harpooned whale's flurry. Otha disappeared down a shrig's maw, and its companion ate Shrighunter. The unfed third shrig sounded a deep moo of disappointment.

All at once, the second shrig's tiny winged legs began fluttering in spasmodic agony. It snapped its body, slapping its fan-tail against its underside with a sound like an iceberg falling into the sea. The force of its tailsnap drove it away from us. Its gaping mouth was bellowing a hideous cry of anguish that stopped—all at once. A balloon of blood appeared at the doomed beast's slit throat, and then the powerfully kicking body of Shrighunter could be seen heading out into safe air. The dying shrig lashed its body this way and that, its opened windpipe whistling a cracked shrill tune.

I looked for Otha's shrig, but it was gone. He'd been too slow! The other hunters were pointing outward toward a dwindling black speck whose vibrating tail suddenly blossomed with bright flame. Otha's panicked shrig was going to gas its way clear back to Htrao!

Moving quickly, Lightrider got on a lightstream and shot out after the fleeing shrig. It was pulling steadily ahead of him, but then, all at once, the flame-tipped black dot exploded into a great ball of brief fire. Shortly there came the boom of the blast and a shockwave carrying chunks of debris.

With the lack of tekelili, nobody could tell me what was going on—and then they'd all headed outward on their boards. Unsteadily, I mounted my curved shield of *ballula* shell and tried to ride out too, but I kept losing control and falling off. Finally, I put the board on my back and furiously kicked my *pulpuls*. I had to save Otha!

Just when I thought my heart would burst from exertion, I heard laughter above me. Looking up, I saw Seela, the black gods, and Otha—a bald Otha, with his hair and eyebrows singed off. Lightrider, Watcher, and Jewel had the blasted carcass of Otha's shrig in tow. About a third of it had been lost in the explosion.

This far from the Central Anomaly I could no longer sense the mentations of the black gods. Without tekelili, their spoken speech seemed an arbitrary system of grunts and squeals, like any human language. But Otha and I knew the same tongue.

"Ah seen a haint in dere, Mason," called Otha. "Ah seen Quaihlaihle inside o' dat shrig! Lissen here, cause cain't none ob dese odders unnerstan' me. Fust dat shrig swaller me and ah git all twisted aroun', and den 'fore ah kin cut its throat, it done swaller me *all de way down.* It were all full of fart an' rocks an' rotten junk in dere, Mason, and wust of all ah done rubbed up gainst Quaihlaihle. Don' aks me how ah knowed it were her, but ah do. Ah were so skeered, ah cut me a great big hole in de side ob dat shrig. Looky here, Mason, ah still gots de knife! But all dat fart from inside ketched on fire wid de outside and de shrig blowed up like a bomb."

"Good God, Otha! I thought you were done for!"

"Ah were right in de center, ah 'speck."

I began to laugh, while bloody Shrighunter whooped for joy. We'd slain two leviathans today.

It was easy towing the carcasses down to the Umpteen Seas, as they were falling thither anyhow. Quantities of pterodactyls and hummingbirds shrieked about, snatching off scraps of flesh. The hummingbirds had iridescent blue bodies, with red markings at the throat. The pterodactyls were brownish-green. The tekelili intensity of the birds' small-brained greed was in some way amusing. On our approach, scores of black gods arrived to help skin and butcher the shrigs in midair at a spot near the watery end of our sea. Eddie ventured out of his fried egg to look and listen, while Arf gorged himself on offal from the shrig. Otha told everyone his adventure in full tekelili detail. Shrighunter couldn't get over the way Otha had made his shrig explode. She'd had no idea our knife could cut so big an escape vent in a shrig's body.

To round things out, Otha's tale of encountering Quaihlaihle was quickly confirmed when a black god with the icon of Offerer told us he'd found the partially unwrapped body drifting in the air near our sea. Offerer's function was to take certain special kinds of debris inward to the Great Old Ones instead of outward to the shrigs. He and a few others fed human corpses to the Tekelili; also did they haul in the offal left over from the butchering of the shrigs. With a mortician's affinity for cadavers, Offerer had come upon Quaihlaihle's body soon after the shrig's explosion sent it to the Umpteen Seas.

When he picked up the tekelili of Otha's story, Offerer contacted Otha to say he'd found the dead queen a mile or two from where we'd brought the bodies of the shrigs. He asked if we wanted to see her before he fed her to the giant sea cucumbers.

"Ain' no way ah go near dat body again," vowed Otha.

"Quaihlaihle a mummy!" exclaimed Eddie. "Come, Mason, we must investigate!"

Watcher and Shrighunter accompanied us. We followed Offerer's mind signals through the mazy congeries of great jiggling waterballs, and finally there Offerer was, with a surprisingly small object at his side—the mummy of Queen Quaihlaihle.

Much of the sappy glue had come loose, and some of the ceremonial money net was hanging free. Quaihlaihle's face was visible. Her lips had writhed away from her red teeth, which were pushed apart by her swollen black tongue. The air near her was pungent with decay. Eddie's eyes grew wide in fascination.

"Do you know her?" I asked Offerer, who was in the process of lashing a rope around the softened body's waist. "Is she of your tribe?"

He was unsure, but Shrighunter said that many years ago a woman had been caught like Otha in a fleeing shrig. The woman's tribal name had been Strutter. Our dead Quaihlaihle resembled Strutter enough so that Shrighunter deemed it likely that after being trapped in her shrig, Strutter had made a small enough airhole to ride all the way to Htrae.

Suddenly remembering Elijah, I asked Shrighunter if a *man* had ever left their tribe in the same way. I showed her our mental images of Elijah. Her reaction was immediate and intense.

"FarMan! You've seen FarMan? Then you really are from the outside! Do you hear them, Watcher?"

Watcher blended his mind with ours and showed us the story of how the one they called FarMan had left.

A few of the black gods were natural explorers. Though the Umpteen Seas themselves were large and various as a small nation, some of the natives were not content. One possibility for breaking out was to try and travel all the way through the Central Anomaly. Watcher's image of being near the Sphere of Anomaly showed the Umpteen Seas spinning past with insanely mounting rapidity. Time slowed down in there and it became difficult to make progress, but once one could get in deep enough, the Teke-lili creatures would assist. They opposed the presence of other living creatures in their realm and would catch hold of an inter-loper with one of their huge fans and fling him either down through the inconceivable heart of the Maelstrom or back whence he came.

The world inside the heart of the Central Sphere was as a mirror image of our side. If a man presented himself to be taken through, then surely his Mirrorself would be on the other side waiting to trade places. This was the natural order of things, and Watcher had been back and forth many times. The journey itself was interesting, said he, but the other side was much like this—with the exception that the MirrorEarth lacked, as he'd told me earlier, North and South holes. Without this signal difference, he would have been hard put to say which of the two worlds he was presently in and which of him was MirrorWatcher.

"But how did Elijah get to the surface?" interrupted Eddie.

More difficult than a passage through the Central Sphere, continued Watcher imperturbably, was the journey outward to Htrae. Evidently, Strutter had made the trip and become Queen Quaihlaihle of the flowerpeople, and a few others had even journeyed out and returned. But the black gods had a low opinion of those who hung and dangled from the roof of the planet's crust. Sooner or later, everything from up there would fall down to the seas anyway, so the trip seemed hardly worthwhile.

FarMan had proposed the greatest exploration of all. After many trips outward to the far reaches of the shrigs' feeding zone, FarMan had formed the idea that the black gods' world was like a hollow bladder. This, Watcher remarked, was the same idea that Otha, Eddie, and I advocated. Reasoning patiently and at length, FarMan had concluded that there must be people out on the "egg's surface" beyond the North and the South holes. Most of the black gods had doubted him, for surely there could be no air out there.

FarMan had insisted that he could break out, as a chicken from its egg.

"How," interrupted Eddie's thoughts. "How did he do it?"

Watcher said that the Great Old Ones had borne FarMan

away on a beam of pink light. First he'd built himself a tight-hatched traveling cabin out of a whole *ballula* shell, and then the black gods had towed the shell far out toward Htrae. FarMan had selected the spot on the basis of visions the Great Old Ones had granted him. Once the shell was in place—with the determined FarMan safe inside—a tremendous lightriver had appeared to push the shell all the way to Htrae. But how an empty *ballula* shell could have carried him through the Rind, no man could say. Perhaps he'd floated out through the North Hole.

"It's time, Mason," said Eddie suddenly. "All the pieces are in place."

"How do you mean?"

"I know how to get us to the MirrorEarth. Offerer, can we be the ones to haul up Quaihlaihle's corpse?"

"You can come along with me if you wish."

"We'll be taking the old metal ship up there, too." Eddie formed a quick image of Quaihlaihle resting on the fried egg's rim like a sardine on a dinner plate. He visioned himself inside the cabin, with Arf and me at his side. He had the idea that the Great Old Ones would snatch us to eat Quaihlaihle and then cast us away because they didn't like the fried egg.

"What about Seela?" I protested. "And Otha?"

"They may come if they wish," said Eddie. "Though I doubt Otha will choose to. Who would willingly change from god to slave?" There were many more thoughts in Eddie's head, but he obscured them by a full-length incanting of his new poem, "The City in the Sea":

Lo! Death has reared himself a throne
In a strange city lying alone
Far down within the dim West,
Where the good and the bad and the worst and the best
Have gone to their eternal rest.
There shrines and palaces and towers
(Time-eaten towers that tremble not!)

Resemble nothing that is ours.
Around, by lifting winds forgot,
Resignedly beneath the sky
The melancholy waters lie.

No rays from the holy Heaven come down
On the long night-time of that town;
But light from out the lurid sea
Streams up the turrets silently—
Gleams up the pinnacles far and free—
Up domes—up spires—up kindly halls—
Up fanes—up Babylon-like walls—
Up shadowy long-forgotten bowers
Of sculptured ivy and stone flowers—
Up many and many a marvellous shrine
Whose wreathed friezes intertwine
The viol, the violet, and the vine.
Resignedly beneath the sky
The melancholy waters lie.
So blend the turrets and shadows there
That all seem pendulous in air,
While from a proud tower in the town
Death looks gigantically down.

There open fanes and gaping graves
Yawn level with the luminous waves;
But not the riches there that lie
In each idol's diamond eye—
Not the gaily-jewelled dead
Tempt the waters from their bed;
For no ripples curl, alas!
Along that wilderness of glass—
No swellings tell that winds may be
Upon some far-off happier sea—
No heavings hint that winds have been
On seas less hideously serene.

But lo, a stir is in the air!
The wave—there is a movement there!
As if the towers had thrust aside,
In slightly sinking, the dull tide—
As if their tops had feebly given
A void within the filmy Heaven.
The waves have now a redder glow—
The hours are breathing faint and low—
And when, amid no earthly moans,
Down, down that town shall settle hence,
Hell, rising from a thousand thrones,
Shall do it reverence.

"Whut dat got to do wid me, Mase?" demanded Otha, impatiently chewing on a chunk of shrigmeat. The great fart blast had flash-cooked a half acre of the second shrig. Though gamey and exceedingly fat, the meat was toothsome.

I had just finished telling Otha that Eddie and I planned to haul the metal fried egg inward. We would carry in the mummy of Quaihlaihle with us to make sure that the Great Old Ones would not mind our intrusion. Our hope was that the Great Old Ones would hurl us through the Spherical Anomaly that divided Earth from MirrorEarth. With luck we would eventually penetrate to the MirrorEarth's surface, and perhaps even reach MirrorBaltimore, where Eddie would help us to a good new start in life.

"Whuffo ah gwine go back be no runaway slave? An' fust haul dat fried-egg shit all de way up to dem *Woomo*? An' de mummy? Fuck dat shit, Mase. Ain' no way." Otha's mode of addressing me had become even more familiar.

I'd found Otha floating near a large glob of pure water in which bobbed two women called Tigra and Bunny. They'd come from halfway around the Umpteen Seas, drawn by the explosion of Otha's shrig.

"We like the shrig that went boom." Tigra laughed. My

Lord, she was beautiful. Being there in tekelili contact with her was as wonderful an experience as I'd ever had. There was something enticingly sinuous and loose about her mentation.

Bunny was rounder, more sensuous, with a sunnier, more direct way of viewing things. Looking through her eyes by tekelili, the full wonder of our surroundings was borne in on me once again.

The filigreed pink light sent highlights off the lovely clear waterglobs on every side. Over our heads was the mighty canopy of the Inner Sky with Htrae. The North Hole was near the Sky's center. As it was late June, the hole was fully illumined, its great watery vortex gilded by the hidden sun. Beneath our feet, the Great Old Ones were closer and larger than I'd ever seen them, for the chaotic peregrinations of the Umpteen Seas had brought us near the inner perimeter of the waterglob zone.

"Virginia's still alive in the MirrorEarth," I told Otha. "And I'm dead there."

"Dat still ain't got nothin' to do wid me. Ah's stayin' here, Mase. Even someone as white and dumb as you is gotta be able to see why."

"He's not white," put in Tigra.

"He use ter be, but yeah, he black now. You done think 'bout dat yet, Mase, dat you goin' back as a nigger?"

"It'll wear off. Eddie's lighter already from spending so much time in the fried egg."

"Sho'. Be Seela goin' wid you?"

"I think so." Recently, our mutual passion had tempered. We'd grown used to one kind of relationship—me as speechless slave—and now here in the Umpteen Seas everything was different. We'd each had several lovers among the black gods, and our mutual bond no longer seemed quite so absolute. Yet for me, Seela was still the special one. "She'll come with me. I aim to marry her."

"Wisht ah could be dere to see, Mase."

The farewell emotions swelled around us, while Tigra and

Bunny kept a tactful silence. If our partnership had been unjustly
unequal, Otha and I still had shared much joy. Building dams,
catching fish, playing in the corn crib. The sickness of thinking
him an inferior slave had not come over me till puberty. "I'm
sorry," I told Otha as he watched my thoughts. "I was wrong."
The memory of the night Pa had raped Turl came welling up.
Otha shared it, and in the sharing of our memories something
new emerged, something that neither of us had ever been able to
think of alone.

"Purly!" exclaimed Otha. "He's yo pa's son!"

"Yes!" said I. "And Turl's his ma! That's why she went
away that summer."

"And why she allus talked about him. Purly's mah bro!"

"And mine too!"

Brothers: Otha and I shared the same blood brother!

He wrapped his arms around me and we embraced.

I found Seela with Smoker and a score of other black gods,
all of them busy tying chunks of raw shrigmeat into bundles for
curing. They were working hard, concerned that the meat might
spoil before they could dry it in the streams of pink light.

Seela's drifting blond hair made a striking contrast to her
dark skin. She was laughing, and her full upper lip crinkled
enticingly. The necklace of gems she's gotten from Jewel spar-
kled against her skin like diamonds. She tekelili-saw me seeing
her and turned with a ready smile.

"Will you travel on with me, Seela?" I thought to her.

"But it's wonderful here! Look how much *koladull* meat
we have!"

"It's wonderful in the world I come from, too." I imaged a
moonlit night, a rainy day, and the flowers of spring. Buildings,
machinery, and books. Oysters, champagne, and stuffed turkey.
Us in a well-appointed city apartment, and us visiting Pa on the
farm. A wedding at St. John's, with Seela all in white. Seela
pregnant, and Seela suckling our child.

The idea of night intrigued Seela mightily, but the inanimate buildings frightened her, and the concepts of marriage and family were—as I'd briefly forgotten—quite alien to her tribe. My suggestion that I might father her child struck her as something like blasphemy. The flowerpeople believed that women were made pregnant by the pink light from the Earth's center.

"But think of marriage," I thought to Seela. "Marriage means we can be together always. Only you and I."

Her reaction was anything but what I'd hoped. Was I then a spoilsport and a tyrant? A selfish self-deluding fool? A slave master intent on forcing her through the insane rituals of my barbaric tribe?

I abandoned this line of persuasion and told her more about the trip Eddie planned. "We'll get inside the metal egg with Arf and Eddie."

"I don't like Eddie."

"And the black gods will tow us up to the Central Anomaly."

"The what?"

"The Central Sphere. The InOut. Where the Great Old Ones live. Right to the source, Seela, where your holy baby-making pink light comes from. It's the bridge to the MirrorWorld. The giant *woomo* will throw us through, all the way to MirrorHtrae. We'll find our way through the MirrorRind and be out on the surface of MirrorEarth before you know it. The nights are lovely, Seela. Imagine what it would be like with no light. And snow, let me show you about snow." I showed her memories of Otha and me sliding down a hill on our wooden sled, with the fluffy white flakes drifting out of the endless sky. Seela liked it.

"But what if you fall into the sky?"

"You can't. Things fall toward the ground on Earth and MirrorEarth. If something's on the ground, it just stays there."

That was the best news Seela had heard yet. If there was anything about the Umpteen Seas she disliked, it was the lack of any stable place of rest. The flowerpeople had a deeply ingrained fear of falling. Pressing my advantage, I drew her close and caressed her. "Please come with me, Seela."

"Maybe."

The next problem was to convince a squad of the black gods to haul the fried egg. An inspiration struck me. What better way to quickly cure a great amount of the shrigmeat than to bear it up to the very source of the sovereign pink light?

Smoker, who had been following our conversation, showed me an image of the meat bundles sticking together and not getting fully dry. I replied with an image of the meats hung from the holes around the fried egg's rim—like tassels around the brim of a gaucho's hat. The fried egg was the perfect rack for mass drying of meat! Smoker came back with an image of a Great Old One darting out a sticky fan-limb that absorbed all our plunder. I wondered if we might hold the fried egg back, just out of the Great Old One's reach. Now Watcher entered the discussion. He of all men knew the capabilities of the *woomo* and the topography of the Spherical Maelstrom.

"The *woomo* move very slowly," Watcher told me. "It is only their light—and their thinking—which is rapid. But why try and scheme against them? They know all. If we ask them to smoke our meat, then perhaps they will. And if they plan to steal it, they will tell us that too. There are no secrets in the One Mind. Ask and ye shall receive."

As always, the mighty chords of the Great Old Ones' thoughts pervaded the background, but they seemed not to be immediately aware of our discussion.

A few beams of pink light had been idly playing over the dead shrigs, probing and feeling them. The lighttubes had the shape of knobby tree branches, twigging out at irregular intervals. Eddie and I had come to realize that these tubes were more than mere light, for they were in no wise bound to the rectilinear urgencies of a lantern's ray. Eddie said that the tubes contained a heated vortical plasm of what he called latent motive craft. As this plasm turned and bent, so moved the light, growing as organically as a vine, as sinuously as the funnel of a tornado, and as palpably as a mounded row of eddies in a rain-swollen stream.

When Watcher suggested we talk directly to the Great Old

Ones, Lightrider kicked over to the nearest column of light and began skittering his board against it until he had its attention. The light bulged out at him, then split off streamers that played over his head. The Tekelili were talking to Lightrider. I peered toward them. Inward from us, the dozen lighttubes that had been fondling the shrig found their source in a bigger tube, which was itself the daughter of a nearby lightstream whose main flow continued forking out past us all the way to Htrae.

In its own aethereal way, the lighttube's plasm was like a rushing river, and I thought of the spring when the James River had run full flood, forty feet above normal water level. We'd gone to see—Pa, Luke, Otha, Turl, and me. It had been too wet for a wagon, so we'd walked. The water had been an ugly light brown color, with hungrily sucking whirlpools. We'd seen trees go past, then two dead mules, and finally a whole house. A house floating down the river, with all its carpentered right angles flexing. The sight of it had given me nightmares about our own unsteady home.

Now the big lightstream sent out a thick gout of warmly wafting light that blanketed all of us. Watcher silently spoke, telling the Great Old Ones that Eddie and I wanted them to throw the metal ship through the center of the Anomaly and out into the MirrorWorld. He showed them our plan to hang the shrigmeat on the ship's rim to dry. The Great Old Ones were but mildly interested. To them we were as gnats—though gnats with a value. They reminded Watcher of their fondness for shrig innards, and he promised that we would bring much and a mummy as well.

So now we went to get the metal fried egg so as to load it up. We found it with the door closed, and Offerer nearby, playing with Arf.

Offerer informed us that Eddie had locked himself inside the cabin with Quaihlaihle's mummy. It had been half an hour. Soon he would have to open the door for fresh air. We waited.

Presently, the door opened and a stained and disheveled Eddie appeared, a ghastly grin on his lips. I was struck once

again by how oddly Eddie's skull was shaped; flat on the top and
with bulging brow and temples. The wild pungent stench of
Quaihlaihle's dissolution floated out of the fried egg. Eddie's
hands were wedged deep into his coat pockets, fondling something. Tentatively, I reached out toward his mind . . . but he was
silently quoting himself again, quoting from his "Berenice," a
gothic tale I remembered from reading it in *The Southern Literary
Messenger* of March 1835.

And why did Eddie recite? I suppose he had some idea of
obscuring his deeds and plans behind a hebephrenic torrent of
inner speech, but knowing him as I did, it was all too obvious
what he had done. Obvious? Far more than *obvious*, Eddie's
newest outrage was made *ludicrously patent* by his selection of
*which* passages to recite.

" 'The eyes were lifeless, and lustreless, and seemingly
pupilless, and I shrank involuntarily from their glassy stare to the
contemplation of the thin and shrunken lips. They parted; and in
a smile of peculiar meaning, the teeth of the changed Berenice
disclosed themselves slowly to my view. Would to God that I had
never beheld them, or that, having done so, I had died!' "

"What have you been doing in there, Eddie? As if I didn't
know. What do you have in your pockets?"

" 'The shutting of a door disturbed me, and looking up, I
found that my cousin had departed from the chamber. But from
the disordered chamber of my brain had not, alas!, departed, and
would not be driven away, the white and ghastly *spectrum* of the
teeth.' "

"You pulled Quaihlaihle's teeth too, didn't you Eddie?"

" 'The teeth!—the teeth!—they were here, and there, and
everywhere, and visibly and palpably before me; long, narrow,
and excessively white, with the pale lips writhing about them, as
in the very moment of their first terrible development. Then came
the full fury of my *monomania* . . .' "

"Stop reciting, Eddie. There aren't any secrets to hide. Everyone knows you pulled the teeth, and everyone knows we're go-

ing through the center. The Tekelili already said they'd throw us through. And all they want for helping us is a mess of shrig guts."

This last was a real surprise to Eddie. He'd fancied the Great Old Ones to be evil schemers, so cut off from their innocent mentations had he become. Now he left off his inner speech and let me into his mind. He had Quaihlaihle's ruby teeth in his right pocket and Virgina's ivory teeth in his left pocket . . . nearer to his heart.

But this was nothing after all I'd already done and seen. "I don't care about the teeth," I thought to him. "Just so I can get back home. But tell me. How will we get out through the MirrorRind?"

Watcher, Seela, Lightrider, Jewel, Smoker, and Offerer were all gathered nearby, all of us in contact. They were listening with quiet interest. "You'll want to weave a necklace around those teeth, Eddie," thought Jewel. "Seela can show you how to do it."

When he stepped out of the fried egg, Eddie's mindset had been that of a criminal and a cringer. But now, to his tremulous delight, we were smilingly accepting him . . . just the way he was. *And* we were ready to help haul up the fried egg.

Flustered and smiling, Eddie pushed himself down from the fried egg's rim to where a large ball of water nestled in the grass. He took off his coat, carefully knotting its sleeves around one of the fried egg's retaining ropes, and began washing himself meticulously. As he washed, he tekelili-chattered to us, presenting his conclusions and his plans.

From his studies of the fried egg's hieroglyphs, Eddie had concluded that Man and the Great Old Ones had come to earth together in the fried-egg ships. Millennia ago, the Great Old Ones had been no larger than humans, said Eddie, and two of them could easily have fit into a fried-egg ship that held two people as well. He called our attention to one of the hieroglyphic drawings that showed a horizontal line with a semicircle on it. This, said Eddie, depicted a fried-egg ship. Inside the semicircle were two ellipses and two branched lines: two *woomo* and two people, as Eddie would have it. He believed that either a) men and women had piloted the ships as slaves of the Great Old Ones; or b) the *woomo* had come to Earth as the slave of Man. He thought (b) to be, on the whole, the more likely alternative.

Watcher objected, putting in a quick image of men, women, and *woomo* together in the fried egg as friendly as Eddie, Seela, me, and Arf. Then Watcher warped the image so that we humans were dogs and Arf was a *woomo*.

"Yes," said Eddie, speaking aloud again. "A symbiotic equality. Perhaps that may be. I have pondered that alternative as well. And if it is indeed so, then perhaps it is that those Great Old Dogs will, as Mason says, throw us all the way to MirrorHtrae for the mere gift of a mess of shrig guts. In my fear, I had planned a less open solicitation."

Eddie now showed us that he'd meant to smear mummy flesh all over the outside of the fried egg so that one of the Tekelili would try to swallow it whole. Finding the carrion-scented object indigestible, the big *woomo* would examine it and recognize it as the fearsome chariot of the old human masters and then, stricken with hatred, or with terror, the Great Old One would fling the fried egg very far indeed.

Thus had Eddie reasoned, having wholly lost sight of the fact that the Tekelili could read our minds—and were in fact reading them right now, as attested to by the hairlike bright pink streamers that drifted through the space around us like roothairs or spidersilk. Eddie had been wrong about some things, but one thing he'd gotten right, this being our means of getting through MirrorRind to the surface: viz., we were to float up through the sea!

I hadn't thought of that. If whales could swim all the way through, then why not we? Given that Eddie could open and shut the fried egg's door, we could use it like a diving bell. But what about air?

"Watcher knows of a plant that exudes air," thought Eddie.

"He pictured it when he was telling us about Elijah, whom they call FarMan. I could see in Watcher's image that Elijah took some of the plants in the *ballula* shell with him. So I deduce that he floated up through the sea. I've been trying to think of a way to ask Watcher for some of the plants." Having finished his ablutions, Eddie turned and faced us. "Watcher? Can I get some pounds of the radially spiked vegetable which you helped load into FarMan's *ballula* shell four years ago?"

Watcher had a noble, arching nose that curved back on itself like a snailshell. He was quite bald. His mouth was broad and mobile, and his figure generously formed. He was nude now, having removed his *pulpuls* so as better to dabble in the water and the grass, and he looked for all the world like a Roman senator in the baths. Yes, he could help us get the plant. It was called airweed. It grew "uphill inward." Lightrider could easily get some on our way in. No difficulties were forseen. Hail and farewell.

Over us hung the saucerlike underside of the fried egg. All about us were man-size, house-size, and dog-size gobbets of clear Umpteen Seawater. A sweet smelling fresh breeze came from one side. Rivulets of pink light played over us all.

"Eddie."

"Yes, Mason?" His dark eyes were clear beneath his over-developed forehead.

"The mummy. You forgot to get the mummy out of the ship."

"Very well. Offerer, can you help me?"

A short while later, we'd lashed Quaihlaihle and what must have been a shrig's liver to the flat underside of the fried egg, using festoons of shrig intestines as the ropes. Some eighty bundles of cleaned shrigmeat were roped to the holes around the fried egg's rim, and four long leather ropes led from the rim to the eight of us—Watcher, Seela, Lightrider, Jewel, Smoker, Offerer, Eddie, and me—two of us to a rope. Arf sat inside the fried egg's cabin, which we'd rinsed out with a waterball.

We kicked our *pulpuls* and slowly, slowly, the fried egg began moving away from the Umpteen Seas and further inward. The gravitational pull back toward the Seas seemed weaker moving in this direction than it had seemed when I'd kicked my way outward for the shrighunt.

In half an hour's time we'd progressed far enough so that I could glance back and see the Umpteen Seas spread out like gems on a jeweler's counter. The space here was warped and stretched in such a way that the zone of the Seas looked flat rather than spherical. It was impossible to see out to Htrae except in the radial direction that went directly outward from the Earth's center. The Central Anomaly looked more and more like a plane and less like a sphere. We were close enough to it so that I could clearly distinguish scores of the Great Old Ones, though the view was a bit obscured by some gauzy green clouds.

These clouds were the airweed plants that Watcher had spoken of. Like a kelpweed, the airweed plants had flotation bladders that kept them here, "uphill inward" from the Umpteen Seas. Each plant consisted of some hundred leathery blades growing outward from its center. The blades were four or five feet long and were densely set with fist-size airbladders that held a breathable gas that was lighter than air—Eddie supposed it to be a mixture of helium and oxygen. With Lightrider's help, we gathered a dozen of the plants and squeezed them into the fried-egg cabin with Arf.

As we pushed further on, the tekelili mind-contact grew ever stronger. Pulling on our rope with Seela, I could actually forget which of us was me and which was her. Strong, happy Seela! It was a joy to be so close to her. Ever since we'd passed the zone of the airweed, the gravitational attraction of the Umpteen Seas had grown weaker, so that now we were practically in free fall. Looking back at the Seas, I noticed something strange: They were moving much faster than ever before.

I caught Eddie's attention and got him to look as well. The Seas raced by like panicked buffalo on the Great Plain, merging into multiple images in the distance, and then miraculously returning from the direction opposite to the one they disappeared in. The directional confusion was the effect of the spindling of space near Earth's center . . . but why did they move so rapidly? "Time dilation," said Eddie. "Watcher told of it. The closer we get to the center, the slower our time goes. This is lotus land, Mason!"

Watcher confirmed Eddie's answer, and I was seized with a panicky desire to hurry. Redoubling our kickings, we carried the fried egg closer to the Great Old Ones. Due to the space spindling, they too looked as if they were laid out on a plane rather than on the surface of a spherical zone. One of them in particular caught my attention—the closest one of all—easily as big as the whole town of Lynchburg. Its antediluvean hide was marked with great rows of flat-topped hills, and flowing out of these hills were vast streamers of pink light that played all around us. The nearer end of this vast trepang bore ten enormous, branching fans. Sensing our approach, the giant sea cucumber slowly, hugely, swung one of its branches our way.

"FEED IT," thought Offerer, and we unlashed the mummy, the shrig liver, and the intestinal strips, pushing these offerings inward. With a massive, writhing movement, the Great Old One's fan caught all we gave it. In gratitude, it steered an intense river of light along the edges of our fried egg, soon drying all our bundles of meat. Smoker cut the bundles of shrigmeat free and fastened them to a series of loops on a long towrope he had ready. And then he and the others were heading outward and away. Everything seemed to be happening very quickly, although, compared to the outer world, we were moving terribly slowly. The high-speed jiggling of the Umpteen Seas was hideous to behold. Only Watcher was still with us.

Eddie, Seela, and I squeezed into the fried egg with Arf and the airweed. Eddie quickly got the door closed, lest one of us tumble out when the Great Old One threw us. Watcher shoved our craft further inward and took his leave as well. As the inward-falling fried egg spun, I could see out to the departing black gods. The further from us they got, the faster they seemed to move.

Now there came a great, sucking slap as the Great Old One took hold of us with its sticky fan. A terrifyingly powerful motion drew us down. With every fathom that we moved inward, the mad jostling of the distant Seas increased. I could see through the zone of the Great Old Ones now, through the very heart of the tunnel between the worlds and out into the MirrorWorld. The MirrorSeas were racing past with bewildering rapidity but in the opposite direction from the Umpteen Seas. Now and then I could glimpse a flash of Htrae, spinning madly and with the summer light flickering on and off in the great North and South holes. Whole years were passing!

Now the mountainous bodies of the Tekelili were all about, great warty barrelshapes bedizened with suckers, puckers, and subbranching fans. They lay in the plane between the two worlds, half here and half there, each of them slowly and steadily rolling over and over about its long axis like a basking whale. This close to the dividing plane, it was very clear that the rotation of the Earth and the MirrorEarth are in opposite directions. This counterrotation is the source, I would suggest, of the biplanetary *vis viva* that powers the plasmic lightstreamers that the *woomo* manipulate with their preternaturally mobile appendages. I believe that the jittering of their undulating and microscopically pileated suckertops is ever in complete synchronization with the whole of the biplanetary tree of pink light that grows from the center out to Htrae and MirrorHtrae, and that the tiniest tendril of the smallest subbranching cannot brush a feather without the Great Old Ones knowing it.

Now our own giant sea cucumber made a huge, wallowing motion, and we moved through the center, through the heart of the world, and for a heartbeat, *time was not*. The fried egg's cabin was suffused with total Light. All was One there, and this One knew All. The name of the creature holding us was Uxa, and

Uxa was two hundred million years old, as man reckons time. Arf was about to vomit. For Uxa and the other Tekelili, the Earth was a kind of vehicle. The fried egg? Man and *woomo* had come to Earth in the fried egg at the instigation of some other planet's *woomo*. Seela was pregnant. I could sense the day old foetus in her womb, a boy, my own child, magically engendered by our lovemaking of the day before. Seela was frightened at the thought of something living within her. Eddie was planning to kill his double, his MirrorEddie. Uxa was pregnant as well; she carried in her mantle the seeds of a thousand new *woomo* to spawn if and when Earth reached its eventual destination, an inconceivably huge space spindle somewhere among the stars. *Woomo* female. A long-buried image of my mother's face flared up in me. Though she'd died when I was born, I knew her face from within. There, at Earth's center, I could see my mother's lined, snub-featured face and her outcurving lips and her strawy pale brown hair . . it was as if Uxa were my mother's head, and seeing this, I worshiped her. Uxa said we'd lost six years on the way in, and we'd lose six more on the way out. She would throw us to land on the MirrorHtraen side of a great ocean hole. Arf made heaving noises. Eddie was racing up mental staircases of piled concepts, shaky idea edifices propped upon mighty teachings from the un-impeachable Uxa. All celestial bodies are hollow, and each of them is umbilically connected, navel to navel, to a Mirrorbody in the MirrorWorld. The Great Old Ones ride the connections and, where possible, they populate their planets with men—just as a farmer might import earthworms to freshen the soil . . . or like another might grow milkweed in order to attract the lovely monarch butterflies. Our small thoughts, particularly Eddie's, were beautiful to Uxa.

All this, and more, I knew in the timeless moment that we passed through the interface between World and MirrorWorld. Uxa rolled slowly over, and now a violent, lashing movement of Uxa's fan snapped us spinning outward.

The centrifugal force pressed us heavily up against the cabin wall. Staring out the thick-glassed view port that was over the ship's ruined control panel, I could see, in rapid succession, views of the Tekelili dwindling behind us and a view of the approaching MirrorSeas. Arf stretched his head forward, retchingly emptying his full stomach. The foul smell of the half-digested shrig offal set Seela, then Eddie, and then me to vomiting as well.

As we drew closer to the MirrorSeas, their nauseatingly reckless slewings relented; we were getting back into normal time. In its godlike wisdom, the great *woomo* had thrown us so as to miss all the MirrorSeas. We sailed past them handily, with barely enough time to glimpse a few of the black Mirrorgods who lived there. We were still whirling too fast to dare reopening the door. I pressed my face down into the mound of airweed and knifed open one of the bladders. The gas within was under high pressure; a vivifying burst of oxygen and helium filled the cabin and our voices grew oddly high.

There was a persistent river of pink light flowing with us, pushing us ever outward. Now the MirrorSeas dwindled behind us, great balls of water arranged as on a sphere. As space opened back up, MirrorHtrae became widely visible. As Watcher had said, this MirrorWorld had no North or South hole.

Finally, the spinning of the fried egg had abated enough so that we could sit up a bit. Eddie opened the door to shove out the vomit and to let some fresh air in. We flew past a herd of shrigs and sent a flock of pterodactyls scattering. Further out, we glimpsed a *ballula*, fortunately not nearby. Save for the lack of North and South holes, the surface of the MirrorHtrae seemed to be laid out just like the surface of Htrae. Having studied the surface at length, Eddie felt that he knew the location of Mirror-America's underside. He had directed Uxa to throw us to a point to the east of MirrorAmerica, off MirrorNorfolk at the mouth of the MirrorChesapeake Bay, because that is where a great hole in the ocean floor allows water to flow *all the way through*.

If there is a hole in the ocean floor, one might expect the

water to drain into the interior of the Hollow Earth, but this expectation is quite fallacious, as at the inner edge of the Rind there is no gravitational pull to drag the water further. Eddie's hope, based on his conjectures about Elijah and on his tekelili contacts with the Great Old Ones, was that we could splash into the ocean near such a hole and be lifted through the sea by the buoyancy of our sealed fried egg.

With the steady pressure of Uxa's light behind us, we made the sea in one day, though not without the attentions of two vagrant *ballula* and a land-based flock of harpy birds. But ringed in the adamantine walls of our ancient skyship, we had nothing to fear.

Seela helped pass the time by weaving. First her agile fingers unraveled some stout thread from my tattered coat, and then she took apart her necklace and reassembled it into two. Each of the two had one of Jewel's bright gems in its center and a variety of Seela's collected shells and seeds on the rest of it. Rather than making them decorative, Seela wove the necklaces so thickly that hardly anything but the string showed. Using the tongue of the flowerpeople, I asked her why. She explained to me that these necklaces were our only treasure, and then she gave me one. More than ever did I feel myself her husband.

Seeing our matched necklaces, Eddie recalled Jewel's earlier suggestion. "Look you," he said, holding out his hands to Seela. "Can you weave these for me?" He held fifty or sixty teeth, half of them white and half of them red. Virginia's and Quaihlaihle's. Seela knotted a tight-meshed little net around each of the teeth and ranged them on a worsted plait. Eddie gladly tied it on.

Seela had a bad moment when we passed close to a giant flower on a mighty vine that stretched up from the land near our chosen sea. There were flowerpeople on the blossom, small as aphids in the distance. She was on the point of jumping out to fly thither, and only my most heartfelt entreaties kept her aboard.

Eddie closed the door for the last time, and our metal fried egg cut edgewise into the water. Due to the singular nature of the gravitational potential at the surface of Htrae, the buoyancy of our sealed ship had the effect of moving us not toward the water's inner MirrorHtraean surface, but rather toward the MirrorEarth sea surface one thousand more miles outward. Instead of floating, the fried egg sank and—which was most unsettling—sank with a speed that ever grew.

Of all of my journey's stages, this was the most terrifying. Picture yourself sealed in a hemispherical room with a dog, a man, and a woman; and remember that your room is a tight-sealed capsule rushing into yet and yet more sunless depths. The pressure grew greater than could be borne, and then grew twice as great again. We were constantly short of breath, and I sliced open a new air bladder every few minutes, hideously aware that I might use them all up too soon. The heavy weight of the air filled my ears with noises and my eyes with fog. The noises— each tiny sound was amplified and left to reverberate like the last scream of a dying demon in the nethermost hopeless hell, and no sound could finish its chiming before a new one set in. With all tekelili gone, Seela and I again had no more than a few hundred words in common; her cries and sobbings were maddeningly incomprehensible. Far from being joyful at the success of his plans thus far, Eddie was grimly brooding over the twelve years it had taken us to move through the slow time zone at the center of the worlds. Again and again, he called out for Virginia. Even noble Arf began to whine. It was bedlam.

As the pressure reached its maximum, I thought surely the portholes would burst—indeed, I half prayed they would, and put an end to our agony—yet still the ancient metal ship held tight.

Throughout all this, nothing was still in the cabin; as we raced up through the water like an air bubble of swamp gas, our fried egg wagged like a fool's mocking head. Where all outside our windows had been utterly dark, I now began to glimpse some luminous writhing forms: fishy denizens of the watery night. A few swam at us, but we waggled upward unarrested. Now, finally, the nightmare pressure on my ears began to slacken. Up and up we rushed, the water gurgling around us, and slowly, slowly, the inky water began to be tinged with brown, with blue, with green . . .

In a final great rush, our sealed ship shot high up into the air, crashed joltingly back down, bobbed up again, and then finally settled itself, rocking on the surface of an unquiet autumnal sea.

# 14

## MirrorEarth

EDDIE OPENED the fried egg's door wide. Right away, two waves came crashing in, scuttling our ship. We barely got free of it before it sank. The situation was grim.

It was late afternoon and growing dark rapidly. Though not frigid, the air and water were cold. Seela readily mastered the trick of earthly swimming, but I wondered how long we could stay afloat. Our clothes were dragging us down; we shed them all. Arf whimpered and tried to climb onto me.

Eddie kicked himself up high in the water, craning to make out which way land lay. But in the gathering dusk and the choppy water, what could he see? Lacking any better plan, we paddled slowly toward the dying sunset. If all was not wholly reversed, then MirrorAmerica lay in that direction.

Night fell, and we struggled on. I kept hoping to hear the sound of breakers. Arf stayed at my side, resting his head on my shoulder as we slowly swam. Seela and Eddie were a bit ahead of me. We splashed fruitlessly onward. Time passed . . . perhaps an hour.

Something in the sound around us had slowly been changing, and now there grew into audibility a low rhythmic thudding. Eddie kicked himself up high and looked.

"Over here!" he shrieked. "Help us!"

I pushed Arf aside and rose up to see as well. It was a steamship—a great two-paddle side-wheeler all lit up like a Christmas tree!

"Help!" cried I. "Help! Man overboard! SAVE US! HEEEELLP!"

Seela joined her cries to ours, and some of the ship's seagazing passengers happened to hear us. An alarm went up, and minutes later the ship had lowered a boat with two oarsmen and a man with a lantern.

"Save us!" cried Eddie. "Save us, for the love of God!"

Presently, a shaft of lantern light fell upon us.

"My word! It's three niggers and a dog! Ship oars, boys, till I pull 'em in."

The speaker set down his lantern and stretched his arms down to Seela. "Ladies first," he said. "What plantation are you all from?"

"*Oonafoonah boolo,*" said Seela. "*Klee ba'am.*" Her wet blond hair clung to her black skin, and when she talked, her teeth shone like rubies in the lantern light.

"Would you listen at her!" exclaimed the man. "Blond hair and red teeth? Can't say as I understand this a-tall." Now he reached down for Eddie. "How 'bout you, boy, can you talk white?"

"I am not a Negro," said Eddie intently.

"What's your name?"

"Edgar Allan Poe."

"You hear that, Henry?" The man whooped, picking up his lantern and surveying the dripping Eddie, who now lay exhausted in the bottom of the boat. "Will? This here's Edgar Allan Poe."

"Edgar Allan Poe's the name of the little fellow on our ship," answered a voice from the dark. "The poet. Got on board in Richmond, slept all afternoon, and now he's been in the first-class lounge ever since dinner.''

"Holding court and charming the ladies," came a second voice. "But I'll be dang if this nigger don't look just like him. Can you read, boy?"

"Hey," I shouted. I was hanging on to the side of the boat, too weak to pull myself in. "Don't forget me. And the dog."

"Here I am saving a nigger's dog," said the man, setting down the lantern again. "That'll be a fine thing to tell the ladies. You 'spect I'll get a medal, Henry?"

I handed Arf over the gunwale, and then finally I was pulled in, too.

"Hello," said I. "I am Mason Algiers Reynolds of Virginia. My companions are Edgar Allan Poe of Richmond, and Seela Flower from Htrae. None of us is Negro."

"Especially not him," said the man, giving Arf a pat. The man had a slow, kind voice that held a hint of laughter in the background. His eyes were piercing, though hooded by puffy lids. He had a full shock of fine brown hair, an aquiline nose, and thin, mobile lips. The general effect was of cheerful dissolution. "I'm Dick Carrington, chief mate of the *Pocahontas*, and these here are officers Henry Langhorne and Will Baldwin. Are you from the Reynolds plantation on the York River? Don't you know there's no free territory anywhere around here? Maryland's a slave state, same as Virginia. Old marse pretty rough on you all? We're gone have to send you back just the same."

"Wait a minute, Dick," put in Henry, a lean man with a small mustache. "We're on the high seas. Practically speaking, it's the same as if we'd caught these niggers in Africa ourselves. We can take 'em to the market in Baltimore and sell 'em. That girl with the blond ha'ar . . . why, she could bring a thousand dollars. What do you think, Will?"

"Too dodgy," said Will. He had bony features and wore his long hair in a ponytail. When he talked, his prominent adam's apple bobbed. "This ain't nothin like the high seas, Henry. This here's the Chesapeake Bay. By the Fugitive Slave Law, we're bound to return them to their master.''

"Damnit, we're not slaves,'' I interrupted. "Check as you will, you won't find a runaway slave report on any of us. We're free men!''

"If that's really true,'' said Will, "then we're legally bound to let them off in Baltimore town, on account of the Personal Liberty Act.''

"Not that they are free men,'' harrumphed Henry, "or why the hell would they be paddlin' around here ten miles from land?'' He unlimbered his oar and dug it into the water. "I say return 'em. Could be a hundred dollars in it for each of us.''

"*Wamgoolo oo'ka tekelili*,'' said Seela. She was complaining that there was no tekelili.

"You'll have to learn English, Seela,'' I told her, placing my arms around her. And then I whispered to her in the language of the flowerpeople. It felt good to hold her. We were chilled through and through

"Wh-what's the date?'' asked Eddie through chattering teeth. "Mr. Cuh-Carrington?''

"Thursday,'' said Dick Carrington easily. "Straight and steady there, Henry and Will. Prepare to cast on.''

We were at the stern of the steamship *Pocahontas*. She was a goodly schooner, with two narrow paddle wheels set amidships, one on either side. She carried some canvas as well, though the sail had been struck for the rescue. Crewmen winched down a sling. Dick and Will made it fast, and then we were lifted up and set aboard, nude and trembling. There was quite a press of passengers there to greet us.

"Runaway slaves!'' cried a red-faced man. "Give 'em the lash!''

"We're not slaves,'' announced Eddie. "We are gentlemen born and raised.'' That's what he tried to say, but he was chattering so badly that few understood him.

"Shackle them,'' said another man. "Shackle them!''

"I'll take the girl in my cabin," offered another.

"I'll pay three hundred for her," yelled someone else. "Five hundred for the whole set."

"Will," said Dick Carrington. "Take them down to the stokers' mess."

Thank God, thought I, for I knew the stokers would be black.

Will Baldwin led us shaking and stumbling down steps and companionways to a low-ceilinged room in the belly of the ship. It was hot as blazes here, and the ship's engine gave a mighty thrum. A wizened black man stirred porridge in a pot. The voices of the black stokers came drifting in. They were shoveling and talking while they worked.

"Ayrab, we picked up these three," said Will. "Let 'em warm up and give 'em a sup. Find 'em some clothes if you can. I'll be back terectly."

Ayrab set down his stirring spoon and gave us a long look. He was mocha-colored, where we three were ebony-black. He had small reddened eyes and only a few teeth. The sight of us seemed to fill him with glee, especially the sight of Seela, with her incongruously blond hair.

"Set ye down," cackled Ayrab. He stepped to the mess hall's other door and hollered down the hall. "Luther! Stop shovelin' and come see!"

The blue-black, bullet-headed, powerful man who appeared was none other than MirrorLuther, the MirrorEarth copy of the Luther who'd gone down the river from Lynchburg to Richmond with me. He showed his age by a certain paperiness of his skin.

"Luther," I exclaimed. "It's Mason!"

"Mason whut?"

"Mason Reynolds. From Hardware. I knew you when you were working with the Garlands, poling that bateau down the river."

MirrorLuther narrowed his eyes. "Sho . . . I wukked dat boat befo' I bought myself free. Cain't say I reckernize you.

Mason Reynolds, you say? There were a white boy ob dat name got shot in Lynchburg, I recall. Who you really be and whar you fum? You be a runaway?"

"We are not slaves," insisted Eddie.

"But they think we are," said I. "There's no runaway slave bills out on us, I swear it."

"Till someone write one up," said Ayrab. "Whut you needs to do is git clear ob de ship fast and lively oncet we land."

"I'll let you out de coal chute," said MirrorLuther. "An' den you go to Jilly Tackler's rooming house down to Greene Street whar it cross de National Road west of town. Jilly take you in. Now, whuffo dis girl got blond ha'ar? Whut you name, darlin'?"

"Her name is Seela," I said. "She doesn't speak English."

"She new fum Africa? Is dat why you run away, Mason? She come in new and you decide to make her all you own?"

"She's mine, yes, as a wife. But I tell you, Luther, she is a free woman and Eddie and I are free men."

"What's the date?" asked Eddie again.

"Thursday," said Ayrab. "Did Carrington say effen he fixin' to gib you all ober to de paddy rollers?"

"What?" asked Eddie.

"Patrollers," said I. "I'm not sure what the officers plan to do. One of them said that if we weren't runaways, they should take us to the market and sell us."

"You be goin' out de coal chute fo' sho'," said Mirror-Luther.

"I know it's Thursday," said Eddie. "I mean what month is it, Ayrab? And what year?"

"Dis still be September, I 'speck. An' de year? Dang if I know. How dat African girl git her ha'ar look so white?" He ladled out three bowls of hot porridge and set them down in front of us. "Hyar."

"The year's eighteen fohty-nine," stuck in MirrorLuther. "Have you been outer de country? You been over to Africa?"

"Twelve years!" cried Eddie. "It is as Uxa said. We have lost twelve years!" He shoved his plate aside, put his head on his arms, and began sobbing. Before we traveled through the Central Anomaly, Eddie'd seen a tekelili vision of a living MirrorVirginia, happy with MirrorPoe. Now he feared we'd come too late.

"Don't mind him," said I, and started eating my porridge. Seela ate as well, but Eddie had no appetite. When his porridge had cooled, I gave it to Arf.

Though the stokers were all free men, they lived in the ship much of the time, so we were able to piece together enough clothing to be decent. Eddie and I each got a pair of trousers, and Seela a long shirt. Ayrab and the stokers were curious about our necklaces, but Seela had woven them over so thickly that the teeth and the two gems were all but invisible. I fluffed and petted Arf until he was quite dry. He curled up in a corner and fell asleep.

After a while, Will Baldwin reappeared. "Feeling chipper? Captain Parrish would like to see you three." Up the stairs and down the corridors we went, then up a final flight of stairs to a mahogany door. Will Baldwin rapped briskly and showed us in.

There were two men in the comfortably appointed cabin: an erect, gray-bearded man, clearly the captain, and—

"The MirrorPoe," breathed Eddie.

The MirrorPoe had Eddie's odd high brow and the same large, dark-lashed eyes set in a pallid face that bespoke chivalry and refinement. Every particle of his clothing was black; and a black cane leaned against the arm of his chair. His upper lip twitched slightly beneath his mustache as he regarded us. He seemed careworn and haggard. Before saying anything, he reached a tremulous hand out for his cup of tea and drank deeply of it. He really seemed quite unwell; knowing Eddie as I did, I surmised that MirrorPoe was recovering from a spree.

"Is she still alive?" demanded Eddie. "Virginia. Is she well?"

"It is not your place to interrogate us," said Captain Parrish. His eyes were blue and sober, and his face was strong and tan. He sat behind a desk on which were laid out navigational charts, dividers, and a heavy metal ruler. "Which of you calls yourself Edgar Allan Poe? You?"

"Of course me," said Eddie. "Are you then blind? I am Edgar Allan Poe and this wasted relic is but my double, the vile MirrorPoe."

"You ask of Virginia," said MirrorPoe slowly. "Are you straight from hell? Black Imp. Virginia is safe from you." He passed his shaking hand across his brow. "Do you have a past at all, or has my evil fancy invented you whole?" Mayhap he took us for unpleasant hallucinations.

"Safe where?" cried Eddie. "I must make amends to her!"

"Safe in the grave," snarled MirrorPoe. "And before you violate it, foul ghoul, I'll send you back to the Father of Lies!" In a sudden passion of loathing, MirrorPoe rose to his feet. He grabbed for his cane, but it fell to the floor and rolled away. Rather than bowing to pick it up, he snatched up the stout bronze measuring stick that lay on the captain's desk. "Imp of the Perverse, at last I see you face to face!" He strode forward, bringing down the heavy stick with all his might.

Eddie shrieked and cringed, but I had enough presence of mind to dart forward and catch MirrorPoe's wrist. The ruler clattered to the floor. Seela picked it up and held it at the ready, in case we were again attacked.

"Please, Mr. Poe," said I. "Compose yourself. This man is indeed your double, or you his, but there is nothing of the satanic in this. We come not from hell but from another Earth, from the real Earth, as we think of it. For us, your world is as a MirrorEarth. You can believe me when I say that our journey has been fantastical in the highest degree. Only calm yourself and let us tell you of it."

"Virginia dead," sobbed Eddie, who had fallen to the ground. "A wretched sinner am I."

MirrorPoe took a stiff step back and regarded us three: beautiful red-toothed, blond-haired, black-skinned Seela, with her strong hand now gripping the bronze ruler; I, in form a fine-featured, smallish black youth of sixteen, exceedingly well-spoken; and unhappy ink-dipped Eddie, so obviously a tortured artist, so recognizably a carbon copy of the younger MirrorPoe. Slowly, MirrorPoe picked up his cane and fondled its handle. I noticed a joint six inches below the handle. Perhaps it pulled out to reveal a sword?

"It is as one of your tales come to life, Mr. Poe," said the captain soothingly. "Perhaps you should write their story! It would be a fine serial for the new magazine you were telling me of . . . *The Stylus*! Tell me truly, you three, how came ye here?"

"We are not slaves," said I. "You must understand that we are not runaway slaves."

"And if I grant ye that?" said the captain. "Whence come ye?"

"We . . . we came up through the sea," said I. "From inside the Hollow Earth."

With Eddie on the floor so defenseless and pitiful, Mirror-Poe's expression had already softened. And now my mention of the Hollow Earth won his interest. The faintest of smiles played over his pallid features, and he perched himself back in his chair, propping the cane against the chair's arm once again.

"Then narrate," said he. "I have no hope of sleep tonight. Pass the hours and tell me your story, young . . ."

"My name is Mason Algiers Reynolds. I am a white man, I am a gentleman. My unparalleled journey started thirteen years ago, when I left my father's farm in Hardware, Virginia."

"Don't tell him," said Eddie on the floor. "He only wants to steal the glory. If anyone writes our story, it shall be me!"

Seela, unaccustomed to MirrorEarth's heavy gravity, had seated herself on the floor as well.

"Let's hear the tale," said Captain Parrish, ringing a bell. The ponytailed Will Baldwin popped back in. "Will, can ye get us three chairs?"

"And some rum and hot water," croaked Eddie. "I've been a year with no drink."

"It is better so," said MirrorPoe earnestly. "Alcohol is death. Bring no rum; bring us more tea." He had the abnegatory urgency of one who has but recently escaped from the pit.

Will and a cabin boy had soon brought chairs and tea. I started talking at ten in the evening, by the captain's clock, and when fatigue forced me to stop at four in the morning, I was still not done. So weary was he from our voyage that Eddie dozed through much of my narration. The account I delivered was nothing like so complete as what you have read in the chapters printed here—salient omissions were all the events touching on Virginia, from the particulars of the Poes' wedding night to the state in which we'd found stowed-away Eddie upon the *Wasp*. With his threatening cane ready by his side, MirrorPoe's condition was far too volatile for such revelations.

He took in my narrative with every outward sign of interest and wonder, yet while I talked, I often had the feeling that he was not really there. He seemed like a hollow tree inhabited by small birds that only rarely peep out the knotholes. One could easily see that he had many sorrows upon his heart—and that he had tasted true madness. He welcomed the flow of my long tale's diversions, but he took them in as a man in a dream, with no real questioning or conviction. Still, the last thing he said to us before we went down to the stokers' mess gave me hope of some further contact.

"I am not quite myself tonight. Your tale . . . if only I could focus on it more acutely . . ." He sighed deeply. "Perhaps we will talk again after I have journeyed to Philadelphia. Pray tell me your name once more?"

"Mason Reynolds," said I. Remembering our plan to slip off the ship unobserved, I leaned close to him and whispered, "You may seek us at Jilly Tackler's rooming house at Greene Street where it crosses the National Road."

"I know the district well," said MirrorPoe.

"Don't tell him the secrets," murmured sleepy black Eddie, touching his necklace. "Don't tell him yet."

We bedded down for a few hours' rest under Ayrab's dozing eye. Shortly after dawn, MirrorLuther woke us.

"We goam dock in one hour," he whispered to me, his black face huge over mine. "Ah gwine show you de coal chute."

Eddie awakened heavily and with difficulty. He was more shattered by the death of MirrorVirginia than I could have expected, and beyond that, he was unnerved by the evident stature of the MirrorPoe.

Though blasted and broken, MirrorPoe had the aura of a great man, and all the remarks of Captain Parrish and the other officers had strongly confirmed this impression. Unlike Eddie, MirrorEddie had stayed and labored in the literary vineyards, building himself an international reputation as poet, author, and man of letters. Eddie was still free to try and do the same, yet how easy would it be for him, with so many Poe tales already old news? And where had MirrorPoe found the will for his adamant sobriety? My Eddie, for one, was ready to drink himself into a stupor. All his plaints and worries he poured out to me.

Meanwhile, MirrorLuther had installed the three of us with Arf at the back of the ship's large coal room, directly beneath a funneled tube that led, MirrorLuther said, to a hatch in the *Pocahontas*'s side. When I could get Eddie to stop talking, I explained our situation to Seela as best I could. So far she did not like MirrorEarth very well.

Somewhat later there was a hubbub in the stoker's mess—an officer had come down looking for us, whether to free us or to shackle us, I do not know. Captain Parrish had given every sign of believing us to be free men, yet perhaps he schemed against us craftily. Certainly, he had stolen many long looks at Seela. It seemed best to hold by MirrorLuther's superior wisdom and to leave covertly.

The search for us was interrupted by the tumult of docking: crewmen's feet pounding around the deck, the roar of the steam engine powering us through tight spots, the clatter of the halyards, and the thudding of the sails. The passengers left as noisily as a herd of cows, and then the stevedores set to work, rolling barrels of tobacco up out of the *Pocahontas*'s hold. Reasoning that if we waited too long we might be found or buried under tons of new coal—I wormed my way up the chute. Some good soul had already removed the hatch cover and I could stick my head right out of the side of the ship. The stones of the wharf lay four feet below! I called back to Eddie to hand Arf up to me. I put Arf out and then scrambled out and dropped to MirrorEarth's solid ground. Eddie and Seela followed after. A few Negroes witnessed our arrival, but they said nothing. Moving quickly, we crossed the wharf area and found our way into a side street. We paused there while Arf shook and shook himself until he had the coal dust all off. I wished I could get my proper color back so easily.

"Where did Luther tell you to go?" asked Eddie.

"He said to go to Jilly Tackler's rooming house," said I. "On Greene Street where it crosses the National Road?"

"The western slum!" exclaimed Eddie. "I used to live there with Virginia and Mrs. Clemm." His brow darkened again. "That is to say, the famous MirrorPoe used to live there. Where I lived, ah Mason, where you and I lived is a world and a world away."

We walked the mile or two to Jilly Tackler's with no great difficulty. To be sure we were half dressed, but as we were black, no one cared. Jilly's establishment was a rickety three-story wooden house with five rooms on each of the upper two floors. The first floor held kitchen, common room, Jilly's own quarters, and one more rentable room. The basement was the domain of Mr. Turkle, Jilly's factotum, handyman, and (the roomers said) paramour.

Jilly was a fat Negro woman with quantities of costume jewelry. Her skin was mid-tan, and she wore bright red lip-coloring. She had a pink turban on her head. I introduced our party and requested a large room. Jilly was willing enough to rent us a room, but she wanted her money in advance. Speaking in the tongue of the flowerpeople, I asked Seela if I could sell Jilly my gem. Seela wondered if I might sacrifice a seed or a shell instead. I didn't think this would cut any ice with Jilly, and after further discussion, Seela gave me permission to sell the gem. Borrowing a penknife from Jilly, I cut off my nuptial necklace and shaved away the fibers that covered my sparkling stone. Jilly was enchanted by the gem's radiance. It was a jewel of limpid transparency, as large as a hazelnut. It rendered light into rainbows with the savage efficiency of a diamond.

"Whar you git dat, Mason?" Jilly wanted to know. She more than half thought us to be runaway slaves. "You steal dat from yo marse?"

"It is not stolen," I promised her. "Although we have no papers, we are not runaway slaves. This gem was mined in a strange and distant land."

"Mother Africa! Is dat whar Seela fum? How she make her ha'ar so white?"

"It is an oddity of her tribe," said I. "Yes, I suppose you could say that Eddie and I are sailors who met Seela in Africa."

"The dark continent," put in Eddie. "Madam Tackler, I can see that you desire the jewel exceedingly, and quite rightly so. This is a gem worn by the African queens. If I give it to you, will you let us live here for . . ."

Thinking of Seela's pregnancy, I named the figure. "Nine months?"

"Na'an month?" She picked up the jewel and tested it with her teeth. "Effen de jeweler say dis be real . . ."

"Perhaps it is best if we take it to a jeweler ourselves," said Eddie, reaching for the gem. "Can you recommend one?"

"Six month," said Jilly, staring into the sparkling gem. "Got a nice big room on de third flo'. Numbah eleben. You go on up while I shows dis to Mr. Turkle. Effen he think it's genuwine, you gits free rent fo' six month."

"With board?" asked Eddie, veteran of many rooming houses. "And can we have ten dollars?"

"Ah gives dinner, but I ain't got me no tin dollar. You bettah go find you a job, Eddie. What else you got in de necklaces?"

I sawed some more of my necklace threads away. Jilly's fancy was caught by an unearthly cowrie and by a lustrously red seed.

"Can we have *five* dollars?" I asked.

"G'wan wid you." She handed me four dollar bills. "Yo room's on de third flo' in de back. Numbah eleben, one-one. Spell good luck. Dere's a water fountain down to de street corner effen you wants ter wash. You gits coal fo' de stove fum Mr. Turkle downstair."

"Thank you."

"Dat dog of yourn . . . is he housebroke? Do he bite?"

"He'll be no trouble. His name is Arf." I trotted out my old witticism, "He's so smart he knows his own name, and he's so famous all the other dogs talk about him."

Jilly chuckled politely and went back to gazing at her new stone.

The room had two beds; pallets on the floor, actually. One for Seela and me, one for Eddie and Arf. The room was very dirty. What a place to bring Seela! Eddie was depressed to find himself in a Negro rooming house with a dog for his bedmate. He badgered me until I gave him one of our dollars and a cowrie shell. He went out. I took our pitcher down to the corner and got water. And then before doing anything else, I scrubbed down the walls and cleaned the dried spit off our stove. After getting a broom from Mr. Turkle—a bald brown man with almost no chin—I threw the rest of the water on the floor and swept much of the filth out into the hall.

Now I lit the stove and put our basin on it to warm. Three trips to the fountain and I'd fetched enough to fill the pan. Seela and I bathed. She enjoyed it; the way water behaved in our gravity delighted her— just as the weightless waterballs of the Hollow Earth had delighted me. For Seela, to trickle water from the pitcher into the basin was fascinatingly novel.

Once we'd washed the trip off ourselves, we went out to buy clothes, Arf at our heels. The shirt and trousers we had were little more than rags. There was a street of Negro shops not far from Jilly's. I got myself a linen shirt and a suit of worsted. Seela was ready to wear the same . . . until she noticed that the other women wore dresses. She picked herself a beautiful yellow dress, with a color like her home flower; and I got her a sturdy blue jacket to wear over it. Shoes, socks, and undergarments we purchased as well. Then we went for a little walk.

Back in the Hollow Earth, Seela had never worn shoes, or really walked for that matter, and her feet pained her considerably. We found a square with some benches and sat down there. The day had started out cloudy, but now it was sunny, though cool. Bright autumn leaves littered the green grass. Arf lay down and regarded us with bright eyes. After so much tekelili with him, I felt like he was a real person.

"*Oofanah goolu.*" I said to Seela, pointing to a red maple leaf drifting by. To help her learn English I had adopted the custom of saying everything twice, once in my broken flower-language and then in English. "The leaf is pretty." I wanted her to like it here.

"*Goolu,*" agreed Seela, smiling. Her blond hair and red teeth had attracted a lot of notice in the shops, but I'd settled on the story that she was an African princess from an unknown tribe. People liked the story.

But now suddenly someone was poking me with a stick. A policeman.

"Move along there, nigger," he told me. "And take your fancy woman with you. The benches are for whites."

As we walked back to Jilly's rooming house, I tried to explain this to Seela. Given her tribe's worshipful attitude toward the black gods, she was having trouble understanding that here on

MirrorEarth, white skin was deemed better than black. For my part, I wondered how many weeks or months it would take us to fade to white.

Jilly and Mr. Turkle served up a greasy dinner of greens, sidemeat, cornbread, and beans. It was filling, if not particularly fine. There was no sign of Eddie. After dinner, Seela and I went to our room and made love. Eddie came in shortly after dark, fiercely exultant. Instead of getting drunk, as I'd expected, he'd purchased pen and paper and had spent his day writing! No white public house would admit him, and the Negro establishments repelled him. He'd passed the day in the back pew of a church, no less a church than MirrorBaltimore's great Basilica of the Assumption. Touched by the half-clothed black man's earnest scribings, a verger had given Eddie shirt and shoes and had provided him a dinner as well. And what had Eddie written? He lit a candle that he'd abstracted from a side altar and handed me two closely written sheets of paper.

I had expected the beginnings of a narrative about our journey, but instead I found that Eddie had penned a long, intricately rhythmic poem entitled "The Raven." I read it twice through silently, and then I prevailed on Eddie to read it to us aloud. Even though Seela could not understand its words, she too was spellbound by the poem's melancholy music.

Even now I find myself quite overwhelmed by the power of the last three verses of Eddie's "The Raven." Whipped into mad imaginings by the strange bird, the poet bares the hope closest to his heart and is rebuffed utterly. Next, he strikes a defiant posture as answer, but quickly the defiance fades to a desperate plea that the bird "take thy beak from out my heart." And then, in the heartbreaking last verse, comes the collapse into a nightmare stasis of oppression.

"Prophet!" said I, "thing of evil—prophet
    still, if bird or devil!
By that Heaven that bends above us—by that

God we both adore—
Tell this soul with sorrow laden if, within the
distant Aidenn,
It shall clasp a sainted maiden whom the angels
name Lenore—
Clasp a rare and radiant maiden whom the
angels name Lenore.''
Quoth the Raven, ''Nevermore.''

''Be that word our sign of parting, bird or
fiend!'' I shrieked, upstarting—
''Get thee back into the tempest and the Night's
Plutonian shore!
Leave no black plume as a token of that lie thy
soul hath spoken!
Leave my loneliness unbroken!—quit the bust
above my door!
Take thy beak from out my heart, and take thy
form from off my door!''
Quoth the Raven, ''Nevermore.''

And the Raven, never flitting, still is sitting,
still is sitting
On the pallid bust of Pallas just above my
chamber door;
And his eyes have all the seeming of a demon's
that is dreaming,
And the lamp-light o'er him streaming throws
his shadow on the floor;
And my soul from out that shadow that lies
floating on the floor
Shall be lifted—nevermore!

For all the poem's sadness, Eddie the man was uplifted by
having accomplished this wonderful creation. He went to bed
almost happy.

Saturday morning, the weather turned bitterly cold, with sprinkles of rain. Eddie proposed that Seela and I accompany him to the offices of the MirrorEarth version of the *Baltimore Saturday Visiter*, a magazine that on Earth had been the first to publish one of Eddie's stories: his "MS. Found in a Bottle." I had planned to spend the morning looking for work, but Eddie's enthusiasm won me over.

"And who knows, Mason," he continued. "Once we tell them of our adventures, they may engage to publish them as a serial. You've an itch to write too, haven't you, boy? Mayhap we'll work together—you can do the rough draft, and I'll polish it! In view of the fact that the MirrorPoe has used up my name, perhaps we'd best publish under your cognomen, at least until the true facts of our journey have been widely disseminated. 'The Raven' and *The Hollow Earth* . . . by Mason Reynolds! Remember, I will do the speaking. I have a long familiarity with the ways of journalism."

Arf and we three were admitted into the office of the *Saturday Visiter* with considerable difficulty, despite Eddie's insistence that he knew the editor, John Hewitt. Hewitt looked up at us with a complete lack of recognition, and when Eddie introduced himself, Hewitt's bafflement turned to truculence.

"Yes, and I'm Washington Irving," said he. "What is your business here? We have no present need for servants."

"Behold," said Eddie, and handed him the manuscript of "The Raven."

Hewitt read briefly, then threw back his head and gave an angry guffaw. "You poor apes," said he. "Have you no concept at all? Is a poem, then, a shiny trinket to pass from hand to hand like a stolen watch?"

"But it's a wonderful poem!" I interposed. "Why don't you read it through?"

"Because I've already read it a dozen times!" shouted Hewitt, throwing the papers at my feet. "Edgar Allan Poe published 'The Raven' nearly five years ago. Do you ignorant wretches really think you can copy out a great work of literature word for word and pass it off as your own? Out! Get out of my sight!"

Eddie gave only a strangled sob. I pocketed the manuscript, and we left. Back on the wet, blustery street, I tried to cheer Eddie with the thought of writing *The Hollow Earth*, but he no longer wished to hear anything of it. Walking rapidly, he led us to a bookstore and hurried in. There we found four volumes by the MirrorPoe: *The Narrative of Arthur Gordon Pym of Nantucket, Tales, The Raven and Other Poems*, and *Eureka*. The Pym narrative was the completion of the sea story that Eddie had been working on before we left. The *Tales* included twelve stories, all of them new. The poetry collection held not only a word-for-word copy of Eddie's "Raven" but also the text of his "The City in the Sea." Reading through the printed "Raven," I was struck by how weak a poem it seemed if I thought of it as written by the effete and condescending MirrorPoe. From Eddie it was (and still is) pure magic, but from MirrorPoe it is plodding doggerel. *Eureka*, as far as I could gather from a hasty glance through it, was a rambling farrago about the nature of the universe. If this was MirrorPoe's latest, the man was in very poor condition indeed. How could he write of the world's structure without mentioning the central fact that *all celestial bodies are hollow*? Old fool.

Eddie struck up a conversation with the bookseller, a common-looking man wearing a green coat and a gray cravat with a stickpin. "You are a friend of Edgar Allan Poe's, are you not?" said Eddie.

The bookseller regarded Eddie with puzzlement. "You are a reader?"

"Yes, I read, Mr. Coale. I am an author. Things are not always what they seem. If you take me and my companions for Negroes, you err severely. We have traveled here by way of the Hollow Earth, and the pink light at Earth's center has burned us black."

"Indeed!" A smile played over Coale's fleshy lips. "To whom do I have the honor of speaking?"

"My name is Edgar Allan Poe." Eddie held up his hand for silence. "I come from an Earth that is a copy of your MirrorEarth. In the early 1830s I spent many hours in a shop that is a copy of your shop. I have every reason to suppose that my actions there were copied by the MirrorPoe who lives here. Of course you think me mad, Mr. Coale, but have a caution." Eddie paused and glanced intently around the shop. Coale turned his plain face to me, wondering. "I have it," exclaimed Eddie. "Mr. Coale, do you remember a rainy April day in eighteen thirty-two when you and Edgar Poe sat here quite alone and played a game of chess? Poe checkmated your king with a rook, a bishop, and a knight. Turning your king on its side, you said, 'Motley, Poe, but well done!' You and he lunched on bread and cheese, and in the afternoon a crate with twenty copies of Washington Irving's *The Alhambra* arrived. Poe whiled away the rest of the afternoon reading to you from it, and then you and he went out for dinner. And *this!*" Eddie pointed a triumphant finger at Coale's chest. "*This* you surely must remember! While eating an oyster, you found a large black pearl. You wear it yet!"

Smiling feebly, Coale fingered his black pearl stickpin. "That I found this pearl in an oyster is common knowledge, good sir. I grant that your account of that April day has verisimilitude. But after seventeen years . . ." Coale shrugged and spread his hands. "Pray be open. What is it you want of me?"

"Books!"

"And you have no money?" Coale shook his head. "Very like Edgar Poe. Very like. Which books did you want?"

"What did you think? I want *The Narrative of Arthur Gordon Pym*, the *Tales*, *The Raven*, and *Eureka*. The total cost is two dollars and fifty cents. I give you my word as a gentleman that I will repay you "

"Your word?"

"Wait," said I, drawing out the manuscript of "The Raven." "This is worth something, is it not?"

Coale peered at the paper for a long time, then glanced up at me. "It is a forgery?"

"You are unable to tell?"

"I know Poe's hand intimately." He stepped to the front of the shop and scrutinized the papers in the light from the window. "If I were to deem it genuine," he said finally, "it could be worth three dollars. Certainly it is a famous poem, but the manuscripts of living authors fetch no excessively high price."

"Can I have another book?" asked Eddie.

"Which?"

"Due to our long voyage, I am ignorant of the past twelve years of literature. Who are the best pens? Who shines? Who . . . who has your Poe reviewed favorably?"

"Nathaniel Hawthorne," said Coale, stepping to the rear of his store and putting the manuscript in his high desk. "Mr. Poe reviewed *Twice Told Tales* so favorably in *Graham's Magazine* that he is quoted in the endpapers. I have a copy over there." He pointed to a spot near me, and I took the book down.

I opened to the endpaper and read aloud. " 'The style is purity itself. Force abounds. High imagination gleams from every page. Mr. Hawthorne is a man of the truest genius.'—E. A. Poe, *Graham's Magazine*. You say we can take this book as well, Mr. Coale?"

"You both read?" marveled Coale.

"Yes, and mayhap someday I will be a writer like Mr. Poe. My name is Mason Algiers Reynolds." I gave a little bow, and Seela laughed to see me move so oddly. She had not the slightest notion of what books were or of what we were doing here.

When we got back to Jilly's, Eddie and I sat down in the parlor to read. Jilly was in excellent spirits—she'd taken her new gem to the jeweler's to have it set into a pin, and the jeweler had offered to trade the gem for a real diamond!

"But ah's keepin' mine!" exclaimed Jilly. "Look at you

two wid yo books. Reglar gemp'men!'' She coaxed Seela into the kitchen and chattered at her as she began to cook a dinner.

We read all the rest of that day and most of Sunday and Monday as well. As Poe had always been my favorite author, the experience was delicious for me. But for Eddie it was shattering. Here in these four volumes were the full-grown fruits of so many of the seeds his soul harbored! It seemed as if all that he'd dreamed of writing had already been accomplished . . . and the joy of creation, the public acclaim, and the income had gone to another man.

This other man, this MirrorPoe, had not forgotten us. He came to us at dawn Tuesday morning, rapping on our door with the head of his cane. I opened to see him there, with Jilly standing anxiously behind him. She supposed him to be an agent for a master we'd fled.

"Dey tole me dey free," she was saying.

"Leave us," said MirrorPoe, "and do not fret. I wish only to speak with them." He stepped into our room and closed the door. He was dressed in black as before, and carried the same cane. A rich cloak rested on his shoulders. His eyes were clear and sober.

"Seela, Mason Reynolds, and . . . Eddie Poe," said he, looking us over with some care. "I was not entirely sure that you were real. That night on the *Pocahontas*, I was not quite well."

"You were recovering from a drinking bout," said Eddie. "There is no need to dissemble before your own double. And Mason knows me as well as anyone ever has. From your appearance I would say that you have been free of the *mania a potu* these last three days. Are you ready to start again?"

"*Mania a potu*?" said I.

"Poe Latin for drunkenness," explained Eddie, laughing. "What did you do in Philadelphia, Mr. Poe?"

MirrorPoe gave a smile that was almost boyish. "I have been courting two rich poetesses. I am raising money to start a new magazine, *The Stylus*."

"Just the name I would choose," said Eddie. "Tell me this. Have you written any tales about Symmes's Hollow Earth?" He indicated our little library of Poe books. "So much of what I might write has already been accomplished by you. I don't remember if Mason told you that we lost twelve years going through the Hollow Earth. Though you are forty, I am still but twenty-eight. Do you know that on my first day here in MirrorBaltimore I wrote 'The Raven'? I took it to Hewitt at the *Visiter*, and he threw it in my black face. He thought me a plagiarist!"

"This . . . this is what drew me back," said MirrorPoe, growing pale. "You truly are my double? The story young Reynolds told . . . it is quite veracious? There is an Earth and a MirrorEarth, both hollow, and the two worlds are connected by a kind of maelstrom at their centers?"

"These facts are incontestable," said Eddie. "The two Earths form a pair which enjoys an exceeding yet imperfect symmetry. For a full symmetry, *you* should have traveled to the other Earth, my home. But you did not do so." He paused, thinking. "Is there a MirrorMason Reynolds?" He pointed at me. "Do you know his MirrorEarth double?"

"No . . ." said Poe, looking at me closely. "I know a *Jeremiah* Reynolds, promulgator of the Symmes theory. He and I once made some plans for outfitting a trip to Antarctica . . ."

I thought back to the day Jeremiah had appeared in Richmond. It was I who'd met him on the porch, and I who'd kept him there talking until Eddie came back from trying to get his marriage license. "It was Saturday, May fourteenth, 1836," said I. They looked surprised, and I smiled modestly. "I've always had a good head for dates. May fourteenth, 1836, was the day Jeremiah Reynolds brought James Eights's plates for the counterfeit Bank of Kentucky bills. Did you counterfeit the money too, Mr. Poe?"

"Jeremiah and I missed our connection," said he. "Perhaps he came by the house when I was not in. I do remember that on Monday, May sixteenth, 1836, I got an advance from Mr. White, posted bond, and married Virginia. The next day we went to Petersburg on our honeymoon.''

"You see, Mason," said Eddie. "You're the cause of it all. What do you think became of MirrorMason?''

"I think he's dead," said I. "Remember our vision? When you saw MirrorVirginia, too?''

"Poor Jeremiah," said Eddie, changing the subject. He had not the heart for thoughts of Virginia. He jerked his thumb at Seela. "*Our* Jeremiah was decapitated and fed to a giant nautilus by her tribe. Mr. Poe, your *Narrative of Arthur Gordon Pym* proceeds to the very rim of the South Hole and then breaks off. I pray that you have contemplated no supplement. Tell me that you have not yet written our tale!''

"No," said MirrorPoe. "I have not. And willingly do I cede this field to you." There was a low hubbub in Jilly's house now as the roomers woke and shuffled off to their jobs. Arf got up, shook himself, and scratched at the door to be let out.

"What should we do next?'' said I.

"Let's get drunk," said black Eddie, grinning at his white twelve-years-older self with easy, jeering intimacy. "Do you have pocket money, Mr. Poe? Some opium would be pleasant, and some good port wine. Laudanum—can we afford laudanum? What if we were to pawn your cloak?''

MirrorPoe's face took on a skulking, haunted cast—but only for a moment. Arf scratched the door once again. MirrorPoe drew himself up to his full height and scrutinized us once again, every inch the gentleman, his crossed hands resting on the head of his ebony cane.

"Come then, you three," said he. "Let us go to the white part of town. I shall await you in my carriage." He drew his cloak about himself and let himself out of our room, Arf hard on his heels.

"He Eddie bro?" asked Seela. "We gwine go wid him?'' Sunday afternoon, she had begun to speak black English. With magical abruptness, our past tekelili, my tutoring, and Jilly's ministrations had taken effect at Sunday dinner. Seela's first sentence had been, "Gimme mo' frah chicken!" Mr. Turkle had passed her the platter of fried chicken, and Seela had talked for the rest of the meal.

"We'll go with him," said I.

With MirrorPoe waiting for us, we hurriedly attempted to make ourselves presentable. I went down to the street to empty our slops and to fetch fresh water. A hackney carriage was waiting at the corner of the National Road. I sped back upstairs with the water, and we cleaned ourselves up.

Ten minutes later we were in the hackney with MirrorPoe, maneuvering our way around great Conestoga wagons, each with a team of four to six horses, setting out down the National Road for the western frontier. "My trip to Philadelphia was not in vain," said he. "Singularly enough, I prosper. I have collected two hundred dollars towards the founding of *The Stylus*. Dear young Eddie." Poe smiled and patted Eddie on the knee. "Guess where I've put up, Eddie!"

"The Fountain Inn?"

"Better! I have a suite at Barnum's Hotel!"

"Hallelujah." Eddie cackled. "The finest hotel in Baltimore!" He glanced down at his black hands and rough clothes. "Will they let us in?"

"For a certainty," said MirrorPoe. "You have only to pose as my slaves. I have registered myself as a Colonel Embry. Simply keep mum and follow me. Mason, you carry Arf."

Set on MirrorBaltimore's Monument Square, the Barnum City Hotel was the biggest building I'd ever seen: a full seven stories high. Our carriage clattered under the elegant, columned entrance. Keeping a respectful distance, we followed the MirrorPoe inside. The doorman grinned and sang, "Yas ma'am!" as he let Seela in. With her yellow hair and yellow dress, all clean and with her red teeth flashing, she was stunningly beautiful.

The rich carpeting of the lobby was thick as the grass of the Umpteen Seas. Heavy red velvet curtains hung at the sides of each of the many entranceways, and great gilt-framed mirrors ran from floor to ceiling on every available wall.

"Ah be glad effen dis whar we live," said Seela, finally pleased by something on the outside of the Hollow Earth. She pointed to one of the mirrors. "Am dat be mo' new world?"

"No, dear Seela, it is a mirror, like stiff water." I walked over to one of the mirrors with her and rapped my knuckles on it. "Not real."

"You an' me?" She pointed. There we were, both of us black as the ace of spades, Seela rather Negroid with her full lips and flattish nose, my face very fine featured for a dog-carrying slave, and tan-and-white old Arfie at ease in my arms, his black lip line looking particularly winsome. Behind us I could see MirrorPoe and Eddie, waiting for us by . . . the elevator! I'd never ridden in an elevator before.

"Come, Seela."

The elevator ride was unpleasantly reminiscent of our trip through the ocean in the fried egg—but of course it was over in a few moments. The slave who ran the elevator eyed Eddie, Seela, and me curiously.

"She yo wife?" he asked me.

"Yes," said I, proudly.

MirrorPoe's fourth-floor suite consisted of a drawing room and a bedroom, placed side by side together at the middle of the hotel's front wall. Each room had two windows looking out onto the street—it was four windows in a row. Magnificent lodgings! Like the lobby, the rooms were richly carpeted and hung with red velvet curtains, and there were several mirrors as well. As if the thick wall-to-wall carpeting were not enough, several Oriental carpets were laid out over it. The bed itself had curtains, and the bedroom had a washroom, complete with a full-size bathtub overhung by a great petcocked tank of wash water, fresh and warm.

MirrorPoe pushed an electric bell-button, and the next minute a servant was at our door, a sympathetic though feeble-looking Negro with white hair and red livery. His name was WIlllam.

"Bring us dinner for four," said MirrorPoe. "The duck we had yesterday, is it still available? Yes? Most excellent. Duck for four and a good supply of Château Margaux. I think three bottles. And could you send a boy out to the chemist's for an ounce of opium? Wonderful." It was ten o'clock of a Tuesday morning.

"Oysters and champagne as well," demanded Eddie. "Four dozen oysters and five bottles of champagne in a tub of ice. Cognac and armagnac. And amontillado."

"It shall be as you desire," rejoined MirrorPoe. "Do you hear, bell captain? And a pint of laudanum, as well."

William recited the order as if it were as harmless as toast and tea. "So dat be fo' dozen oysters, fo' duck dinnah, three bottle margow, ounce o' opium, fi' bottle champagne on ahce, one bottle cognac, one bottle armagnac, one bottle amontillado, an' a pint o' laudanum. Dere be sump'n else, Col'nl Embry suh?"

"Make it a quart of laudanum, Mr. Poe," said Eddie.

"As he says." MirrorPoe nodded, wearing a haunted, skulking air again.

"Yassuh. You 'speck dat be all you gwine need? Is yo serbants gwine put up on de sebbenth flo?"

"I prefer to keep them with me for the present. And let us continually settle accounts straightaway." He drew a slim sheaf of bills from his pocket and handed one to William. The bills were twenties!

"Yassuh, Col'nl Embry. Ah bring up you change wid de order straight away."

While we waited, Eddie and MirrorPoe fell into a conversation about their childhood. Arf settled himself in a corner of the bedroom. Seela and I went into the washroom and enjoyed a full bath together.

By the time we finished our bath, William had reappeared with a maid and a waiter in tow. The waiter stood with back to us, opening the oysters and arranging them on the sideboard. Meanwhile, William and the maid moved a table to the center of the room, covered it with a white linen cloth, and quickly laid out four place settings. William accepted a tip from MirrorPoe, and then he and the maid took their leave.

Thus did our long last feast begin.

# 15

## The Conqueror Worm

"SHERRY WOULD BE the thing just now," said MirrorPoe. "Before the champagne and oysters. Waiter, can you pour us four glasses of amontillado?"

"Yassuh."

When the waiter turned from the sideboard bearing a small silver tray with four glasses, I got my first good look at him. It was Otha?!? No, no, it was *MirrorOtha*, the very image of my Otha, twelve years older and gone somewhat to fat.

"*Oo'm gowow* Otha!" exclaimed Seela. "Why you old, Otha?"

Already puzzled by the sight of a white man taking dinner with three slaves, MirrorOtha was quite dumbfounded by Seela's exclamation. Silently, he served each of us a crystal glass of amontillado sherry: first MirrorPoe, then Seela, then Eddie, then me. As I took my glass, MirrorOtha looked into my face and started back with a shock of recognition.

"Is you fum Virginia?" he asked me.

"I'm Mason Reynolds," said I. "A copy of the Mason you knew."

MirrorPoe and Eddie were busy toasting each other, while Seela stared at MirrorOtha and me.

"It's MirrorOtha," I told her. "Not Otha. Like Eddie and MirrorPoe."

"You ain't nebber seen me befo'?" Seela asked MirrorOtha.

"Ah sees you now," said he. "Is you slave or free? I'se free. Whar you fum?"

"Htrae," said Seela. She tapped me on the shoulder. "He de slave an' ah's free."

"No, Seela, you've got it all wrong, we're both free and MirrorOtha is a slave. I am white," I said, turning to MirrorOtha. "And Seela is my wife."

"Bull*shit,*" muttered MirrorOtha, pushing out his lips.

I thought of a way to convince him. "Hey, Arfie," I called. "Hey, Arf!"

Arf stood up and shook himself so hard that his ears flapped against his head. I could tell that he relished the return to gravity. "Arfie! Come say hello. It's Otha!" Arf twitched his nose to taste the scent of MirrorOtha, and then, acknowledging the verisimilitude, trotted over to jump up on MirrorOtha and to whine hello.

"Do you recognize Arf?" said I. "Boon pet of yore?"

"Arf!" cried MirrorOtha. "How you git here, boy? I left you to home unner de bed!"

"You have a dog like him? You have a MirrorArf?"

"Ain' no mirror 'bout him," said MirrorOtha, rubbing Arf's head but not really looking at him. " 'Ceptin' his ha'ar allus shed. He cain't eat nothin' but mush no more. Don't know how he foller me in here . . ." He happened to glance down at Arf's head, which rested on his thigh as he caressed it. He gave a grunt of surprise and jerked his hand up into the air. "Dis ain't Arf! Dis dog still young!" He stepped close to me and studied my face. He was almost angry. "Stop lyin' an' tell me whar you fum. Ah kin b'lieve dat yo dog is Arf's son an' ah kin see dat Marse Reynolds was yore pa. But who yo ma? Is—is yo Ma be name Turl? Who raise you, an' whar?" He thought I was Purly, the

*Rudy Rucker*

little "nephew" whose mother was Turl and whose father was Pa! The memory of that wretched Christmas night when Pa had raped Turl rushed back to me. I remembered how Otha had broken our new skittles game and run out to crouch crying in our empty field, and I remembered my last farewell to Otha at the Umpteen Seas. My heart gave a little jerk; it felt like a flower unfolding. I seized his hand and pressed it between mine.

"Believe me, Otha, I'm not Purly. I'm Mason Reynolds, from another world. On my way here I went through some strong light that turned me black, and now I can begin to understand what it is to be black. I'm sorry I ever thought you and your folks were slaves. I'm sorry for what Pa did to Turl that Christmas."

MirrorOtha pulled back his hand and stared at me. "You ain't Mason, 'cause Mason been daid since 1836. Ah seen him die. It were me cyarried him back to his pa. You don't got to tell me about no Mason Reynolds. I growed up wid him, an I seed him go inter de groun'."

"Another amontillado, boy," called MirrorPoe to MirrorOtha. "And then quit your crow-cawing and get the oysters ready!"

"Do it yourself!" I yelled. I picked up the sherry bottle and slammed it down on the table in front of Eddie and MirrorPoe. "Go on, you two! Get drunk and go crazy, but don't tell Otha what to do!"

"Set down or leave, Purly," said MirrorOtha to me sharply. "An' don' try an' speak fo' yo elders. Ah's a waiter, and I gots a meal ter serve."

"It's MirrorOtha!" exclaimed Eddie.

"Exactly," said I. "Don't you think he should eat with us?"

"No." Eddie poured himself and MirrorPoe another glass of sherry. "Drink your sherry, Mason, if only as a tonic for blue devils and the mania. Remember—this is the MirrorWorld."

Seela and I took our seats and tasted our sherry. It was sweet and strong. The alcohol mounted immediately to Seela's head, and she began to giggle.

The table was longer than it was wide; we were seated two to a side. Eddie and Seela were across from MirrorPoe and me. MirrorPoe and I had our backs to the hall. We could see out the two windows in the drawing-room wall. A sea breeze had blown away the low clouds of dawn, and then the breeze had died, leaving a calm, sunny Tuesday midmorning, the second day of October 1849. When I looked out the windows, I saw down into the shimmering red and yellow leaves of two maples and an elm. MirrorPoe's cane leaned in the corner. The windows were separated by an oak sideboard, which was a flat-topped waist-high cabinet with griffin legs. Seela and Eddie faced the drawing room's inside wall, which held a wall-mounted candelabra, a door, and one of the Barnum's huge red-curtained mirrors. MirrorPoe was on my left, as was the door to the bedroom. Seela sat directly across from me.

"I'd like to hear another installment of your narrative," said MirrorPoe to me. He seemed greatly invigorated by his two drinks. "On the *Pocahontas* you told of your trip to Antarctica, of your fall through Symmes's Hole, of your time with Seela's tribe, and of your second fall to the Earth's center. Tell me more of what you found there; tell me of the Great Old Ones and of the maelstrom between the worlds."

"Did he tell you about tekelili?" said Eddie. "All layers of the mind become as patent as the strata on a quarried cliff. So wonderful a union with the All . . ." His voice trailed off, and he began again. "Where did you put the opium, Mr. Poe? If we smoke a bit we'll have something very like."

"I prefer to eat it," said MirrorPoe, reaching into his pocket and drawing forth a dark, irregular bolus of the sticky poppy dust. He used his razor-sharp penknife to section out a slice the size and shape of a small orange segment. He divided this in two and gave half to Eddie.

"Champagne, boy!" sang MirrorPoe, and placed his opium on his tongue. I started again to protest on MirrorOtha's behalf, but before I could speak, MirrorOtha turned and glared at me, his hands busy all the while with the cork of a champagne bottle. He pushed his lips out and narrowed his eyes in a way that he had used to do when angered to the point of administering a beating to one of the other black boys. I thought it the better part of wisdom to cease badgering him now and to consult privily with him later.

The champagne bubbled into our fluted glasses with a stiff crackle. Neither Eddie nor MirrorPoe thought to propose a toast, but simply fell to. I raised my glass to Seela. She sniffed her glass, sipped, coughed, and began to giggle again. MirrorOtha removed the sherry bottle and glasses and brought us each eight oysters on ice. They were crisp and fresh, with the taste of the sea. We ate them with a will.

Another glass of champagne, and now came the duck and the Margaux. There were two roast ducks on the sideboard, and MirrorOtha carved us each a red-running medallion of breast and a crisp-skinned slice of thigh. There was a dollop of currant jelly on the side of each plate, and a quivering mound of bread pudding filled with nutmeats, mushrooms, and greens. MirrorOtha brought around a sauce boat of clear gravy and anointed our plates. Then he refilled the champagne flutes and poured out four glasses of the tart, fragrant, richly red Margaux. Eddie, Seela, and I fell on the food like wolves, and MirrorPoe dined as ravenously as if he were no more accustomed to this luxury than were we.

MirrorOtha served out seconds for those who wanted it, refilled the Margaux glasses, served thirds, refilled the champagne glasses, and then went back to the oysters. When we'd quite finished dining, he cleared the plates and brought us snifters and the bottles of cognac and armagnac. Eddie and I had told of the rest of our journey; MirrorPoe and Eddie had reminisced over their common childhood; MirrorPoe had intently and with great fascination questioned Seela over the flora and the fauna of Htrae; and I'd told of my union with Seela and of our child, to be born in June 1850, as I reckoned MirrorEarth time.

By now, believe it or not, it was five o'clock in the afternoon, come and gone. Otha had lit the candelabra on the wall and had placed two candles on our table. All four of us were quite thoroughly intoxicated, Seela so much so that she had kicked off her shoes and lain down on the floor.

MirrorPoe called for his cane, then stood and, with patient hand, poured a heady mixture of the two liquors into three of the cut-crystal snifters.

"A pipe," cried Eddie. "Let me clear my head with a pipe, Mr. Poe."

"Not the laudanum?" said MirrorPoe coolly.

"Not yet."

"Very well." MirrorPoe went into his bedroom and returned with a small brass pipe and a thin shingle of wood. "Waiter!" called he.

"Yassuh."

"Will you sit down and share a pipe?"

"Thank you, suh."

MirrorOtha sat down at the head of the table between Eddie and MirrorPoe, his chair pulled a respectful distance back. While carving and trimming the ducks, he had let numerous gobbets drop Arf's way. Pleased, greasy Arf ambled over to lie at his feet.

MirrorPoe pinched a bit off his ball of opium and rolled the pinch into a little sphere. He put the spherule in the pipe and handed the pipe to Eddie. Then he broke a long splinter off the edge of the shingle and used the splinter as a taper, lighting it from the candle and holding it over Eddie's bowl. Eddie drew in air and the thick, tarry opium melted, bubbled, and began to glow ruby-red at its base. It reminded me of the Central Anomaly, seen from the Antarctica end of Symmes's Hole.

I stood up and stretched. Seela was comfortably asleep on the thick rug. This would have been perfectly natural on the home blossom or among the Umpteen Seas, but here in the slave state of Maryland, it could prove incendiary to social mores. I urged

Seela to her feet. We walked into the bedroom and I tucked her into the clean white linen of the bed, a sheet on bottom and a soft linen-covered comforter on top.

"*Oomo gooba'am*, Mason," said she, smiling sleepily up at me. This is very nice. "You gwine git in, too?"

I studied Seela's full out-turned lips, her perfect nose, the down of blond hair on her temples, the delicate curves of her ears. Why not get in bed with her? I had no special desire to smoke opium with MirrorOtha and the Poes.

"Yes."

I pushed the door closed and undressed. Seela pulled her dress off, and now we lay naked together between sheets for the very first time.

"This is how it's supposed to be," I told Seela. "Once we're white again, we'll always live this way."

"*Gooba'am*."

We made love for nearly an hour and then dropped into a deep sleep.

I woke sometime after midnight to the sound of laughter in the next room. My tongue felt foul and I had a thumping headache. Were those three still at it? I pulled on my trousers and opened the bedroom door to see.

The candle stubs were burning brightly. The dishes and the remains of the duck still sat on the sideboard with the emptied bottles of wine and champagne. On the table were the ball of opium, greatly reduced in size, the brown medicine bottle of laudanum, nearly full, and the cognac and armagnac bottles, three-quarters empty.

Eddie, MirrorPoe, and MirrorOtha sat just where I'd left them, each with a snifter of alcohol and MirrorPoe still with his cane at his side. Eddie was in the act of lighting the opium pipe. His motions were elaborately smooth.

Skin color did not show up so clearly in the monochrome illumination of the candlelight, and as they bent together, Eddie and MirrorPoe looked more like each other than ever with their identical high brows, small mustaches, and delicate chins. Opium smoke curled up from MirrorPoe's pipe, scenting the smoky air with a yet stronger fragrance.

I put my shirt on and pulled a chair over to sit down at MirrorOtha's side. I still wanted to ask him about how Mirror-Mason had died and about how all the others in MirrorVirginia fared. I now realized I had no intention of going there. In the past I'd thought of taking Seela to MirrorLynchburg for a real church wedding—but the longer I had to walk around as a black, the less I wanted anything to do with the slave states. When I left Baltimore, I'd head north or west.

"Hello, Otha." He turned slowly to gaze at me with drugged, reddened eyes. "I've already told you I'm a copy of Mason and you don't believe me, but can you tell me how your Mason died? Who shot him, and why?"

"It were de goddamn stableboy fum de Liberty Hotel shot him," said MirrorOtha slowly. "Mason lost all his pa's gold to de hotel, and when he steal it back, dat damn little wretch done shoot Mason in de back ob his haid."

*The stableboy!* It all came down to that one instant when the stableboy and I had fired our guns; that had been the instant when my Earth and MirrorEarth diverged. I felt fragile as a grain of corn in a gristmill.

"Did you ever get Wawona?" I asked, just to be saying something.

MirrorOtha stared heavily at me. His body was slowly rocking back and forth. "Naw. But I's married just the same. Met me a gal in Bal'more after I moved up . . . been ten years ago. Got three kids wid her an' two mo' wid odder gals."

"Did . . . did Pa set you free?"

"He died two ya'ar after Mason, an' his will set his slaves free. He even left some land to Luke and Turl. He were a good man, in his way. Luke an' Turl stayed down dere, but me, I left dat shithole soon as I could."

My throat felt thick and constricted. If MirrorPa was dead,

could my real pa still live? Not likely. Pa dead, and nobody in the whole world to care for me. I tried to blink the tears out of my eyes. Eddie nudged me now, and handed me the pipe. I'd never smoked opium with him and Otha back in Norfolk, and even now, in my grief, I saw no reason for it. None of these three looked any the happier for their vice. I gave the pipe on to MirrorOtha, who smoked it down to the ash.

The three of them leaned back slackly in their chairs, staring silently at the candle flames and seeing visions. I had a raging thirst. There was no water, but I found some champagne in one of the bottles on the sideboard and filled a glass with that. Arf woke and petitioned me for a few more gobbets of duck. I fed him and ate a bit myself. With the pain of Pa's death in my heart, I was glad for Arf's company. Finished with my snack, I was on the point of getting back in bed when suddenly Eddie spoke.

"Virginia," groaned he. "Where is Virginia?"

MirrorPoe had been sitting there still as a waxwork, but the mention of his dead wife's name set him back into motion. He pinched off a bit of opium and recharged and relit the pipe. Exhaling a blue cloud of tendriled smoke, he breathed the names of the women he'd written of, staring into the smoke as if he saw their faces.

"Annabel Lee. Ulalume. Lenore. Eulalie. Ligeia. Morella. Eleonora. Berenice. Helen."

"Virginia," insisted Eddie. "How did your Virginia die?"

"Insolent fool," said MirrorPoe. "Have you no Virginia of your own in the false world which spawned you?"

"She is dead," said Eddie, choking on the word. "I killed her."

"You did *what*?"

"It . . . it was an accident. I gave her laudanum."

"Laudanum," murmured MirrorPoe, seemingly letting go the thread of the conversation. "By all means." He opened the medicine bottle that held the alcoholic tincture of opium and tipped a heavy dollop into his snifter to mingle with the liquors already present. As he raised his glass, his attention drifted back to Eddie. "What is the necklace you wear?" asked MirrorPoe. "Are you then a savage?"

"It is not for you to know," said Eddie.

"Jewels?" pressed MirrorPoe. "Why do you not give me one?" Suddenly, he shook all over as with a fit of the ague. "I need money for *The Stylus*, let us not forget. Perhaps you and your Mason could write up your adventures for us. Give me one of your gems, you foul child killer." He lurched forward and seized hold of the necklace.

Eddie jerked back, and the threads of the necklace parted. A white tooth fell to the table: Virginia's front tooth.

MirrorPoe cocked his head this way and that, trying to make out what he saw, all the while plucking at the threads of the necklace, which he now held. A red tooth dropped out, and then two more white ones. He picked up the first tooth, and as he studied it intently, his lips began to writhe.

"Yes," screamed Eddie, in an agony of shame. "They are Virginia's teeth. Yes, yes, I pulled them after she was dead!"

Slowly and silently, MirrorPoe rose to his feet, his eyes never wavering from Eddie's face. Now he took his cane in two hands and pulled on the handle. The sword that was hidden in the cane sang softly as it slid out of its sheath. MirrorOtha was too stupefied to interfere, and I was too scared. Eddie screamed and rushed past MirrorPoe toward the hall door, only to stumble on an Oriental carpet and stagger against the mirror on the wall. MirrorPoe came at him with an oath.

The attack was brief indeed. MirrorPoe was frantic with every species of wild excitement and seemed to feel the energy and power of a multitude within his single arm. In a few seconds he had forced Eddie by sheer strength against the floor, and thus, getting him at his mercy, plunged his sword, with brute ferocity, repeatedly through and through Eddie's bosom.

Eddie shook all over; his legs spasmed and beat a last tattoo; and then he was dead.

MirrorPoe wiped his sword on the tablecloth and thrust his sword back into the sheath of his cane. Uttering not a sound, he threw on his cloak, grabbed the bottle of laudanum, and hastened out of the room.

"Whut *happen*?" said MirrorOtha, heavily. "Whut goin' *on*?"

"I'm leaving," I told him. My voice was shaking. "Seela and I are clearing out of here fast."

MirrorOtha forced himself to his feet and went to kneel by Eddie. "Lord, Lord. I gots to git outta here too, less'n dey blame me!"

"Wait," said I, thinking a bit deeper. If we left the body here, then there would be an intensive search for "Colonel Embry" and his three "slaves." Seela above all would be easily found, with her red teeth and yellow hair. "Stay here, Otha, or I'll turn you in."

I pulled the bloodstained cloth off the table and went to kneel by Eddie. He lay in a pool of blood on the small Oriental carpet that had tripped him. I soaked up as much of the blood as I could and tied the gory cloth around his chest to try and hold the rest of it in. Now I put the fateful teeth in with him and wrapped the rug around his body.

"How far is it to the ocean?" I asked MirrorOtha.

"Fi' block. You think we gwine cyarry him all dat way?"

"We have to. We'll be in trouble if the murder is known."

I went and wakened Seela. Numbed by the shocking news, she dressed in silence. I tore our bottom sheet into strips and used the strips to tie the rug around Eddie into a tight bundle. While I did this, MirrorOtha carried a candle into the bedroom and looked through MirrorPoe's luggage for valuables. If he found any, he didn't let me know. Each of us took hold of one of the linen straps around the rug, and then we marched out into the hall, Arf following along. MirrorOtha led us to the back stairs and, unseen, we found our way into an alley behind the hotel.

As we walked down the back streets toward the harbor, the

tugging of Eddie's poor dead body traveled up my arm and into my heart. The jerking of his weight seemed almost to speak to me. For all his faults, he'd been a faithful friend, a wise teacher, and the greatest artist our generation will ever know.

We found our way out to a deserted spot along the Inner Harbor wharves, and there we stripped off all Eddie's clothes, tied a heavy rock to his feet, and dropped him into the sea. Arf let out a cry. As Eddie sank into the deep, I said a prayer for his tortured soul. We made a separate bundle of the clothes, tablecloth, and rug, tied a rock to that, and sank that too. How piteous an end to Eddie's long journey!

MirrorOtha took his leave and hurried off toward his home. Day was just breaking, and a warm land breeze began to blow. Seela and I walked along the docks, talking and thinking. Woeful Arf stuck close to our heels. Now there was no one but us three. Seela and I sat on a bench to watch the sunrise. I found a week-old copy of *The Baltimore Sun* in a trash can by the bench, and until she tired of the game, I tried to teach Seela how to spell out the headlines.

One of the stories that caught my particular attention was about the new territory of California, which the U.S. had won from the Mexicans just a year before. There was a gold rush on in California, and people were heading out there on wagons and on ships. The port of San Francisco had grown from a mere fishing village to a city of twenty-five thousand in the last year. And there was no slavery in California. I was dead sick of slavery.

We walked back along the docks, looking at the ships. I asked a grizzled white dockworker if any of the them were bound for California. He pointed out a clipper ship twice as big as the *Wasp*. "That's the *Ann McKim*. She sails tomorrow. Around the Horn to San Francisco in less than a hundred days!"

"Do you know how much passage on her costs?"

"Got the gold fever, do you, nigger? A hundred dollars a head!"

My thoughts turned to the little sheaf of twenty-dollar bills in MirrorPoe's pocket. In his state of intoxication, he wouldn't get far, particularly if he were nipping at the laudanum. He would collapse somewhere around here, and be found. Not quite wanting to admit to myself what I planned, I told myself that the murder would be even less likely to be found out if MirrorPoe were no longer to resemble "Colonel Embry." The best thing for him, I reasoned, would be if I were to find him and to change clothes with him, and if I forgot to leave him the contents of his pockets—why, it was an oversight anyone could make.

Seela, Arf, and I spent the rest of the morning wandering the streets near the Barnum City Hotel. With no success, I asked for "Colonel Embry" at all the hotels and rooming houses. It would have been natural to seek the besotted MirrorPoe in a tavern, but as it happened, today was Election Day, so all the public houses had been temporarily closed or turned into polling places. By noon we were quite tired out, and still had no success at all. We sat down at the edge of a stream-carved gully called Jones Falls and I thought back on yesterday's many conversations.

Up until the day when I'd appeared at *The Southern Literary Messenger*, Eddie's and the MirrorPoe's lives had been entirely the same. Yesterday they'd passed a pleasant hour or two reminiscing and marveling over their identical pasts. Across Jones Falls I could see Baltimore's great Shot Tower—a huge cylindrical brick building in which spheres of lead gunshot were made by dripping molten lead through colanders and letting it fall into tubs of water at the bottom. It was easily two hundred feet high. Eddie and MirrorPoe had spoken of the Shot Tower and of having lived near it in the early 1830s. *Wilks Street*, that was it! They'd lived in the block of Wilks Street known as Mechanics' Row, happy with Mrs. Clemm and little Virginia. I had a sudden conviction we'd find MirrorPoe there.

I found a bridge over Jones Falls and, asking directions of passersby, soon led Seela and Arf to Mechanics' Row, an L-shaped block with perhaps a score of small two- and three-story brick townhouses, each of them sharing a wall with the house next door. There was an alley that led in behind them. Leaving Seela at the entrance to the alley as a lookout, Arf and I sauntered in, staring keenly at the little houses' yards and outbuildings. Sure enough, we hadn't gone more than fifty feet before Arf singled out a disused carriage shed. A low muttering came from within. I entered to find MirrorPoe seated on the ground and wrapped in his cape. His cane and his bottle of laudanum lay beneath his limp hands on his lap.

He gave a low moan when he saw me—he thought I was Eddie. "Oh damned Imp," groaned he. "Can I never get free?"

Eddie had been my friend and this man had killed him, yet I felt no anger toward him. If it made me unhappy to think of the death of MirrorMason, how very much unhappier must it have made MirrorPoe to know he'd killed his double with a sword? He was more than halfway to suicide.

No, I was not here to punish MirrorPoe, but neither had I come to aid him. I was here to rob him—for robbery it was. While he watched in befuddled wonderment, I took off all my clothes and then pushed him onto his back and stripped him of his vestments. It was a personal point of honor for me not to look in his pockets. Poe was slightly larger than me, which meant that getting his clothes onto me went easier than putting my clothes onto him, but in only a few minutes the deed was done. He struggled a bit, but not much—I think my actions quite stunned him by their unexpectedness.

"I do this so the authorities won't find you, Mr. Poe," said I when I was done. I'd donned his cloak as well, though I'd left him the laudanum and his cane. "It's a disguise." Still did I keep myself from feeling in his pocket. If there were two hundred dollars there, we could be on our way to San Francisco tomorrow!

"Reynolds," said he blearily, finally recognizing me. "Young Mason Reynolds. Where's Eddie gone?"

"I tied a rock to him and threw him in the sea."

MirrorPoe shuddered and raised the laudanum to his lips. He sipped a bit, and then he began to retch up clear liquid. "Are you going to leave me here in peace?" asked he when the retching stopped.

"Certainly."

"Thank you." He sipped again at his laudanum, and this time kept it down well enough to feel some of the drug's euphoric effect. "So happy," said he, pointing vaguely toward the back of one of the houses. "So long ago."

I left him then and went back out the alley. Just as I reached the end, I heard him calling for me by name: "Reynolds! Reynolds! Reynolds!" But I never turned back.

The end of Poe's story is public knowledge. Joseph Walker, a compositor on *The Baltimore Sun*, found Poe lying on the sidewalk in front of Gunner's Hall, a public house two or three blocks from where I left him. As it was Election Day, Gunner's Hall was being used as a polling place. Poe was taken to the Washington College Hospital in a state of violent delirium, which lasted from that Wednesday until Saturday, October 6. Saturday night he began again to call for "Reynolds," and Sunday morning he died, his last words being, "God help my poor soul!"

His funeral was the afternoon of Tuesday, October 9, 1849, at the Presbyterian cemetery at Fayette and Greene streets, only four blocks from Jilly Tackler's rooming house. I went to the funeral, or tried to, but one of the grave diggers called me a damned nigger and chased me away—perhaps because with Poe's fine cloak on, I looked as if I were putting on airs.

And how much money did I find in Poe's pants? None. By the time I got to him, he'd already lost it all.

"And much of Madness, and more of Sin, and Horror the soul of the plot." So runs a line in one of Poe's last poems, "The Conqueror Worm." The poem tells of a "gala night within the lonesome latter years" wherein a throng of angels sit watching a play. A crawling fanged creature appears onstage and kills all the actors. For weeks after the funeral, I couldn't get the last lines of that poem out of my mind:

> Out—out are the lights—out all!
>     And, over each quivering form,
> The curtain, a funeral pall,
>     Comes down with the rush of a storm,
> And the angels, all pallid and wan,
>     Uprising, unveiling, affirm
> That the play is the tragedy, "Man,"
>     And its Hero the Conqueror Worm.

Right now as I pen these words, it's the evening of Saturday, March 2, 1850. All winter I've worked on this narrative and waited tables at Ben's Good Eats, making just enough money for our clothes and our pleasures. Seela and I are almost white enough to pass now, except for the fact that all the people who know us are used to thinking of us as Negroes.

Tuesday morning we'll be shipping out for San Francisco on the *Purple Whale*, a clipper ship even faster than the *Ann McKim*. We have a cabin for two, and Arf will come with us. In the end we had to sell Seela's necklace jewel for the ticket money; the gem brought three hundred! We'll start a new life as white people out there; we'll be in San Francisco in time for our son to be born white and to have it easy. Maybe I'll find work at a newspaper out there.

Meanwhile, I'm going to turn this manuscript over to Mr. Coale at the bookstore. He says he'll try and get it published or, failing that, send it on to me in California when I have an address.

I'm excited about sailing around the Horn and being so close to the South Pole again. It's too bad this MirrorEarth doesn't have a hole down there, because if it did, I think I'd be tempted to go back inside, back to the wonderful Hollow Earth.

# Editor's Note

SINCE I AM GUILTY of the occasional science-fiction novel, I'd better make clear right away that *The Hollow Earth: The Narrative of Mason Algiers Reynolds of Virginia* is an authentic nineteenth-century manuscript and was *not* written by me. The original is available for inspection as catalog item *PS2964.S88S8 in the Edgar Allan Poe Collection of the University of Virginia in Charlottesville, Virginia. I first saw the manuscript there on March 7, 1985. It consists of 378 pages of parchment, handwritten in black ink. I have edited *The Hollow Earth* from a notarized Xerox copy of the manuscript.

I'm sure it would boost my desultory half career as an author to present *The Hollow Earth* as my own creation, but I'd be doing a big disservice to everyone. The simple fact is: Every word of *The Hollow Earth* is true, and we must all question our beliefs about the planet we live on.

My confidence in the legitimacy of *The Narrative of Mason Reynolds* grows out of the research I've done over the past five years. I've traveled to Hardware, Lynchburg, Richmond, Norfolk, and Baltimore. Every single thing I've looked into checks out completely, right down to the courthouse documents.

Simplest to confirm were the facts about E. A. Poe. In the years 1831–1833, Poe lived in Mechanics' Row on Wilks Street in Baltimore with Mrs. Clemm and Virginia, next moving to a house on Amity Street in the western part of Baltimore. From 1835 to 1836, he was editor of *The Southern Literary Messenger* in Richmond. Upon visiting the Poe shrine there, I was able to examine the marriage bond of Edgar Poe and Virginia Clemm, which is indeed dated Monday, May 16, 1836. At that time Eddie, Virginia, and Mrs. Clemm lived in a boardinghouse on Bank Street at Capitol Square. The reader can check many of these facts for him- or herself in any reliable biography of Poe. The biography I know best is Arthur Hobson Quinn's beautiful and meticulous book, *Edgar Allan Poe: A Critical Biography* (New York: Appleton-Century, 1941).

After the marriage, Mason's information about *his* Poe does not, of course, correspond to what we know of our *own* Poe, the one whom Mason calls MirrorPoe. But the information Mason gives us about our Poe from September 27, 1849, through his burial on October 9, 1849, accords perfectly with what is known. Poe *did* take a steamboat from Richmond to Baltimore on that September 27, and he *was* indeed found dying near a polling place on October 3, dressed in cheap clothes.

With respect to the last period of Poe's life, *The Hollow Earth* solves one of the riddles of Poe scholarship: Why did the dying Poe keep crying out for "Reynolds"? Till now, many had thought that Poe might be thinking of Jeremiah Reynolds, who also appears in *The Hollow Earth*. But now that we can read *The Hollow Earth*, we learn that Poe's last days in Baltimore were far, far stranger than anyone had ever imagined, and that the Reynolds he cried for was the one who'd brought him his deadly double, all the way from another world.

Who was Jeremiah Reynolds? In our own "MirrorEarth," Jeremiah Reynolds was a follower of John Cleves Symmes, Jr., of St. Louis (Missouri Territory), who on April 10, 1818, began proselytizing his doctrine of the Hollow Earth. The best surviving accounts of Symmes's ideas can be found in James McBride, *Symmes's Theory* (Morgan Lodge & Fisher, 1826), and in Adam Seaborn's novel *Symzonia, A Voyage of Discovery* (Cincinnati: 1820). These books heap so much praise on Symmes, by the way, that I agree with Mason's suspicion that Symmes actually wrote them himself and published them under pseudonyms.

Jeremiah Reynolds was an accomplished traveler. On one of his voyages he went as far as the coast of Chile, where the mutinous crew put him and the officers off. He seems to have *walked* all the way back to the U.S. An excerpt of his journals appeared as "Mocha Dick, or, The White Whale of the Pacific," in *The Knickerbocker* in May 1839. This excerpt is thought to have been one of the inspirations for Herman Melville's *Moby Dick*, of 1851.

For us, of course, the most important thing that Jeremiah Reynolds did in his lifetime was to agitate in Congress for the funding in 1838 of America's first scientific expedition: the United States Exploring Expedition. The seal hunters of that time had penetrated far to the south but had always been stopped by a "wall of ice." As a follower of Symmes, Reynolds believed that beyond the wall lay a great hole, leading to the interior of the Hollow Earth. He was able to interest enough congressmen in this proposition to obtain funding for the expedition, as is well described in William Stanton's monograph *The Great United States Exploring Expedition of 1838–1842* (Berkeley, Calif: University of California Press, 1975), and in Charles Wilkes, *Narrative of the United States Exploring Expedition* (Philadelphia: Lea & Blanchard, 1845).

Although, thanks to *The Narrative of Mason Reynolds*, we now know that Symmes and Reynolds were right in all essentials, our planet seems regrettably to lack a South Hole. But what of the undersea hole through which our heroes' saucer floated up? I find it suggestive that the hole is in the general area of the Bermuda Triangle. It is my fervent hope that the publication of *The Hollow Earth* will inspire some modern day Jeremiah Reynolds to step forward and convince Congress to fund the construction of a deep-sea diving apparatus capable of locating the hole and retracing Mason's path.

During the end of his time in Richmond, our Poe finished work on his only novel, *The Narrative of Arthur Gordon Pym of Nantucket* (New York: J. & J. Harper, 1838). For information about the southern seas, Poe drew much of his information from Benjamin Morrell, *A Narrative of Four Voyages* (New York: J. & J. Harper, 1832). *The Narrative of Arthur Gordon Pym* tells of a journey to the very high southern latitudes and ends with a description of what could be Poe's vision of a huge South Hole in the sea: "I can liken it to nothing but a limitless cataract, rolling silently into the sea from some immense and far-distant rampart in the heaven. The gigantic curtain ranged along the whole extent of the southern horizon. It emitted no sound. . . . The summit of the cataract was utterly lost in the dimness and the distance. Yet we were evidently approaching it with a hideous velocity. . . . Many gigantic and pallidly white birds flew continuously now from beyond the veil, and their scream was the eternal *Tekeli-li*!''

I puzzled for some time over how it could have come about that Edgar Poe and Mason Reynolds seem independently to have arrived at the same word, which they write, respectively, as *Tekeli-li* and as *tekelili*. Did Poe somehow have a vision of the language of the black gods at the center of the Hollow Earth? I think a simpler explanation is possible. Before Mason actually set pen to paper on his own *Narrative*, he had already read Poe's *Narrative of Arthur Gordon Pym*. It is likely that the book influenced him in subtle ways. Never having seen the word *tekelili* written down—it was, after all, merely a sound that he had heard—it is natural that Mason might have adopted a spelling similar to that used by Poe.

I might mention that the poems and passages Mason Reynolds quotes from the works of Poe are all faithfully transcribed. He quotes the poems "To Helen," "The City in the Sea," "The Raven," and "The Conqueror Worm"; and he quotes brief passages from the stories "Berenice" and "William Wilson." All of these are attributed in the text, save for the quote from "William Wilson," which consists of the climactic paragraph, where MirrorPoe stabs Eddie. I can find no other places where Reynolds has directly plagiarized Poe for more than two or three words at a time.

Granted that all the historical facts jibe—and, yes, there really was a Cornelius Rucker—the modern reader must doubtless wonder if the physics of the Hollow Earth are plausible. Apparently so. The spindle— or Central Anomaly, or Central Sphere—that Mason finds at the center of the Hollow Earth is nothing other than what today's cosmologists call an Einstein-Rosen bridge (ER-bridge, for short). One of the better popular accounts of such a space structure is to be found, I may say, in my own book *The Fourth Dimension* (Boston: Houghton Mifflin, 1984). Not only can an Einstein-Rosen bridge function as a kind of wormhole between the insides of two worlds, but it can also bring about the varying gravitational fields that Mason and his friends encountered on their trip from Htrae to the Great Old Ones.

It is well known that many ER-bridges are unstable and must collapse in on themselves, effectively "pinching off" the vortical connection in question. A simple, nonrotating, uncharged ER-bridge collapses in depressingly few computation cycles. But if an ER-bridge carries a large static or dynamic electric charge, then it is in fact stable due to the charged hyperwalls' mutual electrical repulsion.

Whence comes the charge that fills the spindle and enables it to send out the streamers of pink light? If we consider the Kerr solutions for the ER-bridge configuration, we find that if the two ends of the bridge are counterrotating, then the bridge becomes a source of electrical energy; like a dynamo or, more appropriately, like a Wimshurst machine. I first understood this refinement of the theory when examining a "plasma sphere" toy for sale in a San Francisco gimcrack shop.

In these plasma spheres, which presumably many of my contemporary readers will have seen, a fractally branching electrical discharge connects an outer sphere of doped glass with a small metal sphere at the center. To visualize the model that Mason describes, we need to suppose that, slightly displaced in the fourth dimension, there is another outer plasma sphere, whose only overlap with our sphere is the small metal sphere at the center. Set the two glass balls into opposing rotations, break the small metal sphere up into squirming Great Old Ones, and you have Mason's model.

What of the time dilation that is experienced near the Central Anomaly? The phenomenon dovetails correctly with modern astrophysical theory as well, for Kruskal has shown that a charged, rotating ER-bridge must engender exactly the time-dilation effects that Mason describes. I have carried out extensive calculations, which confirm all these harmonies to a high degree.

Although the concept of an Einstein-Rosen bridge was utterly unheard of in the nineteenth century, Mason Reynolds's descriptions make it very clear that an ER-bridge is what he has in mind. To me, this strongly confirms that *The Hollow Earth* is in no way a hoax or a fabrication by Mason Reynolds but is rather a true account of things he really experienced and saw.

What was the eventual fate of Mason Algiers Reynolds? The March 6, 1850, issue of *The Baltimore Sun* reports that the *Purple Whale* did indeed set out for San Francisco on March 5, but the June 10 edition of the same paper reveals that, tragically enough, the *Purple Whale* never made it around the Horn of South America and was presumed lost with all hands in a gale off Tierra del Fuego.

Grim news—but somehow I find it impossible to believe that Mason, Seela, and Arf could have died so simply. Surely, in the grand scheme of things, Mason's breaking of the great symmetry of the worlds must have had some higher goal. Even in a screaming gale and a shipwreck, would not Mason's uncanny luck and ingenuity have found some way to keep him, Seela, and Arf alive? Would not the Great Old Ones, who know all, have preserved them?

I am presently continuing my investigations and would greatly appreciate information about any post-1850 manuscripts that mention, or could possibly be attributed to, Mason Algiers Reynolds of Hardware, Virginia, born February 2, 1821.

—Rudy Rucker